Praise for Jay Parini's

THE DAMASCUS ROAD

"Jay Parini has found his own uniquely potent way of remaking the historical novel. He digs into the layers of history, into so-called real characters. They become more real in his work, hyperreal, parts of our own conflicted souls." —Gore Vidal

"Jay Parini has written a blockbuster destined to become a classic. A thrilling story of spirituality in the midst of fire and torture, a page-turner that takes the reader from the gutter to the heavens. . . . A book for our time and our transcendent times to come." —Erica Jong

"*The Damascus Road* has all the hallmarks of a great new Parini novel and contains a solid balance of drama and reverence. An extraordinary work. Engaging, informative, and deeply moving. This is a book, and a voice, for our times and is highly recommended." —David Bunn, bestselling author of *The Pilgrim*

"Of all the many books I have read about this 'Apostle to the Gentiles,' Parini's was the most helpful by far. . . . Splendidly readable. . . . He made Paul live for me." —Harvey Cox, Hollis Professor of Divinity Emeritus, Harvard University

"Fantastic. . . . Parini has produced a stellar novel that humanizes the Christian message and its messengers." —*Publishers Weekly* (starred review)

"Parini enlivens a narrative familiar to many with fine scenes and writerly touches. . . . An exceptional character study."

—*Kirkus Reviews*

"Sweeping in scope, yet as intimate as a breath. . . . Few [stories] are written with the intense detail and keen insight that Parini provides. . . . The beauty of [Parini's] language is everywhere. . . . A deeply intimate portrait. . . . Earthy and transcendent."

—*Booklist* (starred review)

JAY PARINI

THE DAMASCUS ROAD

Jay Parini is a poet, novelist, and biographer who teaches at Middlebury College. His six books of poetry include *New and Collected Poems, 1975–2015*. He has written eight novels, including *Benjamin's Crossing*, *The Apprentice Lover*, *The Passages of H.M.*, and *The Last Station*, which was made into an Academy Award–nominated film starring Helen Mirren and Christopher Plummer. His biographical subjects include John Steinbeck, Robert Frost, William Faulkner, and, most recently, Gore Vidal. His nonfiction works include *Jesus: The Human Face of God*, *Why Poetry Matters*, *Promised Land: Thirteen Books That Changed America*, and *The Way of Jesus: Living a Spiritual and Ethical Life*.

www.jayparini.com

THE DAMASCUS ROAD

Also by Jay Parini

FICTION

The Passages of H.M.
The Apprentice Lover
Benjamin's Crossing
Bay of Arrows
The Last Station
The Patch Boys
The Love Run

POETRY

New and Collected Poems: 1975–2015
The Art of Subtraction: New and Selected Poems
House of Days
Town Life
Anthracite Country
Singing in Time

NONFICTION AND CRITICISM

The Way of Jesus: Living a Spiritual and Ethical Life
Empire of Self: A Life of Gore Vidal
Jesus: The Human Face of God
The Selected Essays of Gore Vidal (edited by)
Promised Land: Thirteen Books That Changed America
Why Poetry Matters
The Art of Teaching
One Matchless Time: A Life of William Faulkner
Robert Frost: A Life
Some Necessary Angels: Essays on Writing and Politics
John Steinbeck: A Biography
Gore Vidal: Writer Against the Grain (edited by)
An Invitation to Poetry
Theodore Roethke: An American Romantic

THE DAMASCUS ROAD

A Novel of Saint Paul

JAY PARINI

ANCHOR BOOKS
A Division of Penguin Random House LLC
New York

FIRST ANCHOR BOOKS EDITION, MARCH 2020

The Library of Congress has cataloged the Doubleday edition as follows:
Name: Parini, Jay, author.
Title: The Damascus Road : a novel of Saint Paul / Jay Parini.
Description: First edition. | New York : Doubleday, 2019.
Identifiers: LCCN 2018021318
Subjects: LCSH: Paul, the Apostle, Saint—Fiction. | Bible. New Testament—
History of Biblical events—Fiction. | Apostles—Fiction. |
GSAFD: Christian fiction. | Biographical fiction.
Classification: LCC PS3566.A65 D36 2019 | DDC 813/.54—dc23
LC record available at https://lccn.loc.gov/2018021318

Anchor Books Trade Paperback ISBN: 978-0-307-38620-5
eBook ISBN: 978-0-385-53840-4

Author photograph © Oliver Parini
Map designed by Jeffrey L. Ward
Book design by Maria Carella

www.anchorbooks.com

146119709

For Devon,
my companion on the road

Jesus calls those who follow him to share his passion.
How can we convince the world by our preaching of the
passion when we shrink from that passion in our own lives?

—DIETRICH BONHOEFFER

One man will step into the holy fire,
Unfailing in his mission, unafraid.
He travels light, now driven by desire
From sundown into dawn, from pyre to pyre.

—ION OF CHIOS

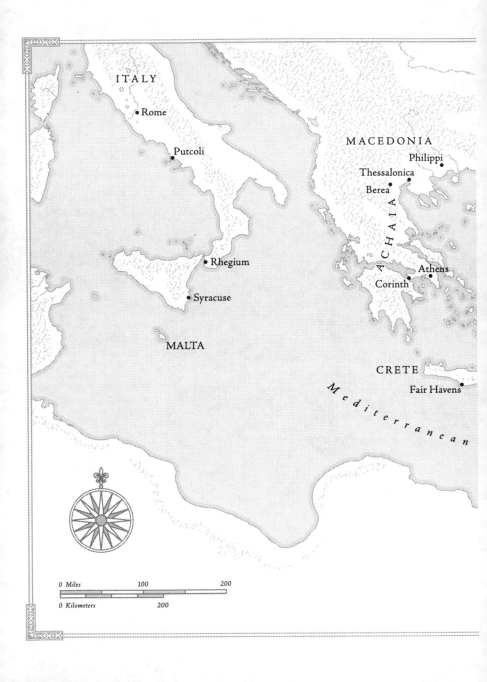

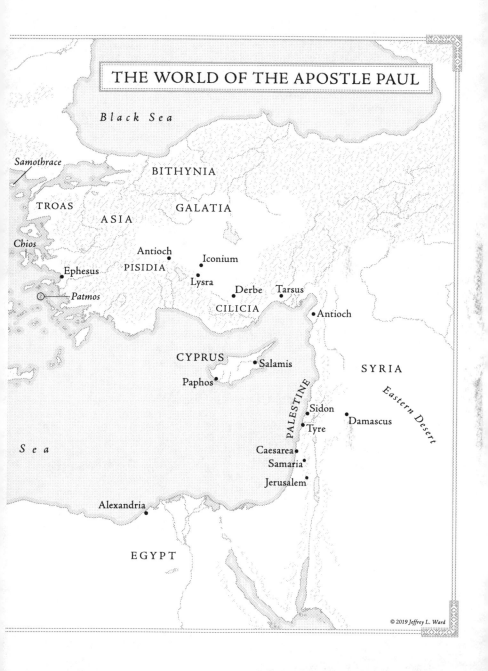

THE WORLD OF THE APOSTLE PAUL

Black Sea

Samothrace

BITHYNIA

TROAS

GALATIA

ASIA

Chios

Antioch
Iconium
PISIDIA
Lysra
Ephesus
Derbe
Tarsus
Patmos
CILICIA
Antioch

CYPRUS
SYRIA
Salamis
Eastern Desert
Paphos

Sidon
Damascus
PALESTINE
Tyre

Sea
Caesarea
Samaria
Jerusalem

Alexandria

EGYPT

© 2019 Jeffrey L. Ward

THE DAMASCUS ROAD

Chapter One

LUKE

The city began to burn on a quiet hot day in midsummer under the bluest of skies, fanned by dry winds from the northeast. The conflagration had already destroyed much of the capital as it swept from the mercantile district to the imperial city and scoured the valley between the Palatine and Aventine Hills, climbing and rolling over them, lunging into depressions and byways, setting ablaze the houses of rich and poor alike. It had even destroyed several of the emperor's beloved palaces, which were now nothing more than burned timber and rubble. In wooden tenements and mansions alike, floors tumbled through floors, windows billowed with tongues of flame. The sky at midnight became a huge vermillion dome with sparks showering from heaven.

This was, many said, God's revenge on a people who rejected his love.

But I doubted this. Paul had warned us not to imagine we could comprehend God's plan for his creation, even when catastrophes struck. "We can't see what God can see," he said. "One day all will become legible."

Everything was surely illegible now.

I fought my way through a scrim of hot smoke, past the charred remains of villas and public buildings. Since coming to Rome two years ago, I had made this trek countless times to sit with Paul in his room to take the dictation of his letters, to talk and pray with him, often recalling our decades on the road. He was the great apostle of our Lord, the man who, more than anyone in the Way of Jesus, had understood the meaning of the Christ in this world. He was a man changed forever on the Damascus Road, one who had proclaimed the unfolding Kingdom of God throughout the empire, a Jew preaching mostly to the Greeks, who had joined our circle in increasing numbers.

I had wished that after decades of rough travel, abuse, triumphs as well as failures, Paul could settle for a time. Nero, our grotesque emperor, had for years ignored the Jesus movement, and this had given us a feeling of security. But now he chose to blame us for this all-consuming fire. And why not? We were perfect scapegoats, an eccentric fringe, and few Romans had even heard of us. They would never object to our vilification, nor would they doubt our culpability. Our rude demise would perhaps satisfy their need for revenge.

Carts and barrows passed me, one after another, each loaded with household goods as families retreated into the Italian countryside, hoping to slip beyond the circle of their ravaged city. I was headed in the opposite direction, toward the house near the river that Paul shared with our friends Junia and Josephus. Normally this was an hour's easy walk. Today I would be lucky to make it at all.

Junia and Josephus were key figures in the Way. As such, they would be among the first taken into custody during any sweep of the city by Nero's men. I knew as much, but as I pushed through hot flaky smoke I tried to persuade myself that they would never arrest Paul, a lame old man with poor vision and threadbare hearing. Even if Junia and Josephus had been arrested, Paul would still be at the house, waiting for me to rescue him. I would find him sitting in his room and looking out his window at the plum tree in the walled garden, much as before. He had lived past the time when anyone should consider him a threat.

His legal status remained a puzzle. Was he really free, as we'd been told? Our troubles began in Jerusalem four years ago, on a sun-drenched day when he brought a Greek friend from abroad onto the grounds of Herod's Temple to show him the grandeur of this holy place, which as a boy he had first visited with his father and always loved. A few days later, a crowd accused Paul of violating Jewish laws by allowing a gentile to step across the forbidden boundary into a place where only Jews could pass. A riot broke out, and Paul was seized by Roman soldiers, who mistook him for a dangerous zealot who had been plotting against Rome. It was all so maddening and complex. After Paul spent two years in prison in Caesarea, the port of Judea, he asked the procurator in that city to send him to Rome for a hearing before the imperial courts. As a citizen, he had the right to this appeal, and they seemed only too glad to get rid of him. Paul's escort to Rome, the centurion Julius, had become our friend on the way. And, to be fair, Julius had tried to warn us that Paul might not actually receive a hearing. He had conferred with an acquaintance at the imperial courts and was told frankly that Paul's case could only be seen as a highly technical, incomprehensible, and obviously petty squabble among Jews. The courts would assume Paul had been sent away by the local authorities in Palestine to rid them of a nuisance. "You should simply disappear into the crowd," Julius told Paul. "You're a free man."

This suggestion only irritated Paul, who wished to justify himself before the law. There was no truth in the accusations made against him in Jerusalem, and it still rankled that the Jews—his own beloved people—would humiliate him in this way. Was he not a righteous man who loved the Temple with all his heart? "Those who accuse me have no idea who I am, or what I represent! Almighty God speaks to me! They're scoundrels!"

It dismayed me to hear him talk in this way. That was the old Paul, the fanatic who at times became so obsessed with his own righteousness that he lost track of his grand and beautiful vision of God, his connection to the Holy Spirit. He forgot that he did not need to justify himself before the imperial courts or Temple authorities. The only judge who mattered was, of course, Almighty God.

Discouraged though he was, Paul had continued to work on behalf of the Way. He had moved freely among the house meetings in various parts of Rome and surrounding villages, presiding over the sacred meals that occurred on the First Day, offering words of encouragement, cautionary tales, digressions on scripture, and reflections on the meaning of the Christ and his "perpetual resurrection," as he put it. His mere presence had excited those in our movement, which grew day by day.

"I'm just beginning to understand," Paul had said to me the last time I saw him, only a week before the great fire began.

"You're always a beginner," I said, teasing him.

"A perpetual beginner. Aren't we all?"

Though his body crumbled in the usual ways, he had retained his voice, a resonant if gruff instrument, which had sounded through the empire. Abundant lung power fed its amplitude, and he could be heard above any crowd. "Not since Cicero have we had such an orator," I heard a man say after Paul had addressed a gathering only a few months before the fire. Indeed, Cicero was a figure in Paul's mind, and I could see the parallels, even if Paul lacked the guile of the famous Roman consul. Though subtle in his thought, he did not possess Cicero's lawyerly precision, his way of patiently making a case and refusing to wander into byways of reflection. Paul said whatever he thought, whenever he thought it, often with an obscurity that dismayed his listeners. And yet he never purposely deceived anyone.

Now I was desperate to see him, to speak to him, at least one last time. I prayed: *Oh Lord our God, protect your great apostle.*

The air grew hotter, the smoke thicker as I walked toward his house, with ill omens along the way. I saw a rat stupefied in the gutter, staring at me with fiery red eyes, with a burning tail. A donkey lay by the road, dead, its hide blackened with soot, its teeth bared and grinning obscenely. A vulture lifted from the hot dust with the carcass of a dog in its talons, and it flapped its wide leathery wings over the burning rooftops of government buildings. Abandoned children wandered in the streets, exhausted, unable even to cry, and I had to assume their parents had succumbed to the fire.

Smoke curled around a stone embankment where I crouched to catch my breath and sucked in air through a piece of wet muslin. I watched helplessly as a young man walked without hope into the flaming doorway of a villa, as if unfazed, his arms stretched out with sleeves of fire. He had, I supposed, lost everything already, so losing himself meant nothing. The sorrows in his heart canceled the anguish of his charred and melting flesh. I wondered if, for him, the fires didn't create a gaudy equilibrium of sorts, an unholy balance of forces.

The firestorm had already killed thousands of Romans, mostly the poorest of the poor, who could not find places to hide or means of escape. From what I heard, the open fields and orchards around Rome had become trampled-over encampments, with legions of displaced people scrambling to survive as best they could, the more fortunate ones living in tents or makeshift shelters. The army did its best to provide water and food to those in great need, but it felt as if nobody were in charge.

And where was Nero in all this? Some accused him of hiding at his summer palace in Actium and paying no attention to our troubles. Others suggested he was in Actium in frightful agony, worried about the fate of his beloved people. Nero was evil, but never stupid. In a ploy to elicit public support, he had set up a shelter on the grounds of one of his few remaining palaces by the river, where bread and water appeared, as if by magic, laid out on tables and rationed by soldiers. I shivered to imagine his mind, its recesses and tar-black depths. This was, after all, the man who encouraged and fed the public taste for gladiatorial combat, gratifying their wish to see animals rip human beings into mounds of flesh. He himself often appeared at these contests and cheered on the vengeful displays.

And now he had spread this vile rumor about the Way of Jesus, saying we had lit this fire. And for what reason? Could anyone imagine that we hoped to gain anything from the destruction of Rome?

I pushed ahead as best I could through the purple smoke and glitter of sparks, arriving at Paul's house much later than expected. Two small boys, the children of Junia and Josephus, cowered by the fiery wall of what had been a happy home. Their white eyes drilled through soot-glazed faces. They froze when they saw me, though they had welcomed me into their home countless times in the past two years. How could they think I would harm them? Their minds could hardly begin to fathom the horrors that flared around them and wrecked their lives.

I had a few figs in my sack, and I held them out for the boys. They stared, unresponsive, though I could only guess how hungry they must be and what terror held them down with its hot thumb.

"Come on, boys," I said. "I'm Luke, Paul's friend. Remember?"

As often as I'd come to visit Paul and their parents, I had not quite formed a bond with these boys, not as Paul had. He was good with children and enjoyed telling them stories of his travels, exaggerating his adventures. He had never encountered "slimy monsters and fire-breathing serpents and bears with lightning in their claws," as he told them with a straight face, yet he purveyed these stories with relish, even suggesting I should write them down.

"I will only tell the truth," I said.

This produced deep-chested laughter, even tears, in Paul. "I do love you, dear Luke," he said. "But what do you mean by 'the truth'?"

Did the apostle of our Lord have to ask such a question? Was he pretending to be Plato, the Greek philosopher he admired so much? I must have looked a fool to him.

Occasionally he would do magic tricks for the boys, such as making a flower appear in his ear, which he would then pluck and present to the child, who watched dumbfounded. When I asked quite innocently how he did this, he replied without hesitation, "I grow a flower in my ear."

At last the younger boy, a twig of a child with cropped hair and flinty eyes, took a fig from my hand.

"That's it! Good boy," I said. "Eat."

As he chewed it deliberately, the roof of the house fell through with a whoosh and spray of gold-vermillion sparks. The heat of it pulsed. The boy and I locked gazes.

"Where are your parents, son? And Paul the apostle?"

The boy chewed and held my gaze, but no answers came.

"They're not here, are they?"

"Took them, they did."

"All of them?"

He nodded slightly.

I knelt before the boy, squaring up to him. "How long ago did this happen? Try to remember."

My urgency made no impression on him. He simply ate his fig, chewing very slowly. His life had become all cinders, smoke, and flame, and nothing mattered now, not even this morsel of nourishment. He and his brother were being licked by the fires of the world, and if their parents failed to return, they would become slaves or servants, at best. More likely, they would starve to death at the edge of the city, becoming one of thousands of unnamed bodies turfed into mass graves at the bottom of the Esquiline Hill or dumped into the

Tiber. Many times I had sat on those sad banks and watched miserable scraps of human debris float by on the brown river.

Now the elder boy, who had resisted me, stepped closer, and I handed him a fig as well. "Did you see who came?" I asked.

In my heart I knew that something hateful had befallen Paul. I imagined him with Junia and Josephus, all three of them locked in a fetid jail, where they would be tortured and murdered without ceremony. I had witnessed the ingenuity and brutality of Roman torture firsthand, and it was never pretty. Once, on a dusty trail in the provinces of Asia, I had seen a traitor staked out for hours until he died, a fat rusty nail driven through his anus and sticking him to a plank with his belly to the board. And that, unfortunately, was hardly the worst thing I saw.

"Did your parents say anything to you?" I asked the boy.

It was quite pointless, I could see, to persist in this way. The children had no information, and whatever they had witnessed, they couldn't say. The words would never come. So I put a coin into each of their hands, a weak gesture of thanks.

A thick swirl of ash blew toward us, a cloud of red-hot cinders, and I fell to my knees. My face felt on fire, and I couldn't see. When the cloud passed, I looked up, but the boys had vanished.

"Boys!"

I staggered to my feet, rushing into the nearby alleyway between their house and another building. I could not let them go. But another whirlwind caught me with a blast, and I fell to the pavement, and I could not move.

But the boys!

I dragged myself toward an opening in the smoke, leaning into what I thought was the direction they must have gone. But the alleyway branched in three directions, and there were flames at the end of each, massive clots of fire. Turning back, I hoped to follow them another way. The streets in this part of Rome all circled upon each other and, at some point, converged. For an hour or more I searched through the smolder before abandoning hope of finding them.

In a quiet spot apart from the fire, near the river, I sat on a rock and prayed. Prayer was my only refuge. And I begged God for guidance. I could not possibly discover a way forward without divine intervention. But I could not bend my will to God's will, accepting that Paul had vanished and that I might never speak to him again. *Do not let this happen!* I prayed.

It was late afternoon by the time I rose, exhausted, to cross the capital on foot once again. The flames had spread from the slave quarters near the base of the Circus Maximus, where it caused a claustrophobic huddle of human misery. I pushed ahead through the imperial city, where the Temple of Luna was reduced to blackened stones and smoldering char. Vesta's shrine was damaged too, and flames licked the edges of the Forum.

Was this the apocalypse that Paul had predicted? "He is coming soon," Paul would tell gatherings in the early days of our efforts. "Waste no time! You might not even get to sleep through the night!"

Many in Rome would not sleep through this night.

✝

Somehow I made it back to my room in the house of Atilius, a young friend and follower of the Way, on the other side of Rome. That I was alive at all surprised me. Though exhausted, I could hardly sleep, and my thoughts turned to all the ways I had failed Paul, small and large. How could I even pretend to be his physician? In the past few months he had spent many days in bed, complaining of vicious headaches that shot from temple to temple and distorted his vision. I treated this condition—not unfamiliar to those who practice medicine—with an herbal compound, a mixture of ginger bark and clove, with extracts of willow. Yet he slept badly, and the headaches continued without pause, though it helped a little to apply a wet cloth soaked in the dust of eucalyptus leaves to his forehead. I would sit beside him, listening to him gasp until he fell asleep.

Some nights, as Junia told me, he wandered alone in the city streets, returning with the next day's sun on blistered feet, which she insisted he soak in brine. Walking in pain with a stick at night, he told her, was preferable to tormented sleep. I objected to these nighttime prowls, too. "Rome is full of thieves and murderers," I told him. "One night you'll disappear, and we'll have no idea what happened."

Paul would shrug and say, "Luke, you're a physician. My dear friend, summon your magic!"

But I was not a magician, and I could not rescue my dearest friend. I could not make him sleep soundly, without pain.

A few weeks before the fire began, Paul and I had visited a gathering of the Way near Ostia, a port some miles to the west of Rome, where we spent a few nights with Lucina. She had been a Godfearer—that is, she was a Greek like myself, a gentile drawn to the God of Israel, to the richness of Jewish traditions and the glorious Hebrew scriptures, where God had spoken with eloquence and force. Like me, she had turned to the Way of Jesus, as had so many Godfearers over the years. (They had become our richest source of converts.)

She owned a fine villa on an estate that had belonged to her family for generations, and had become our close friend and benefactor. She suggested that Paul and I retreat to a small house near the coast that belonged to her. This could, she said, become our "final refuge" after years of wandering on the distant roads of empire, over mountains and through long valleys, from city to city, by ship or foot, donkey, cart, or camel.

"Your work is done," she told us.

Paul thanked Lucina, saying that he liked the idea of a peaceable time by the sea. It would not, of course, mean the end of his work. His trenchant, eloquent letters to followers of the Way often provoked controversies and required elaborations and clarifications; he could easily spend the rest of his life responding to their questions and clarifying his positions. For my part, I would try to finish my life of Jesus, which had preoccupied me for decades. And I would write, if God permitted, an account of my travels with Paul, our journeys through the empire with the Good News, as we called it, in hand, this message of God's love.

In safety and seclusion, in Lucina's seaside refuge, we might finish our projects.

That was the dream, now scorched by flames.

Paul had envisioned the end of history in fervid and often beautiful dreams. But the sky had not opened with brass trumpets and voluptuous choirs of angels, with the eyes of the Christ burning into the world as he descended from the clouds. The bodies of the dead had not risen through the packed dirt over their graves, becoming light itself. We had not been transmogrified, turned into angels.

Not without the pain of loss, Paul had begun to modify his sense of what Jesus meant for us and how the final days might unfold.

"Stay calm, and love God," he had said, when I pressed for answers. "He will know you when he returns. Time does not concern us."

But I wanted and needed more. I needed to find Paul.

✝

The next morning Atilius, a kindly soul whose ministrations always surprised me with their gentleness, brought a plate of orange slices to my room. His hand trembled, and he sat beside me silently. I could see that something troubled him. I forced myself to eat and did not ask for news, as it could only discourage me. Only when I had chewed and swallowed the last segment did he tell me, in tears, that Nero's soldiers had herded dozens of our friends into a stadium, stuffing them into the skins of beasts. Wild dogs had been set upon them, tearing them apart for the entertainment of crazed onlookers, many of whom scavenged in the crowd for a crust of bread or drink of water.

"I'm leaving Rome," he said in a low voice, as if even within his own house he might be overheard and seized. "And you should too, Luke. It's not safe."

"I'm going to look for Paul."

"This is foolish." But he saw I could not be dissuaded, and he sighed.

✝

Near sunset, I headed to the foot of the Aventine, by chance meeting Marcus, another Roman convert to the Way, who told me that only the night before, in a garden called the Circus of Nero, the site of chariot races in recent years, they had burned our people alive, transforming them into human torches. They were likely to do the same again tonight.

I knew the garden well, as Paul and I had often gone there to pray in that green enclosure, once a shrine to Cybele, with its tidy rows of poplar, its fragrant oleander beds, yellow roses, and sword lilies. It had been a tranquil place for us.

"I must go there," I said.

Marcus looked at me with fear. "It's not safe for any of us," he said.

But what did safety matter? What was my life anymore? Paul might be there in the Circus of Nero, ablaze, in agony. Though my skills were hardly equal to this outrage, I would do whatever I could for him and assist the others as best I could. If they arrested me and burned me to death as well, so be it. Paul's words came back to me: "The suffering of the present moment is meaningless, especially when we think of the glory to come, with the Christ, who is revealed in him." Helpless though I was, I would be glad for a way to show my allegiance to the Kingdom of God and my affection for his son.

Marcus grasped my hand to say goodbye, and I set off toward the garden by myself.

As darkness dropped, I fell in with a Roman mob, folding myself in their chaos, hiding amid their raucous cheers and bellowing. They surged through the streets, some of them lifting torches. Their violent energies, and hatred, appalled me.

And then I heard it: The agony of voices peeling over the rooftops. The sound cut my heart into strips.

"They're burning them," said a toothless man beside me in demotic Greek.

"Who? Who are they burning?"

"The Way," he said. "The ones who set this fire. They follow the Christ."

He used the Greek word for messiah, "the Christ," and in spite of my terror I felt a rush of satisfaction: Jesus was indeed the Christ and not simply the Jewish messiah. He was the Word itself, before and after time, the pulse of consciousness, the shaping spirit of the Almighty. As Paul had written, "Our Christ is one in whom all things come together."

The garden blazed with dozens of human torches. Soldiers had poured black pitch over our people and set them ablaze. Not even Gethsemane had known such anguish.

I pulled the cowl over my face and crouched behind a glistening ivy. My nerves rippled, hot lines in the sleeves of my arms and legs. I burned with my friends, ablaze myself and screaming inside.

The lucky ones were, thank God, already dead, so beyond this horror and anguish. The flesh had melted from their faces, and the black eyeholes in their skulls outstared infamy.

I took this inferno as a sign from God and could hardly doubt its meaning. Paul was right: The end of time had drawn near. It was, perhaps, here. Our Lord would at any moment appear, and the mighty of the earth would collapse beneath the weight of his glory.

But where was Paul?

Chapter Two

PAUL

Y ou're lazy," my father said, as he pruned an olive tree in our garden. "God hates lazy people."

He was slightly stooped, his head sloping forward like a vulture, with his shoulder blades like folded wings; the back of his neck glowed like a stalk of cinnamon, the consequence of long days in the sun. His name was Adriel, and he had a pronounced dimple in his chin, deep and dark, that had carried over generations. I had the same mark in my chin.

I was twelve years old, with the first hint of a mustache dawning above my lip, and too old to treat like a child. The charge of laziness passed through me like a hot blade. Had I not been piling branches on a heap for him, stacking them all afternoon under a ferocious blast of sunlight?

"Goddamn you," I said.

It was not the best choice of words.

He knocked my head to one side with a flat palm, drawing a welt along my jawline.

I tried not to cry, bending forward to conceal my pain. I never cried, though my neck would hurt for a week. And this wasn't the first or only time he had slapped me, though it felt like an assault on my dignity.

For whatever reason, I remember that slap, even as a fully grown man who has been stripped, flogged, stoned, and beaten many times over. But none of that violence stands out more vividly than the day my father swatted me in the garden.

Though I loved my father, I never liked being home. It was more than comfortable, even among houses on the western fringe of Tarsus, where the wealthiest merchants had a wide view of the green sea below. We had four bedrooms with raised beds and two public rooms, including a peristyle with tapestries on the wall; there was an expansive garden and a spring-fed well. A dozen guests could dine comfortably in our tablinum, and my father often brought associates to meals there, where they would recline on soft cushions and discuss business matters. Our three slaves went to the market every morning and cooked and cleaned the house. They treated me, a motherless boy, like their own child, especially Gila, a white-haired woman with astonishingly wide hips, her hair pulled back and tied with a ribbon. She considered me her son, and laid out a fresh tunic for me every day and made sure that I ate and slept enough. "You must eat more fruit," she would say.

My mother passed when I was eleven months old, so I have no memory of her. Not even the haziest image survives, however much I try to envision her. My sister, Esther, was ten years my senior, but I hardly knew her, as she went off to Jerusalem at seventeen, where she married a man twice her age, a rabbi who had been my father's friend. Her letters were infrequent, and we saw her only on periodic visits to Jerusalem.

My grandfather came to Tarsus from a village near Jerusalem as a young man hoping to study philosophy as well as Torah. This had been a center of learning for centuries, the Athens of Asia, the birthplace of Antipater, the Stoic writer and exalted teacher.

Much as he liked the idea of it, my grandfather had no head for study, and he eventually turned to business, gathering from valley farmers the skins of goats. After buying a mill on the Cydnus River, he engaged dozens of slaves to work the fine goat hairs into a durable and coveted fabric, which he sold throughout the world. Large bundles of this cloth were shipped in wooden crates as far as Greece and Egypt, even to Rome. He also made tents that could easily be rolled and carried on the backs of mules by Roman legions on military expeditions. His assets accumulated, with profits in profusion, and he soon bought land on the outskirts of Tarsus. Before long, he had several villas, factories, warehouses, and a fleet of vessels in the harbor.

All of this wealth would eventually come to me, though my only interest was to spend everything I had in the name of Jesus. I would happily become a poor man for his sake.

My father would never understand this. He had no depth of spirit, even though he became a figure of weight in the local synagogue, where he would read from the scroll on the Sabbath: an honor in this city, where scholars often wandered into Sabbath gatherings, many of them gifted linguists. He would shift to the rostrum slowly, gazing through eyes like slits, furtively. His performance impressed the congregation, as he could utter the sacred words with some authority, though Greek was his first language, like mine. In truth, I could detect a stiffness and inexactitude in his Hebrew even before I myself knew the language well enough to be discerning. Then again, a boy is always skeptical of his father's public face, and I felt his incompetence in every performance. I vowed that nobody would ever have cause to doubt the depth of my knowledge, the range of my learning, the ferocity of my devotion to God. I would become everything my father only seemed to be. I would inhabit fully the reality I dreamed about as a boy.

Each morning at home my father read the scriptures aloud, in the Greek translation. Because of its familiarity, this version felt to me more like God's revelation than the Hebrew original. Its strong and beautiful if bracing words dug grooves in my heart, and my feelings flowed naturally in those grooves.

I was a Jew, and would always remain a Jew, even as my mission to the gentiles grew wider each year.

In my early years I sometimes traveled with my father, who had business in distant parts, with visits to Alexandria and throughout Asia. We would occasionally visit Esther and her husband, Ezra, during the week of Passover in Jerusalem, and attend the Temple worship. How could I forget that overwhelming vision of gold-and-white marble that Herod had built? As we approached its steps, the full-throated choirs of the tribe of Levi welcomed us with their angelic singing, and even then I had visions of God on his throne, the king of heaven, and I wanted only to bathe in this glory.

My father explained that the tribal elders, the Sanhedrin, met in the Hall of Hewn Stones. "They are great men," he said. "You will sit among them one day."

This seemed inevitable to him, at least during my childhood, when the evidence of my scholarly abilities grew abundant, and tutors praised my gifts. "Your son is a bright star," they would say, pleasing him so well that he would lavish gifts on them.

This approbation only made my life difficult, as expectations rose. And I kicked against them, feeling reckless at times, wishing to revolt. I would steal fruit from the market or go abroad at night, often walking down to the harbor when my father assumed I slept safely on my pallet. I became a nocturnal creature for a period, a vagabond at heart, and thought of escaping to sea. I vowed to myself that I would wander in the world, no longer the pride of Adriel. No longer the perfect son whose life gave flesh to his father's fantasies.

But my scholarly nature kept reasserting itself. I could not deny the appeal of learning, the lure of the Greek and Hebrew languages, and the shimmering light of truth reflected there.

When I was twelve, my father took me with him on a trip to Jerusalem and, much to my surprise, he introduced me to Gamaliel, a well-known Jewish scholar (who was the grandson of Hillel, the famous rabbi). Quite terrified, I held my father's hand tightly as we walked into Gamaliel's school, where young men chanted portions of the Psalms. They nodded as they prayed, some of them dipping to the floor in their avidity, even kissing the tile with their foreheads. I caught sight of Gamaliel himself at the end of a colonnade, a marvel with his bountiful and hoary beard and purple skullcap; the voluminous robes he wore failed to disguise a multitudinous belly that he pushed before him like a cart. At a glance, I worshipped him and wished only to serve his needs.

"You'll attend this school one day," my father said. "I have already written to Gamaliel about you."

This startled and impressed me. My father had, on his own, taken my intellect seriously. He would put me on this path as best he could. Of course, he could send me to a school like this because he could afford such a luxury, which fed his own feelings of importance in the Jewish community. He would proudly tell his friends in Tarsus that young Paul sat at the feet of the grandson of Hillel. In his mind, I would take my place in this tradition, a scholar of the Hebrew scriptures, perhaps as a great rabbi. He nonetheless insisted that I learn to stitch and fold tents like any one of his workers. I had nimble fingers, taking to these tasks eagerly, and my affinity for this work pleased my father.

It was lucky for me that my father had so many projects in his business to oversee that I could escape his surveillance. Tarsus was a splendid playground, as pagan temples could be found in every quarter, all of them seething with the devotees of strange gods, and this spiritual frenzy appealed to me. The worshippers of the god Mithras, for example, caught my attention, as they met in underground vaults and sacrificed bulls, bathing in their blood, which became for them a redemptive gesture that helped them to purify their souls. I knew one boy, Fabian, the son of a Roman guard, who had contacts with this group, and once I stepped beside him into a cave at the outskirts of the city.

They huddled together in the dark, which only a handful of large candles illumined. Most of them wore long white robes, although one of them, a kind of high priest, had purple robes and a diadem of flowers. He held a scepter in the air, chanting in a language unfamiliar to my ears. They had lifted a living bull to a makeshift platform, and one of the votaries slit its throat. One by one the worshippers stepped beneath it, allowing the stream of blood to cover them. The women among them trilled their tongues, and the men sang together, accompanied by a hollow drum. I had never heard such peculiar music.

Fabian had said, "We must all be washed in the blood of the bull."

I had no wish to do anything of the sort and stepped away with my back to the cave wall.

"These people, they are worse than mad," my father said, when I asked what he knew about the Mithras cult. "Stay far away from them, son. Do you hear me?"

Often I felt like a thief in my own house, scarcely welcome, taking what was not mine; and yet some of my happiest days unfolded in Tarsus. I loved to see the mountains in the northern distance, the peaks with snowy scalps lifting through the tree line in early spring. I dreamed of climbing those peaks, rising in a snowfield, white as the sun, all radiance and dissolving into light. I longed to get out of this world, my life, my body: to rise and rise.

I was, in fact, a dreamy child, one who loved to sit by the harbor in the early morning, watching merchant ships depart for Cyprus or the farthest ends of the earth. Memories of that quayside lingered. I once, for instance, saw a lightly bearded young man kissing an older sailor, and the image unsettled me. It's odd how certain recollections will stick, while others—more significant—just fall away. I would shelter under a tarpaulin, listening to the talk of sailors, absorbing tales of adventure, of foreign tribes and customs, exotic sea creatures, of unlikely and miraculous landscapes with vistas of snow or sand. These travelers had been to Spain and Arabia, to Athens and Macedonia, to Alexandria and countless seedy ports along the Black Sea.

Everyone talked of Rome, of course: the center of the world. And I dreamed of going there one day.

The odor of spices—cloves and coriander, nutmeg and cinnamon—lifted from dockside stalls, and the quayside itself churned with prostitutes, girls and young men as well, who seemed inoffensive to me. I didn't know for certain, not yet, what they offered for a fee. Yet I understood only too well that my father wouldn't approve of their behavior, and heard him talking to one of his assistants about the "vile creatures" who approached sailors and visitors, taking money for "the use of their filthy bodies."

I often thought about that phrase: *the use of their filthy bodies.*

"Your body is God's temple," my father told me, quoting the Tohorot.

He was always quoting something, usually getting it wrong. But I never forgot many of these sayings. And he would remind me of our status.

"We're Roman citizens," he said, as if I might forget. "Your grandfather purchased our citizenship at a very dear price. So we may appeal to the emperor when it's necessary, and they know this, the authorities. Never be afraid of them. Ask to speak to the emperor yourself if you should find yourself in trouble. You have every right."

This sounded improbable, as the Son of God in Rome (as Tiberius fashioned himself) probably had better ways to occupy himself than listening to the complaints of minor subjects from the provinces; but my father never let go of this. He was himself an emperor in his world: an iron-fisted man, a man of commercial influence, a godlike figure who didn't allow fools room for their foolishness.

He was a lonely man as well, especially after the death of my mother, and I rarely saw him with friends. We never met for meals with neighbors, as others did. It would be difficult even to call our little household a family, in fact. It was just my father and me, with a sister who lived far away and rarely saw us, and three slaves.

I did, however, have my friend Simon, whose father worked closely with mine as a shipping agent and might have been considered a friend since they very occasionally dined together, though nobody thought of them as equals. I know my father didn't. But that didn't matter, and I grew fond of Simon, an orange-haired boy with gray-green eyes. He caught everyone's attention, as nobody looked quite like him in Tarsus.

My father whispered that Simon must have slave blood in him, "possibly Egyptian," though I had never seen a slave with orange hair or green eyes. He was taller than me by a good measure: I doubt that the top of my head ever reached his chin. Strong and lean, from the age of ten or eleven he spoke with the authority of a man, in resolute tones, with a knowledge of the world around him. I had never observed such confidence in a boy.

We both liked swimming and knew the good places along the banks of the Cydnus, some miles above the city. My father had taken me to a rock pool in this river when I was five or six, teaching me to feel comfortable in the water as we played in the shallows. I never felt closer to him, not before or after. In the course of my instruction, I discovered that after a while I didn't need his big hand under my back. I could float by myself and would seek out places to swim on my own. The gift of swimming was perhaps his most precious offering.

One swimming hole beneath a waterfall near Tarsus became a favorite place of escape for Simon and me. The waterfall crashed into an icy pool below the river, fanning out in ripples, obscuring the sharp blades of rock that sometimes flashed below the surface. My father would never approve of my swimming in this place, nor would Simon's father. But we didn't care what they said. It was enough that they couldn't see us, and that both had better things to do than worry about where their sons went to swim.

Indifference to children is also a grant of freedom.

On hot summer mornings Simon and I walked there together.

Unlike me, Simon was a fine diver, an arrow shot into the stream between its rocky blades. I would follow in his path, but nervously, jumping feetfirst, as I sensed the danger. But danger was part of the thrill of this activity, part of us now.

I was beginning to learn to live with peril, even to crave it.

By the edge of the pool were gray rocks, warmer than the water below or beside them. We crawled onto them like lizards after paddling in the swift gurgle of the stream, and would lie in the sun, letting pearly beads of water evaporate from our skin, saying nothing, needing to say nothing, just listening to the water tumble below us, fizzing and churning.

I loved its hoarse voice, its throaty rumble.

Simon himself had none of my scholarly or religious instincts, and he wondered politely about my devotion to reading the scriptures or my interest in Greek poets. Once in a while I allowed myself to think aloud in his company about philosophical matters, as if testing the waters. But he would bat away these ruminations.

"Do you care nothing for this earth?" he asked.

"What do you mean?"

"This world, the earth, a running stream. Not the clouds!"

It was an odd thing for him to ask me, and I quoted from David: *The earth is the Lord's and the fullness thereof.*

This drew an approving grin, and I can still see the happy opening in Simon's face, his brilliant white teeth with uneven spaces between them. With his smile, he blessed and welcomed me, even when I went overboard in conversation. He didn't mind if I was silly with philosophical affectations and quotations, as long as (like him) I took pleasure in the cool stream and the hot stones where we lay. I think friendship itself was everything to Simon.

One day at the far end of summer, when it was too hot to breathe and one could not sit anywhere comfortably, Simon and I hiked out to this waterfall, our secret place. I had turned fifteen that summer and felt like a man, with a silky beard darkening my cheeks. I let my hair grow to a fashionable length, and wore only the finest linen tunics and leather sandals with glass-studded straps, an affectation that annoyed my father, who once said, "I've seen girls in those slippers."

The remark stung, and it hurts to recall it. How could he humiliate me like that? But my father clung to every convention and had no tolerance for youthful attempts to separate oneself, to express uniqueness.

As Simon and I approached the waterfall, I began to speak about the existence of the soul, its name and nature, or the possibility that our bodies might one day inhabit a different form, something quite unlike what we understood as human. The soul itself, I said, was possibly like a bird, high in the heavens, and in its soaring left these passing shadows on the ground, these bodily traces of its existence.

These ideas had come to me in a dream and troubled me. My friend Fabian had mentioned that the votaries of Mithras believed in the divine re-creation of life in some cosmic realm, and this had excited me. I wished that the Hebrew scriptures had talked more explicitly about such things, the shape of the life that lay beyond us, whatever glistened at the horizon, beyond the edge of every visible thing.

Simon let me ramble. But then he sighed loudly.

"I think I'm boring you," I said.

"It's a little sad for me to see you troubled," he replied, as we approached the cliff above the rock pool. "You should know, I don't really mind what you say. You're interested in these notions."

"But I'm dull," I said.

"Or mad," he said. Then he laughed, and it pleased me that he would laugh and not simply shrug or turn away from me.

We stood for a while in silence on the bluff above the pool, taking in the beauty of the place, the churned-up freshness of the air, the crackling water, a wistful breeze. I watched a large and colorful bird hover, then drop into the river, rise with a fish in its mouth. I wiped my face with the back of my hand, and the salt of perspiration ran into my mouth as I tilted my head upward. Quite literally, I seemed to be melting away and drinking myself.

I watched as Simon slipped from his clothes and plunged head-first into the water below. Many times I had watched him arrowing through the air like this, always so agile, unafraid of diving from a height.

Now I leaned over the cliff, slightly dizzy. The sun blinded me, and I had to shade my eyes, expecting a shout. He would usually draw me into the water within minutes, forcing me to abandon my fears.

I called out, "Simon!"

When his head didn't break the water within moments, and no voice called from below, I was only confused, not frightened. He had probably come up in a different place, farther downstream than usual.

I shouted again, but his name hung in the air, unanswered, as the sun tucked itself behind a cloud as if ashamed of something.

And then the day darkened.

Sick with fear, I jumped, and was sucked through the air in the downward draft, breaking the hard glass of the water with a slap that stung the soles of my feet. My heels dug into the sandy bottom, stirred to a muddy cloud. When I opened my eyes, it was impossible to see: the water opaque, a hail of bubbles and swirling sand. Lifting my head above the surface, I scanned the river and its banks without seeing him.

"Simon!"

I must have called his name a dozen times but recall only a blur, the watery fizz, an upturned sky, and sharp black ledges covered with moss. I saw a mass of scudding clouds, an innocent bird that had strayed into this terrible scene without knowing what it had happened upon by chance.

I climbed onto nearby rocks to scan the pool, hoping that Simon had come up in some unexpected place or, perhaps, lay quietly under a ledge. It was like him to play games with me, although this was a step too far.

The waterfall thundered in my ears, and my whole body shook. Could it be suddenly so cold?

I called again and again for Simon, but with a faint voice now.

After a timeless time of searching the shoreline, I saw him at last, in the distance, the unmistakable orange hair, in a pale wad of reeds. I didn't understand at first, or dare to understand, what this could mean, even as I approached. I waded slowly into the shallows, talking to myself, praying. I could hear my voice, oddly removed from my body, calling out, "No, no, no . . ."

I lifted Simon to a bank of dry grass nearby. A wide gash in his forehead explained what had happened only too well. He had caught the left side of his head on a buried rock blade, and it had sliced away a part of his skull. I could see into the cavity itself, its tangle of blood and gristle and soft sponge.

I knelt over Simon's limp body, putting my face against his chest. And held him for a long time, my maimed dear friend.

I whispered his name to myself, letting it hang in the air above us as his bloody head lay against my chest.

I wanted him back again. Back, back, back.

But he was not coming back, not in the same way.

Ever.

※

Chapter Three

PAUL

I recall one horrific day on the outskirts of Jerusalem.

"Help me," a voice cried.

A man quivered on a cross with pain, hung by the wrists.

I had seen crucifixions before, especially near Jerusalem. Crosses were a common sight on dusty roads leading into the countryside of Judea or anywhere in the empire, with miserable creatures strung up, fly-bitten, bruised, dying, or dead: thieves and runaway slaves, rebels and bandits, adversaries of empire beside those falsely accused. This serial ordeal of milestones along any Roman road warned us, Jew and Greek alike, to behave as they told us.

"Help, sir!"

"I can't do anything," I said, though his black eyes caught me on their hooks. What had he done? Steal a handful of nuts, a loaf of bread? Prayed too loudly? Thrown a stone at a Roman soldier? It took very little to condemn a Jew to death in Palestine. And I should have known better than to pause beneath a cross or to engage with a dying man. The consequences for assisting a wretch in these circumstances would be horrific. I might hang next to him before long. The law was the law.

On the other hand, I saw no soldiers in sight, nor anyone else.

I found a suitable stone, about the size of a hammer's head. With an energy that appalled me, I lifted it twice, hitting him squarely on each of his kneecaps, which crumpled under my blows like eggshells. He sighed, a mixture of anguish and relief, staring ahead in fixed agony.

"It works," a friend had explained to me. "You speed them on their way by breaking both knees. There is no better solution."

I watched in agony as the poor man quickly proved unable to support himself with his legs, so all weight shifted to his upper body. Within minutes, the shoulders slid from their sockets. His elbows and wrists gave way, elongating the arms. He sighed again, his mouth distorting, his eyes bulging. With his rib cage lifting, the wretch gulped for air, in a state of protracted inhalation. Suffocation came quickly. Within less than fifteen minutes, he was dead.

We all suffered with this Roman bit in our teeth, and I myself could take no pride in my Roman citizenship.

This was especially so in Jerusalem, with the imperial guards in the streets and sprawling military encampments at the edge of the city to the southwest. The camps swarmed with boisterous troops who spoke a rude dialect of Latin that few of us understood. The officers rode tall war horses through the markets, taking whatever pleased them without paying. I'd seen any number of protesters cut down brutally with a sword, their bodies left for the buzzards, since it was dangerous to reclaim the corpses. And the Antonia Fortress, which had held Jesus briefly on the night before his crucifixion, bulged with Jews who had, for any number of reasons, dared to resist Rome, even in small ways (like spitting in the path of a soldier or refusing to nod in respect when a centurion passed).

It had never been like this under Herod the Great, who had rebuilt the Temple almost by himself. But under Herod Antipas, one of his measly and self-serving sons, a Jew could be arrested for anything: stealing a handful of dates or figs, even praying in public. Almost any gesture of defiance could offend the empire, appear treasonous, and lead to imprisonment. Public trials had become sideshows. A simple word from above (and one could never tell who spoke on behalf of Rome) could send a man to his death by crucifixion or beheading—the latter reserved for Roman citizens like myself, though I had witnessed beheadings with a dull blade, a sight not worth calling to mind.

They had executed Jesus after a cursory hearing, seeing him as one of countless troublemakers and petty criminals who must lose their lives at Golgotha, especially as Passover approached and the potential for mob violence loomed. Unrest terrified the Roman authorities, and potential rebels died without the opportunity to appeal their sentence, as they were aliens in their own country. The only way to keep order, in the Romans' small minds, was to threaten violence, even brutality.

More than once I made my citizenship clear to a soldier who approached me with a challenging glare. It was rare for a Jew to have this status, so they believed me, knowing that the penalty for lying about this was death. They assumed I meant what I said, and backed away.

I didn't tell them—or any gentile—that I was a student of Gamaliel because they didn't care about any rabbi or understand what it meant to study at the feet of an illustrious man. But I took shelter in the comfort of this status, wherein I felt some protection from the Roman world, although I seethed, thinking about the crucifixions, the imprisonment of Jews for no reason, even their petty derision, and how they laughed at what they considered our peculiar customs. I had, I confess, murderous impulses, which I did my best to contain. I would have slaughtered the Roman army wholesale by myself if I could.

I did my best, however, to maintain a sense of equilibrium. An intense study of the scriptures must replace my wish to kill the Romans and protect the Jews. Even Gamaliel had said that our only hope was in God, and that our work in his school helped to preserve what mattered in our tradition.

"Never be distracted," he would say. "See only what God wants you to see. Listen to him."

My father had written: "To see God, look into Gamaliel's eyes." This was, for him, a rare poetic turn.

I did love the Rabban, as we called Gamaliel: this genial, quick-witted man whose beard recalled the white bristles of a boar. His teeth were dark brown, almost black, but the mint he chewed gave his breath an unexpected sweetness. He was perhaps the most respected scholar among the Jews, the author of numerous commentaries on scripture, a rabbi steeped in the legal codes. He rocked back and forth vigorously when he prayed, sitting in a straw-backed chair while a few dozen boys (and not a few men) gathered in a circle on the blue-tiled floor of the study hall to listen as he recited the Psalms in a voice that pinged off the walls and doubled in volume:

> Bless the Lord, O my soul. O my God, thou art very great and
>   clothed with honor and majesty.
> Who covers thyself with light as with a garment: who stretches
>   out the heavens like a curtain:
> Who lays the beams of his chambers in the waters: who makes
>   the clouds his chariot: who walks upon the wings of the
>   wind:
> Who makes his angels spirits; his ministers a flaming fire:
> Who laid the foundations of the earth, that it should not be cast
>   away forever.

A reflection always followed, as with the above passage, when he said: "Remember that God creates all forms of life. He made everything: the hills, the trees, the wildlife that runs in the desert, in the forests. He is the voice in every bird. He makes the rivers race to their conclusion in the sea. He rains on us. He fills us with breath. He brings the honey of life into the delicate combs of our minds. He is the light we seek."

I aspired to speak with such clarity, in such natural metaphors.

The Rabban was a poet himself, and when he discovered my early training in the Greek writers, he allowed me to pursue this vein. (None of the other boys even knew about this interest of mine, nor would they easily have understood.) With Gamaliel's encouragement, I took it upon myself to memorize passages from Homer and Sophocles, Plato, Ion of Chios, and Apollonius of Rhodes. The latter, in particular, appealed to the Rabban, since Apollonius had been the librarian at Alexandria and, he said, "almost a Jew among pagans."

The idea that one might be among God's chosen without being a Jew intrigued me. It was something I knew I must try to understand, since my father had taught me the opposite, saying God would embrace only his own, the descendants of Moses, one of the twelve tribes, with particular affection for our tribe, the tribe of Benjamin.

"And what of the rest?" I once asked him.

"And what of them, boy? What of them?"

It somehow comforted me to know that our tradition, based in the scriptures, had been revered in faraway places. As we learned from Gamaliel, the library in Alexandria had acquired multiple copies of the Torah. In his wisdom, Ptolemy—a truly great king—had summoned seventy-two scholars, six from each of the twelve tribes, from Judea; he confined them on an island, in what had once been a fortress, in separate cells, asking each of them to translate the Torah into Greek. It was miraculous, how they summoned the scriptures— each translation exactly the same, word for word, with no variations. The result was "the second great miracle," as the Rabban taught us, the first being the original in Hebrew.

"Try not to rely on the Greek translation, however wonderful," Gamaliel told us. "A translation is always an interpretation. Go to the Hebrew for prayer, for deep study. Study God's tongue."

I would fail him in this, relying in later life on the Greek text, which sang in my head, the luminous music of the Greek scriptures, which I still hear in my father's voice. It was the language of Homer and so many fine poets, dramatists, and philosophers. On a walk with the Rabban through the Lower City, I once quoted Anacreon, hoping to impress him with the range of my knowledge. But this produced only a wince and was followed by a clear rebuke. "That is a drinking song, dear boy," he said. "Profane!"

I never referred to Anacreon again, at least not in his presence.

We were taught to seek God's face in dreams, to listen for his voice. "Be still and know that he is God," Gamaliel would say, echoing the psalmist. One evening over dinner he explained in surprising detail to a group of us about the layers of heaven, and how one might, while still in bodily form, visit the spirits above us, penetrating those august layers.

Quoting Daniel, who understood the meaning of Nebuchadnezzar's dream of the many-layered heavens, he said, "God gives wisdom to the wise. He gives knowledge to those who sit, who discern."

I questioned the Rabban about this and other matters—inquiry was encouraged. The school of Gamaliel was designed to lead us in the path to wisdom, to teach us to write vigorously, without fuss or vulgarity, and to instruct us in the techniques of rhetoric and argument, where conflict arose naturally and was a good thing. "You must question everything," Gamaliel said. "Nothing is beyond interrogation. If a thing is true, God makes that plain to the reasonable mind. If any man is truthful, he will be uplifted. If any man is false, incapable of reason, without the fire of God in his heart, he must fail. The man who does not abide in God will crumble into dust. The man who enters the mind of God will rise like Elijah in the chariot of sound judgment."

I had developed a deep prayer life during my years in the school of Gamaliel, and would rise before dawn, pulling a shawl around my shoulders before reciting a few psalms from David, or perhaps a passage from the prophets. I often prayed the set prayers, as taught to us by Gamaliel, and would listen for God—sometimes for an hour or more in silence like a desert mist.

This voice I heard only a few times, but it came distinctly, unexpectedly, much as the voice that had come to Samuel in his sleep. "Paul, you are mine," I heard, quite late one night, after I had nearly fallen into a dream. "Let my own voice be yours!"

I sat up, sweating, and pledged obedience for life. What else could I do in the face of the Almighty?

"I am yours!" I cried.

I realize how much I gathered from Gamaliel and made into my own. We inhabit our teachers, and they are changed in our own flesh. We become their voices, even if they would hardly recognize us.

When my time with Gamaliel came to an end, my father instructed me to remain in Jerusalem, which surprised me. I had fully expected to return to Tarsus and work beside him in his business.

"You will join me in commerce, but not in Tarsus. In Jerusalem, at least for now," he wrote. "You will enlarge our business in that city."

I agreed to this readily, pleased by his confidence in my powers. A young man needs the confidence of his father: It's the ground he walks on.

At his insistence, I boarded with my sister's friend, a robust widow called Hadar. Her black hair was streaked with white, and she had skin like yellow parchment. My brother-in-law, Rabbi Ezra, had known her husband, and my father approved of her as "a pious woman, with a fine reputation." And this reputation was widely shared, as Jews came from different parts of the city to consult her, often bringing problems that she would solve as she passed out chunks of unleavened bread that had been baked in her clay oven and smothered with a paste made from dates and seeds. My father explained that she would provide shelter as well as meals: often a segment of barley loaf with goat cheese or sesame paste with dry fruit on top. Sometimes she boiled sun-dried locusts in salty water or baked a honey cake with cinnamon or cumin. She made delicious pigeon pies and would occasionally roast a shank of lamb over the wood fire in her courtyard. I did not complain about any of this.

Her husband had been close to her, and despite her usual bravura she retained quantities of unresolved grief, as I realized when I heard her wailing at night. She would call her husband's name, and this unsettled me. I liked to imagine that my own mother, had she survived, would have possessed a stoic nature, and could not have been overwhelmed in this manner.

As Ion once wrote: "A good mother cuts with a keel through clashing waves, and her gunnels rarely dip."

✝

Jerusalem in those days was exactly the right sort of place for me to begin my life, within the amber limestone borders of the city walls, in the shade of Herod's Temple. The city had advantages for a young man of my disposition, who imagined himself sitting among the Council of Elders one day, where Gamaliel had presided as Chief of Court for many years. It would not take long before my contacts there multiplied, and I would use them wisely. (The counterfeit gold of worldly approbation attracted me, as it does in the hearts of most younger men who have not yielded to God in full submission, learning to rest in his presence.)

My father sent clear instructions: I was to assist our cousin Amos, an associate in the family business, in whatever ways I could. Our enterprise had done reasonably well in Palestine in past decades, and Amos understood the growing market for tents as well as anyone. He explained that shipping good hides to Tarsus was our primary task, thus agreeing with my father.

Setting about this work in earnest, I noticed that they slaughtered countless sheep each day for sacrifice at the Temple. I told Amos I had an excellent contact there, a young guard called Aryeh, whom I'd known in school. His uncle sat among the Council of Elders, adding to his luster. I had a hunch he might be willing to assist me.

Amos snickered at me; my bold approach failed to convince him. He said, "Let's be careful not to upset anyone in the Temple. One could do damage, and that is never good for business. Always remember that."

"I'm a careful person," I said.

I liked Aryeh more than he knew, and had spent long evenings in conversation with him, arguing over commentaries much as we had done under Gamaliel. He had a quick smile, an easy and energetic manner. Long russet-brown hair cascaded over his shoulders. His strength of will impressed everyone, and the fact that his nose had obviously been broken in a fight spoke to his combativeness. It bent sharply to one side, although this imperfection did nothing to lessen his attractiveness. To my dismay, he showed little of a scholar's passion for the specifics of a given text and had only a glaze of learning. On the other hand, he didn't worry about this insufficiency, which mattered little to him or others in his circle.

Aryeh had acquired the necessary gifts for a young man with Temple aspirations, and everyone marveled at the way he would talk in rambling sentences that nearly lost track of themselves as he spoke, disappearing around obscure corners of thought. Sometimes his language would unexpectedly cohere, and this could delight his listeners. ("He's quite brilliant," one of his friends said in my presence, much to my amazement.) One often saw Aryeh in the marketplace with a group of young men straining for his attention. And, indeed, I envied his outgoing nature and admired as well his presence and storytelling powers, with never a ponderous moment. I invited him back to my room one day, where he gently mocked my tendency to speak of Plato and Antipater of Tarsus.

"Don't talk of Greek philosophy," he said, in a way that reminded me of my old friend Simon, who dismissed my allusions to the Attic poets and thinkers. "I would have disliked Athens," Aryeh said. "That sort of elevated chatter gives me a headache."

I put before him the issue of getting good hides for my father's business, aware that the prospect of a problem to solve usually excited him. He glowed now with the satisfaction that comes from needing to find a good and practical solution for a friend with a dilemma. Within days, he had spoken to friends in the Temple, working his charm, and soon it was possible for me to buy large numbers of excellent hides cheaply. Taking advantage of the arrangement, I had them tanned in Bethany and shipped to my father from the port of Caesarea. The quantities surprised him, as did their quality, and he wondered about my sudden gift for commerce. How had I managed to acquire this valuable stock, and so quickly—more than Amos had managed in many years in Jerusalem? If I could sustain this level of supply, there were few limits to what we might achieve as a family, my father told me.

His letters became more affectionate, full of praise. One of them ended with "your loving father."

Could this really be Adriel?

One day Aryeh asked me to accompany him and other members of the Temple Guard who had been charged with ferreting out Jewish heretics, and the invitation appealed to me. I hated heretics, those who dared to contradict God's word, who threatened our very being as Jews. This paramilitary group had flourished in the last few years, when a number of dangerous cults had taken root. Some were followers of Apollonius, or Simon of Peraea, or Athronges—each of them fiery self-appointed prophets with a following. Among these was the rustic Nazarene called Jesus, whom they had crucified recently. His followers claimed he had actually been raised from the dead by Almighty God and that he continued to dwell among them in some fashion. From what I learned, Jesus had numerous disciples, including Peter and Andrew, whom I had met in passing when they attended some of Gamaliel's prayer sessions. Jesus's brother James behaved like a pious Jew, and he could often be seen in the Temple in prayer. I had noticed James in animated conversation with Gamaliel in the Temple only a few weeks earlier, and this puzzled me. My old teacher had often talked about cultic groups and the dangers they posed, and I thought he should have been wary of James.

Peter had caught my eye. A flat-faced man with massive lips and mottled ears, he would crouch with his back against the whitewashed wall of Gamaliel's school, his arms folded, grunting in prayer. He had become a loud voice in the Jesus circle, but James was obviously their ringleader. Followers of the Way (as they called themselves) had increased in numbers and enthusiasm since the Nazarene's demise and supposed resurrection. I laughed at their stories—they were absurd—but worried about the political implications of this cult. It was bad enough for the Jews in Palestine without this sort of nonsense, which could only draw further contempt from Roman authorities.

"Jesus never claimed to be the Messiah, not himself," Aryeh said to me, when I asked about him. "He was an ordinary man with extraordinary gifts of perception, a man of God perhaps. But surely not the Christ."

This was the first time I heard the Greek word for Messiah, the Christ, applied to Jesus of Nazareth.

Like most Jews, I felt sure the Christ would come as a warrior, another Judas Maccabaeus, who led a triumphant revolt against the wide-reaching and overbearing Seleucid Empire so many years ago. (We now lit candles every year to recall the rebirth of worship at the Temple, which Maccabaeus had delivered back into our hands.)

"The Christ will arrive on a white horse, raising a sword of steel," Aryeh said, mouthing what every Jew believed, however improbably. "And they will beg for mercy, the heathens."

Anything to get the Romans out of Palestine, I thought. They hated us and forced us to follow their laws, to adjust to their harsh and bureaucratic ways while they consumed our resources, which is always the point of empires: They feed without mercy on those they conquer.

Jews had seen this before, successive empires rolling over us, ripping us apart. The Babylonians burned the splendid Temple that Solomon had built, taking the best of us into captivity, and we had wept by the waters of Babylon for decades, although we never forgot Jerusalem, singing the great line from our Psalm: *If I forget thee, O Jerusalem!* Somehow we survived their brutalities, just as centuries later we survived Alexander on his violent eastward march and, still later, the wicked Seleucid kings, who killed Jews like pesky insects, beheading mothers and children and well as fathers and sons. We would survive Rome as well.

"We must defend the Jews," I said, feigning gruffness, hoping to match Aryeh's tone.

"Wayward ideas always fail," he said.

"We must take them seriously."

"We do. Come with me."

At this invitation I followed him into the Upper City, where we heard that an eloquent speaker would appear on behalf of the Jesus circle. This was Stephen, whose preaching had already roiled the Jewish population in Judea and Galilee. We stood at the back of a surprisingly large and buoyant crowd, listening to Stephen, a handsome fellow of twenty-five or so with thick chestnut hair and black eyes, a narrow face, and the whisper of a beard. He had an appealing manner and overflowed with miraculous tales of Jesus, who apparently had healed the lame, caused the blind to see, and had made lepers whole. He was even said to have raised the brother of a friend from the dead at Bethany, summoning him from a tomb. According to Stephen, Jesus did not distinguish among kinds or classes of people, preaching radical equality between men and women, between free men and slaves. He conversed freely with whores, beggars, and petty criminals, even tax collectors.

Stephen wore a white tunic under a scarlet cloak and stood with his arms outstretched, his hands lifted.

"It's Isaiah come back!" I said to poke fun. Aryeh looked at me with satisfaction, and one or two of his friends laughed.

"If Stephen isn't careful," said Aryeh, "he will float away to heaven."

I laughed perhaps too loudly, and heads turned toward us. A thin man with a red beard glared at me. Was he not someone I had seen before? Perhaps a visitor to Gamaliel's school? How was the Jesus sect attracting such a range of people, some of them quite respectable? It worried me that so many intelligent and devout Jews could find this man and his ideas plausible. They apparently failed to realize how dangerous this was, that the Romans would seize on any chance to make us look ridiculous and round us up. Wasn't the Antonia Fortress already filled with Jews?

Stephen's tone darkened as he began to talk about the Jews in terms that worried me: "We have heard the prophets from centuries ago, and how they spoke about the coming of the Christ, the Righteous One, a man whom God would anoint. But I tell you now: God anointed Jesus of Nazareth. He is living among us, though crucified. He is alive!"

"Not so much," said Aryeh, winking at me. I responded with a smile and a shrug. The poor fellow was mad, alluring but mad.

I said, "Stephen is alive."

"Not for long," Aryeh replied.

At this point Stephen told us an astounding story. He claimed that Jesus, during his "years of wandering and teaching in the countryside," had accepted a cup of water from a whore at Jacob's famous well near Sychar, in Samaria. This wicked woman had taken any number of men into her bed. Not surprisingly, her own tribe in Samaria had rebuked or shunned her.

Could any man with self-respect, a spiritual leader like Jesus, speak to a whore, accepting water to drink from her filthy hands?

Jesus told her to bring her husband to the well, but she insisted she had no husband.

Jesus apparently knew she lied. "You have five husbands," he told her.

"The Lord Jesus could see into her heart," said Stephen.

The Nazarene explained to her that God was spirit and that the hour of his kingdom would arrive any day. Everyone would be called into the presence of God, the living and the dead as well. Jesus told her that no one would ever again feel thirst, as he had supplies of water that she could scarcely imagine.

"Sir, give me this water," she said to him, trembling.

She understood that the Christ stood before her, Stephen explained.

A young man shouted a question from the crowd: "Did Jesus teach the Law of Moses?"

Stephen paused, then told us that Jesus had overturned Moses, preaching a "New Covenant" between God and his people. "The old world must pass away," said Stephen. "Everything must change. *You* must change!"

"He's insane," Aryeh said. "And wicked as well. He must pay for this wickedness. Blasphemy!" He looked at me hard. "Do you hate him as much as I do?"

"I hate him," I said.

"We should kill him."

"Yes," I said. "Death is the right response to blasphemy, as the scriptures say."

I could feel a peculiar and pleasurable sense of righteous power, and believed at this moment that Stephen posed a danger for all Jews. He threatened the fabric of our lives. And those who wished to defend our cause must show an alertness, a readiness to kill for whatever was true and good.

Aryeh quoted from David: *When he shall be judged, let him be condemned, this wicked man. His prayer itself has become a sin.*

This Jewish sorcerer, Jesus, apparently considered himself a god of some kind, and many regarded him as a king, a rebel hero, another Maccabaeus.

And that was dangerous.

"Jesus will restore our kingdom," Stephen told his audience.

Approval rippled through the air, a cool admiring wind that stirred the leaves of attention in this small forest of onlookers. And I myself found Stephen appealing as a speaker. He had an ease that surprised me, with a clear eye and bright, calm demeanor: Hardly the booming orator or mad zealot I'd been led to expect. His voice carried the crowd and caught the ear.

I did wonder privately about the risks of killing the followers of Jesus. Already we had Jews fighting Jews, one sect denouncing another. Slaughter might not always work to our advantage. But Aryeh was not alone in fearing Stephen and his message, and within days the Temple Guards seized Stephen on religious grounds for spreading false teachings, and—worse—for blasphemy. I found myself uncertain, afraid to put a foot wrong, and minding my words. This was a dangerous moment in Jerusalem.

As Jews, we had survived for many centuries under perpetual siege but only because of our steadfastness and vigilance. Now the Romans wished to see us disappear or walk with our eyes to the ground, obedient, even subservient. I knew we must not provoke a violent response from the Romans, who would eventually—as had our enemies for millennia now—move elsewhere. The land of Israel belonged to God's people, the Jews.

+

When I came home late, Hadar was sitting in her chair by the door, as ever waiting for me. She made a cup of linden tea, and we sat in the garden under a flaming torch, and I told her about our encounter with Stephen, including his peculiar story of the woman at the well.

"Perhaps this man, Jesus, had an open heart," she said.

"What is open?"

"Without preconceptions. He accepted this woman with many husbands as a human being, one of God's own."

"She rejected God."

"But God didn't reject her. He rejects nobody."

I didn't know what to make of Hadar's surprising comments. Either the Law of Moses had been established for all time—the single rule of morality, unwavering and eternally true—or it had not, in which case chaos would prevail. God had spoken to Moses with absolute clarity, once and forever. And Moses had come down from Mount Sinai bathed in a terrifying gold light, as if touched by God himself. And so Torah must not be overturned. I felt I must do whatever I could to stop this evil from rooting in our soil.

Hadar didn't quite share my affection for Aryeh. "He is a decent young man," she said, "but perhaps headstrong and limited in certain ways. Be very careful, Paul. Violence will never help any cause."

I understood her point, yet I agreed with Aryeh that those who worshipped this false Christ should be weeded out. They blasphemed God, and the punishment for blasphemy was death by stoning. "Whoever blasphemes the name of the Lord, the people shall stone him, according to Leviticus," I said to Hadar.

"Don't be so sure of yourself," she said. "Our God is a forgiving God."

It was easy to dismiss this thought because Hadar was a woman. Could one trust a woman to make hard choices?

I arrived the next morning at the Temple in time to find Stephen kneeling on the steps, with his wrists bound. He had apparently given himself up without even trying to resist—a fact that disgusted me in itself. Did he have no self-regard? The guards surrounded him now, with Aryeh in control. He explained to the mob—suddenly silenced in anticipation—that a brief trial had produced a sentence. The Court of Elders decided that Stephen would be buried to his neck in sand, in the usual manner, outside of the walls of Jerusalem. The guards would crush his skull with stones. (I had seen any number of these executions since my arrival in Jerusalem, but always stood apart, not wishing to look too closely.)

A gathering of Roman soldiers watched us from a distance, their swords drawn. They didn't want a riot, as one could never tell where violence of this kind might lead. But it was impossible for them to intercede in Jewish affairs, which they didn't, I suspect, even understand. A judgment had been rendered by the Temple authorities, who had appropriate jurisdiction in cases like this one. This outspoken Jew would be stoned to death by other Jews.

Our ways puzzled them.

"Come with us," said Aryeh, taking me by the arm.

I kept telling myself it made sense to rid our city of any man who threatened the Law, who preached the power of a Christ figure who stood above others, even the Romans, a rabbi whom some of his followers considered a son of God when (as we knew) only the emperor could lay claim to this title.

A throng followed the execution party, gathering into a frenzied mass at Golgotha, with its stench and aura of fear. I had always avoided coming anywhere near these grounds. Several crosses stood nearby, with vultures pecking away at the loose guts of the unfortunates who hung there, probably thieves, most of them dead for days.

A cross was a feast of carrion, and the sky above us darkened with black wings.

It didn't take long for the guards to pack Stephen up to his shoulders, pushing the dirt around his neck carefully—a collar of sand. The victim assumed a passive manner, never asking for mercy, not begging for a reprieve, saying nothing. His face settled into an angelic softness, and I could detect no fear in him. Death clearly did not intimidate Stephen.

A young man in the tunic and belt of a Temple Guard approached with a heavy stone, ready to strike. Before he began his deadly work, he said, "Have you anything to say, Stephen?"

"Thy will be done," replied the victim.

The crowd cheered as the guard heaved the stone at Stephen's skull, ripping away skin but not quite doing the job. Another followed, and the poor man's brow caved to the blow. His features dissolved in a mash of blood and bone.

"It's your turn," said Aryeh, handing me a stone.

My hands trembled, embarrassingly, as I stepped up to the spot. Did I really want to do this? Could I even avoid it?

I hurled the stone with everything I could muster, crushing the skull in a way that would end Stephen's misery at once, though I hoped he had lost his senses already. Aryeh followed suit, casting another large stone, and soon there was nothing but splinters of bone and blood in the sand, with ragged bits of flesh and brain within a small circle beyond the pit. An eyeball lay to one side, dislodged and staring.

Feeling removed from this world, a ghost of myself, I walked back in the direction of the city, my eyes on the ground, its sparse grass and gravel. The city walls loomed ahead of me. An old man passed me leading a goat, and he looked at me hard, even through me. I glared back at him. My head spun, and I stopped to gather my wits, to breathe. I grabbed a post by the road to steady myself. What had I done?

"Paul!"

The voice startled me. It was Gamaliel who walked toward me. He was larger than I remembered: tall and broad-shouldered, a vast hoary presence. I looked up into his face. What was he doing here?

"Paul, my son . . ."

"Yes, sir?"

He hesitated, then he said, "You know, I've been reading a collection of the sayings. The words of Jesus. Do you know them?"

"I don't," I said.

But I knew the followers of the Way quoted from these sayings at their gatherings and regarded them as holy words.

"You should study them. There is more wisdom there than I would, at first, have suspected. Truth lives in this language, I'm quite sure of it. Study them."

Study the words of Jesus? Did he say that to me? Was this not the foremost scholar of the Hebrew scriptures in Jerusalem, a man whose commentaries had traveled far and wide? Wasn't this the man whom my father worshipped like a god, sending me here to sit at his feet?

"I don't understand, sir."

"We should meet one day for a talk, and soon," he said. "I believe that the Messiah may have arrived in our midst, and we have failed to recognize him." His lips quivered as he spoke, and his eyes widened. He opened his hands to the heavens, quoting from David's Psalm: "*Teach me your way, dear Lord, that I may walk in the truth of your words, for I am afraid.*"

I was afraid myself.

When I looked back toward Golgotha, the crowd had already begun to scatter, while three or four vultures fed on the remains of Stephen, dipping their beaks into the pool of his skull. A few bystanders, perhaps followers of the Way, lingered and would probably fetch his remains and bury him.

"The soul is eternal," Gamaliel said.

I had never been less happy with myself, or more confused.

"Will you come to visit one day soon?" he asked.

"Yes, of course. I will come."

I went back to my room at Hagar's house, and my unease, even my fury, grew day by day. I tried to convince myself that I had behaved correctly, and allowed myself to blaze with anger, as in Exodus, where it says: *Let me alone so that my fury can flame, and I will burn in my righteousness, and destroy those who worship idols.*

It was good, I told myself, and the right thing to destroy those like Stephen, blasphemers who worshipped false gods. God was God, the Almighty One, the circle and center. He would allow no other gods before him. He wished us to destroy those who pretended otherwise. I would, I said to myself, become a warrior for God. I would defend him with all my strength.

It felt good to express my hatred of the Way in the company of Aryeh and his comrades, and they suggested one day that, with the blessings of Caiaphas, the high priest of the Temple, I should go as their emissary to Damascus, where the Jesus circle had increased quite dramatically in the last few years and threatened to spread to the far ends of Arabia. They would send me there with two guardsmen as guides and companions on a mission of denunciation. I would warn the Jews in that city about this false Messiah and explain the dangers.

And so we moved into the desert beyond Jerusalem on the road to Damascus one morning in the middle of summer.

It would take a week to get there, stopping by the roadside at well-known watering holes, sleeping under palm trees to avoid the worst heat of the day. I had in my possession a letter from Caiaphas, which I would deliver to the synagogue. It allowed us to find and arrest key members of the Way of Jesus in Damascus. We could not arrest everyone, but if we took away the ringleaders, this movement would wither and die.

✝

It was on the fifth day of our journey that the midday sun began to swell in the sky, even to pulse, a fist of light clenching and unclenching. I had never encountered such heat and light before, nor had my comrades, and we paused to drink water from an oiled leather sack. Never having spent much time in the desert, I shrank as the white sands whipped suddenly around me, stinging my cheeks and forehead like sand flies. I covered myself with a hood, eager for shade from the sun and whirling dunes, but this only made things worse, and I found it nearly impossible to breathe and groaned.

"What's wrong?" asked one of my companions.

"I feel quite dizzy."

I got down from the donkey to walk with a sense of anticipation— much as a field of corn will whisper and tingle before a burst of rain. After only a short while a sandstorm blew up, wrapping a white sheet around our small caravan, forcing us to the ground. We understood the dangers of these unexpected storms, which could bury a man in less than an hour. The most experienced of my comrades said we must get to the floor of the desert and wait out the storm in a prostrate fashion.

As I lay flat against the ground, the earth itself began to tremble while the storm passed beyond us. Now a hard blue sky rang out like an anvil stung with birds. And a brassy sound like a chorus of trumpets filled the air as if to announce the arrival of a king or prince. The sky then reddened, a vermillion blaze.

The others lay on the ground, still covered, but I rose. I could feel an opening in the heavens. And I felt drawn, opened, emptied of myself.

A voice boomed: "Paul! Paul! Why do you persecute me?"

"Who speaks?"

"Jesus."

Was the voice beside me? Was it above or below?

"What do you want of me?"

"Everything, Paul. Follow me. Follow . . ." The voice dwindled.

"Where? Who are you?"

Did I hear trumpets? Did the sky crowd with angels?

Time passed, with nothing forthcoming.

I cried out, "Speak again!"

No answer came. I looked around to see what my friends made of this conversation, as the sky pressed on me, turning white and hot.

One of my fellow travelers, a young man named Jarib, rose from the ground, taking my hand, asking what troubled me. He was a sympathetic fellow, and I could sense his distress.

But I could not see him.

"I am blinded, Jarib," I said. "Did you hear anything? Jesus has called to me from the heavens. You heard him!"

"I heard wind and sand."

Another man agreed that the wind had been loud, "a wolf's voice in the desert, rising on a leash, a howl of anguish." The sand, he said, "scraped along the ground, a grating noise."

"It was Jesus the Christ," I said. "He called to me. He asked me to follow him."

This produced only confusion, a feeling of dislocation, even fear.

They could not understand what I said to them. Was I not on my way to Damascus to punish those who followed the Nazarene?

"Jesus is not the Christ," Jarib said emphatically. "The desert can play tricks. The wind and sand, the swirl. It's easy to lose one's bearings."

They assured me that I had simply absorbed too much sun, that my sight would return, and my balance as well.

"I see nothing!" I told them. "I am blind!"

"You have lost your wits," said Jarib, putting a wet cloth to my forehead. "The sun can do this. It's not uncommon for this to happen on desert journeys."

His words meant nothing to me. I knew what had happened. God had punished me for what I did to Stephen. But for reasons beyond understanding, Jesus now called to me. I had been singled out, chosen. My life was forever changed.

They helped me onto my donkey, and I clung to the stubble of its neck.

I shuddered and wept as we proceeded, utterly lost. I could see nothing but a glaze of indistinct light, a smear of yellow, and shadows, and thought I must soon die. My associates simply didn't understand what had happened and how I felt. But how could they? It was all too peculiar, upsetting, upending. I would never be the same, that much I knew in my gut. I was no longer the same man who had left Jerusalem.

Chapter Four

✖✖✖

LUKE

Paul talked a good deal, even in his sleep, and told the story of his first encounter with the Christ many times. I grew quite tired of the road to Damascus after a while.

I heard the anecdote in various forms, as the details, and the emphasis and tone of the story, shifted. The audience mattered, and he possessed a keen sense of his listeners and could alter his presentation in mid-flight, adjusting to the responses in the room: a laugh, a sigh of boredom, even a snort of contempt. For all this, I had no doubt that his experience on that legendary road changed everything for him.

"I'm not the man who set off from Jerusalem to Damascus," he said to me. "Not the man who stoned dear Stephen."

"All true," I would say. "You changed course, reversed direction."

"No," he would say, argumentative as ever. "That doesn't go far enough."

Paul wanted everything framed in terms that measured his ideas of reality, and yet he clung to strange notions about himself. Often he would push back at me, resisting the shape of whatever I proposed, as if my version of Paul the apostle could never quite capture his reality.

"It was a transformation near Damascus," he explained, "but not what you imagine. On that road I discovered what I already possessed, which is eternal life. It had been there all along, in my hand but concealed. I simply opened my hand, and there it lay."

All very brisk and fetching, that comment, but I'm not sure his explanation was logical. Logic was never his gift. "It only leads to untruth," he would say. "I never liked the syllogism as a form of thought. Aristotle be damned!"

What remained true was that he had wished to persecute followers of the Way. A friend had enlisted him as an adjunct of the Temple Guards: an unlikely prospect for a small, stumbling, stooped man with a squint who had no martial training, no gift for violence. They accepted him only because they imagined he would advance in elite Jewish circles and sit among the Court of Elders one day. His pervasive learning, skills of persuasion, determination, and blunt expressiveness boded well.

It must have disappointed them to see Paul reverse course, becoming an apostle of Jesus, especially among the Greeks. What puzzled many in the Way, however, was Paul's lack of interest in the actual life of Jesus.

"Jesus never talked about his childhood," he told me. "He stepped into the world at the moment of his baptism in the River Jordan. Anything before that was irrelevant. I suspect that his mother annoyed him."

Mary had become a leading figure in the Way, and her role as the mother of our Lord gave her a special status in Jerusalem. With my plan to write a life of Jesus, I had a strong wish to interview her. What a thing it would be to have her voice in my head. But Paul discouraged me.

"Write as the spirit inspires you," he said. "Let God push your fingers. A good story obliterates the material it serves. It creates truth."

I did my best to convince him that a narrative of the events in the life of Jesus could be useful, providing a portrait of man perfected by God, a man chosen by the Almighty to express his voice. Followers of our Lord would (and did) have many questions: Where did he come from? What were the conditions of his birth? How was he different from other teachers who claimed a special connection to God?

Paul insisted that nothing mattered but the crucifixion, followed by the resurrection. Only this was relevant. Even the relationship between Jesus and the Law bored him. "He was himself the Law," he said, a comment that didn't go down well in Jerusalem with Peter and James, the Pillars. Of course he hoped to retain their approval, even thought that he required it. They gave him their approval, yet remained uneasy about his approach to gentiles like myself. He argued that the Kingdom of God would embrace the world at large, Greek and Jew alike. "There is no boundary," he would say.

Paul's mind often played over his youth in Jerusalem at the school of Gamaliel. I think one always recalls the days of yore with fondness, and perhaps trepidation as well, as this is a time of misplaced affections, unexpected turns, fancies and fantasies, inklings and excitements. (I often pushed away thoughts of my own distant childhood in Antioch, which had never been especially happy. Is there such a thing as a happy childhood?) I understood that Paul's training with Gamaliel had formed the basis of his broad learning, and I could feel his gratitude to this old teacher, who had taken him in hand—and recently joined the Jesus circle himself, much to everyone's astonishment.

If anyone understood the matter of reversals, of changing course in mid-flight, it was Paul.

Recollections of the Damascus Road became the opening gambit in most of his sermons, especially when he met an audience for the first time. And the tale adapted readily to local conditions, accumulating fresh dimensions in the moment of its telling. Paul usually failed to say that he had spent a good deal of time in Damascus before this visit because his family had business interests there, believing this somehow lessened the drama of his tale. He was in fact widely known to the Jews in that city. This fateful journey was a return of sorts, and he expected a bright welcome in the synagogue near the market, where he would be called on to read the scriptures aloud and comment as well. Paul knew the Torah well, and it was a rare thing for a scholar trained in the school of Gamaliel to appear in their midst, so they would have taken full advantage.

"I was halfway to Damascus when the ground beneath my horse began to tremble," he might say, although I knew from other conversations that the "horse" was in fact a donkey, as he confessed one day. But a donkey doesn't play well in public. "I clung to the quivering mane of my tall white horse," he would say, "sure I would be thrown and mangled underfoot." Sometimes he would begin: "Not far from the pink city walls of Damascus, the sky began to brighten. It was almost night, so this seemed odd, even ominous." Another time he opened with: "One morning, as I mounted my small gray horse to begin the fourth day of my journey to Damascus, the clouds above me parted, and the face of our Lord shone like the sun itself, only brighter. I could see his eyes!"

The animals disappeared from the anecdote on many occasions. "I went by foot from Jerusalem to Damascus," he could say. (I always missed the donkey.) He was with or without companions on this journey. Once he moved through the desert in a train of camels, which seemed highly unlikely, but he enjoyed talking about camels, which he considered "the most amusing of all God's creatures, a divine joke."

Did he actually meet the Christ, our Lord?

That cannot be doubted, although the exact nature of the manifestation and the meeting varied in the telling.

"A great light wavered in the desert, and a voice spoke to me," he would often declare. *"Why do you persecute my people? I am Jesus. You know me, I'm quite sure. You have always known me. I will make you my apostle."*

I took notes, as was my habit, accumulating a range of Damascus Road stories. The narrative might vary in detail, but the message was firm. The Lord had made contact with Paul, shaken and blinded him. He had been transformed.

The face of Jesus may or may not have glistened in the sky, but there can be no question about the intensity of the light or its effect on Paul. "As if lightning flashed and failed to fade," he said. "It was steady, a bright surrounding glow, overwhelming." Once he said, "My own flesh seemed to melt," but that image displeased him and I never heard it again.

Somewhere near Damascus, Jesus appeared to Paul—the persecutor of the Way—in a blast of light, and Paul fell from his horse. Or fell to the ground as he walked. Or tumbled from his donkey. And the men who accompanied him fell beside him or didn't. It was significant that the earth itself shook violently, as this detail drew gasps from the crowd, whatever their disposition. And the voice of Jesus, with his appointment of Paul as apostle, mattered to everyone but especially to Paul.

One night, as he lay next to me on a straw pallet near the Galatian town of Derbe, he recalled the Damascus experience with less bombast: "We slept beside the road each night, our donkeys tethered to a tree. When I woke one morning, before sunrise, there was the body of Jesus—a glorified body—crouched beside me on the blanket. I sat up, and we talked face-to-face, and he asked me to direct my attention to the mind of God. He said I could become like him, part of the Eternal Mind. He told me that time only existed for those who were lost. To be 'found' was to find myself outside of time." He paused. "And he asked me to follow him."

That was a singular monologue, possibly accurate, though I much preferred the image of Paul riding on a white horse, perhaps a warhorse, charging toward Damascus with anger in his heart, eager to slaughter those who belonged to the Way. The ground shuddered beneath him, tilting in air. A mighty wind arose, lifting the sand in a cloud. The sky turned blood-orange and gauzy. At once a brilliant and blinding light enveloped Paul, and in the midst of this effulgence came a voice telling him to stop persecuting people of the Way. Instead, he must join them. And spread the Good News about Jesus and God's kingdom.

I quite preferred that version, although I perhaps have combined the details of many versions in my own way. A good story is a running river that never empties itself.

✝

"Listen to what I say to you, my son," Jesus said to Paul in one often-repeated version. "Go into the city now, pray, and ask for forgiveness. You will be told what to do by someone within the walls. Do not be afraid."

In the course of years, the death of Jesus became the focus of Paul's thought, the still point at the swirling center of his imagination. "Everything follows from the cross," he would say. But it was the life and ideas that interested people in the Way, not so much the humiliating death. This was also true for the Jerusalem leaders, who regarded Jesus as the anointed one, the Christ, a man who asked his followers to turn their eyes to the heavens and to their community, where the need for service arose. "Love God and love one another. These are my commandments," Jesus said.

I liked the simplicity of this formulation: *Love God, and love others—much as I have loved you.* That message could be taken into the world, and it would change the world as well.

The death of Jesus and his resurrection didn't concern many of our circle in Jerusalem, especially those who admired James. But Paul, raised in Tarsus, understood the range of meanings one could discover in the imagery of blood and torn flesh: It was Mithras, after all, who held Tarsus in thrall. Paul knew the usefulness of suffering, how it served as an invitation to the spirit, a path to resurrection in life. Over time, he uncovered a language for thinking about Jesus that stuck in our heads and helped us to understand the meaning of the cross.

The slaying of a sacred bull obviously intrigued him: an aspect of Mithras and his cult that acquired a ritual significance in the time of Paul's boyhood and mine. We had both seen hot blood poured over the heads of the devout. With a gift for symbolism, Paul acknowledged the power of blood as a sign of rebirth. And he used this symbol in ways that linked it to the execution of Jesus, focusing on the crucifixion as an act of self-sacrifice, with the symbol of blood granting new life to those who held Jesus dear, who valued his teachings, who believed that the soul undertakes a passage through a dark tunnel before resurfacing into what Paul called "the glorified body," which is radiant and changeless.

I settled back with pleasure to hear Paul turn rhapsodic, as he often did before a gathering, especially on the topic of the resurrection, which was not the Great Resuscitation, as he would say: "It was so much more than simply that and more confusing, too. Even Mary Magdalene and Peter did not, when Jesus returned to them, recognize their teacher and spiritual master."

This intrigued me, especially when I heard about the disciples who, only a couple of days after the crucifixion of their Lord, headed out of Jerusalem on the road to Emmaus. Two of them talked of the death of Jesus, shaking their heads sadly, when a third appeared beside them, someone they didn't recognize. This stranger asked them about their stories, and they said, "Haven't you heard about Jesus, and his execution?" He feigned ignorance, listening all day to their lamentations, absorbing their grief. At the end of the day they asked this sympathetic stranger to dine with them, gathering around a fire pit. Jesus said, "Would you mind if I offered a word of prayer?" As they listened, it dawned on them that this was actually their Lord. "Rabbi!" one of them cried. At which point Jesus disappeared in a puff of smoke.

Paul adored this story, and he implored me to include this exemplary tale in my life of Jesus. "It will teach your readers the truth, that we can't know Jesus fully in this life, and that his resurrection is mysterious. The new life we find in him is nothing like the old life. It's a transformation, and it's complete."

Paul's way of talking entranced his listeners, even if he wasn't necessarily the most polished of speakers and often seemed baffled by his own message, almost babbling in tongues. He could lose his thread, backing around a narrative rather than moving through it, fumbling and fussing for the right word, occasionally settling on the wrong anecdote or parable. But there was a thrill in this, too: watching the mind of a prophet at work as he stumbled toward the truth.

"They don't understand," he would say to me, frustrated when listeners didn't catch what he meant. "I was clear, wasn't I?"

I would reassure him. Nobody doubted the force of his message, even when the exact meaning eluded his listeners. The proof of his power was in the number who turned to the Way of Jesus because of his rhetoric. And it surprised me how rapidly we grew, with pagans and Godfearers coming to our gatherings, not infrequently demanding baptism in the nearest river or lake. We would sing hymns and hold hands, standing up to our waists in water.

"The Word is alive in my mouth, and in yours as well," Paul told me one evening before bed, kissing me on the forehead as if to confer apostolic powers.

He knew the power of ceremonial gestures, though I resisted the idea that I had any special access to God. I was, always, an ordinary man, another follower of Jesus. No more and no less.

I watched with fascination as Paul developed ceremonies that seemed to draw our communities together, giving us a vision. He broke bread and shared cups of wine with gatherings in ways that generated reverence as well as loyalty. "We become one body in the breaking of this bread," he would say, lifting a tiny loaf above his brow, breaking it. The phrase proved durable and moved from outpost to outpost along Roman byways as our movement spread. "We who are many have become one body," they would say.

Were those Paul's words or the words of Jesus? When I asked, he glared at me.

Blunt questions proved an inconvenience. Did I somehow not realize that Paul could speak for Jesus? "Are you with me, my dear Luke?" he would say, raising his voice. "Have I lost your confidence?"

I didn't doubt him, as I had seen the strength of his utterances, even felt God growing inside me, overwhelming me, in his presence. Paul stood among the prophets, a true descendant of Moses and Ezra, Isaiah and Daniel and Jeremiah. Of course no prophet was perfect except in the quicksilver moment of prophecy.

I loved Paul and his perfervid ways, but he could be awkward and demanding, a human thorn. A look of his could whither a fig tree, I once told him, and he laughed to think I compared him in this to Jesus, who had supposedly cursed a fig tree in Bethany, for reasons I never understood.

"You want everything explained," Paul said. "This annoys me."

He knew that I, as a physician, sought explanations. In the pursuit of healing, I must take into account causes and effects. I didn't often speak in metaphors or parables, preferring the plain sense of things. Nor did I traffic in abstruse thoughts: a trait better left to garrulous Athenians, who made fools of themselves in the public square with arguments and counterarguments, with gaseous musings.

I lay beside him night after night on the road and listened to his stories, hearing them unfold in the dark. It occurred to me that, in living so close to Paul, in listening with such attention to his conversation, I absorbed his way of thought, even his language. Sometimes I could hardly separate myself from him.

The tale of what happened *after* he got to Damascus rarely varied, and it had about it the exactness of truth. I myself witnessed these events, so I could judge this part of the story. I had come from Antioch to visit Ananias, my uncle, a leader of the Way of Jesus in Syria for some years, and to pursue some business connected with the salves that I had begun to sell throughout the empire, although in small quantities. I had been in the city for only a few weeks when Paul thundered into view, a figure who raised considerable terror, since word had traveled to our ears about the death of our friend Stephen in Jerusalem and the role Paul had played in that grisly execution. He was, my uncle said, "something of a holy madman" with a "vengeful nature."

The combination of elements here caught my attention. A holy madman?

I must see this for myself, if I could.

+

Having lost his sight, Paul was led by a kind soul to a house on Straight Street, near the loud, frenetic market where merchants sold spices and leather goods, silk and wool, knives of Damascus steel, trinkets, meat, eggs, and pigeons. Paul knew the city from earlier visits, and he sensed his whereabouts, hearing people shout and laugh, the cluck of chickens, the wheels of carts grinding through dirt and gravel ruts. Someone played a wooden pipe nearby.

In a hot room, with the shutters drawn, Paul sat on a low divan, unable to understand what had befallen him. Had he committed such a miserable transgression that blindness and isolation would consume his future? Would God ever forgive him?

Ananias had told me about Paul's intention to punish our circle of blasphemers and heretics, which is how he viewed us. Peter in Jerusalem had forewarned my uncle about this fellow, saying in a note that a messenger delivered in the nick of time: "Beware of this rabid one, Paul of Tarsus. He is quite unhinged, a fanatic, possibly deranged and homicidal. He may do great harm to our movement." Another member of our circle had studied with him at Gamaliel's school and spoke of his intensity, calling him a fool who nevertheless had a command of the scriptures unlike anyone he had seen before.

But God spoke to my uncle in a dream, informing him that Paul had arrived a couple of days before, and that he would find him in a particular house on Straight Street, which was more like a cave than a comfortable dwelling: the sort of place that attracted no attention. This was important because the followers of Jesus already felt threatened by the Jews in Damascus, who dismissed their fanciful stories about a Christ who had come without a sword, who asked Jews to ignore the Law of Moses.

For three days Paul ate little, rocked in prayer, and begged God for mercy. He saw nothing but flickering spikes of light that actually hurt when they flashed, digging into his brain. He lived on bread and water and was sucked into an empty space, a deep mind well with no bottom.

I arrived with my uncle, and we sat on either side of him on the divan. My curiosity was piqued, and I will never forget my first impression: This wild man was clearly a prophet. A strange glow surrounded him, as if he were a fallen angel in human flesh. His eyes rolled like empty orbs, apparently seeing nothing. He winced and smiled and frowned. He spoke in an excessively loud voice, with authority, even in his great distress.

"I scoured the pit of darkness, below this earth," Paul told us. "I was tempted. But God is faithful. He never allows temptation to exceed what a man can bear. He shows us how to endure it, how to find a way out." In the depths, he told us, he spoke face-to-face with Ha-satan, the Adversary, who tempted him with glories. He was offered empires, principalities, a golden throne, a kingdom of his own to rule. But he resisted these enticements. He didn't want an empire, he told the Wicked One. He wanted the eternal life that had been promised by Jesus, if Jesus wanted him.

"Does Jesus want me?" he asked Ananias.

"He does," said my uncle, grasping one of his hands.

The room smelled of mud and sweat, and green flies swarmed with their brittle buzzing wings, and I could not breathe. My uncle stood over him, and Paul lifted his chin, as if looking into the sun.

"You persecuted the saints in Jerusalem," Ananias said, with an unlikely hint of kindness in his voice.

"It is my shame," Paul said, after a long pause.

Tears gleamed on his cheeks, then sobbing overwhelmed him. And yet Ananias made no effort to comfort him or intervene in this necessary struggle; he merely sat again on the edge of a bed and watched Paul weep, listening as he began to mumble phrases in an alien tongue. Foam seeped from Paul's lips before he finally spewed

a rank green vomit onto the floor. He knelt like a cat, then fell sideways, shuddering, and drew his knees to his chest. More foam ran
from his mouth, dribbled into his beard. He had slipped back in time,
returning to childhood. Or fallen into complete madness.

As a physician, I could not help myself. I knelt beside him and
lifted his head slightly.

"I'm Luke, a physician," I said. "And I'm visiting from Antioch,
here with my uncle, who is beside you."

"You are with the Christ?" Paul asked.

"Yes, the Christ lives in my soul."

Paul began to shudder again, quaking so violently that I thought
he would break his neck, so I held him to the floor, pressing myself
upon him until he grew still.

When the fit ended, Ananias whispered in his ear, "Do you wish
to turn away from evil?"

"I do."

"Will you pray with me, Paul? And Luke?"

"Pray for us, uncle," I said.

"Pray for me, sir, yes," said Paul, with a spiritual hunger in his
voice that moved me.

Ananias put his palms on the blind yet beseeching eyes, pressing
his thumbs into the lids. He prayed intensely, lifting his voice: "This
is your servant, Lord. This is Paul. You invite him now to preach to all
the children of Israel, and to the Greeks as well. He will stand before
kings and queens, proclaim the news of your kingdom, your advent in
the world." He waited for a moment. "You will do this, Paul?"

"I will."

"As Jesus himself became the servant of his father, you shall be
his servant. Remember that Jesus humbled himself, obedient even in
death, losing himself in the flesh, finding himself in the spirit."

With that, light filled the room for Paul, and the face of Ananias
wavered into being. He saw the old face smile at him.

"I see you!" said Paul.

"Of course you do."

+

I was present at the moment when Paul's sight returned, and yet he seemed to forget my witness in the room, the fact that I could supply evidence from memory. In later years, I often heard him talk about how his sight returned to him that day on Straight Street. At times he claimed that actual scales fell from his eyes onto the floor like goose feathers and "disappeared miraculously" when he stepped on them. Once in a while he said that Ananias broke into an angelic voice, summoning the angels with a chant. "We heard tambourines, Luke and I, and Ananias—the tinkling of bells, and wonderful strange horns," he declared, though I never heard these instruments of heaven. "Even the cherubim sang my name, a chorus of welcome."

So odd, to hear these embellishments, which he could not resist, lifting them into the air as if to test their meaning, truth, and force. And yet the core of the narrative didn't change.

At the end of this particular story about the experience in Damascus, he invariably intoned: "And the Light of God flooded the world, and I could see at last. There stood beside me Ananias my deliverer and Luke the physician, my dear friend Luke."

Paul insisted that Ananias take him to the synagogue, only a short distance from the house of Judah, as in his new state of transformation he felt the urge to preach, to declare himself a changed man. The synagogue was familiar to him from earlier visits to Damascus, and he recalled the names of many Jews who worshipped there, and he thought they would never turn him away.

I followed them, curious to see what might occur. As it happened, we found only a handful of elderly Jews in the room, and they did not respond to Paul's enthusiasm for the fabled rabbi from Nazareth. One or two raised a skeptical eyebrow at Ananias, a Greek whom few of them trusted, and the leader of what they considered an eccentric sect that had drawn too many Jews away from the fold.

I, a Greek stranger, meant nothing to them.

"Do you know the Christ has come?" Paul asked.

They shrugged, looking more with curiosity than anger upon this intrusion, although rage would follow.

"Who is this Christ they speak of?" one of them asked.

Paul blurted out his message, which was not so well refined at

the time. I can recall their baffled faces looking up at him. Why was
he breaking into their prayer circle in the synagogue? Was this the
Jew supposedly sent by the Temple priests to help them deal with
the Way, which had caused a good deal of annoyance and threatened
their own existence by appealing to Jews and Godfearers alike? Had
something gone amiss?

At this point a young man in a filthy tunic walked into the room
with the help of a cane, his right leg withered from an affliction of
early childhood. It could bear no weight, and he nearly toppled as he
leaned forward. Paul saw an opportunity.

"Sir, the Lord Jesus can heal you."

"What's he saying?" the poor fellow asked, looking around the
room.

The elders shrugged. They had no idea what Paul meant by this
assertion.

"Come to me!" Paul cried.

The young man thumped toward Paul, and the elders sat forward
in their seats.

One often saw magicians in this synagogue, sorcerers who laid
claim to healing powers, but the thought of Paul in this role probably
worried them. He looked possessed, his eyes flashing like hooks. His
mouth twitched, and he blinked rapidly. I feel quite certain that a
light surrounded his head.

"Come," said Paul, motioning with a hand to the benighted fellow, who approached to within arm's length, allowing Paul to lean
into his face. "Will you kneel with me, sir? And what is your name?"

"I am Jesse."

"Then kneel, Jesse. You are a gift to this community."

With difficulty, Jesse knelt. He had learned how to do this in
a manner that allowed him to crank himself to a standing position
with the good leg while leaning on his cane. It was a maneuver he
would avoid, or so I assumed, but he felt drawn to Paul and sensed an
opening in his life.

"Believe me, Jesse, that Jesus is your Lord and Master. He can
heal this leg, if you put trust wholly in his goodness, in the great
goodness of God, our father in heaven."

The young man dipped his head forward, and Paul put a thumb on his brow.

"Jesus is here," said Paul. "He's inside me, inside you, Jesse. I invite the spirit of the Christ to enter the body of this young man and to heal him! Heal him, dear God in heaven! In the name of your son, Jesus!"

Did the walls begin to shake at this point? Did the ceiling lift? Paul claimed they did, although I saw no such thing. But he often felt tremors that eluded others. I don't doubt that, to him, the ceiling would *appear* to lift. His world frequently succumbed to trembling. It shook, even splintered and broke apart.

"Say aloud, with me: *I love you, Jesus. God, make me whole!*"

Jesse repeated this. And he wept now.

Suddenly throwing his cane to one side, a gesture that startled us, he rose and walked across the room with confidence and ease.

"I love God," Jesse said.

The others murmured, and one of them left the building quickly. Perhaps he wanted to tell others about what had happened to Jesse. Nobody in Damascus could have expected this young man, whom they all knew, to walk again without great pain and the assistance of a cane.

Soon others came to meet this Pharisee who they assumed was an enemy of the Way of Jesus, an emissary of the Temple Guard.

"You are Paul?" someone asked. "You come from the Temple?"

"I'm Paul of Tarsus," he said. "And yet the Temple of God is here." His hand touched his breast. "Your own body is a Temple."

✢

That evening, a gathering of nearly two dozen Jews arrived at the synagogue, several of them upset about what they had heard, questioning the motives of this emissary from Jerusalem. They could not tolerate the idea of Paul as an advocate for the Way of Jesus and had never expected this turn, not from a Pharisee, a student of Gamaliel, an associate of the Temple Guard. To most of them, miracles were off-putting, and Damascus teemed with magicians and mountebanks who made outrageous claims for themselves. Their behavior invited scorn from the authorities, even censure. On the other hand, a man who can heal is always welcome, and several Jews brought relatives who were lame or sick before Paul, who prayed with each of them in turn. In many cases they were healed, though he made it clear that he did not actually do the healing.

"I heal no one," Paul explained. "Only Jesus the Christ heals. He does so from within. He heals the soul first, then the body."

The chief rabbi in Damascus at this time was Jacob ben Isaac, who called a number of elders to his house the next day, warning them that trouble might follow from the disruptions of Paul. "I'm not happy about what I hear," he said. "Those from our tradition who turn against us, these are the ones who create the most trouble." It was difficult enough to pursue the faith of their fathers in a city overseen by Aretas, a barbarous king who found enemies wherever he looked and punished them swiftly, without mercy.

No Jew felt safe in Damascus now.

Jacob's council unanimously agreed that Paul must die. They could not afford to let him stir up trouble in Syria, and he had clearly become blasphemous, claiming to heal people in the name of Jesus and not the God of Israel. The sooner they killed him, the better.

They summoned a number of rough young men, laying a plot to kidnap Paul that night. They would take him outside the city walls, where he would be buried in the sand, stoned, then covered over. And nobody would complain to the authorities, who would be only too glad to see the end of this troublemaker from abroad, an alien from Tarsus, another crazy Jew.

But word of this scheme reached Paul, who often talked about what happened that night. I heard many versions over the years, and this again dismayed me because I had been there and seen everything with my own eyes. Did he not believe I had eyes and ears? And why could he never stick to one story, the true one?

"A woman in a white veil told me about this plan to kill me," he might say. Another time: "God woke me in a dream while I was sleeping and warned me that I would soon be captured and murdered." The messenger often changed but not the message. There was a modicum of consistency, at least. "I was packed into a laundry basket, then lowered over the city walls at night," he would say. Or: "I insisted that they put me in a crate, which they tied with ropes, and pushed over the walls of Damascus." Sometimes the basket went crashing to the ground. Sometimes it seemed "almost to fly" and landed far from the wall in a bed of reeds, although reeds would have been unlikely there, without a river nearby. The "bed of reeds" became "high grass" in due course, and this was probably not inaccurate. The reeds, perhaps, were a bid for an association with Moses in the bulrushes!

Once Paul told an amazed crowd in Antioch that he flew over the city walls. "I stretched out my arms and glided softly in the star-filled night after riding the wind for a good while. And with a company of angels as an escort."

The angels ruined the story, I explained to him, and he never in my presence used that sullied version again. It was sheer megalomania, even madness. A basket would do, as I had been the one to fetch it, to attach the rope, and to help a few others lower him carefully over the city wall.

As I learned the hard way in later years, it didn't pay to question Paul too closely, as it could cause him to bristle and fall silent for long periods. He disliked challenges, and the last thing I wanted was to alienate this servant of God, an apostle of our Lord, who had done so much to spread the news of Jesus to the far ends of the earth. Better just to let the stories breathe and carry the crowd, as they usually did.

I learned never to raise my hand in objection, saying, "But I was there . . ."

My assistance was useful to his missionary work, especially toward the end. He often drew on the sayings of Jesus and the parables I had culled from a variety of sources. The story of the lost sheep and the prodigal son were not broadly in circulation at the time, nor was the tale of the Good Samaritan, which Paul adored and frequently employed. With ease, he folded my notes into his sermons, quoting my versions of the sayings:

> Knock and he will open the door, seek and you shall find.
> God will always give exactly what you require. He is your own
> dear father, and will a father deny a fish if his child asks for a

fish? Will he offer a snake instead? Of course not. So imagine how much more generous will be your father in heaven than your father on earth!

I heard myself—my own voice—talking in Paul's public addresses and didn't mind this eerie ventriloquism: Jesus speaking with the help of scribes, his voice caught and fed through me to Paul, on and on. This is how the spirit moves, around us and within us. I had to trust in this fact of life, to accept it. God had something in mind for me, as he did for Paul. Our meeting in Damascus had been revelatory for me, and it determined the course of the rest of my days, though I didn't know this at the time.

Chapter Five

PAUL

I could not afford to dawdle, given the hostility around me in Damascus, where both the Jews and the king's men wanted me dead. Either of these groups, or some ruthless offshoot, might drag me behind the city walls, and I knew how this would end.

"Go now," Luke, my new friend, had said. "And may God be with you."

"If I could stay a few more days . . ." I didn't know how to complete the sentence. Even saying it, I understood that to remain in this city was not possible. I had only begun to regain my sense of balance, and my vision needed to clarify. I could see, but not well, with streaks of orange-and-red light jabbing into the periphery. I would reach for something, and it would disappear. I stumbled over objects in my path. I mistook one of my sandals for a massive pit viper, which terrified me one morning when I woke, and my high-pitched scream horrified the others.

"You can't stay," Luke said. "They will find you soon. The city is small."

That evening at sunset he and a few others lowered me over the wall in a wicker crate. There was a violet glow on the western rim of the desert, and clouds stretched in broad blue-vermillion lines like veins in a wrist. I landed in high grass that smelled heathery and sweet, then hurried away into the dusk, following a crease through scrubland. A path opened beneath my feet, with the moon casting a shimmer on the pink limestone walls that receded. Where to go?

A return to Jerusalem was unthinkable. The Jews, my former friends and allies, would consider me a traitor, a blasphemer, no better than Stephen and perhaps worse, as I had been an agent of the Temple Guards, sent on a distinct mission. It seemed unlikely that Peter and James, who worked patiently and with ingenuity to maintain good relations with the Jewish community, would find it in their hearts to forgive me for everything I had done. The Jesus circle would never open their arms to one who had so recently been their persecutor.

I must go into the desert, as Jesus had done.

Ananias favored this plan and explained that I would find a stream after two days of walking beyond Damascus, and I should follow it into Arabia. But the wilderness spread in every direction, and I wondered if I could find this rumored stream or, in the end, anyone at all. The company of friends seemed like an impossible shore, and I could feel my body softening, breathing from every pore, as if changing into air as I moved forward. Scuffling sounds in the nearby brush alarmed me, and I feared I could be torn apart by jackals before dawn.

It was all unfamiliar, and I couldn't think how I had stumbled into this situation, whatever it was. What had actually happened on the way to Damascus?

Possibly I should never have left Jerusalem.

I replayed the scene again and again, but the truth eluded me. No matter, I told myself: I was not the same man who had rushed toward that city with a few comrades, eager for vengeance against those who lived by the name of Jesus and threatened to disrupt the Law of Moses. Now I had been touched by Jesus himself and turned in another direction. And I could not tell where any of this would lead.

From my earliest years I had been enamored of Mosaic Law. It had built bones in me, created my body, and formed the foundation of my soul. I had become its knowledgeable defender. Yet I was a new creature now, a kind of Christ myself—that was my distinct feeling, however hard to understand or fully absorb. Was I deranged, unstrung? Had my companions really not heard the thundering voice that afternoon on the road to Damascus?

"Jesus has spoken, the Lord himself, the Christ, and I'm blinded," I had said, and wept.

They stood above me, a haze of concern. What did I mean? How could I have lost my sight, and without apparent cause? Who had spoken?

I would often recount what had happened that day, trying to understand the meaning of this holy encounter. I needed to find a narrative sufficient to the experience itself. But what language could suffice, could hope to describe and embody what happened to me that day? A spiritual wind had whirled the desert of my own heart, scattered the sands of my soul, but how could I explain those feelings, which even now churned inside me? How could I account for the radical intervention of God's presence in my life?

The elderly Ananias had prayed beside me with his nephew, Luke the physician, a dear man from Antioch. They had told me more about Jesus of Nazareth, about his simple birth on his mother's farm in Galilee, and his long apprenticeship to his father. He and Joseph walked from nearby Nazareth, a tiny village, to the major city of Sepphoris each morning, where masonry skills were in demand, as it recently had become the seat of Herod Antipas, whose royal court drew visitors from distant parts of the Roman Empire. Ananias had any number of anecdotes about the Christ, some of them contradictory. But I was eager to learn more.

Others told me that Jesus had gone off into the Arabian desert by himself, encountering any number of teachers along the way, including magicians who unlocked secrets and recited sutras from hidden scriptures. After forty days of fasting and prayer, and a fiery encounter with the Adversary, Jesus assumed a ministry of healing and teaching, having been immersed in the Jordan by his cousin, John the Baptizer, a man who lived on dry, salted locusts and wild honey and wore only a sackcloth made from the long, bristly hair of camels. He lived in prayer, rejoicing in each moment of life, saying that every step he took was an answer to God.

I enjoyed all stories about this wild man of the desert, this ascetic who lived on the simplest food, who had no pretense or worldly possessions, whose fasting drew him closer to God each hour of the day. I, too, must rejoice and pray without ceasing. "This was the way of John the Baptizer and the Christ as well," Luke had said.

"And what was the nature of Jesus's teachings?" I asked him. "What did our Lord ask of us?"

I knew so little about him then. But one must begin somewhere.

"He went among the Essenes," Luke had told me. "They are a

mystical group who live in desert caves, who read the scriptures, every kind of scripture. They meditate, and they sing hymns of their devising."

I had heard of this sect, a gentle people devoted to reading and all-consuming prayer. They lived in small communities, and would chant together from ancient writings, and had in their possession many versions of the holiest books, as well as esoteric texts, and believed one could find eternal life in death itself, dying into the flesh to emerge in the spirit. I had heard such language before from Greeks in Tarsus, who sometimes carried stories of Eleusis, where sacred mysteries had been celebrated from the beginning of earthly time. Those who worshipped Mithras understood these mysteries as well, which centered on renewal of the spirit.

"It's like Persephone," I said to Luke and his uncle, "the descent into death, the awakening in spring. A kind of rebirth."

His uncle laughed when I suggested this, tugging my ear as if I were a child trying to speak like an adult.

"You've spent too many years in study," Ananias said. "Go into the desert, where all things begin. Luke is right. You will find guides, and they will instruct you in the Way. I can only begin, pointing my finger in a direction that may help, but you must walk that way yourself."

Ananias told me about a particular community of Essenes who lived near Mount Sinai in the eastern desert. A number of them belonged to the Way of Jesus, and they had key insights that would help me along my own path. "Go there," he said. "Ask for Musa. They will take you to him. And he will know you are coming."

"How will he know?"

"Don't ask this," he said.

It made no sense to question him, I could tell. But I did wonder how many people in the desert near Mount Sinai might answer to the name of Musa, a common name. On the other hand, Ananias knew something, and this was part of my humbling. I must withdraw and not wish to understand. Nor should I attempt to control outcomes. Instead, with effort, I must learn to pray as Ananias taught me, after the manner of Jesus, crying, *Thy will be done.*

This concept dizzied me, as I had lived by getting my own way from earliest childhood. I might as well have prayed, *My will be done.*

"Jesus emptied himself out," Ananias said.

The phrase played on my ear, beautiful and mysterious.

I found myself thirsty for instruction, having only begun to empty myself into Jesus the Christ, who had emptied himself into me. I would go into the desert, as Ananias suggested, although this would not be undemanding for someone who had spent most of his life in cities. I had never slept like a shepherd under a shower of stars in the company of wild beasts and biting insects. I had never crouched in caves or moved through evergreen forests or across silent deserts. My life had been spent in churning streets and noisy markets, in school-rooms and synagogues, in the society of rabbis, scholars, merchants, men of trade.

A letter to my father needed writing, that much I knew. I must explain that I would not be shipping hides from Jerusalem to Tarsus, not for a while. I would tell him that Amos could manage. Amos understood exactly where those hides came from, and the supply would not shrink without me. My father would be furious with me, of course, having raised me to meet his expectations, and disobedience never entered his mind as a possibility. Sons did what their fathers required of them. Just in case I felt tempted to stray, he often quoted one of the Proverbs of Solomon: *A foolish son is a grief to his father.*

But I must seek the face of God, my real father, going into the wilderness as prophets had done for centuries: Ezekiel and Ezra, Miriam, Aaron, Isaiah and Huldah. I must go among the gazelles, jackals, lizards, sand cats, vipers, badgers, scorpions, and fire ants. I must learn to listen for God in the roiling midst of his creation. Live in the whirlwind, listen to the icy choir of stones.

As night settled, with a full moon, the desert opened before me, and I sank happily into the accumulating silence, grateful for the directions of Ananias and the encouragement of his nephew, whom I knew I would see again one day. For now, I would walk myself out and sleep in full exhaustion, spent of myself and my small worries for personal survival. I was nobody, nothing. And it was good to know this in such a visceral way, with the world around me a reflection of my emptiness.

What little I understood of wild places I could trace to Simon, the friend of my youth, who once suggested that a man could live for months in the desert as long as he found something to drink. "You won't notice at first, but water is everywhere," he said. He showed me how to suck at the roots of the saltbush for moisture, or tear into the soft bark of the boras tree. He forced me to fill my mouth with juicy red-and-yellow insects and to sip at rock pans in the shelves where water pools at dawn.

I had done all of this in the country beyond Tarsus, though it was long ago.

Late on the second day of my journey, when I had seriously begun to worry about quenching my thirst, I heard the flourish of a stream behind a thicket. A trail moved beside it, and I assumed I could follow this route into the desert. It was the path by the stream that Ananias had mentioned, and God had led me here, as promised in the Psalm: *I sought the Lord and he answered me.*

I kept to the north side of the stream, stopping occasionally to dangle my feet in the cool water, letting it catch and frill around my ankles. One evening I stopped well before sundown, falling asleep on a patch of moss, drifting in a timeless time. When I woke, I drank as much as I could from the stream before filling my waterskin. I told myself that God had opened his hand for me, and I could nestle in his palm. I felt safe in his presence.

But was I fooling myself?

After eating a handful of nuts and dates, I bathed in a pool where the stream had caught in a backwash of silt, and I remembered Simon, who had plunged headfirst into a swirl. I would never forget how I found him, his limp body in the reeds, and how I lifted him to shore. After the briefest rest, numb with grief, I pulled him over my shoulder and carried him into Tarsus. For a while blood continued to seep from his wound, where the bone of his head was exposed. Then it clotted and caked. The eyes stared ahead, as if he had begun to look beyond his life on earth. Perhaps he had seen eternity, its ring of light. My forearms and hands were stained, sticky and somehow burning. After a couple of hours of walking, I brought my friend to the door-step of his family house and knocked, wishing myself anywhere else in the world but there. His father opened the door casually, with a slight frown, as if annoyed by having to deal with a visitor.

He looked at me without fear. The poor man.

"Simon has drowned," I said.

The dead body of his son lay on the ground beside me, where I had gently put it down.

There was a pause as he gathered into himself this blunt and brutal fact, allowing it to seep into his bones and sour the honeycomb of his brain. Like all grief, it had to become physical in order to become real. And yet I never knew horror could take such proportions. In an instant, Simon's father understood his life was utterly changed and could not settle again into its former texture. He would never sleep without the horror of dreams that could unmake him and never count on eating a meal without thoughts of an absence, a hole ripped in the tissue of his spirit.

He fell on his son's body with alarming force, burying his face in the child's stomach.

I caught sight of his mother in the dark shadows of the house as she peered from behind a curtain, her face covered with a shawl. She would never recover, as one does not recover from such a thing.

Some impossible phrases by way of explanation stuttered from me. These fragments hung in the air, dissolving as I stepped backward, eager to get out of their sight.

That afternoon, when I told my father about Simon, he said nothing for a while, walking into another room to collect himself. When he returned, he told me to follow him to Simon's house. I admired this aspect of my father, his willingness to step into the anguish, not hide from it. "It's our duty to go there," he said.

The forlorn parents grieved in silence with a few other friends, the body propped on straw cushions on a table and covered by a linen burial cloth. I could smell the cinnamon and cumin, eerily fragrant, perhaps too sweet, which had been pressed into Simon's skin. He would be put into the dirt and covered before sundown, as was our custom from the time of Adam and Eve, who had been taught by a raven how to bury Abel, their beloved son; the black ragged bird had scratched in the dirt, and they knew what they must do.

God teaches by symbol and semblance.

I sat behind my father, avoiding the afflicted parents. Nobody spoke, but soon a broad-chested bearded man from the synagogue appeared, a beautiful singer from the tribe of Levi. He lifted a Psalm into the air. *Oh God, my God, why hast thou forsaken me?*

In his anguish on the cross, feeling abandoned by heaven, Jesus himself had quoted from this poem by David.

Why hast thou forsaken me? I would ask this question myself so many times in my life.

But there is an honest wildness in such inquiry, facing into pain with an inward rage that works to equalize the violence coming from without.

I wanted this for myself, a wild bravery of spirit.

As I resumed my trek, I thought of Aryeh, who I assumed I would never see again. I longed to hear the timbre of his voice, the eruption of his laughter at unlikely moments, his bluff, easy approach to life. I liked the way he leaned against a doorjamb in his own fashion, watching others at work with a wry wincing smile. His childlike manner contrasted my own looping, convoluted thoughts, my tortuous ruminations, and I wished only to simplify what I thought, to live by a few bold assertions. But this seemed impossible now.

Suddenly a pillar of sand swept toward me, whirling in midair, and I stood amazed before it. In the swirl itself, the black eyes of Aryeh burned, ice and fire.

Was I awake and dreaming?

"You disappoint me, Paul," a voice said.

Was it possible?

"Why have you not come back to us?"

"I have met Jesus," I said. "He came to me on the road."

"You must kill him."

"He is my Lord."

"I didn't expect this, Paul. I thought you and I would fight together—for the twelve tribes, and the one God who rules the universe."

"I've been called by Jesus," I said. "Let me go!"

He raised his arms in the air, and I could see the auburn hair under his arms, a bare torso. The wind rose in a girdle about him, absorbed him. And soon the air was clear, with no evidence of a sandy pillar.

Was it Aryeh who spoke to me? Or had I met the Adversary, who had assumed this familiar and alluring form? No matter. I felt sure of myself now, and looked at the open horizon, and began to walk into my new life with fresh energies.

Before my escape from Damascus, I had filled a sack with bits and pieces of food, and could feed from this cache for any number of days, maybe weeks, eating as little as possible. Hunger was good, I told myself, as it forced an alertness. I felt nimble and adroit, quick-witted. I had met the Adversary, or some specter, and not been over-whelmed or deceived.

The crude map of the desert that Ananias had drawn led me forward. I would follow this route, avoiding "soldiers and small gather-ings," as he warned me. The news of my change of heart would have traveled, and condemnation would greet me in territories governed by Aretas, who assumed that all of Judea was his. At least for the time being, I would stay far away from towns and villages as I moved into the pink sand and silence before me. The less contact with people, the greater my chances of survival.

Surely my former associates in the Temple Guard would puzzle over my transformation, my apparently traitorous turn, and I did not doubt that Aryeh would feel betrayed, even furious. The fury I had just heard in Aryeh's voice—real or unreal—rang in my ears.

Stopping to pray by the wayside, I allowed myself to sink into God's presence, saying nothing. I recalled that my father, a pious Jew, rarely departed from set prayers, which he recited in a low grumble, a scowl on his face as he rocked before a scroll that had belonged to his own father. I tried to imagine a different way of praying, allowing the flames of love to kindle inside me. And I would seek this fire in the desert.

After a week or so, I stopped counting days and simply watched as constellations banked in the sky at night, and I grew more com-fortable with sleeping under that luxurious canopy, wrapped in the blanket I carried as a bedroll, my head on a mossy patch or tuft of grass. Sleep enveloped me in its blessing, cushioned me, carried me to a space where I could escape from the hardness of life in the wild, could evade my own terrifying but exhilarating solitude.

I slept in stone huts when I could—one came across them now

and then—but mostly it was open air around me or a lee of sand. My sandals barely covered the soles of my feet, their straps wearing thin. My clothes turned into clouds, mere threads that traced the lineaments of flesh, however vaguely. But none of this mattered.

Nobody knew where I was.

I barely knew.

And so I prayed, spending an hour or more in devotion each morning after dawn. At night I would talk to God freely, appealing for mercy. I thought about Mary, the mother of Jesus: Ananias had dwelled on stories of her purity and faithfulness. God singled her out, of all the people in history, as a portal through which his radiant power would pour, an intersection where a timeless vertical beam passed through horizontal time. Mary was chosen for this mission of love and would suffer with him as well.

"She is our mother, too," said Ananias.

I wanted to find her in Jerusalem one day, to speak to her, as I knew she still lived somewhere in the Upper City, an elderly widow. She was looked after by James and his brothers and revered by many in the Way. And when I dreamed of her, I could see my own lost mother, whom I never knew, with her smile of sweet unending compassion, with a maternal heat that could warm me still.

From the little I knew, I guessed that Jesus had been a tiresome child to raise, determined to gain access to his heavenly father, willfully dismissing his earthly one. I could understand his frustrations. He would have felt the spirit at work in his soul, and this would have both thrilled and terrified him.

I had myself been thrilled and terrified. I began to hear voices more frequently now, many of them suspicious. Devils? The Adversary? I decided to ignore them, unless I sensed that Jesus approached again and wished to communicate with me. I felt quite sure that he would, and that my encounter on the Damascus Road had not been singular, an incident that would never occur again. I expected more from the Lord now, and knew I would get it.

But I must be alert, open to every possibility.

As I knew, angels inhabit unlikely forms, often taking you by surprise, such as when I encountered a hermit in a cave where I took shelter from a particularly nasty sandstorm. I had thought myself alone but heard him snoring only a few feet from where I crouched against a wall in meditation. This ill-shapen creature had an angular jaw, a large crooked nose, and blue scars on his face, as if he'd been through many battles. His look unsettled me, but apprehension turned to gratitude when he offered me a drink of water from his skin and food from a satchel of sycamore figs and raisins mixed with walnuts.

He asked about my destination, aware that most of those he met in the desert were in flight. Why else would anyone be here?

When I told him that Mount Sinai was my goal, he brightened, telling me about the communities that lived in caves. I had made the foolish assumption that, given his odd visage and isolation, he must be illiterate or mad, a lost soul. But he spoke with surprising eloquence and seemed aware of the scrolls in their possession. He wondered if I had any interest in what he called "esoteric learning," and I nodded, although I didn't like the term. What was esoteric to one inquirer, the fruit of some foreign tree, might be common fare to another, if we took "esoteric" to mean abstruse and possibly profound as opposed to simply rare and perhaps from another tradition.

I asked if he knew of Musa.

"Musa ben-Zakkai!" he said, with a grin.

He introduced himself as Abel-Sittim, which (according to him) meant "meadow of acacia." He said he was born beside such a meadow, in a remote part of Judea, where his father had been a shepherd. "But that was long ago," he said, "in the days when stars applauded us." I didn't know what he meant, but it didn't matter. He appeared well-meaning, intelligent, and kind. I didn't worry he would stab me while I slept or rob me of my few possessions.

The sandstorm made travel impossible, so I spent two days in conversation with this unlikely new acquaintance. Abel-Sittim was a connoisseur of desert survival, and he told me that almost any insect was good to eat, though I should avoid scorpions. One could feast "quite happily," he said, on rodents and snakes. Lizards tasted "wonderful when roasted over a fire." As he pointed out, there were locusts everywhere. "They are the gift of God to anyone who hungers, a feast for our pleasure."

I wondered about dead snakes, having seen any number of them recently.

"You are not a vulture," he said. "Carrion may kill you."

Quicksand was another hazard, he explained, and this was especially so for those unfamiliar with desert ways. He said not to panic
should I get stuck. "Lift your knees, lie back and paddle to a dry spot.
It is only water and sand, and those who drown in these puddles do
so from panic." Dust storms could also prove fatal, he told me while
we hid ourselves from a particularly nasty one that whirled about the
cave with a massive whining like a thousand jackals. "Storms suck the
goodness from the air," he continued, appreciating my receptive ears.
"Get somewhere you can breathe, into a cave or behind a large rock.
Avoid dunes, even though you may feel tempted to shelter against
them. It never works. The wind carries sand like waves over any crest,
and it may prove impossible to extricate yourself. If there is no shelter,
sit with your back to the storm, covering your head and face, keeping
low to the ground. Put a wet cloth over your nose and mouth, even
your eyes, if you have enough water."

We talked about water. It is the primary subject among desert
people, and he mentioned sources I had never imagined. "The speck-
led cactus plant will be found everywhere, and it's clever at collect-
ing moisture," he said. "You can break off its spikes, and suck on
them. But be careful, as they're sharp!" He mentioned several beetles
that acted like sponges and could fill the mouth with an "explosion
of moisture." He said to "pay attention to the birds, and the insects.
They know where to find water. Follow them."

The most dangerous element in the desert was the sun, with its
lethal radiance. "Walk by night," he advised. "It's the first lesson of
the wilderness. Daylight is your enemy."

I knew this but adored the sun and preferred to walk in its rays,
although never in the middle of the day.

With so many pitfalls, it might not be easy to make my way to
Mount Sinai unscathed. But spring was an especially good time for
desert walking. The weather had yet to begin to blister the rocky
ledges, and I could make progress in the early-morning hours, moving
in the predawn dark as it faded into light and burst to flame. I would
sleep through the midday, taking shelter where I could, under a cliff
or ledge, in the lee of a dune, under a date palm, or, ideally, in a sycamore grove. One could create a shelter with dead leaves, too, though

I didn't want to spend much of my time creating shady hutches for myself, which I would abandon after only a few hours of rest. The conservation of energy mattered.

When the storm abated, I thanked Abel-Sittim and set off again, following a narrow trace in the desert that he had recommended.

Hours later I saw the oasis he had told me lay ahead. It was bordered by tamarisk, with a flourishing of date palms. Alas, a caravan watered their camels there: never a good sign. I approached the men warily, as desert people jealously guarded sources of water, and one could easily cause offense, which could lead to violence, even death. Nobody in the desert worried about courts of law, so murder was unimportant, simply a reflex. This was a savage world, and you survived by your wits, or didn't.

I approached a thin, dark man who stood by a camel with its long neck dipping forward toward the water. He knew some Greek, much to my relief, and asked for my destination. I didn't fully trust him but had a hunch this caravan might help me along a potentially treacherous way, where you could easily be waylaid by thieves or worse. Abel-Sittim had been quite explicit about what dangers lay ahead.

For a sum, Dumuzi—he had given me his name—said I could join the caravan. He stated this with authority, so I assumed he didn't have to consult the others. And soon I discovered that nobody objected to my presence. Nor did anyone welcome me. They hardly seemed to see me, though one prune-skinned older man brought me a cup of barley beer one day after we set off. Perhaps I was not as offensive to them as I had thought.

Without reason, I began to trust these rough-hewn men, and the routines of caravan life soothed me, with travel beginning in the middle of the night and continuing through the first part of morning. During the midday hours, they lay in the shade of their tents, sleeping on cushions or under trees when possible. As the sun tilted into evening, they would begin again, pushing ahead on their camels until dark, sleeping for a while, then beginning again. It was as if they had been traveling for centuries and, in a way, they had.

I fell into these rhythms, in the soothing cradle of long-established routines, and found that, like them, I could sleep heavily without notice. Too heavily perhaps, as I woke one day with Dumuzi hovering near. He breathed deeply, rumbling like a cat, watching to see if I would waken. It relieved me to find my coins intact, and from this point on I slept with my pouch under my head for a pillow. I must guard my few possessions, especially this little cache of money, which might provide a lifeline at some point.

Dumuzi and I exchanged a few words each day, though nobody else spoke to me or caught my eye; loneliness didn't trouble me, however. I savored my independence and worked to bolster my prayer life. Praying (which I could do as I walked or, more easily, before I slept) became a source of nourishment and a place of refuge. I could feel the presence of God flow through the rooms of my mind like the odor of jasmine, those aromatic tiny white flowers that open in the wilderness at night to become low little stars.

When I felt pain, exhaustion, or fear, I told myself that these feelings were just the cracking of a shell that enclosed the truth. It might hurt to break through this shell, but it must be done—just as a chick must shatter its eggshell to emerge.

My Lord, Jesus, I would pray, *take everything from me. Fill me. Make me your vessel on this earth, your hands in the world, your voice.*

After four weeks of travel, when mostly I walked beside the camels and once or twice rode high on their humps, I found myself in the depths of Arabia, somewhere in the purple foothills near Mount Sinai that Abel-Sittim had described. And one morning, at the outskirts of a village, Dumuzi said, "We arrive for you." He winked and grinned, ever so briefly, before turning away.

I understood what this meant.

The caravan rested in the shadow of clustering palms, and nobody seemed to notice as I gathered my few things and, as unexpectedly as I had joined them, walked off by myself. One man, posted as a kind of sentry at the edge of their encampment, saw me go. I didn't trust this fellow, who had a dark semicircular scar on his cheek and one tooth (his only one) that reached over his bottom lip in a most disgusting fashion. I had nodded to him a few times before, without a response; now I glanced at him casually, as if nothing was amiss, and moved ahead steadily, my head down, half expecting a hand on my shoulder.

But I was not their prisoner and nothing happened. I didn't need to take my leave of the group in any formal manner, as they had largely remained indifferent to my presence. Whether Dumuzi shared any of my payment with them, I could not know. Nor did I care now.

In the village itself, which was much larger than it appeared from a distance, I found the local synagogue, where I spoke with a man who directed me to the house of Milka, a widow only too glad for a paying guest. We sat together in her garden with a cup of wine, and she told me that she had never been to Herod's Temple in Jerusalem, but hoped one day to make the journey for Passover. Her spiritual hunger impressed me, and I explained that new voices had emerged among our people.

She welcomed my stories about Jesus, whom I carefully described as a "great rabbi."

I often referred to him as Rabbi Jesus, especially among Jews, telling them that as a boy he had discussed the scriptures with the wise and erudite scholars of the Temple, and his knowledge had amazed them. He seemed to have read and fully absorbed the five books of Moses, the prophetic writings, and the Ketuvim as well— those poetic anthologies of wisdom that included a variety of psalms and proverbs. (As I would learn, Jesus had a special fondness for the prophecies of Daniel.)

Milka knew something of Musa and said that she could get word to him about me. This amazed but didn't surprise me: Everything in my life felt improbable now. So I made a plan to sit still, often in prayer, waiting for Musa. I might have stayed for several months with Milka and it would not have troubled me, as great happiness flowed in me and her kindness and hospitality pleased me.

But after only a few days, at daybreak, Musa himself stood at the edge of my pallet, waking me with a sharp cough.

"I've been expecting you," he said.

His gold eyes darted around the room, but he was not shifty. The world inside him expanded, growing wider with each breath. His long face was made of putty, caked and cracked by the sun, flaking when he grinned. His nose swelled at the tip, a fist of purple veins. His toes bulged from his sandals, knobs of flesh with black nails, and his hands were yellow with a parchment-like pallor—the large callused hands of a man who had lived rough for most of his life.

"Gather yourself and come," he said.

Milka stood in the background and looked at me, perhaps a little sadly, putting dried meats into my sack and then touching my forehead with her thumbs as a form of blessing. "I will miss you," she said. And I would miss her, more than I could ever miss the invisible mother I never knew.

I followed my new master on foot beyond the village into the mountains, drawn into the wake of his long strides. He carried his own food, which he shared: stale bread, nuts, seed cakes, raisins. He said he would take me to a settlement near the holy mountain, where I would meet his friends and fellow Essenes. "They have been expecting you," he said.

Exactly how that could be the case eluded me. But what did I really know?

We talked of Jesus that evening beside a small fire, and it startled me how much he knew.

"He lived among us for a few years," Musa told me. "He studied our scriptures. But he knew most of them already by heart. Even the lost songs." He added: "What a beautiful chant he could lift to the heavens. The stars would gather overhead to listen."

He referred to the hundreds of psalms in the vein of the Davidic hymns. They were gorgeously framed, mystical, and moving, and I would learn many of them myself and recite them before sleeping or when, in the middle of the night, I woke with terrors: *Lord, my master, fill me now and find a place in this world. Lord God Almighty, make me whole and make me hale, a part of your deep and vegetable kingdom, acceptable and lovely in your sight, your own forever.*

I was glad that I committed that one to memory, as I never found it again, not in any other scroll.

Musa took a special interest in my education, telling me about the Garden of Twelve Palm Trees, in Bethany. Jesus had gathered his disciples there and taught them the secrets of deep affiliation with God through prayer. He demonstrated before them a form of communion that he perfected among the Essenes, who spent much of their lives deciphering ancient manuscripts, meditating or praying, forging their connection to heaven. "We are the sons and daughters of God," Musa told me. "Jesus understood that God is presence: *I am that I am.* This is what God said to Moses. *I am the Way, and also the Light."*

Musa unsettled me when he would burst into laughter at odd moments, shaking and even salivating with amusement, as if suddenly aware of some private and quite hilarious joke.

"You have no sense of humor, Paul," he said one day. "It is your principal defect."

I objected, but there was a point in his remark, and it was probably true. Humor had never been one of my gifts, and I regretted this. It's better to laugh than to weep, as laughter is a balm for wounds of the heart.

Musa would talk a lot to himself or to God—or possibly the angels. Alone with him, an otherwise empty room felt crowded, with invisible ears and eyes all around. In a cave as I slept beside him during our first night together, I heard strange laughter in the dark.

At his bidding, I soon found myself absorbed in translations of ancient texts from the Chaldeans. "The holy sages of Babylon passed along these revelations. They understood the figures in the constellations. A few of them traveled a great distance to find Jesus the infant, who was born beneath an especially bright star." This was among many stories that would circulate in various forms in the decades to come, and Luke often extracted them from me. To be frank, I invented variations at will, depending on my mood, although I trusted in God to guide my imagination on the paths of righteousness. I heard many contradictory but often credible and illuminating things about Jesus, and learned to accept them as ornaments, to treasure them, holding them in my hand like fruit from a strange tree.

But not every piece of exotic fruit should be eaten.

"Study the scrolls," Musa said, "and pray over them. Then we can talk about their meaning."

These teachings had been handed down over generations, carried by groups of men and women from as far away as the legendary Kush and preserved in dry caves, now treasured and examined by this community.

"Once you absorb our teachings, you will never dream in the same way," Musa told me.

Musa called Abraham our "true father," reasoning thus: "He was not a Jew—not in his own mind. God's commandments came to Moses many years later, as we know. But Abraham was the father of everyone, Jew and gentile, the beloved of God. He worshipped God as the single master of the cosmos."

This rhymed with my own preference for Abraham over Moses as the true father of mankind, the source of our longings, our dreams, our ideas of justice and redemption. (I had to work very hard not to dislike Moses, whose arrogance worried me.)

With his odd and discomfiting thoughts, Musa jolted me out of the complacent ideas with which I had lived so comfortably for much of my life. He didn't let me fall back on facile thinking or received wisdom. "That is not wisdom," he would say. "Wisdom allows for the unexpected. It feeds on error, which it modifies into truth." And so I began to read again as if for the first time the opening movements of the Torah, marveling at the work of God as delivered by Abraham our father.

A long period of study, prayer, and meditation followed, and gradually I found my place in this community, which had welcomed me without reservation, asking no questions about my past, taking me for who I was.

The Essenes worked and studied with an impressive stillness. Musa told them about my father's trade, and I was glad to pass along my skills at tent-making: how to sew the seams in a way that would form a barrier against sun and rain, how to find the most durable materials, what tools worked well. We sat together in silence, studying in the pink-and-gray early hours of the day, and prayed together in the evenings. And we kept the Sabbath, a time for deep prayer and rejoicing.

Musa and most of the others here had encountered Jesus, many of them personally, and they often would talk about their experience. This was useful, as I continued to try to understand and absorb what had happened to me on the Damascus Road. This was probably the work of my life, as I knew. What did Jesus want of me? Obedience? Was the Christ simply another god who needed my fealty? I put this last question to Musa.

"Jesus doesn't want or need your allegiance."

"So what does he need?"

"The universe has no need. He is the Logos."

"Meaning?"

"He directs us to an awareness that was here before and after everything. He is understanding itself."

"That is cryptic," I said.

"I don't wish to confuse you."

I pondered what he had said. "I must pray to God?"

"No," he said. "You must learn to pray *through* God."

It would take time for these ideas to make sense, for them to settle into that depth below depths, where we no longer ask questions but sit beyond any need for understanding or logical thought. A thought, to become your own, must taste of acacia and fresh figs. It must have an aroma, the sharp smell of reality. It must sting like nettles.

"We live in a thousand minds at once, in the Christ," said Musa. "We unleash ourselves, let go. We are one body, not alone. Not ourselves."

After a day of labor, in my case working to repair canopies, I sat with Musa and the others around a fire, and we broke bread together, then passed a cup of wine, and the heavens opened inside us.

"I give you this, the resurrection," said Musa, intoning. "We rise together."

And everyone said, "We rise together."

I said it myself, over and over. And I would rise, with them, that day.

Chapter Six

PAUL

Musa came to me one morning when I was reading the Psalms of David, basking in the straw-colored rays of the sun, sitting with my back sealed comfortably against a stone wall. He sank to his haunches, eye to eye with me—as he often did when he wished to instruct—and told me I must go.

It was time for me to visit the synagogue in Petra, he said. This would become the starting point for a longer mission. "You will travel to the ends of the earth," he told me.

"So far?"

He smiled. Once in a while I did manage a small joke, and he liked this and touched my shoulder.

I looked into the dirt to think, pushing the sand to one side with a stick. My three years in the desert had been edifying, and I could hardly bear the idea of leaving this circle of friends, such lively and compassionate spirits. I had learned so much, and it was likely I could learn more if I stayed.

"I don't want to go," I said. "I feel at home here. I can study and pray, as everyone does."

The thought of remaining permanently among the Essenes had consumed me in the past year, and I didn't wish to live anywhere else. I had no desire to resume work in Tarsus with my father. Jerusalem was impossible, even dangerous, for me. And I didn't know that traveling to the ends of the earth made sense for one of my disposition. I liked being in the same place, among congenial friends.

Musa was unresponsive.

"I have something to contribute, to you, to everyone here," I said.

He nodded, as if to confirm what I said.

"We worship God together," I added. "There is a lot of work to be done with the scrolls. I can help."

"You have already helped," he said.

My linguistic skills and long training under Gamaliel had served me well here, and I knew my way among hundreds of psalms now. My new friends hadn't encountered the visions of Daniel, and I opened this material to them, quoting from memory: *And those who have wisdom shall shine like the brightness of the heavens above, and those who turn many to righteousness shall glisten, taking their place among the stars.* I could actually see the words in my mind. And so they often asked me to talk of Daniel, who had risen to the third heaven: ever the goal of deep prayer, although a further turn remained, which was to bring back into daily life the insights of any revelation.

As ever, Musa read my thoughts.

"God has something in mind for you. Petra is only the beginning of your journey," he said. "You will find many guides in your life, and you will add to the store of inspired writing." He read my mind closely. "Nothing is enough. Not for you. But that is your nature. To lie under open skies, to think, to move, to talk and persuade others about the truth—the full meaning—of the Christ. We are each given separate gifts, you see. Some will feed the poor and heal the sick, or sit beside them unto death. Others will teach. Others have the gift of prophecy." He paused. "I see you as a prophet. Your time will come."

Did he really say that? It was unlike Musa to exaggerate.

But I resisted this idea. I didn't want such a lofty place in the universe. "I'm at home here. I can make a contribution."

He stared at me, squeezing his fingers in that peculiar way of his. "Move on, Paul. In Petra, you will find a group of pious Jews and Godfearers—and they will listen to what you have to say. The ground is fertile. Say what you say boldly, even when it comes out misshapen and provokes anger. Your true work begins in Petra, but it extends to the farthest regions. The power of your voice, it will carry you over many mountains, deserts, and plains. You will walk in valleys of the shadow and find yourself in bright and noisy cities. You will tell the world what you know. And some will listen."

I looked up with interest, knowing he told me something I must hear.

"You will go to Rome one day. Even Spain, perhaps. I can't say where. But you must go quickly to Petra. When the fruit has ripened, it withers if not plucked at once. Fill God's basket!"

Occasionally I teased Musa when he offered ponderous sayings, and sometimes I responded with a favorite old Syrian proverb that my father often repeated: "The dogs bark, the caravan moves on."

The caravan, it seemed, must move on.

Now Musa gestured for me to come close, and I leaned forward to accept his direction, looking into the green-gold glistening stare, seeing his nostrils widen like a bull before the charge. "Mark carefully," he said. "As you approach the city of Petra, you will see an overhanging red rock—it is blood-bright stone, unmistakable—with a thin spire like a crooked finger pointing at the sky. On the eastern side of the long and narrow entry. Wait there, and a voice will come. You will have further instructions. Don't be impatient. You are always impatient!"

"I don't know why you say this."

"Don't expect too much. Try not to want so much."

Easy to say, of course. I thought back to my first days with Musa. He evidently found me insufferable, full of my own opinions, wishing to argue. He took me aside many times and said I must allow the well to fill, must not always drink so greedily. He asked me to find the silence in which the spirit prospers, to wait on God, who would find me at the appropriate time.

I was sure that I grew stronger in the desert, richer in the spirit, able to accept the quiet of God as my foundation and the place to begin my real work. I had sought his face, as the scriptures commanded, but it blurred whenever I tried to examine his features. Even the voice eluded me.

"Remember that he comes when least expected," Musa said. "But he comes. Depend on this."

Musa had been my guide for more than three years, and I found it painful to leave him, possibly forever. It was hard to believe I would return, as a child can't return to a school once he has finished his studies, at least never as a participant. Parting is life's work. We are always leaving someone or something.

This was the first truth, and I must embrace it.

I must go.

✝

This was a bad time to be a Jew in Arabia—or anywhere. All rulers owed allegiance to Rome, who looked for the slightest signs of insurrection.

"It's the Jew!" they would cry.

It was always the Jew. Everywhere in every situation.

Being of the resilient tribe of Benjamin, and a Pharisee by affiliation, I embraced my tradition and spoke first as a Jew, much as Rabbi Jesus had done. His trust in God became my trust, and I tried to emulate this devotion, allowing my dependence on him to grow, not wane.

Musa took my hands in his. "In the Christ there is neither male nor female," he said, "neither slave nor free man, neither Jew nor Greek." He paused. "This is the teaching of Jesus, and you need only remember it and repeat it. Tell all the world! I believe you will do this."

Neither male nor female, neither slave nor free man, neither Jew nor Greek.

This radical equality of every class and kind startled me. And I knew it would take a lifetime of prayer to assimilate this teaching properly, as it was deeply strange and far-reaching and profound.

"Go, quickly," Musa said. "Hesitation is a little death. If you don't act, you will never act."

I didn't even pause to say goodbye to the others, as the agony of separation would convulse me, upend my leave-taking. Musa would explain everything to them, and they would understand and accept his reasoning. And so, with a few belongings in my sack, I left this circle of friends, this holy community, my spiritual family.

"Your time is upon you," Musa said.

With that, I set off into the sun, which burst over the lip of the desert, a bright red ball, departing with just a slight nod to Musa, who ignored me as he crouched by a tree and chewed his ganza, the sweet grass that had browned his teeth over the decades. "It is always arriving," he said, more to himself than to me, the last words I ever heard from him.

Certainly "it," whatever that was, was arriving now.

I pushed back tears. It felt impossible to leave my friends, to discontinue our conversations. But I would go where I must go, and learn by going.

God's path opened, as Musa predicted. A sense of well-being lifted me as I walked across the Valley of Bones stretching into the eastern desert, passing tent villages that had no name or fixed location. These nomadic people drifted with their animals as the grazing season shifted, at home nowhere and everywhere. They would roll their tents onto long poles, then carry them on the backs of donkeys or camels for days and weeks on end; a small village would manifest in the midst of a plain, near an oasis, in the leeside of a cliff.

There was no need for a map, as I simply followed the ruts of caravans that had left decades-deep impressions in the dirt, with Petra a magical destination: this fabled pink fortress carved from sandstone. Nobody went through this part of the world without stopping there. I recalled that Aaron, the brother of Moses, lay buried nearby, and his tomb attracted votaries from as far away as Egypt and Spain. Petra itself was the hub of Nabataean authority—the earthly power I had escaped several years earlier, in flight from Damascus. Should they discover me, I would be arrested, tortured, and killed.

Or perhaps they had forgotten me.

I drew upon a small caravan of char-faced travelers with half a dozen camels and a donkey or two, but followed from a slight distance, not wishing to engage them, as they might be Bactrians or Turkmen, who could prove hostile. I assumed they were headed for Petra, since the red hills appearing on either side of the valley suggested that I was moving in the right direction. As I walked, I was buoyed up by God, with the Holy Spirit rising within me like a geyser.

When the caravan paused to rest, I paused as well. I knew the rhythms of these travelers well and mimicked them.

Once I fell asleep during one of their resting periods at an oasis—I kept off to one side, out of view in a nest of shrubs—and they pulled far ahead of me, out of sight. But I felt confident about the route to Petra, since the trail showed signs of centuries of travelers, with hoofprints, wheel ruts, dung droppings, and refuse that proved oddly reassuring.

As I drew near, I tried to imagine this legendary city of the Nabataeans. Over the years I'd heard many travelers describe it: this massive narrow canyon of rose sandstone, sculpted by human hands, the walls of the canyon transformed into dwellings, temples, public spaces. It was a busy thoroughfare, too, because so many of the world's roads converged here.

I followed a path above the main route on the eastern side of the valley, as Musa had suggested. A goat bell tinkled in the distance, and I saw sheep on the hillside, these white grazing peaceful blurs. A shepherd boy looked up at me, then continued to move in the opposite direction. Soon I passed the carcass of what must have been a donkey, though the hawks had already had their way with it; even the eye sockets were empty. Only the ears remained, barely attached to the skull. The long dorsal spine had settled in the dirt, and a bit of gristle clung to the bones. The smell was musty, not putrid. Time purifies everything, and soon this poor creature would exist only as a layer of dust on rocky soil, an outline in chalk.

As I surveyed the ruins of this beast, a voice sounded above me, with an edge of steel: "Paul, Paul. I am the son of the Lord your God."

When I looked up, the face of Jesus materialized, with distinct features: not a ring of light. Nothing hazy about this now. The face hovered, ablaze in its unique beauty, the features sharply etched and yet welcoming. I could almost reach up and touch the cheeks of my precious Lord had I dared.

His eyes burned a hole in the sky.

"Lord," I said, kneeling in the dirt.

The late-afternoon sun paused on the far west rim of the cliff on the other side of the valley. And I knew that dark would never overhang this day. It would shine and shine. Jesus had come before me, face-to-face.

"There is a rock," he said. "Do you see it?"

It loomed, rising not more than thirty paces away, redder than the surrounding stone, nearly sanguine, with a golden spire that caught the sunlight and glittered.

"I see it, Lord."

I could feel a warm pressure like an approving hand on my shoulder.

"Pray in the shadow of the red rock. And you will know what to do before darkness falls."

I looked up again, but the face had disappeared. Only the blank sky now. Jesus had vanished as rapidly as he had appeared, leaving a gap in the air. I rubbed my eyes, staggering toward the overhang, and sat in its shadow with my legs braided in the position Musa had preferred for "deep prayer," as he called it. In the yellow afternoon light, I welcomed this shade, the sense of enclosure.

I was overwhelmed, having just seen the face of Jesus.

One can't look into the sun without going blind, much as one can't look frontally at God. Such intensity of light is overwhelming. And so the Almighty gave us the gift of his son, a deflecting shield upon which we might gaze without flinching. The human face of God, as Musa called him. And now I had seen that face myself, although I tried without luck to reconstruct the exact image.

I recalled the words of Musa: "Jesus forms the image of the invisible spirit, and becomes in this the firstborn of creation. By God's strength, all things came into being. God was before all things, and all things hold together in his being. Jesus calls us into this reality, which is before and after, the durable kingdom. Open yourself to these true things. Allow yourself to settle into his unseen hand, which will hold you and keep you strong. Then rest in God."

My skin blazed as I sat under the rock, feeling my skull opening to the sky, to the heavens. I shone, entering a world aflame with love, and blazed with my newfound freedom, released from what had been my life and now held by unseen hands.

This was the fiery love of God.

So I repeated those beautiful words delivered by Musa: *In the Christ there is neither male nor female, neither slave nor free man, neither Jew nor Greek.* The language would always draw me back to the source, refresh me, give me the courage to move forward to the next step, however perilous or beyond view.

The boundaries of male and female were artificial. Perhaps essential for the perpetuation of humanity, and for incidental pleasures— that was all too imaginable. Lust had its purposes. But I could not see how any of this mattered, given that the final manifestation of the Kingdom of God loomed. Procreation must cease, as it was irrelevant. No child born today would see adulthood but, in the hope of the Christ, would live forever.

All boundaries and antinomies—male and female, slave and free man, Jew and Greek—lost their meaning in the shimmer of God, as did so many other distinctions. Neither rich nor poor, neither jailor nor prisoner. Not heaven and not earth.

Everything was dissolving. I was moving but unmoved, flying but still.

Without the ability to control my experience, I began suddenly to float, swept into a vertical movement as I rose into and through the skies above me, my soul unleashed. I sailed through the first heaven of blue rock and black water into the second, where bright and tingling star-hairs dangled in an ebony sky. I brushed beside them and quivered with the shock of their cold heat. Then I passed the orange moon and moons beyond this moon, pausing only to look back at this good earth, its mountains and valleys, lakes, rivers, and deserts. I didn't need those green fields of corn, the glint of rock faces, lush oases, palms, nuts, dates, men and women, children. I didn't need the grand, gleaming Temple in Jerusalem, as I had fashioned one of my own body. *In my father's house are many mansions,* Musa had told me our Lord had said, and this made perfect sense. I had many rooms for prayer, mansions of meaning, a tower from which I could sing out, blow the ram's horn, shout: *I will exalt you, God, my king. The heavens belong to thee. Praise to the many-layered kingdom within the kingdom of your making, the last breaking of the shell, the radiance that goes on forever and ever, this world without beginning and without end.*

I spoke in Hebrew, the tongue of King David, my holy tongue. As David had humbled himself before God, so did I. I emptied myself, becoming nobody, nothing.

And rose—kept rising—aware of the separation of limbs, bone from bone, the disintegration of my soul into pieces, a scattering of self and skin, the fine dust of meaning shaken free, loose in the universe.

Neither width nor depth, up nor down. None of that made sense. Words—what are words? I write these for myself as a way to recall, but so feeble is each utterance and every phrase.

All language dissolves into silence, its goal. As the chattering streams descend into the sea.

I had not the slightest need for words this glorious day when I found myself in a crystal globe of light, and before the great throne of the Ancient of Days, which was not a throne but more an emerald dais. Choirs sang around me, such surpassingly beautiful but unfamiliar hymns, in a bliss of scented light, with green folding melodies, and louder than the brightest radiation, and with Jesus there as well as Mary his mother and my mother, too, and my father, and all dear friends of long passing. Oh Simon, Simon! He came toward me with his green eyes, and we laughed and maybe we sang and danced—I don't know what happened in this flickering, unfooted and free.

It was all uncounted time and beyond measure. It filled me though I wanted to fill myself again and without quantity. I was satisfied yet still yearning, hungering. Eager yet full. I don't know what this meant in ordinary hours and days, where I commonly dwelled, in the usual cascade from dawn into dusk, the rude passage into night. This was uncharted infinite and unrestricted time.

By the grace of the Lord my God dear savior, I rose and rose, and was met, and needed never again to think about life in the same way. Or fear the prospect of death.

"Go into the city," said the Lord, kissing my forehead suddenly, though I didn't see his face. Not this time. "Whatever you imagine shall be yours."

My forehead was damp and burning as I began to descend into flesh again, into the world of human frailty and confusion, the counted hours. I found my footing again in the world of creatures, night and day, death and dung, the howling of wolves and goat bells and the sharp cries of children from dark windows cut from the red stone of Petra.

I didn't want to leave and would have stayed in the third heaven forever. But it wasn't possible, not yet. I knew that, but I would return, that much I also knew. Maybe often.

Now I would do as the Lord had asked, would humble myself before the world. Take on this flesh again, these pale body rags. I would fall to rise and to bring others, my dear brothers and sisters in the Christ, with me.

To rise and rise again.

Chapter Seven

Walking with Paul, asleep beside him in caves, in leafy groves, in mountain huts abandoned by shepherds, in rank unspeakable prisons, I came to know him as a brother. He might be odd, yes. He was distinctly odd. Humorless and temperamental, unpredictable, even irrational. His temper could lick the night sky like desert lightning running along the far hills. He might speak at length in the most abstruse language, quoting passages from alien scriptures or the Greek poets—Ion of Chios. But I always felt alive in his presence, closer to the truth, called to that Messianic flame, to the breath of our Lord Jesus the Christ.

He was mad, yes. An irritant. But he saw things nobody else saw, and did things nobody else could do.

He told me about what happened in Petra, where he actually saw the face of Jesus, not just a haze or numinous glow but the features distinct and shimmering with, as he said, "a clarity of expression." Soon after this experience, he rose through the ether itself into the third heaven, as Isaiah, Elijah, and Daniel had done before him, coming back to earth with quickened energy and without fear, a different man.

He walked with fresh courage into the pink city, visiting the nearest synagogue, which lay at the end of a cul-de-sac. And he was lucky: It was the Sabbath, and a dozen elderly Jews sat reciting prayers, bending in a helter-skelter fashion. "It was a gallery of disconnected supplication," Paul said.

He sat among them, attracting little notice. Then a leader of the group, a rabbi in a purple caftan, with a curly white-and-yellow beard and wild red eyes, walked to the front of the gathering and read from the scroll. He had a melodious dark voice that filled the small room, although Paul doubted that his fellow listeners would know much Hebrew. (Their nodding and grunting could easily be misconstrued as understanding.)

A knowledge of the Hebrew scriptures was uncommon, except in Jerusalem. And even there most Jews preferred the Greek or Aramaic translations.

Paul stood as the reader continued his recitation, then—seeing that this impertinent visitor refused to sit—the rabbi paused to look down as if to say, "May I help you?"

A tall man stood and shouted at Paul, "Sit down!"

The rabbi continued, and Paul waited patiently until he finished. Then he walked to the front of the chamber and stepped onto the wooden stool, where he said, "I am Paul of Tarsus, a Hebrew, born of the tribe of Benjamin, a Pharisee by affiliation. I was educated in Jerusalem under Gamaliel."

This statement brought everyone to attention.

"I come as a messenger of Rabbi Jesus."

This was an unfamiliar name, but they had no trouble imagining that some new and popular rabbi would have emissaries. Any number of them had come and gone over the years, and most seemed harmless, afflicted with enthusiasm for some obscure text or charismatic teacher.

"Have you heard of Rabbi Jesus? If so, stand. I shall count."

Nobody stood, of course.

"Ah, this is unfortunate. Yet I bring good news. A great rabbi was born from a maiden, Mary, in the city of Bethlehem, a son of the House of David, from the tree of Jesse. His learning was great, and scholars of the Temple revered him. He was a messenger from heaven and spoke about a New Covenant between God and man. The Law of Moses remains in place, but it has to be understood in the light of this fresh covenant. Jesus announced a new heaven, a new earth. He was the promised Christ. As we just heard from Isaiah: *Our God shall give a confirming sign. Look out, for a young maiden will give birth to a son, and you will name him Immanuel, God-within-you.* Immanuel has come in the name of Jesus. He was arrested in Jerusalem, fastened to a cross by nails, crucified under Roman authority. Within three days he rose to new life in a heavenly body. He walked among his family and friends. And he brings us all to life, as we—like him—learn to trust in God."

There were gasps and some derisive laughter as well. It must have seemed a fabulous tale, moderately well told.

"I don't think I impressed them," Paul said to me much later. "I stuttered quite a lot and my throat felt dry. My knees grew soft and quivered. I was not heroic."

He went into the western part of the city, where poor Jews sheltered in tents, and managed to make a little money by mending leather goods. His dexterity in this craft would increasingly prove useful, a skill in high demand wherever he traveled, and he managed to acquire funds as necessary and gain respect among ordinary people by stitching seams. It would be a few years before he had the inheritance from his father that allowed him to finance his travels and missionary work with considerable ease. And Paul always liked the idea of contributing to his own sustenance. "A man who supports himself lightens the roof above him," he said, quoting Ion of Chios.

A week later he returned to the synagogue, determined to speak more clearly and forcefully, even to win their hearts.

"Their faces turned in my direction," he recalled. "One of them, a man of astounding height, approached me. His eyes drilled down into mine. He said I should leave or he would pitch me through the door, then step on me. At once, I appealed to the elderly rabbi in his purple caftan, who stood to one side. He nodded, then told everyone to be still and patient, quoting wisely from Deuteronomy: *Love ye the stranger, he said, for you were once strangers in Egypt.* With courage, he invited me to the front of the room for what he termed 'a final statement.'"

Paul stared at the assembly, tongue-tied, frightened.

"Do say whatever you wish," the rabbi said. "This is your time."

Paul spoke, but it was, he said, "as if I must propel the words through a thick gauze." After a pause, during which he surveyed the room, he said, "I come, as I have said, in the name of Rabbi Jesus, who was of the tribe of Jesse. He is lord of heaven, seated next to the Ancient of Days, his dear father. He is the Christ."

"But he was crucified!" a man shouted.

They would know that according to Deuteronomy only an outcast beyond the pale of redemption would be executed in such an ignominious and shameful way: *A man hung on a tree is cursed by God.*

"But he rose from the dead," Paul replied.

This drew laughter from the back of the room. Several heads shook in disgust.

"There is more to say," Paul said, lifting each word like a heavy stone. "The end of history approaches, and Jesus has shown us the way to enlightenment, a peaceable kingdom. We shall live there together, all of us, Jews as well as gentiles."

The rabbi said, in sonorous Hebrew, *"Yemot Ha'Mashiach."*

Paul understood: The "days of the Christ" approached. Yet nobody but Paul understood what the rabbi had said, and I suspect nobody cared. This talk about the end of times maddened and amused them in equal measures. Had they not heard all this somewhere before?

Taking Paul by the arm, the rabbi led him to a door at the side of the room, saying, "You have the gift of the spirit, but the proper time for your message hasn't arrived. You must go quickly. Petra is dangerous. Someone will kill you if you remain, believe me. But I will pray for your safekeeping." His bloodshot eyes narrowed and he said, "Go!"

Paul had no wish to fight with the Jewish community in Petra, and even less of an inclination to die before his work had properly begun.

"I shall write from Jerusalem," he said. "But what is your name, sir?"

"I am Elah," the rabbi said.

Three men moved toward Paul and the rabbi, and Paul understood the precariousness of his circumstances. Seizing the moment, he slipped into an alleyway behind the synagogue and ran to a thoroughfare, where he fell into a broad stream of people. The crowd absorbed him nicely, folding him into their flow. Paul had a gift for hiding in plain sight and made use of it now. When it was safe, he gathered his few things and left the city along the rose-dark valley, disappearing into the dusk.

He set his mind on Jerusalem.

✝

The visit to Petra, with its ruckus at the end, agitated Paul. Yet the Lord had urged him to carry forward his mission at whatever personal cost, and Paul would never shrink from that commission. He knew that the soil of God's kingdom would moisten, grow fertile and sweet in the spiritual waters that heaven poured out. Before he took this message into the wider world, however, it seemed wise to gain approval from Peter and James, the Pillars, in Jerusalem. Their consent would lend an air of authority to his undertaking.

He found a caravan moving north and, as before, hid himself in their company. These nomads who carried a variety of precious goods along the Silk Road would accept him as part of their cargo, and for only a few coins. That was good, but there was a danger in this as well. Paul knew he could easily be knifed, robbed, his body dropped along the roadside. The vultures would remove all evidence that a human being had lived and moved in this body. The bones themselves would turn to dust and sand before long, and there would be nothing left of Paul but his soul.

He survived the journey, crossing the Jordan at dawn one day in a raft, feeling himself at home in Palestine, although he knew that nobody would welcome him. The important question was, would they murder him? He must get to the Pillars as quickly as possible and make a case for himself. And then depart.

Peter was the first disciple of our Lord, a man who had walked with him in Galilee and Judea. Jesus had loved him, and Peter knew the teachings well, in their many iterations, and had seen the risen Christ more than once. The Way depended on him for counsel and direction, and many considered him the final authority. Yet James, the brother of Jesus, refused to grant Peter so much power, having closer ties to the Lord than his other brothers—Jude, Simon, and Joses—who considered Jesus a madman whose activities and death had brought only shame to the family.

The ironies here did not escape Paul, who knew that James had come late to the realization that Jesus was God's son. Apparently after his return to life, Jesus had kissed James on the forehead and urged him to carry the mission forward. *You are my brother,* Jesus had said, *and you will speak for me now.* James repeated this in public, and it was widely accepted, although not by the disciples who had actually walked beside the Lord in Galilee. By now, most of them had scattered to distant parts of the empire, and their stories remained unobtainable. This was a pity.

But James was very much present and had considerable sway in Jerusalem circles. Even by his outward habits and appearance, he conveyed his authority and uniqueness. He refused to cut his hair or eat meat or drink wine. He never married and forswore carnal relations of any kind. He wore white linen tunics that had darkened with sweat and grime over the years, and he never washed them. They trailed him like clouds of soot. He went into the Temple every day to pray for the sins of his fellow Jews (gentiles were not his concern), and his knees resembled those of camels, enlarged and knotted with gristle. He smelled horrid, like onions that have softened into moldy pulp, as was evident from Paul's first meeting.

James believed that his brother taught that trust in God was impossible without the active pursuit of justice in the world, and he repeated his favorite saying: "Faith without works is dead."

In the course of years, he wrote many letters to members of the Way, and these had been collected in a book that continued to circulate, although James and Paul would repeatedly clash on points of principle.

"Why do I so dislike James?" Paul would ask, with a sigh.

I pointed out that even those in the Way who revered James as the brother of Jesus considered him peculiar and prickly, possibly an impediment to the Kingdom of God. He spoke in a thin, reedy voice without the usual manly registers. His broken-toothed smile failed to inspire confidence or put anyone at ease. It was said, in disdain, that even the poor refused his alms.

Peter, on the other hand, had poise and grace. He connected to those around him in ways James could never do in a thousand centuries. Peter had been the favorite of the twelve, although James disputed this, saying his brother loved John above the others. (John was conveniently silent on this matter and had not been seen by anyone in several years, having retired to a remote island far from Palestine.) Jesus had certainly encouraged Peter at every turn, even if his dear disciple frequently misunderstood the point of his teachings and had actually denied his affiliation to Jesus during the last days.

Now Peter devoted himself to efforts on behalf of the kingdom. He led gatherings in prayer, and would commonly speak after the holy meal, often at length, with an eloquence that astonished those who heard him. All who wished to lead a gathering in the city sought his blessing as confirmation of their stature, and this eventually became ritualized, with a laying on of hands.

Paul approached James first, having caught sight of him in the street.

"I am Paul of Tarsus."

"I know you," said James, coolly.

"I've spent three years in the desert, and met Jesus twice."

"You're a sinner, and I shall pray for you," said James. "Do you keep the Sabbath? Moreover, do you really understand the importance of Sabbath-keeping?"

"Is it so important?"

There had been stories about Jesus and the Sabbath that did not convince Paul that it weighed significantly in the mind of our Lord.

"Did you really ask me such a thing?"

"Your brother would gather food on the Sabbath to feed his disciples."

"You have been misinformed."

"I want only to serve."

"Speak to Gamaliel. I remember seeing you in that school. He is one of us now. But he may not be glad to see you. You murdered Stephen."

"I have changed direction," he said.

James studied Paul as if a strange new planet had appeared in the sky.

"What do you want?"

"I want to follow in the Way of our Lord."

"Give everything you have to the poor," said James, without conviction. "Pray for forgiveness. Go home to Tarsus. Observe the Law that has been given by God through Moses."

He wished simply to get rid of Paul, that much was clear.

"I want to do more," Paul said.

"You don't listen. Are you so ignorant?"

Paul realized he would get nowhere with James, an unpleasantly self-righteous man, deeply convinced that he understood better than anyone else what Jesus had intended for his people, the Jews. Those who disagreed with him were at best an annoyance, at worst an enemy of God.

Having sought out Peter, Paul found the disciple in prayer beneath an olive tree by a house on the street called after the prophet Schmuel. He sat with his palms facing upward, his lips quivering without audible words. His eyelids fluttered but were shut.

Paul sat opposite him, waiting.

When Peter opened his eyes, he asked, "Do I know you?"

"I am Paul of Tarsus."

Peter absorbed this information slowly. Then he said, "You've had a change of heart, I was told. You spent time with our friend Musa in the desert."

"I met our Lord as I traveled to Damascus, three years or more in the past. Jesus has asked me to speak on his behalf."

"This is so?"

Paul nodded.

"Jesus speaks very well on his own behalf," Peter said.

Paul looked at the dirt and said, "Jesus is alive."

"I know this."

"I hope to speak about him to the Greeks. I'm alive in him, as you are. And lost to myself. I know the Greeks, as I grew up among them."

Peter applied his long fingers to his temples and seemed to massage them. I suspect that he had rarely encountered a young man with such coiled energy, with a thrust of being equal to his own. And one who spoke in this urgent manner.

"I should warn you," Peter said, "that they recall your violence here. Your name is soiled among us, though stories of what happened in Damascus have reached many ears." He looked around, as if frightened someone would overhear this conversation. "Is Musa well?"

"Very well indeed."

"Oh, that's good. We depend on Musa."

Paul thanked him for this conversation, and arranged to see him again. But he saw clearly that it would not be easy to join the Way in this city. Not perhaps for some years.

Later in the day, he went to see Amos.

"The wastrel returns," said Amos, with an ironic twang that irritated Paul. "Your father has been furious these past three years. He was in Jerusalem last month, to visit your sister and Joshua, your nephew. He told me you were no longer his son."

"I'm sorry to hear this."

"Are you going to get more hides?" Amos paused. "I haven't done so well, not since you left. I don't know what I'm doing wrong. You had a gift."

"I don't think so."

"You're still a Jew, I hope?"

"I'm a Jew."

"Good. There are rumors," said Amos. "They say you have become enamored of the Nazarene, the unfortunate magician."

"He is our Lord."

Amos shook his head, not being an especially devout man, although he kept the Sabbath and celebrated the major feasts. He had a wife in some village outside of the city, and visited her and their three children now and then. He supported them in all the ways a man should support his family, except emotionally. He worked hard, without looking to the left or right. And prayed loudly, but in public.

"Go back to Tarsus," said Amos. "I doubt your father will remain hard of heart. He is not an unkind man." After a considerable pause, he said, "And he loves you. Do you know this?"

Paul knew only that he must further God's kingdom, which lay at hand. Exactly how he might go about this business puzzled him. He decided to pray and await direction, although an urgency propelled him.

"The world will end soon," he said to Amos.

"For me, I'm sure. Look at me!"

"For everyone. Jesus will sweep us into his army."

"It's a battle, then?"

Paul had misspoken and knew it. "He invited us to give ourselves to him. We do not live in this world."

This only confused Amos, who launched into details of the hide business, as if Paul had never been gone. He had a trove of figures in his head and disgorged them. He said that although profits had dwindled since Paul's departure, opportunities remained. He spoke with animation about their commercial prospects, noting that the Roman legions needed more and more tents, especially as their numbers in Judea and throughout Palestine had increased in recent years, but Paul brushed this aside.

"Profits mean nothing to me," he said. "We might gain the whole world but lose our souls, and where would that get us?" He was quoting a line from Jesus that Musa had conveyed to him, and which he would often repeat in years to come.

Amos didn't take any of this personally, and considered his younger relative a fanatic who could nevertheless prove useful in the family enterprise. He invited Paul to stay with him as long as he wished and, as he said, "ease your way slowly back into the business." To assist him, he ordered a servant to provide for Paul whatever he needed, and also gave him a small bag of gold coins.

Paul's sister, Esther, soon welcomed her younger brother to her house, and he delighted in the presence of Joshua, his young nephew, though found his brother-in-law, Ezra, wary of him.

"You must understand," said Ezra, "that we have no time for the people who follow the Nazarene. Yet another of those fools who trouble our faith. We are the people of Moses, the Jews. Never forget that."

"And of Abraham," Paul said. "More Abraham than Moses."

Rabbi Ezra did not like this, but he would not argue with his sister's impetuous brother, whose dire reputation in Jerusalem dismayed him. It was awkward for him to have this family association, and he worried that the connection would inhibit him as he rose in the Temple hierarchy.

The following Sabbath, after a period of prayer, Paul entered a synagogue where he had gone often in earlier years, in the Lower City and just inside the Valley Gate. Many in the small, hot room knew him, and they gasped upon seeing him. Could this be Paul of Tarsus? His face had grown thin, his back had begun to curl forward, and he had lost most of his hair. The smooth skin of his youth had dried, wrinkled, and hardened. Could three years have made such a difference?

Paul wasted no time, striding to the front of the congregation, where a scroll had already been unfurled. He still considered himself a Pharisee and read a few lines about the exile of the Jews in Egypt, then broke off in mid-recitation, saying, "Rabbi Jesus is the fulfillment of the Law. Believe me, friends: He is our king, the promised Christ of Israel, and this is his kingdom." He thumped his chest with his knuckles. "We have a New Covenant with Jehovah, and must not be chained to old ways. We must—all of us—go beyond this material world by seeking God through the spirit of his prince, our Christ, who is God's son."

The gathering listened with rising anxiety, having never heard such talk in this circle of pious Jews. A young man at the back, no more than twenty, shouted, "He needs a good thrashing!"

One of the respected elders lifted his voice to concur: "He speaks with a devil's tongue. This is blasphemy! God is God, and he has no son!"

Paul knew the punishment for blasphemy only too well, and felt unexpectedly drained of the courage that had propelled him to the front of this room. Backing away carefully, he moved toward a side door. As he had done in Petra, he would slip from the room into the noisy street, and it would not be difficult to lose himself in the familiar byways of Jerusalem. But half a dozen younger men followed on his heels, one of them stepping around him, stopping him.

"Let me pass," said Paul.

"You must die," said the fellow, who as Paul often recalled had a face like an ax blade. He recognized this rogue as someone who had studied with him under Gamaliel and had joined the Temple Guard.

"You are Jabin," said Paul. "Did we not sit together in prayer, many years ago? I recall those days."

From the side came a sudden blow as another man's fist caught Paul sharply below the ear, cracking his jaw. He fell to his knees on the flat stones. Then the world darkened.

Time blurred as he woke in what he assumed was a prison cell, with a loud banging in his head, a swelling at one side of his jawbone. He had been kicked hard, and a cavernous vault of discomfort opened in his skull. He guessed his nose had been broken, as that hurt even more than his head. Blood caked on his lips, crusted on his chin.

His jailor sat at the entrance to the cell on a small wool rug. He looked across the room at Paul.

"I need water," said Paul, drawing himself up to sit.

The jailor grunted, then sloshed a pail of water over his head, bringing a cup to his lips. Paul shuddered as he drank.

"Why am I here?" Paul asked.

"Under arrest. That's what it usually means."

"By whom?"

"The authorities!"

This was disconcerting. The rowdy Temple Guards felt quite free to take a man into the country and murder him at their pleasure if one of the high priests simply agreed to sign a writ of execution. He guessed that those who brought him here had gone to find one of these priests, who would certainly remember Paul and probably delight in ridding the world of this blaspheming rebel. But surely this was a Roman jail?

The Jews played a delicate game with the occupier, much as the Way played their cards with the Jews carefully. The Jesus circle had survived in Jerusalem by keeping strictly to the Law, and James had earned the respect of everyone in the Temple, so the priests kept a certain distance from the Way. Followers of the Nazarene, as they called Jesus, were allowed to have their meetings and holy meals, as long as none of this interfered with traditional observances, and as long as they remained invisible to the Romans. As a consequence, Jesus was not loudly proclaimed as the son of God or king of the Jews. Such titles rang of treason.

The Way now lived a fairly safe if subterranean life at the fringes of Judaism.

But who had arrested Paul, and why?

"Eat," said the guard, pushing a plate of stale bread and green cheese covered with red ants before the dazed prisoner, who slumped on the packed-dirt floor with his back to a wall. The stench of shit and piss suffused the cell, and this did nothing to increase Paul's appetite. He understood, however, that his jailor was being kind.

"What will they do to me?"

"It will be unpleasant."

Paul groaned, feeling a jab of pain behind his eyes as he bit into the stale bread. His jaw hurt too much to chew. He felt dizzy and sick, and couldn't think to think.

Did he hear a calm voice telling him to have no fear or did he imagine it?

"I love you, Lord," he whispered. "Remember me."

Some hours later, in confusion, he woke from a muddled, unsatisfying sleep. Something or someone had startled him. He forced open his eyes, where he saw the heavily bearded face of Aryeh, who held Paul's head in his strong hands.

Paul tried to smile.

"They want to kill you," said Aryeh.

Paul reached up and touched his old friend's face. He had come as an angel.

"Can you possibly stand, Paul? We must go. Quickly!"

Paul drew a breath, then moved to stand. His legs supported him as he leaned on Aryeh. Those years of walking in the desert had strengthened him, and he benefited now from the residue of hardwon brawn, combined with his natural resilience and pluck.

Beyond the prison walls, a cart awaited them, with a donkey and driver.

"Get into the back, and I will cover you. Aaron will take you to Caesarea."

Paul kissed Aryeh now. "Thank you, thank you."

"Tell no one that I helped you. Do you understand? I would be in very great danger."

Paul said, "Your secret will die with me."

Aryeh handed him a small bag of coins in a hemp purse. "This will secure passage to Tarsus," he said.

"You are such a good friend," said Paul. He was happy now, even with the pain. "I promise to return, Aryeh."

"Not for a long while. The longer, the better. Stay away!"

"I will think of you every day," said Paul.

Aryeh said, "That's too often." Putting a hand on Paul's wrist, he said, "Go!"

✢

Paul sat in the tablinum of his father's house, absorbed in prayer. He had forgotten that he had grown up in such embarrassing luxury, and it felt peculiar, even unnerving, to sit here in this familiar splendor. On the other hand, the atrium was cool, bright, and pleasant in the late afternoon, with a sea breeze puffing through and feathering the curtains. Mottled lemons sat on a plank table nearby and scented the air and, just beyond, a doorway opened into a garden, with only a veil across it. The wind parted this flimsy curtain to reveal an old tamarind tree. As a boy, Paul had spent hours in study there, his back to the bark of the trunk, reading the Greek version of the Torah. ("Or sometimes Ion," he would say.)

Gila, the elderly slave whom Paul had known since childhood, welcomed him home with tears as he awaited the return of his father, not sure how this encounter would unfold.

"You've been gone for too long," said Gila, who could not stop sobbing. By now she had not a single tooth left in her mouth.

It had been nearly four years since his trip to Damascus, and his father would not be easy with his wayward son. Adriel had a prickly and self-important way about him, and disloyalty of any kind made him furious, even irrational. His reaction at seeing Paul again could not be predicted, and yet Paul knew he must accept his father's response.

Adriel came into the house as the evening sun turned red in the sky and changed the colors on the interior walls and tapestries. The tile floor gleamed. Paul heard the tapping of the old man's stick and the familiar cough as his father approached. He seemed to be talking to himself.

As the only son of a widower of means, Paul had led a privileged existence, with tutors and slaves, nursemaids and miscellaneous attendants. He had never lacked for attention but had not known his father especially well. Adriel rarely talked with him, although his reticence came naturally, part of a temperamental strain that played a large part in his reserve. But he was a patriarch, sure-footed in his world, eager to conform to whatever laws, secular or religious, obtained. He would consider his son's rejection of Jewish traditions irritating if not blasphemous. That Paul had become hostile to the Temple must have seemed unimaginable, especially as he was a Pharisee and student of Gamaliel. Adriel had been so proud of that.

Amos had written to "explain" Paul's unlikely turn a few years earlier, basing his information on the rumors that flooded Jerusalem. Of course this letter had clarified nothing. Amos had no real sense of what had driven Paul into the Arabian desert. And Paul's letters, only two of them in so many years, had made everything worse, such as when he offered a long critique of Jewish legalisms dear to his father and argued that his great new master—the untutored son of a mason from a remote village in Galilee—had created a New Covenant that swept away what Moses had sealed with God for the people of Israel.

"My son is an imbecile," Adriel had written to Amos, asking about this rabbi who had deprived Paul of his senses.

"What I know about this teacher from Nazareth isn't much," Amos had replied to Adriel. "There are too many rabbis with opinions."

Failing to get much from Amos, Adriel asked friends in Tarsus for information about Jesus, and it surprised him to learn that this Nazarene had acquired an ardent following, however few in number. That Jesus had written no commentaries on the scriptures did nothing to ease his mind. A collection of sayings—supposedly by Jesus— came into his possession, and they upset him badly. "Do not lay up for yourselves treasures on this earth," this insolent and impoverished rabbi had said. Elsewhere, he suggested that one should sell all one's possessions, giving the money to the poor. Could Paul imagine doing such a thing? Was it not his father's money he would be forfeiting in this case? Where was the gratitude for everything that Adriel had given to his son? Was there no loyalty?

Questions multiplied and hung in the air.

Paul felt his father's presence before he saw him, an odor of persimmon, manly but oddly distinct, as if aged in the cask of the old man's body.

Adriel saw Paul as he turned in to the room.

"You!"

"Me, father."

Adriel didn't touch him but sat on a plump mauve cushion, unable to stop looking at his son. Could he trust this vision? Was it really Paul or had some rascal spirits conjured this phantom?

"I had no time to write," said Paul. "I should have given a warning. It must be shocking to see me."

It was an arrival that Paul had not planned, and he could probably not have outpaced a letter. The removal from Jerusalem to Caesarea, and the voyage out, had been swift, dizzying, unexpected.

He looked at his father, hungry to see how time had fallen on the narrow bony shoulders, weighed them down, distorted them. Adriel was thinner, and his head lurched forward. The curve in his spine had deepened, and a large hump protruded between his shoulder blades. His legs had dark purple veins that branched from his ankles to parts of his calves. His nose, too, had grown oddly bulbous and become a lobe of magenta-tinted flesh. The elderly lips looked dry and flaky, and his cheeks recalled a desert mudflat, parched and spidery with cracks. A deep horizontal fissure had opened in his brow, a crevice above his untamed expressive white eyebrows.

It remained an interesting face, however, a text Paul had once memorized and which, upon rereading, revealed fresh contours, added significance; it was familiar and weirdly calming.

"I have disappointed you," said Paul.

His father rose with difficulty and walked toward his son, letting the stick topple to the tiles. Paul watched the old man quaver, his right hand lifted to the level of his chin, as if uncertain what to do.

Paul swayed, rocking from side to side. "I really didn't mean—"

"Stop!" said Adriel, lifting his hand over Paul's head as if raising a flag. "I forgive you."

Paul welcomed this response, but all was not forgiven. It would take time, and he would never quite repair the breach that had opened between them. His father could never fully understand what his progeny had done, not only to him but to himself. Adriel had raised Paul as a son of the tribe of Benjamin and sent him at considerable expense to Gamaliel's school in Jerusalem. He had been convinced of his son's capacities and potential. And this was his reward? Paul had spat on his inheritance, his sacred heritage and everything that came with that, including a position in the world. The Jewish community in Tarsus would never warm to him or trust him fully.

They embraced and stood for a long time with their arms wrapped around each other, with tears on their cheeks, in their beards. Gila stood to one side, weeping. There was too much to say even to begin to talk. And, given Adriel's natural reticence, the conversation could hardly begin.

"I never understood the old man," Paul would say to me, "and he never took any pleasure in my renewed faith, my contact with God through Jesus, whom he persisted in calling my 'peculiar rabbi.'"

The break between father and son had insufficient time to heal, as Adriel died in his sleep a few months later. In the meantime, Paul occupied himself with the family business, taking control when his father passed away, making sure that all assets were secure, as he planned to use them judiciously to support the Way. He also made inroads with the local Jewish community, a number of whom actually welcomed the news that Paul offered of Rabbi Jesus. This was especially true among the Godfearers, who had grown in number since Paul last visited Tarsus.

Paul understood that the future lay among the Greeks, especially those who—like me—already worshipped the God of Israel and felt drawn to the Jewish scriptures.

Soon Paul's house became a meeting place in Tarsus for the Way. His gatherings on the First Day of each week attracted many of those who had worshipped Mithras and understood the language Paul had only begun to formulate, seeing the death of Jesus as a kind of atonement for the sins of many. Together they sang hymns and read passages from the Jewish scriptures in Greek; a meal followed, one that involved the breaking of bread and the sharing of wine as symbols of the body and blood of Jesus, using many of the phrases that Musa had developed. Paul often recalled that God had dropped manna on the starving Jews in their exile and hunger. And so men and women ate the bread of angels, as David had written. Paul would hold up a small loaf before his gathering and echo the son of Jesse: "This is the bread of angels. It is the body of the Christ, which becomes your body when you eat. We take him into our body, and we become one with God. We become the Christ ourselves, as Jesus did before us."

It was an elaborate idea, which in his mind deepened and took on various hues and contours, and which he developed in letters to various gatherings in Greece and Asia.

"I'm a tree with many birds in my head," he said to me. "One chirps, cries out, even shrieks. Then another, and another."

"A black cloud of thought," I replied.

"Luke, shut up," he said.

I knew, or thought I knew, he was teasing me.

Now the business of cloth production and tent-making in Tarsus prospered, as Paul made sure that good men were in place. He gradually disentangled himself from all daily operations, diverting profits as he could to those in need. An array of orphans and cripples, lepers and destitute widows with hungry children came to his doorstep every day, and they rarely vanished without help, including prayers. And Paul continued for a couple of years to read from the scrolls on the Sabbath in the local synagogue, as his father had done, assuming what he considered his rightful place within this congregation. They could not dislodge him, and nobody had the will or knowledge to discredit his ideas, which they could not even understand.

⸓

When I first met Paul in Damascus, some years earlier, the impression I got was indelible. His body was bathed in nearly invisible light. He had clearly been struck by God, and he blazed with the spirit. Even in his great distress, I could see that here was another son of God, a man in whom the Christ had rooted and would blossom. He spoke with authority. It was evident in every sentence that fell from his lips.

When we lowered him over the city wall and watched him disappear into the desert, I said to my uncle that I would spend my life in his company.

My uncle looked at me with hard, flat eyes. "You must never say things like this," he told me. "Language envelops us, it creates us. What we say, we become."

I knew this, but I liked it, too.

My wife had recently died in childbirth in Antioch, and my son had drawn his last little breath only a few hours later in my arms. Chara and I had been friends since childhood, and to lose her like this, and my son as well—it was impossible. The medical practice I had established in Antioch had grown nicely, and I had developed a business in salves that brought me to distant parts of the empire, where sales of my products flourished. I had foolishly thought nothing in my life could go wrong, then everything went wrong. My life closed, and nothing made sense.

An old friend called on me one evening, months after this tragedy, and insisted I go with him to a synagogue where Joshua, a powerful young rabbi, had attracted a following of Greeks who wanted to know more about the God of Israel. I still remember that Sabbath, when I entered the darkened room and could feel God's presence. The candles flickered with messages for me, these mysterious tongues of flame seemed to call my name. I listened to readings of the Jewish scriptures, in Greek, and could hear the divine voice in them.

Joshua invited me to come back, and I did, again and again. I loved it when he read from the scriptures, the strong words of the prophets, Isaiah and Ezekiel and Daniel. The lamentations of Jeremiah moved me deeply and spoke to my own pain. I took to praying at home and reading the Greek scriptures. And Jeremiah's promise from God called to me: *Know that I have plans for you, plans to make you prosper, not to harm you, plans to give you hope and a future.*

Could I really believe such a thing? Hope and a future?

I was trying to find my way in the world after the death of Chara and my tiny son. But was this a way forward?

Joshua came often to dine with me, and held me by the shoulders with his strong hands, insisting that God knew my heart, saying that I would prosper. Once he suggested that I undergo the ritual of circumcision as a way of drawing me closer to the Jewish people and to enclose myself within the covenant. But I resisted this act of mutilation, thinking it could not matter to God. I prayed intensely about it, and knew I had made the right choice. Then, one Sabbath, our rabbi introduced Phoebe—a wealthy woman with black hair falling across her forehead. Her eyes glistened like raisins. She brought news of Rabbi Jesus, whom she called "the son of God." She read from his sayings, and told stories about him, and suggested that he was the long-awaited Christ.

I spoke to her afterward, and she invited me to a gathering at her house the next day, the First Day of the week. She asked me to share what she called the sacred meal. And it pleased me to see the energy and spirit of these people, who surrounded me in love when I told them about my wife and son. They lifted me up, and we prayed together. "God heals," Phoebe said to me. "He wants you to be part of our movement, the Way of Jesus."

For some months I wavered between the synagogue and this gathering of the Way. Joshua understood my dilemma and told me I should make my own decision, although I could not help but notice that he—a rabbi himself!—found the Way appealing. He often attended Phoebe's gatherings, sitting at the back of the room with his head bowed, praying for clarity. One night he came to my house and said, in blunt terms, that Jesus was our Lord. "He is the Christ," he told me. "I have heard his voice in the night."

From that moment, I belonged only to the Way, which had by this time gathered strength in distant cities in Asia, in Palestine, Egypt, Syria, and beyond. On a sunny morning in late spring, Phoebe baptized me in the Orontes, with five others. So I can date my new life, my eternal life, from the moment I rose through that flaming bronze sheet of water under a blue sky. "You and the Christ are one now," she said to each of us. "Tell the world what has happened, that we are alive in him! Alleluia! Alleluia!"

My medical practice flourished, as it had for some years, although I wondered how long I might continue on this path. All I wanted now was to proclaim the Good News of the Kingdom of God. But it's hard to break from a profession like medicine, especially since I could help so many others in the course of a day, using the knowledge I had slowly acquired in my youth.

It was not just physical knowledge I had learned, the working of the body. I had studied the *Hippocratic Corpus*, and the anatomical work of Herophilus and other Greek physicians. Each of them had stressed the intimate connections between the soul and its ambience, its habitation within flesh and bone. The elaborate distinctions that Paul would make, naming flesh and spirit as contradictory elements, always seemed pat to me, not subtle enough. I wished that I knew more, could elaborate, even for my own purposes.

When I mentioned these classical physicians to Paul, he quoted Ion of Chios at me: "The mind is air, and air itself is mud and motion, clouds and sunlight."

Always Ion of Chios!

Antioch was home, and would be home again, as I had inherited a family house there, which in my absence was filled with many cousins and their lively offspring. I loved this city, which boasted half a million people: Romans at heart, with a Greek inflection. We were, I would tell visitors, the eastern capital of the empire, having overtaken Alexandria in everything but medicine. Our position on the Silk Road near the Orontes made traffic through our streets exotic and thrilling, with ideas pouring in from the West and East. Julius Caesar had confirmed our freedom more than a century ago, and we boasted temples on every hill. "There are a thousand gods," my whimsical father used to say, "if you count the monkeys." We had a forum, where philosophical and political arguments clashed and prospered or failed, and where received opinion was perpetually challenged and reformulated. Our hippodrome equaled the Circus Maximus in Rome, and we boasted theaters and bathhouses, colonnades, even terra-cotta aqueducts: all the amenities of civilization.

My early days in Antioch often coursed through my dreams, that time when I went about my work as a physician with mild optimism, helping where I could, aware that my limited knowledge of the body and soul could make only small differences in the lives of my patients. I saw I could make a decent living by treating wealthy clients and, on the side, making and selling a variety of salves that proved useful for skin rashes and muscle pains. One uncle, an ambitious merchant, supported my enterprise with enthusiasm, and we hired a dozen workers to concoct these emollients according to my recipes. His eldest son had taken over this business upon my departure from Antioch, and it prospered, so I did not lack for money.

After my baptism I became a pillar of sorts at the house of Phoebe, who occupied a Roman-style villa with a panoramic view of the Orontes. We drew more than two dozen men and women to our sacred meals on the First Day, and Phoebe spared no expense, providing so much food that her slaves could feed happily for the rest of the week on our leftovers. The Holy Spirit moved upon us, through us, lifting us. I felt that, sooner rather than later, I would reunite with my dear wife in Christ, and Phoebe assured me that even those who had never encountered the Way of Jesus could, in time, move beyond time into the Kingdom of God. God was generous in this way, never vindictive, wanting only the best for us.

I adored Phoebe, whose name in Hebrew meant "bringer of light," she told us. This bright widow had business interests in Rome and Jerusalem, where she had met Peter and James. She was, like them, devoutly Jewish, and had at first conceived of the Way as simply a reformation within Judaism itself, a necessary transformation. I loved our meetings in the walled garden at her villa, where we sang newly minted hymns and read passages from one of many books of sayings by Jesus. Her friend Chloe, another leader in the Way, would frequently visit Antioch, and she would lead us in prayer, breaking the bread for us, passing the wine: the high priestess of our gathering. This large, tall, profoundly intelligent woman would visit other assemblies, too, where everyone treated her as a prophet; in keeping with this, she often recited passages from the writings of Ezra and Esther, foretelling the emergence of new prophets. "They are coming among us soon, with their own language and visions," she would say.

She argued, as Phoebe had, that scripture was not "closed" but ongoing, active, emerging. We had only to listen with open ears.

As if summoned by her voice, Paul appeared one day at the back of Phoebe's house at the sacred meal. It was a crowded room that afternoon, with more visitors than usual, some of them from Jerusalem.

Paul, once again! I had prayed for him earnestly after he disappeared into the Arabian desert, and I longed to see him, but we had received no word of his whereabouts. Many went into the desert and didn't return, so it would not have surprised me had I never heard his name again. But there he stood. He nodded to me like an old friend, casually, then seized the attention of the room, asking in a loud voice to speak to the group.

Phoebe said, "Come to the front, sir."

Paul stood on a slightly raised dais, with everyone seated. He said, "An angel of the Lord woke me, some weeks ago, in Tarsus. I am a son of Tarsus, where I run my father's business in the manufacture of tents. But I am a child of the Christ as well. I have met Jesus himself, and was appointed by him as an apostle. I was told by an angel to come to Antioch."

The gasps around the room suggested a mixture of awe and confusion. Who was this peculiar little man, this slightly hunched, hawknosed fellow with narrow eyes, and what angel would seek him out? He had this idiosyncratic way of raising his hands when he spoke. The eyes blazed in his long, thin face, and he had a profound dimple in his chin that set him apart: a sign of character, I thought. But there was a wildness in him. His ruff of a beard was in need of grooming as were his eyebrows.

In a breathless, stuttering manner that I would come to know, he told us that he, a Pharisee by training and inclination, a student of Gamaliel, had stoned Stephen, our first martyr, delivering the final blow outside of the city walls of Jerusalem. He had been stricken by our Lord on the road to Damascus, permanently changed. He lifted his fists in the air and shouted, "God, Almighty Jehovah, we worship you, and we thank you for the voice of your son, for his living presence. May we hide ourselves in the Christ, in his bosom!"

"Dear God, this is peculiar," Phoebe whispered in my ear.

That day I sat with Paul under a spreading laurel, with its pale yellow leaves like hands waving in the breeze that circled Phoebe's villa. Chickens gabbled in the yard, and I saw a peacock spread its feathers by the garden wall. The gathering had dispersed, and we drank mint tea that a slave had brought to us in warm cups.

"We met in Damascus, some years ago," I said.

"I know you, Luke."

"Ah, yes, but I thought perhaps—"

"Never think. Know."

My first instinct was to say: *Who are you to speak to me in this way?* But he made quick amends, his face softening, the eyes baleful.

"I should not have spoken like this. I'm impetuous, they tell me."

I leaned toward him, listening.

"This agitation of spirit," he said. "Sometimes I feel the Lord—the spirit—rising inside me, quivering, making my flesh melt. I lose the governance of my own tongue. At other times I fall away, fade to silence, and God's door closes. But I knock and knock again."

"Knock and the door shall be opened," I said. "Those are the words of Jesus."

He looked interested. "I have never heard this."

"It's in many of the books of sayings."

"You know about them?"

"I've got several scrolls in my house. You see, I'm planning to write the life of Jesus—an account of his days, his time on this earth."

"His death and resurrection?"

"Of course."

"Does the life matter so much?"

"He is our example."

Paul closed his eyes. His voice became otherworldly now. "*In my vision at night I looked, and behold, before me was one like the son of man, and he came with all the clouds of heaven. He approached the Ancient of Days and was led into his presence.*"

"I love Daniel's words," I said.

It was a test, and I had not failed to recognize the prophet's visionary statement. Paul reached for my hands and held them, even digging his thumbs into the loose skin at the top. It was growing late in the day, and sunlight sifted in the leaves, with a dapple of light-and-dark on the ground beneath our chairs. It seemed as if the sun had poured into Paul's head and shot through his body, as his hands became small flames, difficult to hold, but I held tight and would not let go. I could feel the surge of the spirit there.

"I love God," I said.

"And we know God through him, our Christ. You know this, as you are one of his own."

"Pray with me, Paul?"

We knelt in the dirt and lifted our hands in the dwindling light, and Paul prayed for my soul, for his soul, that we might tell out our souls, summoning a new world into being. "We must create the Kingdom of God," he said. "In him, by him, and for him."

I repeated these words slowly: "In him, by him, and for him."

"You will go out with me soon," he said. "I hear the voice of God in your voice. I see him, our Christ, in your eyes."

I had not felt such happiness since before my wife and son died. But now a flood of joy passed through me, and I shook with joy. I would go with Paul wherever he saw fit. I would do the Lord's bidding with him.

Chapter Eight

PAUL

The work that Luke and I would accomplish lay ahead of us, but I resolved to test the missionary waters first with Barnabas. Peter had suggested I go with Barnabas to his native Cyprus, where opportunities for the Way of Jesus could be found. This appealed to me, as I was an apostle to the Greeks and this would make an appropriate beginning. I could test these waters, formulating our message. Barnabas and I would circulate through the island, pushing ahead into Asia, then return to Antioch, where I would join forces again with Luke, who was making preparations for a more ambitious journey into the western provinces.

Luke had impressed me in Antioch. He was meticulous where I was casual, a man of quiet passion, his mind as still as the bottom of a well, which I found calming. He had convinced Phoebe (with encouragement from Chloe) that she must finance an elaborate mission to the West among the Greeks. We would delve into virgin provinces, bringing the Good News with us. The Kingdom of God must be discovered on earth, and preparations made for the arrival of our Lord. The more I searched the holy scriptures, the more convinced I became of the sanity of the task before us. God spoke through me and, most important, through Jesus. It was only left for us to deliver this message of transformation, allowing the spirit would pick up where we left off.

Let it be said: I did not from the outset find Barnabas an easy companion. We met briefly in Antioch to discuss our journey, and he insisted that we bring along John Mark, the immature son of a woman from Jerusalem who had become a leading presence in the Way there (and, I thought, something of a nuisance).

"You will like John Mark," Barnabas said. "His mother—I believe you know her—is a force."

"We should, in this case, enlist his mother," I said.

He shook his head, disliking my little joke. Barnabas was a tubby fellow with rippling jowls, fond of colorful tunics, although he often walked with bare feet. He wore many rings on his fingers. He chose to finance this particular mission himself, and so the logic of our partnership was sound—if I could tolerate his companionship. Not being stupid, he sensed my hesitation, although he misunderstood my reservations.

"We have a clear mission, do we not?" Barnabas asked.

"The path of our journey is well-defined, and this is something."

"That is nothing," he said. "What spiritual energies we bring to the task, this is what matters."

I nodded, and found him difficult to oppose. He had a soft quality that made arguments pointless. He blundered ahead in his own fashion, insisting that we should travel with John Mark, who would be my scribe. I didn't see that I had much choice in this.

Barnabas was a Jew with strong connections to the Pillars, and he supported the Jesus movement passionately, having sold a large quantity of family land in Cyprus and donated these funds to the Way. He struck me as self-serving, but perhaps this is true of anyone who pushes forward in life and lifts his head above the parapet. He was only five years my elder, but I regarded him as an old man. Certainly the premature grayness of his beard radiated age if not sagacity. He was neither agile nor fit, and his belly jiggled ahead of him as he walked on precariously skinny legs.

He might well become a liability on this mission.

At least John Mark was lean and quick. He had the slightest wisp of a beard yearning toward manhood, which to me suggested an innocence I liked. His soft brown eyes widened with intelligence and curiosity about the world, and his skin smelled of sea salt. I liked the pale smoothness of his brow, like a robin's egg, and his delicate fingers.

I preferred to travel with a slave as my attendant and scribe whenever I could find a suitable man to take my dictation on commercial trips. I wasn't foolish, of course, and knew that Peter and James wished to surveil me from a distance, and that Barnabas and John Mark would become their eyes and ears, reporting back to the Pillars in Jerusalem. My past as a persecutor of the Way still troubled many in that city, and they wondered if I could be trusted. My behavior in Cyprus would confirm their view of me, in one way or another.

It made good sense to begin the search for Greek converts in Cyprus, and Barnabas knew the island well. He still had relatives in both Salamis and Paphos, the port cities, and one close childhood friend served on the staff of Sergius Paulus, the Roman governor, and Barnabas thought he could secure an invitation to his palace.

"Paulus has a mystical bent," he said, "but he's under the sway of some magus. A vile and dangerous man."

"Magus?" asked John Mark.

"Sorcerer," I said.

"I have never met a magus," he informed us.

"Life is full of possibilities," I said.

John Mark had come to the attention of Peter because of his penchant for note-taking. Like Tiro, the Roman scribe who took near-perpetual dictation from Cicero, the boy had perfected a style of abbreviation that allowed him to get down anything I said. This was convenient, as I took great care with my letters and often rewrote them. I found it useful to formulate and refine my ideas in this way, proceeding without caution. With so little time left in the world, it was important to think fast, to gather thoughts quickly. And John Mark worked with a kind of scrupulous vigor, writing down my words with his tongue pushing through moist lips, occasionally slurping. As my scribe, he carried a quantity of soot in a leather pouch, which he mixed with gum arabic to create an ink that adhered nicely to vellum or papyrus. He packed a quantity of thin sheaves, acquiring more along the way, which were plentiful if expensive. It was necessary for us, however, to record the key moments of our journey and send reports to Peter and James. I also planned to write to our gatherings in Antioch and Tarsus and elsewhere.

To my dismay, Barnabas wished to compete with me as the narrator of this journey. "I will have my own record," he said.

History exists only in competing narratives, much as in "real life," that oddly compelling and parallel narrative that absorbs most people like a colorful dream. And so Barnabas would have his own dream, although he probably didn't see that what is written is just as real as life, perhaps more.

"Remember, John Mark is not a slave," said Barnabas. "Be careful what you ask of him."

"In Jesus there is neither slave nor free man," I said.

Barnabas flinched, as he often did when I would separate the thinking of Jesus from traditional Jewish thinking. He tried to adjust my musings, alert to any divergences from what he considered sound judgment in all things. I didn't mind so much, as I never worried that my own thoughts could be tainted by his, or anyone's.

He liked to quote the original Hebrew scriptures at me, and this was intimidating because my slight unease with Hebrew remained a flaw, one that I would labor (with more or less success) to erase. But at least we had the splendid Greek version, a product of Alexandria, now three centuries old. It's the version of the scriptures I knew as a child, and I still preferred it.

"I know you much prefer the Greek to the Hebrew," said Barnabas.

"The translation was a miracle," I said.

A slight exchange of glances between John Mark and Barnabas followed, but it didn't pay to acknowledge such slights, as I would learn in decades on the road with Luke, who invariably questioned my version of a story or, if he didn't, kept an even more offensive silence on the topic.

So we set off, the three of us, from Antioch, with its crawling markets, clamorous streets, with the clash of commerce and races that is part of any major port. It was the city where, not long before this, I had made a spectacle of myself before Phoebe and her gathering, and where I had come to know Luke as a brother. I was only beginning to find my footing as an apostle and preacher.

"I shall recall your life and work in a book," Luke said to me, bidding me farewell.

"You will make them up," I said.

I only said that to annoy him, but I knew that—being a physician—his methodical nature would limit his inventions. And he wrote so well. To be sure, his Greek was gloriously rich, full of images and apt turns of phrase, and I envied his fluent style, being one who struggled to make my thoughts lucid and persuasive. God does not always apportion talents in ways that are comprehensible or seem fair.

I loved dear Luke and yet on one hand wished for a wider range of thoughts in him; on the other side, his dependability proved indispensable in the long run, as did his good humor. I certainly preferred him vastly to Barnabas and John Mark, who might well diminish the effectiveness of our present journey.

We set off one morning from Seleucia, with its long green slope to the sea. The harbor lay below, where ships from Cyprus, Egypt, Sicily, and faraway places anchored offshore. Merchant vessels making for Ostia and Rome huddled in the docks, most of them heaped with staples—wheat and olive oil as well as scents and spices, dyes, jewels, glassware, silver, gold, ivory, and silks. I marked the wealth afloat below us, and it reminded me of Tarsus.

"It is easier for a camel to pass through the eye of a needle than for a rich man to enter heaven," said Barnabas.

His solemnity was offensive.

This remark by Jesus—which I think had an edge of impishness to it, a wish to shock—had been included in most of the books of sayings. Peter had, I was told, explained that our Lord had simply transposed an old Persian saying about elephants, substituting camels, which had more currency in Palestine. It was certainly one of the more arresting things that Jesus either said or was supposed to have said, and it retained a certain irony, given that so many of our leaders in the Way, such as Phoebe or Chloe or, if truth be told, myself, even Luke, had ample wealth.

Perhaps the point was to give it away but with clarity and direction, aware that everything belongs to the Lord at last.

We had brought a good deal of money with us on this journey, as it often made travel easier. One could bribe officials, pay for ferries or rides on the backs of donkeys or horses, and hire a room for the night in a large and comfortable house. Food was always expensive, and walking made one hungry. Moreover, it made no sense to preach on an empty stomach.

John Mark sensed my unease with Barnabas—I was never much good at disguising my feelings.

"I don't like it when you disagree," he said to me, within earshot of Barnabas.

"You're an innocent," I said.

John Mark wrinkled his brow, unhappy. He was an earnest fellow, almost like a girl with those searching and moist eyes, with hands that showed no sign that he had ever lifted an ax or mallet. The hair on his skinny legs was pale, hardly visible.

We came down into the harbor and boarded a small ship bound for Cyprus. I stood in the stern, my hands on the rail, facing east as the thin brown line of Syria faded, listening to the wind as it caught and cracked the sails. The sea was radiant, a sprawl of diamonds.

Barnabas sat in a cross-legged position on the foredeck, praying, while John Mark was preoccupied with the activity of the sailors, these tightly muscled dark men who worked briskly about us, untangling lines, rearranging crates on deck in preparation for our departure.

"In my next life, I would like to be a sailor," he said to me.

How could one respond to such a remark?

We set off briskly and sailed through the night under a full moon, a time of gentle rocking and sweet air with only a slight tinge of salt. I knew from experience that we should be grateful for these passages, as they were hardly the norm. But it seemed pointless to mention such a thing to John Mark. It actually pleased me to keep his illusions about life afloat.

That morning we trolled a seine net, gathering a catch of silver fish—mostly sardines—which we grilled on the deck in the late afternoon. Each one seemed sweeter than a fig or date, but salty as well. Such a delectable crackling morsel, and I enjoyed watching John Mark as he devoured them. There was wine, too, rich and dark, almost granular in texture, from the vineyards in the low hills beyond Antioch.

That night I slept beside John Mark on a straw pallet, in a soft wool blanket that I carried, while Barnabas found a quiet spot of his own below. "I like shelter, when possible," he said. "What if it rains?"

"We would hate to see you melt," I said.

I knew the heavens and understood that rain was impossible that night. But I didn't want him to sleep near me, and so it pleased me to see his head dipping below the deck.

On that first night out, on the open foredeck but nestled against the starboard bow rail, it soothed me to lie beside John Mark. We talked of Jesus under stars that seemed to fall like snowflakes and whiten the deck. He knew so little about our Lord, but this was, for me, an opportunity to hone the message I hoped to take forward into the world. I told him about the Kingdom of God and explained that the Christ principle had been uncovered within himself by this spirit-saturated man from Nazareth, and it had consumed him—"a holy fire obliterating selfhood." I surprised myself with this phrase, knowing I must use it again. And I could hear Musa talking as I talked, his quiet way of gathering ideas into phrases as he fished for, and found, meaning.

"You have such a peculiar way of talking," John Mark said. "I don't know what you're getting at."

It was wonderful, the way he said that. I found his manner delightfully innocent and wondered if, some years ago, I might have seemed quite so simple to my elders. Perhaps Gamaliel had simply tolerated me as well as my classmates while we blundered our way toward a knowledge of the scriptures or an understanding of Jewish Law in its rich complexities and historical contexts.

The boy fell asleep heavily beside me, perhaps bored by my talk, and I watched with pleasure as his chest rose and fell, his lips slightly parted. Occasionally he mumbled to himself, though I could not understand what he said.

Once, very lightly, I touched his forehead as one might do with a beloved child. He winced slightly and rolled over, with his back to me.

✝

In the morning we came ashore. I loved islands but only visited them briefly when I traveled with my father on business. Cyprus was isolated, cut off from the larger empire, being a clutch of fishing villages and port cities with a tiny population of Greek-speaking natives whose dialect I liked to hear, especially with their elongated vowels and explosive consonants, which made it seem like they were spitting in your ear as they spoke.

The port of Salamis impressed us, the entry to this bright city crowned by a temple to Zeus—the king of Greek gods. My father had known a Cypriot merchant and middleman in this city named Schemuel, to whom over many years we had shipped large, rolled tents in crates, which he sold in remote parts of the empire, where he had many contacts. My father used to say, "If Schemuel doesn't know the man, the man doesn't know himself." We found him in his expansive house overlooking the harbor, and he seemed delighted to see me, inviting the three of us to remain with him as long as we liked.

I quoted my beloved Ion of Chios: "A visitor should stay only long enough to clean the larder."

This amused him, and he patted my back.

Schemuel understood from me that we had come on behalf of a special rabbi, and he asked sensible questions about Jesus, neither approving nor disapproving of our answers. The following day he took us to a synagogue near the center of the commercial district, where we discovered a pious, polite congregation. I was introduced as a student of Gamaliel and a Pharisee. This drew the usual nods of approval, and the rabbi invited me to read from the Torah. It was the opening passage from Isaiah where the prophet envisioned God on his throne, with angels—the seraphim, with their fiery wings— singing: *Holy, holy, holy is the Lord of hosts, and the whole earth fills with his glory!* Isaiah was struck dumb at first by his own sinfulness before such splendor, and remained speechless until the Lord asked who would go for him among the people. Isaiah cried: *I will go! Send me forth!*

God led me to read these words on that day, which marked the true beginning of my life's work of going among the people of the wider world with God's word on my lips. And it seemed fitting that I began with a passage that Jesus himself had read when he began his ministry in earnest in Nazareth.

"I bring news of a great rabbi, Jesus of Nazareth," I said, taking the occasion to speak, as was customary after a reading. "I met him on my way into Damascus. He called to me from heaven, as the angel had called to Isaiah: *Your sins are forgiven!*"

There was a hush in the room as heads tipped forward. I had exceeded the usual boundaries of such commentaries, and they probably wondered where this might lead.

"Jesus was crucified," I told them, "sacrificed at the hands of the Romans. But death failed to silence him. He rose from the dead after three days. And he lives within me now. He will live within you as well, the only Christ, a true son of God."

One had to be careful using that phrase, as every emperor since Augustus had laid claim to that title. Yet the Romans had a natural tolerance for cults and what they considered wayward pieties. Earthly power alone concerned them, and they would suppress anyone who challenged their authority. And so I frequently maintained in public that Jesus had no wish to overthrow the imperial government. Only the Kingdom of God concerned him. And when he returned, as soon he would, history would come to its natural end, at which point his rule could begin.

My commentary unnerved a few in the assembly, that much I could observe, but Schemuel liked my talk, and he suggested I meet with other Jews in the city. "I think you have good words," he said. "It's a strong message. Your father would be proud."

"We didn't necessarily agree," I said.

"That's as it should be. Fathers and sons. Often troublesome, as the one supplants the other."

This struck me, the idea of every son as his father's executioner.

Schemuel invited half a dozen leaders of the Jewish community to his house the next day, and Barnabas and I spent the afternoon with them, talking about Jesus and his message of radical love. But the message of Jesus was disruptive, and these intelligent listeners asked the right question, wondering if what I told them went against the Law of Moses and God's promise to Israel. I said bluntly that Judaism could never be the same again, not from Jesus's point of entry into the world. This, as it must, gave them pause.

John Mark offered very little, as was appropriate for a young man. Yet his gift for taking notes added to his value, and I wondered if one day he might not amount to something as a writer—the fluency of his prose struck me at once. We talked at length about the art of rhetoric, which interested him, and I recommended that he study the early Romans and Greeks, who had written shrewdly on this subject.

To spread the gospel, I knew I must perfect the art of rhetoric, which was as much about persuasion as presentation. I had to lure in the audience by the novelty of my approach. Dazzle them with my focus, my memory of detail. I would overpower them with the inevitability of my arguments, the deft arrangement of points. If I irritated many listeners, I could not help this. The truth is often irritating.

"You are not consoling in your speech," Musa had said, "but that isn't important. Your style is your own. Style is the exaggeration of one's temperament. You take what God has given, and you burnish it."

When I mentioned this to John Mark, he asked, "What has God given to me?"

"We shall have to wait for that," I said. "The answer will come."

We left the Jews of Salamis in a state of openness to Jesus, with one or two men in place who might lead a gathering of the Way there as we waited for the Lord's return. I promised to write to them, and—if possible—to join them again. But we felt an urgent wish to press on, as Paphos awaited us, on the southwestern side of the island. It was the seat of government, and because Barnabas had a friend at the palace, the governor himself would greet us in this city that had arisen under the gaze of Aphrodite, the goddess of beauty, described by Sappho as "the enchantress, wily, gleaming," the lover of "both men and gods."

According to legend, Aphrodite rose from the sea near Paphos. That a goddess of fertility and earthly love should dominate this coast made good sense when I thought of Paulus, whose reputation for lechery preceded him. I could foresee a massive challenge.

"One must never trust rumors," said Barnabas. "I've been surprised on many occasions."

It was better not to question Barnabas when he lifted up such empty rhetoric. There was so much less to him than met the eye.

"Paulus is certainly a man of the flesh," Barnabas added.

I had never been one to pursue the flesh. Which is not to say that lust didn't trouble me at times, even ruin my sleep. It did, repeatedly, and much to my annoyance. It was a wound in my character that no amount of prayer seemed to heal, and yet I wanted badly to liberate myself from this and every form of desire. I think the idea of Paulus and his amorous pursuits upset me more than I realized. But I knew that real freedom lay in wishing for nothing. Only to rest in God, never in the body. So prayer was essential now.

My life in prayer only increased, and it helped me to temper my worst impulses and calm myself. I knew the psalm tradition well, and could draw from that deep well almost at will, relying on David's wisdom. And the words of the prophets, too, bolstered my meditations. If only an angel of the Lord had "put a hot coal to my lips to redeem me," as one read in Isaiah! Like the rest of humanity, I was mostly forced to carry the considerable burden of myself by myself. It felt at times as if God had abandoned me to my passions, the lurid theater of mind where I often lived so unhappily, with its colorful tapestries and florid chambers. In my dreams there were no boundaries.

I could see that John Mark also suffered painfully from lust. He had gazed at the young women in the marketplace in Salamis with an intensity that embarrassed me, and I worried that he might lose his footing. I recited the opening of the first great psalm of David for him, hoping to uplift and inform him: *Happy is the man who never walks in counsels of the wicked, never shelters in the way of sinners, never sits with those who scoff.*

"I am quite happy, Paul," he replied, unaware of my intentions.

Barnabas took me aside one day. "Try not to oppress the boy. There is a heaviness in your expression of concern. This kind of talk unsettles him."

"He has yet to waken to the Lord, in the deepest sense."

"It's not your concern."

"My brothers are my concern!"

I could see this journey would soon prove tiresome, even arduous. And we had scarcely begun.

+

We set off for Paphos early one morning, aided by a donkey that Schemuel had bestowed upon us, making our way along the zigzag coast, as the rocky mountainous interior held us at arm's length. I would never worry about scrambling over passes, however precipi-

tous, but I could see that John Mark would dislike climbing anything
steep or challenging. He complained already about his feet—in his
view we had done nothing but walk in the city of Salamis.

In later years, I relished the stillness of mountain passes, the
silence when the air thins, with the wind more like a soft sigh than a
moan. I liked snowfields, black lakes, pebble-strewn paths, and long
arid stretches of parched grass. But now we kept close to the shore,
moving through flowering wild meadows or along ridges that fell
off sharply to the sea. The sun lofted over us, golden-faced, and the
island dazzled with its profusion of scarlet, orange, and yellow flowers. I found myself muttering praises to God as I walked.

After several days, the approach to Paphos led into a narrow valley, with stony outcrops pushing through the cinnamon-red dirt of
our path. The air stung of brine, growing more intense as we drew
near. We saw below what looked like a flotilla of merchant ships
offshore, dozens of them, anchored and asleep. And the infamous
Temple of Aphrodite rose above the city, a site where any number of
prostitutes found refuge and community.

"It's a city of whores," said Barnabas.

"The young must beware," I said. "These women will be tempting."

"We have no money for whores," said Barnabas, in a rare moment
of levity.

"I've never slept with a whore," said John Mark.

"You've never slept with anyone," said Barnabas.

"But if I should want children . . ."

An idiotic exchange, especially as I had explained to John Mark
that, with the coming apocalypse, it made no sense for him to think
about the prospect of having a wife or children. Families belonged to
the past, to history. The cycle of generation must stop. Saying this,
I realized he was only eighteen, and it's not easy to separate a young
man from his lust.

We found lodging in the Jewish quarter of the city. The keeper
of the inn was Avital, a woman of seventy with the enviable calm that
may accompany age in the right circumstances. I sat with her in her
garden late into the night, under the stars, and she told me about the
sins of Paphos.

"It's the goddess," she said, saying that Aphrodite had cast her spell.

Many Jews acknowledged (even worshipped) the pagan gods, especially given the spirit of Roman open-mindedness to all cults. I myself doubted that Claudius, the emperor, believed in any spirit higher than himself, and yet most of his subjects thought of him as a divinity as well, one capable of changing the seasons if he wished. Such notions played into the hands of astrologers, sorcerers, and religious fanatics, who fleshed out the marketplace of ideas in a place where the stars and planets held as much sway as the God of Israel.

Barnabas sent a note to his friend at the palace to announce our arrival, and we were invited to dinner the next evening.

Avital, her cheeks and forehead scored with crevices, scoffed at the news of this invitation. "You will see for yourself," she said. "Any self-respecting Jew in Paphos avoids the palace."

It was pointless to explain that we had come to Paphos with a message for this particular and rarefied audience. If a man in power—in this case Paulus—would turn to Jesus, there was no limit to what God might do. Nevertheless, we had no idea what lay in store and approached the palace cautiously, intimidated by the armed guards at the gates, who nevertheless let us onto the grounds and inside the palace without interrogation. We had obviously been expected.

Interior doors swung open, taking us deeper into the palace, where the opulence amazed us. Gold and silver fixtures blazed in the candlelight, as did the painted tiles and statues of Aphrodite in every niche. The walls had been hung with tapestries, and one had been embroidered with scenes of men and women in embrace, with animals in copulation, and assorted cultic practices. Whores eyed us from doorways as we passed through the chambers, led by a muscular young man in a loincloth, who had obviously been assigned to us.

"Let me suck you," one of girls said, tugging at my arm.

I looked sharply away from her, but it was more difficult for John Mark.

For his part, Barnabas tuned out their piping voices, taking the lead behind our guide.

The ill-clad courtier ushered us into a grand reception room, where the governor squatted on a cushion with gold brocade. Palm fronds waved in the air, and the music of a lyre played from the corner of the room, the musician herself perhaps a votary of Sappho: naked, with a necklace of shells, legs crossed with her bare knees spread, the soles of her bare feet touching. Her small breasts held my attention, with their upturned nipples. I took the deepest of breaths.

This was more difficult than I'd imagined.

"Welcome, friends!" cried Paulus, coming toward us in a hail of good humor.

He was a large man, with a wide, monumentally flat head graced by a dense outcrop of short hair in the style of Pompey the Great. He had no perceivable neck, and his nose was blue-veined. His fingers sprouted white hair above and below the knuckles, and on either side of many gold rings.

He gripped my wrist, and the vehemence of his greeting puzzled me. We were hardly well-known or influential guests, and "friends" didn't describe us. That Barnabas had a connection to the governor could not have mattered.

Perhaps God was at work here?

Sometimes the ground is fertile, ready for seed. Ready for water and sunlight.

Something was surely afoot.

As we introduced ourselves, it proved difficult not to look over the governor's shoulder, where a lean young couple engaged in sexual congress on a low divan by the whitewashed wall. The girl sighed, gasped, and moaned luxuriously as the man—a slave, no doubt—plunged deeply into her from behind. He had a shimmering sword, as I recall.

John Mark froze in place.

"We've come to talk about Jesus," I said, putting a hand on John Mark to draw him back among us.

"Ah, the Christ," said the governor. "I have heard of him, your Jesus of Nazareth."

At which point Bar-Jesus appeared, the magus also known as Elymas.

"Bar-Jesus!" the governor announced, as if laying down a challenge. The sorcerer stood at least a head above the rest of us, with a

muddled face and sharp, crooked nose; his fiery upturned eyes had
been heightened by charcoal rings. The eyeballs themselves revolved
in a yellowy liquid, almost rolling back into his head as he mumbled
unintelligibly.

"He is praying for you," the governor said. "He told us about you.
And said you must come to meet us. Jesus is his Lord."

I didn't think so.

"I am the son of God," the magus said.

Barnabas acquired a puzzled look, wondering what was unfolding before him. It was a claim he had never heard from human lips
before.

John Mark said, "You're a magus!"

The governor smiled at him. "Dear boy, he can make serpents
sing. He has turned water into wine—a very useful trick in these
parts."

I had heard tales of Jesus doing this at a wedding feast near
Capernaum, although accounts of this miracle varied. It worried me
that Bar-Jesus claimed to have done the same thing, as if challenging
us. This would soon become a test of powers.

Slaves appeared at our elbows unbidden, bearing cups of wine in
silver goblets. John Mark was only too happy to receive this gift, and I
accepted a goblet as well. We were guests and must behave as guests.
Wine settles the stomach and opens the mind. And I preferred it to
water of unknown origins, which often made me sick.

The young woman on the divan shrieked, an expression of pleasure strangely akin to agony. I put a hand over my eyes.

"Pay no attention to them," said Barnabas to John Mark. "They
are rutting goats."

"I will summon the spirits," said Bar-Jesus.

Any number of cats swirled about our feet, and fresh couples
emerged from behind curtains, all naked, with the men in various
states of arousal. I could see that the governor enjoyed this continuous demonstration of perfervid lust. Aphrodite was, I saw, alive and
well in this city—and much venerated. Her presence blazed from
every wall, every orifice, in a wilderness of mirrors.

"Sit, please," the governor said.

Slaves drew cushions in a circle, and we reclined, as platters heaped with delicious fruit—melons, pomegranates, oranges, figs, and dates—appeared. I realized that, to my surprise, I was hungry. Insanely hungry.

So was John Mark, who moved greedily to devour a handful of sticky dates.

Bar-Jesus flushed and swayed before us with feeling, in a stupor of ecstasy, chanting in a language I could not recognize.

"He has summoned the dead for us," said Paulus. "My own lost brother, he came to speak to us only yesterday. Quite remarkable! He stood before us. And spoke at length."

This caught John Mark's attention. "Your *dead* brother?"

"This was nothing for Bar-Jesus. He taps the underworld," said the governor. "He's truly a god."

Bar-Jesus smiled; he was missing several teeth, and those remaining were rusty nails driven into his gums. Dressed with a purple silk pallium over his tunic, he rocked, now chanting in what I decided was some dialect of Latin, hieratic to a fault. His feet were bare—the large toes were as purple as radishes.

"I will speak to my father, the Almighty Lord," he said.

I inclined an ear.

"Jesus, Jesus, Jesus," he said. I could not tell if he referred to himself or my own Lord and master. "Almighty One! Father in heaven!"

We waited patiently, but it took some time for him to gather his thoughts. A slave girl offered to refill my cup, but I waved her away.

"What do you ask of Jesus?" I said, drawing out the magus.

"He is the son of Aphrodite."

"Not so!" Barnabas said.

I put a hand on his arm to silence him. We must let Bar-Jesus condemn himself by his own words.

He raised his arms, saying, "Aphrodite, goddess, we acknowledge you are the holy mother of fertility. You inhabited Mary, mother of the world. You are my own dear mother!" This vaguely comprehensible sequence of statements dribbled into incoherence, as he began to speak in tongues, trilling his consonants.

The young couple by the wall continued to writhe and exhale with pleasure, and the mere mention of the goddess quickened the pace of their copulation.

John Mark sat with a hand on his crotch.

Bar-Jesus drew a smile like a tight bow, the tip of some invisible but poisonous arrow aimed toward us. "God invites us to love," he said. "It is the freedom of love he preaches. Love everywhere. Love everlasting."

"But not copulation!" Barnabas exclaimed.

"Copulation is the essential posture of man and beast," said Bar-Jesus.

The governor smacked his lips, delighted by his perverse teacher, whom he had doubtless encouraged by his patronage.

I saw I must step in aggressively or lose my position altogether.

"*My* Jesus has not preached physical love, although he allows it," I said. "It is a sacred rite of marriage."

"And everywhere as well, Lord have mercy. We marry each time we mate," said Bar-Jesus. He stuttered: *jug jug jug* . . .

The Holy Spirit seized me, and I had no control over my movements. I felt my hand rise, my right finger extending toward Bar-Jesus. A bolt of lightning leapt from the tip of my finger and blinded him.

Bar-Jesus gasped, his head on fire. The eyes sparked and sizzled in his skull.

"What have you done?" the governor asked.

"God has blinded him. I was only his vessel."

"But why?"

"He doesn't tell the truth about our God, or the Christ who lives in Jesus of Nazareth!"

The governor motioned to a slave, who stepped forward to lead Bar-Jesus in all his misery and muttering from the room. Paulus understood that God had empowered me to blind Bar-Jesus in this ghastly way.

With a sharp clap, Paulus sent the young copulating couple from the room, then sat cross-legged, asking me to tell him more about my Jesus. Questions tumbled from him. What had Jesus—the real Jesus—actually taught? Where had he lived? What were the circumstances surrounding his fabled execution? Did I know him? Had he truly been raised from the dead?

I told him that I would be speaking the next day in a synagogue, and that he should come.

And Paulus did, attending our small gathering near the harbor. He sat among the Jews, who looked at him with amazement. Could this really be their governor? What on earth brought him into their company?

I delivered the news of Jesus and the unfolding Kingdom of God, and marveled at the unqualified acceptance of this holy message in Paphos. This would, as it happened, prove a rare specimen of general assent, perhaps a gift to me from God. Yet the occasion startled me. The Lord had found me afresh that morning, and I spoke with an angel's tongue and not my own. I lifted the assembly up to the roof beams, and then came bountiful singing and praying—everyone joined in, and somehow they knew prayers and songs that had never before been spoken or sung, and we all wept together at the end.

I led the group—more than a dozen, including Paulus—to a beach near the harbor, where Barnabas and I baptized each of them in turn. As their heads emerged from the salt spray, we shouted: *Alleluia! In the Christ there is neither male nor female, neither slave nor free man, neither Jew nor Greek! Alleluia!*

✦

This improbable week in Paphos ended with the baptism of Bar-Jesus, whose sight immediately returned as he burst from the water. He kissed me on either cheek and acknowledged that a dark spirit had inhabited him. He was free now and would worship God through Jesus of Nazareth. He would study the scriptures closely, would pray, and would do what he could for the Way in Cyprus. This was, I think, another miracle.

Our work here accomplished, we set off for Asia on a lumbering square-rigged merchant ship from Thessalonica that carried a miscellany of cargo in crates and sacks. I heard geese and chickens gabbling about belowdecks and one braying donkey. As the green scalp of Mount Olympus receded, I had no wish to look back. Fresh triumphs for Jesus lay ahead, I felt quite sure. Who could have imagined our successes in Cyprus, especially at the court of Paulus in Paphos?

When people are hungry for the experience of God, God happens. The crew spoke a rude dialect of Greek with many unfamiliar words, and they kept their distance, occasionally glaring at us. But with a few gold coins, we added something to their profit, paying more for this passage than seemed appropriate.

"They hate us," said John Mark.

"I doubt they have an opinion, certainly nothing so strong. We've paid them very well."

As we sailed into dusk, a purple bruise darkened in the western sky and deepened in the water. A low wind skipped over the straits from the north, and it felt chilly for late spring. The waves before us rushed to form white running horses, and the boat rocked miserably from side to side. Soon Barnabas, no sailor at the best of times, turned quite pale and went below with a bucket, nearly losing his footing on the ladder.

I began to worry about John Mark, whose cheeks quivered, and one hand drifted to his belly.

"Does it hurt?" I asked.

He nodded, and I sat with him before the mast, where we sheltered behind a wooden crate covered with a tarpaulin that smelled of rancid beeswax and a crusty white mold. I spread our blankets in the lee, making a soft cushion for his head.

"I don't know why I'm here," said John Mark.

"God has called you."

"I didn't hear a voice. You're the one who hears voices." After a pause, he added: "Perhaps I should make my way to Damascus?"

I let this rudeness pass. He was young, after all, and unaccustomed to proper conversation. His mother had, I believed, indulged him, and he expected his elders to smooth the way on every excursion.

"Do you trust in God?" I asked. "And do you love Jesus?"

It was important to speak frankly, as we would rely on him in the coming months, perhaps in less than easy conditions.

"I hold him dearly."

"That is belief," I said. "It's an affection kindled in the heart. It allows us to feel his presence through the Holy Spirit, which moves in each of us, a quiet river."

"Why do you say 'river'?"

"I speak in metaphors."

"What is that?"

"It's to say one thing in terms of another."

"I don't understand."

"As in the hymns of David, it's a common turn of thought. *My soul thirsts for God.* Do you know that line? I doubt the soul actually feels thirst. It's a way to stimulate thought."

"Stimulate?"

Once in a while I felt tongue-tied around John Mark, as he revealed few intellectual dimensions, though he was obviously intelligent and skilled as a scribe. I spoke to him with care, aware that he regarded me as an old man and, as such, inherently tedious. I thought back to Gamaliel, and how he had been so patient with the young. It would have been difficult for me to teach in a school like that.

"I don't feel well," John Mark said, as the boat continued to rock. The captain had lowered the two long steering oars in the water on either side at the aft to stabilize the vessel, and the mainsail came down hurriedly. When it began to rain—a cool slantwise drizzle—we crawled beneath an awning that reached from a beam, a perfect little cocoon. As long as John Mark suppressed the sickness in his gut, we should be fine here, sheltered and relatively dry.

The ship drifted, without direction, as night drew upon us. One could hardly anchor in these depths, so we had few options.

When John Mark began to shudder, I covered him with a rough blanket.

He had never been at sea before we left Syria for Cyprus and was lucky that his first experience had been with a flat sea and steady wind on the way to Salamis.

"I feel quite awful," he said, and I sensed the urgency, leading him to the gunnels, where he spewed a green bilge overboard that smeared his tunic. A fit of coughing followed as I patted his back.

"I'm dizzy," he said.

"Lie down and close your eyes. Pretend you're elsewhere."

I settled him on the blanket, wrapping him as tightly as I could. But his shuddering disturbed me.

I pressed as close as I could, to keep him warm, putting an arm around his shoulder.

To my relief, the wind settled before long, and the rains gave way to a clear night with a cascade of stars. I could make out through a gap in the tarpaulin a slice of moon in its waning phase, and one could see the rest of the moon, too, in faint outline. It was much like the mind, most of whose contents—memories, ideas, dreams—remain nearly invisible. Whatever one sees or feels represents only a sliver of content, the visible manifestation of much that remains unseen or barely seen.

John Mark shuddered into sleep and began to snore, smelling lightly of vomit. I watched him breathe, noting the rise and fall of his chest. His lips parted since he could not get air through his nose, and he gasped now and then, as if choking. I found myself caring for him, loving him, and wondered if this mirrored the experience of fatherhood, something I would never know.

I may have slept but can't be sure. Certainly in the early dawn I lay awake and felt the lovely sleep-warm presence of John Mark beside me, his head against my chest.

Had he put his head there during the night?

The sky slowly drained itself of dark. The sea moved below us with the slightest waves now licking against the hull of our ship. I took this waking slowly, letting it arrive in its own time. Nobody moved aboard the ship, which pleased me. I wanted only to linger in the gathering of dawn, to savor the silence, and to let the night crumble into dawn.

John Mark's head slipped from my chest, and he nestled beside me. I studied his face, the dark eyebrows and pink lips, still slightly parted. His sleep was deep, the breathing soft and regular, though it occasionally caught and held. A faint smile passed on his lips, and I assumed that a dream must have pleased him. An aura of purity, even innocence, bathed him, a nimbus that one cannot earn. It is grace itself.

I could not resist touching his hair, chestnut brown, silky. I touched him in the way a father might touch a sleeping child, with complete affection.

One eye opened unexpectedly, and John Mark winced, sitting up.

"What are you doing?"

"I like to watch a young man sleep."

John Mark glowered at me.

"I meant no harm."

"You dislike me, and try to embarrass me."

"Nothing in that remark is true," I said, drawing back. "This is preposterous!"

"Listen to yourself. Preposterous! Dear God . . . I must go home."

"But we have work to do, for the kingdom. We have to trust and love each other, much as God loves us."

"I can't, and I won't." John Mark stood, looking down at me. "You're peculiar. I will tell Peter and James that we are incompatible. I won't tell them the truth."

"Which is?"

"That you are, as I just said, too peculiar. I've had enough."

A familiar tingling of shame began in the soles of my feet, stung my heels, and rose along my spine, breaking over my skull.

Soon enough, two muscular Greek sailors lifted a sail, which caught the breeze and snapped. There was just enough wind to move us forward.

Later, I explained to Barnabas, who resurfaced and looked well again, that John Mark had taken an odd turn and didn't wish to proceed with us.

"But why?"

"It's a matter of youth," I said. "The young are moody."

"I was never moody."

I suspected Barnabas didn't want to travel alone with me, and he tried to persuade John Mark to continue, underscoring the promise of our mission. "We have accomplished so much in Cyprus," he said. "An auspicious beginning, I would say. We may do wonderful things in Asia as well."

But there was no changing the young man's mind.

"I'm going back to Jerusalem," he said.

I detected clarity and resolve in his voice, and wished I had seen this sooner.

"There is so much work to do," Barnabas said. "And Paul's letters—"

"I don't need a scribe," I said, waving off any attempt to persuade John Mark to shift his position. I knew it would not be difficult to find a slave if I needed one, although he would never copy my words with such speed and accuracy, and would almost certainly not improve upon what I said, as dear Luke would do in years to come, taking my rough drafts and polishing them, expanding them, clarifying what often remained unclear in my own thoughts.

Later that day, our ship thudded into dock in an unknown harbor (at least to me) that smelled of dead fish and brine. While the men unloaded crates and animals, we sat like three separate trees on the bow, not speaking. A green scum on the water oozed around the hull. And I worried about what lay ahead for us, especially with Barnabas as my sole companion.

⁜

We exchanged our sailing vessel for a barge that crawled along a brown pelt of water. It slipped almost silently through vineyards and stony fields, past villages of mud huts and tents. The dark-skinned pilot said nothing to us, although he took our coins. He would ferry us most of the way to Perga, from which we planned our trek to Pisidia through a high mountain pass.

John Mark remained set upon returning to Jerusalem, and I could see that his disgruntlement and disloyalty perturbed Barnabas, who had not imagined this turn of events. "I shall have a word with the boy's mother one day," he said. "She needs to know she has spoiled this child."

It was too hot by noon, the deck like a griddle in the sun, with no place to shelter. I wiped my face with a cloth, watching crows settle on the carcass of a sheep along the bank. The breeze whirled the smell of rotting sardines, and—did I imagine this?—I saw the corpse of a shepherd boy on the banks of the river as well. It was propped against a mossy stone, smiling and open-eyed.

"The dead live everywhere around us," I said to Barnabas.

My poetic observation fell flat, and he sighed. I think he wished he had not accepted this assignment from Peter and James.

In Perga, we made our way to a synagogue where Barnabas had been given the name of a well-known rabbi, Ezra ben Ezra, who already seemed to know about the purpose of our mission and to approve, although when I questioned him, he referred to Jesus as "the magician from Tyre." I dissuaded him from this over dinner, and he didn't seem to mind. "God sends us many of these messengers," he said. "I have witnessed such wonders. Voices! The gods speak, and abundantly."

"Only Jesus is Lord," I said.

"A Nazarene magician, is that it?"

"He is not a magician."

This puzzled Ezra ben Ezra, but I saw no point in trying to sort it out for him. His mind was not unlike a sponge that absorbs every kind of unnatural liquid and, itself, begins to stink in time.

John Mark slept by himself that night, as far from me as possible, and I saw that Barnabas had grown pensive, angrily so, as if his abstract and grand idea of our journey had collapsed. I don't believe he knew what to make of whatever had transpired between John Mark and me, and I wasn't sure myself what to make of it.

After an early breakfast, John Mark announced his departure.

Thinking of potential pitfalls, I offered him a small purse. "You will find any number of ships to Caesarea, even Jaffa. These coins will help."

He held the purse in his hand, considering. Then threw the money at my feet.

After he disappeared, Barnabas shook his head. "It makes no sense," he said.

"He's a child."

Barnabas sighed. "Perhaps we should return to Antioch?"

"We do have a plan," I said.

"But it's gone amiss."

"Not at all, although I can go by myself, if need be."

Barnabas waved a hand as if wiping away the foolish idea of ending our journey now.

"Pisidia awaits us," I said.

"Pisidia, yes," he said. "And Iconium. Derbe."

"And Lystra. I have heard good things about Lystra—the people are ready for God in that city, ready for the love of Jesus."

In truth, I was glad to see the last of John Mark, who posed a distraction for me on many levels. Focus was essential: The end of history loomed, and we must do whatever we could to spread the Good News while there was yet time.

Chapter Nine

⨯⨯⨯

LUKE

I had evasive conversations over the years with Paul about Barnabas and their tumultuous journey to Cyprus and parts of Asia. It had begun well in Cyprus, where the Way took root as a result of their deft and early planting. The conversion of the Roman governor Paulus altered circumstances on the island, and gatherings multiplied in Paphos and Salamis and spread to villages around the coast, on the plains of Mesorea, even into the high mountain regions of Troodos and Madari.

It was largely among the Greeks, not the Jews, that the Way of Jesus prospered in Cyprus, making it a model for future missions.

But something had gone amiss, and the matter troubled Paul. A young man recruited by the Pillars had taken against the apostle for reasons Paul never understood. "He challenged my friendship, my affection," said Paul, in what I took as an elusive remark with enough truth in it to deflect further inquiry. Whatever happened, the boy abandoned this mission after Cyprus, returning to Jerusalem, where he did nothing to enhance Paul's reputation among the Pillars.

"I don't know what passed between Paul and John Mark," Barnabas later said to me, "and I would never ask. Paul is, in my view, an awkward fellow, at best."

There were unfair innuendos in that comment, but I didn't press him.

Certainly Paul could be irascible, even peevish, which I knew better than most. As a companion on the road, he tested one's patience, insisting on his own diet, sleeping arrangements, and directions. I knew enough not to contradict him on many things, and the backlash would foul our relations. He could be intrusive, too, asking personal questions in the way that children do. But there was nothing black in his soul. He might well have behaved toward John Mark without complete respect, only to have his actions (whatever they were) misconstrued.

This unhappy turn after Cyprus bothered Paul, but I stayed away from his occasional efforts to talk about it. Why pick at old wounds?

Paul didn't lose sight of the mission at hand, and realized after the boy's departure that two could travel more easily than three. They could change directions quickly, hide, or flee. Lodging became less complicated, and the need for food diminished. (Paul occasionally mocked Barnabas about his plumpness, he told me, calling him "our fat angel.")

Because Barnabas had no talent or even inclination for public speaking, the burdens of oratory fell exclusively on Paul, who began to hone his skills in front of audiences, trying various tactics to hold their attention. Poor Barnabas struggled to understand Paul's ideas, especially the notion that one actually became Jesus by following him, by emptying oneself and taking on what Paul memorably called "the mind of the Christ."

But Paul was Paul, a man who could not resist thinking in complex ways in public, pushing ideas to the point where the normal lines of argument broke down. He could excite and inform listeners but might also leave them confused as he outrode their capacities, and even his own. "What I don't know defines me, not what I know," he said.

I suspect it was Paul's unguarded and natural intimacy that offended John Mark, as it did many others. In conversation, he pressed too close, his nose hairs spiking though his nostrils. He touched you when he talked, often poked and jabbed to make a point. The garlicky rankness of his breath could prove overpowering. When he met you, he locked gazes, and it was impossible to evade him or pull away.

I heard from Barnabas that Paul had mercilessly teased John Mark about women, making insinuations. "She's a pretty one, no?" he might say. Or "Don't get your hopes up," when a nubile beauty passed in the street. This must have upset the young man terribly. In fact, I met John Mark a few years later, and I could understand Paul's discomfort. He was an arrogant fellow, one who lived in a shiny sphere of his own, deaf to the wishes of others and consumed by his own voice, which perhaps sounded loudly in his head. His needs whipped him about, and he took offense easily and often.

After the departure of John Mark, Barnabas and Paul proceeded, following the eastward itinerary established at the outset: Pisidia, Iconium, Lystra, and Derbe. Traveling on foot, they slept when possible in huts along the way, these lonely outposts used by shepherds. Or they went to sleep under the stars, which had its charms for Paul, who could not cease from speculating on the nature of these gaudy pinpoints in the heavens above, this spectacle that nature offered on a nightly basis. He would lecture Barnabas on the poetic efforts of the pagan Lucretius to understand the meaning of the heavens. "We all derive from that celestial seed," Lucretius wrote, and Paul recalled in a sonorous voice: "A selfsame father generated all, / And gave this earth, our mother, drops of rain / To bring forth this luxuriant bright world."

Barnabas had not heard of Lucretius, but he worried that a heathen should be granted so much leeway to interpret the nature of the heavens. "He would not have known our God," he said.

"Our God is infinite, and shows himself in various faces. Even the heathen can find God."

Barnabas would never get used to Paul's curious dicta, these "sayings" of his, which adorned the letters he would write to gatherings throughout the empire. I did my best to make a note of wise or interesting things that he said in passing. Indeed, I hated to imagine how many were lost, as I could not write everything down. And often, when I did, I discovered later that he simply quoted (or slightly misquoted) the ancient authors, usually the Greeks.

Once I complained to him about this passion for quotation, and he said, "What is the universe but God's quotation of himself?"

The idea was ever to seek out Jewish communities first, as Paul knew very well how to approach Jews, being one himself. He respected them and didn't overwhelm them with intricacies of the gospel. Jews clung to their routines, their ancient practices and legalities, and they would not easily see the advantages of a new way to regard the world. Often enough, they expressed skepticism about the emergence of yet another rabbi, especially one who seemed to overturn the edicts delivered to Moses on Mount Sinai.

After weeks of tramping, Paul and Barnabas arrived at the gates of Pisidia (called Antioch of Pisidia by some), this walled Roman town with a strong military presence and a small but persistent Jewish community. It had long attracted retired officers from the imperial legions, and campaign banners waved from the towers as a stiff wind crackled the surrounding brush.

"Augustus knew what he was doing," Paul said to Barnabas. "The army set up bases throughout Galatia and brought Roman order to bear. Governance by extension, propelled by good roads. An excellent formula!"

Paul admired Roman order, which placed him distinctly at odds with many in the Way, who wondered how he could remain loyal to a government that had crucified the Christ. Jews in turn denounced what they considered his apparent loyalty to the emperor, failing to see that Paul simply and sincerely believed that history would end soon, making all imperial claims to earthly power superfluous.

Paul and Barnabas expected questions, but nobody even noticed them as they stepped through the city gates. Why trouble over a plump, gray-bearded, middle-aged Jew accompanied by a skinny, stooped, balding companion who leaned on a stick for balance? Visitors were common enough here, and so these unremarkable travelers aroused no suspicion.

In the market, where chickens and pigeons gabbled under the feet of donkeys, Paul asked a seller of melons, figs, and dates (which were displayed in a wooden barrow) the whereabouts of the synagogue. The merchant gestured to a nearby house, doubtless recognizing Paul as a fellow Jew.

A venerable, toothless rabbi named Zebadiah welcomed them as if he had waited decades for their appearance. (Paul thought he surely mistook them for someone else.) In any case, they were fed sumptuously that night; the rabbi offered them unleavened bread from his oven, grilled hare, green almonds, and small clay bowls that brimmed with chickpeas mashed with oil and cumin, with plenty of good wine in clay pitchers. A slave girl waited on them, and later that night several elders from the synagogue arrived to ask questions, having heard that an "important scholar of the Torah" had appeared in their midst. They listened with astonishment as Paul once again recalled his experience on his journey to Damascus.

Paul's status as a former student of Gamaliel impressed them in Pisidia, and they invited him to speak at the synagogue on the upcoming Sabbath. He was, as ever, happy to oblige, and for two weeks in a row he attended these gatherings—a dozen or more men of various ages—standing in the midst of them and expounding on the scriptures in a rapturous voice, often reciting long passages from memory. The Greek version came to him swiftly and verbatim: the preferred translation of these Jews as well. It also suited the Godfearers, who rarely knew any Hebrew.

Most of them listened politely to Paul, but one of the elders, Micah by name, upbraided him at the end of the second Sabbath meeting. "I've never heard of this Rabbi Jesus," he said.

"You will hear him now, but only if you listen," Paul said.

"Hear him? He's not in the room!"

There were smiles, which Paul expected.

"But he is!" Paul declaimed. "He's alive!"

Paul continued without pause, calling Jesus the Christ, the anointed one, who had been sent by God to establish a kingdom without end. "He is the son of God and our true king," Paul added.

Micah said, "The emperor won't like this."

Paul refused to back down. "Let me tell you more. Jesus will soon return from the heavens to judge each of us. And those found wanting will sink into the muck, the black pit." He elaborated on the idea of the pit, which he filled with vipers and maggots for good effect. It was a rare dark turn for him because he didn't commonly think in these punitive terms.

"There is no pit," said Micah. "With death, we die."

"We never die," Paul responded, raising his arms like Moses preparing to part the Red Sea. "In Jesus, we live!"

This language perplexed them, but Paul and Barnabas experienced none of the anger in this room that would meet them soon with force. For the most part, his listeners nodded or grumbled. Only one man stood to ask in a polite but pointed fashion, "Does this have anything to do with the Law? I'm not sure I see your point."

"Jesus revises the Law," said Paul. "His way is a new way. Radical equality—this is what he preaches. Radical equality! No Jew, no Greek! No man, no woman!"

A small number of this congregation met with Paul separately, and they began a circle of the Way that would prosper, although they often fell into division in later years. Paul called them "the quarrelsome Galatians," and yet he retained an abiding fondness for them, especially a teacher named Adam, one of those rare Jews who had studied philosophy at the Academy in Athens. Paul immediately found kinship with him, and they spent two or three long nights in conversation, working their way through the intellectual byways of Godly thinking, trying to understand how Greek theories (especially the reforms of Solon, the great lawgiver and poet) might function in the context of Jewish traditions.

In later years, Paul swore it was in Pisidia that his ideas about radical equality in Jesus—an idea that would reshape the Way and its thinking—began to emerge with clarity, when he grew alert to the full weight of its implications. "I saw such bright lines," he would say. "I wish I could have spent years, not days, with Adam."

Fears that Paul was corrupting young Jews arose, and Rabbi Zebadiah suggested that it might prove dangerous for them to remain in the city for long. Hearing this, Barnabas insisted that they depart for Iconium the next morning, and Paul didn't object. He could not see taking unwarranted risks, and he did hope for a return to Antioch before too many months had passed.

Iconium was a Greek-style democracy, almost a city-state like Athens in the age of Pericles. Paul thought they might find in this community any number of gentiles who were ready to begin the work of creating God's kingdom on earth. As ever, however, he and Barnabas knew they must begin their mission with the Jews. So they sought out Onesiphorus, whose name had been given to them by Adam. He was a wealthy merchant, a Greek turned Godfearer, known for his spiritual energies and warm manner.

Onesiphorus struck Paul as a man who could be turned easily to the Way. He knew nothing of Jesus but was immediately able to grasp what Paul told him. He invited Paul and Barnabas to his house for a dinner the same day he met them, asking pointed and useful questions. As he, too, had once studied in Jerusalem with Gamaliel, he and Paul talked at length about the roots of Jewish mystical thinking in the Merkabah school, whose scholars dwelled on the prophet Ezekiel and his vision of a divine chariot, of angels and seraphim.

I suspect that poor Barnabas was left out of this discussion.

Soon Paul baptized Onesiphorus in a brisk stream on the outskirts of the city. This impressive man, elegant in every way, occupied a light-filled house on a hill overlooking the city, which was conveniently attached to the much larger villa of his sister, Theocleia, a widow who lived with her beautiful daughter, Thecla. This girl, who had luxurious chestnut hair and olive-hued skin, was betrothed to Thamyris, a shockingly handsome boy, the son of a local magistrate.

Paul later told me that Thamyris was "among examples of the male form the most exquisite version" that he had yet seen. He compared him to Paris and Adonis, two legendary men of beauty.

Onesiphorus invited this mother and daughter, with Thamyris as well, to a gathering at his house, where a number of local Jews and Godfearers met for an evening of prayer and conversation, now amplified by the enthusiasm of Onesiphorus himself. The betrothed couple sat on cushions at Paul's feet as he talked, bewitching him with their rapt gazes, drawing from him what Barnabas (without irony) called "long and rhapsodic divagations on the meaning of the risen Christ."

Thecla and Thamyris had a shimmer about them, their faces lit from within, as Paul told me. Thecla, however, fastened her gaze on the apostle with an intensity that was noticed by the others, including her betrothed, who looked coldly to the floor when he realized the extent of Thecla's absorption. Surely this man's wild theological diversions could not be taken so seriously?

That night Paul told everyone in the room that the end of history drew near, and therefore it made no sense to marry. Young people should "forswear copulation, the dream of children, all hope of generations to come" because Jesus would soon return to earth, thus making "fantasies of family life" irrelevant. "Train your affections on God alone," he said. "Keep your eye on heaven."

Barnabas remembered the discomfort in the room as he spoke. He recalled that Paul continued with such vehemence that many of his listeners gasped, and one elderly Godfearer fanned herself and fainted. (Two men carried her from the room, and yet Paul continued to talk without pause, as if unaware of what had occurred.) Thecla sighed as Paul neared the climax of his talk, drawing rapid breaths as she leaned toward him. Thamyris continued to look away in distress. What had at first seemed interesting, even amusing, now annoyed and dismayed him.

"Let the young be young," Barnabas said to Paul later that night.

"I will not! There is neither young nor old in the world. Age is meaningless. The king will return soon, and time will become irrelevant. It's already meaningless."

Barnabas didn't disagree, but he urged caution. Did God really wish for every member of the Way to rearrange his or her life? He remembered that resonant line in the book of Psalms: *For a thousand years in thy sight are but as yesterday when it is past.* When Jesus suggested he might come "soon," that could mean thousands of years from now!

Paul discarded this suggestion. "He has whispered to me in my prayers, and quite recently I could hear his voice in my sleep. Believe me, Barnabas, he will draw near, and soon. And soon is soon, not a thousand years!"

Drawn to Paul, Thecla became a regular visitor to her uncle's house, appearing in the afternoon with fruit or freshly baked bread, eagerly seeking out the apostle's attention. His arguments persuaded her that the Kingdom of God was at hand, and she opened her heart to God in the name of Jesus. Like her uncle, she was baptized in the nearby stream.

She had asked Thamyris to join her, but he scoffed at the idea. "I'm a Greek. This man, Paul—he is a Jew!"

When Paul heard this from Thecla, he countered: "Tell him I speak the same language as Homer and Plato."

"But you *are* a Jew."

Paul replied, almost chanting, "In the Christ there is neither Greek nor Jew. You must explain this to your betrothed, whom—I fear—you should abandon. There is no point to marriage. That pleasure must be forsworn. The end of time is upon us."

Thecla agreed, saying she would not go forward with the marriage. She would devote herself to the Christ, to the work of bringing his message forward in the world. Thamyris would understand.

In fact, nothing of this set well with Thamyris or his family, who were influential in the city, and it surprised no one to learn that three soldiers soon arrived at the house of Onesiphorus looking for Paul of Tarsus.

"What do you want with him?" Barnabas asked.

"It's none of your business."

"Paul and I are associates."

"Is he home?"

"He is not."

"Then we shall wait for him."

The soldiers made themselves comfortable under a lemon tree in the garden. They had brought with them bread, cheese, and a jug of wine. It was clearly their intention to stay until Paul returned, whereupon they would seize him. Barnabas feared they might kill him, too.

Paul was asleep in the back room, and Barnabas had to slap his cheek. "We have a chance to go, but now!"

Onesiphorus came in, breathless, to say someone had taken away Thecla.

Paul reddened. "She is one of us!"

"I suspect they want to get her away from you. She belongs to Thamyris. His father is enraged, and I'm very worried about what will become of you." He looked genuinely frightened.

"I won't allow this," said Paul.

"It's not your decision, I'm afraid. I don't want your blood on my hands."

Barnabas sided with Onesiphorus, who assured Paul that he would not abandon the vision of Jesus, nor would he lose sight of their common purpose. Paul had already achieved what he set out to achieve in Iconium.

Unexpectedly, as if unmoved by anything that his companions said, Paul fell to his knees and began to pray under his breath, lifting his palms to the heavens. He shut his eyes, and the lashes quivered. He mumbled now, drooling slightly, incoherent. Then he opened his eyes.

"Jesus spoke to me."

"Now?"

"Lystra awaits us," he told me. "All of Lystra!"

"Good," Onesiphorus said, relieved and helping Paul to stand. "Go quickly, and to Lystra."

He mentioned that the soldiers lay in wait in the street and suggested that Paul and Barnabas dress as women—he had several slaves who would help to clothe them—and exit through a servants' door at the back. "It sounds foolish, but it's perhaps the only way."

"We shall make ugly women," Barnabas said.

They slipped on the ankle-length tunics that women in this part of Asia wore, with long veils covering their heads. It was not unusual for modest women who walked in public to hide themselves from view, and they would take their chances in this disguise.

"We look a fine pair of ladies," Barnabas said to Paul before they stepped into the afternoon sunlight.

Paul recited a passage from the fifth scroll of the Torah: *The woman shall not wear that which pertaineth unto a man, neither shall a man put on a woman's garment: for all that do so are an abomination unto the Lord thy God.*

Barnabas did not find this either funny or pertinent, but he was relieved to see Paul going along with the plan for their escape.

They passed through the garden behind the house, noticing the three men sitting by the lemon tree, who paid no attention to Paul and Barnabas, as a game of chance (and the wine) absorbed them. Only one of them turned slightly to the passersby and, with a show of respect, nodded slightly. He watched, perhaps puzzled, as these peculiarly shy women stepped through the doorway into a narrow street.

Nobody took notice as this pair of unappealing older women—one of them stout, the other like a rail and stooped—limped by with their satchels, one of them leaning on a stick. They hurried to the stream where Paul had baptized a number of people in the past week, stopping to bathe their feet in the icy water.

Feeling disburdened, Paul drew attention to the yellow spikes of asphodels that lined the banks as the sun flashed in the quick water. "God is shining on us," he said, removing his tunic. "And Lystra awaits. I have a feeling in my stomach: This will be a turning point for the Way. Mark my words, Barnabas."

✝

The wide plains swept them forward on the two-day journey to Lystra, another walled Roman city. They slept that night perhaps ten miles from their destination in a mountain hut, where an elderly herdsman fed them bread and goat's milk. He spoke no Greek, and Paul realized they had come into a region where less Greek would be heard, at least among working people and slaves, who had dialects of their own.

"They strangle when they try to speak," Barnabas said to Paul. "I can recognize a word or two, but not much more."

In the morning as they approached the city, its pink limestone walls topped with crenellated parapets and turrets, children and dogs began to run in circles around them. They heard the bleating of sheep and goats. Deep-throated bells rumbled over rooftops, and soon a number of men and women emerged from behind the trees and bushes.

"There must be an occasion," Barnabas said.

"We're the occasion," Paul said. "I sense God's hand at work in Lystra."

This was, as they both knew from advance reports, a city with few Jews, although they had a contact in Lystra—a woman called Eunice, a Jew formerly from Antioch, whom Phoebe knew well and admired. She and Timothy, her son, were already followers of the Way, and they had formed a tiny gathering at their house. But the name of Jesus meant nothing to most dwellers in this city, where innumerable temples and altars to pagan gods and goddesses could be found. The chief deity here was Zeus—the god of thunder, the mighty one of Mount Olympus.

As we know from the ancient poets, who never tired of writing about this god of thunder, the mightiest figure on Olympus, nothing could restrain his erotic energies. He sired endless progeny over the centuries, including Athena, Apollo, and Artemis. Even gods who were not his actual offspring called him father, bowing in his presence.

Now a crippled man scuttled crabwise in the dirt and mumbled to himself as he approached Paul and Barnabas.

"What's your name, sir?" asked Paul.

The fellow grinned, a toothless slice of a smile. His tongue slithered in and out of his mouth like a lizard, and he spat in the dirt.

Paul waited patiently. Then he shouted, "Speak to us!"

"Ariston," he said.

Paul lit up. "Which means 'the best.' I do believe that's what it means."

Barnabas enjoyed this. "So are you the best they have in Lystra?" he asked.

The crowd that had gathered around them, a dozen or more, laughed, enjoying the mockery. A piece of unexpected theater is always welcome.

"I'm from a good family," Ariston said. "Very good, my parents, they are. But my legs never did carry my body."

"And do you wish to walk?" Paul asked.

"I do."

Paul considered him. "Let me tell you that my God can help."

"Who is your God?"

"Jehovah. He is the only God, the God of Israel."

"There are so many gods . . ."

"There is only one God. He is here, there, and in all places around us. In the air and grasslands, in the walls of this city, every stone and crevice cries out to him. He lives inside of you, Ariston. He makes you the best of the best."

"In me?"

"Feel him in your breast, I beg you. Feel him!"

Paul put his right hand on the forehead of Ariston. This brought stillness as well as curiosity. The crowd could not imagine what lay in store, but several of them grinned in the expectation that this mysterious visitor would soon reveal his fraudulence, and everyone would laugh.

"Rise," Paul said, unworried that the poor fellow might prove incapable of lifting himself from the ground. "Rise in the name of Jesus the Christ!"

A crack of thunder came, although not a cloud could be seen anywhere in the sky, and fear rippled through the crowd, moving from one person to the next, as when a cold wind moves through a deep forest and each leaf suddenly trembles.

Ariston looked thoroughly befuddled, afraid.

"Rise!" Paul said.

"I can't do it," Ariston whispered. "I cannot get up. My legs—"

Paul spoke sternly: "Rise and walk, in the name of Jehovah, the only God. Rise and walk in his holy name!"

The poor man asked for a stick from a man beside him. Using it for balance, he drew his legs beneath him and, with a grimace, pulled himself to a standing position. He wobbled for a few steps, then truly walked, even casting aside the stick.

As Paul recalled at a later time, "I saw him dancing! Dancing Ariston!"

The crowd gaped at this spectacle, and one of them shrieked, "The gods have come to us! This is Zeus! This is Hermes!"

A dozen of the citizens of Lystra groveled before them. One young man lay prostrate on the ground at Paul's feet, letting his face drop into the dirt. A woman fell before Barnabas on her knees, lolling her tongue. She lifted her arms to him, as if beseeching.

"They believe you are Zeus," said Paul.

"It must be the beard," said Barnabas.

A small girl appeared with a bouquet of yellow wildflowers, which she gave to Paul, and then a hoary-headed man, possibly a priest at the Temple of Zeus, stepped through the crowd, which opened for him with a hush of respect. A number of heads bowed in his presence and mumbles of adoration could be heard from several women in veils. The priest wore a pristine linen tunic and a necklace of glass and silver shards, and he carried a long staff. He wore no shoes, but the bottoms of his feet were as thick and brown as old leather.

He pointed to Barnabas. "We acknowledge your presence among us, bearer of thunder. We have long expected your visit."

Barnabas looked at Paul with confusion, as the true meaning of this commotion still eluded him. He thought Paul had been joking when he said they thought he was Zeus. On the other hand, when did Paul joke about anything?

"Great One, you have come to us for a reason, and you honor us," the priest continued. "We shall sacrifice a bull." He tilted the top of his staff toward Paul. "Oh, messenger of the gods, you are welcome, too!"

The crowd multiplied, with townsfolk rushing to see these visitors. Rumors of this miracle of healing spread like seeds in the wind. And people began to chant and circle around the visitors, holding hands, dancing. Paul recognized the chant as an ancient hymn to Zeus, one that—he would tell me—"was known well before Homer sang of Troy."

The priest shouted above the canticle, "The gods have come down to us in the likeness of men. We are blessed, Lycaonians!"

Several young men lifted Paul and Barnabas on their shoulders, parading them through the city gates, bearing them aloft to the Temple of Zeus with the beating of brassy cymbals and hollow drums. They set them down gingerly before what seemed like an altar, whereupon a chorus began to sing their praises in the odd language of the region, which neither Paul nor Barnabas could understand, although they could sense the veneration. One wild-eyed woman with curly auburn hair threw herself at the feet of Barnabas, weeping, mumbling.

"She would like to kiss your feet," said Paul.

"So I am Zeus," Barnabas said, "and you are Hermes."

Paul found it difficult to accept this confusion, or to understand what it meant for the ultimate success of their mission here, but he could do nothing. The crowd swelled, chaotic, numbering several hundred devotees of Zeus within less than an hour. A band of young men with painted faces whirled with their spears in circles, with one of them pirouetting in the middle. An old woman knelt, issuing a tremulous and unearthly howl—as if the world had come to an end before her eyes. There was a choir of small girls who sang what seemed like a sweet if inappropriate tune. And soon a pair of oxen in garlands trod to the slaughter behind a young votary at the temple in a salmon-colored silk robe, with the sound of tambourines and loud copper barrels rung by hammers.

A thin woman in a headdress began to kiss Paul's feet, but he pushed her away. "I am not Hermes!" he shouted. "Away, girl!"

The woman turned to Barnabas next. Her eyes filled with tears as she began to claw at his garment.

"Let go!" he said, as she clutched his belly.

"I worship you, Great One! Listen to my prayers!"

"Don't touch me, please!"

Paul ripped off his own tunic, exposing his bare hollow chest. "I am Paul, a man. I am like you. I am a man!"

It was evident that they understood little of what Paul said as they lifted him, then Barnabas, back onto their shoulders and carried them to a handsome travertine house behind the Temple of Zeus.

"This is for you," said a man in yellow robes, another votary, in vaguely comprehensible Greek.

"I am not Zeus," Barnabas said.

The man shook his head sadly. "You must accept your greatness, my Lord."

They left them with baskets of food—assorted meats, fruit, honey, and bread—and amphorae of wine.

Paul knew he must pray for instruction.

The house was still, which came as a relief after a time of such commotion and confusion. They had been provided with soft pallets and cushions of silk, and Barnabas, exhausted by the scramble of the day, soon fell into a consuming sleep while Paul prayed.

As often happened when he prayed, Paul slipped into a trance— eyes closed, hands apart, palms upturned. He swayed forward and back, pivoting at the waist, his lips moving. Once in a while he sighed or seemed to wince. Prayer, for him, was agonistic, an effort of listening, with his attention spiraling inward. He grunted at times. He wrestled with whatever dark angels presented themselves. Sometimes, he told me, he could actually see a brilliant rank of seraphim, with the Lord himself, the Ancient of Days, perched on the edge of an alabaster cloud.

After a while, Paul could not help himself but fell asleep beside Barnabas. God had offered no instruction.

They both awakened to shouts on the street below and saw dozens of angry faces.

In an unexpected reversal, a furious mob had come to kill them, or so it appeared. Paul saw Thamyris below, with a cluster of young friends, and immediately understood that they had followed them from Iconium to seek revenge. Apparently it was not enough simply to disappear. Paul and Barnabas must suffer.

The door had never been locked, and so a crowd seized Paul and Barnabas, taking them to separate locations in Lystra. And Barnabas found himself in a small cell with a damp floor.

"We have done nothing," he told his jailor. "Let me go at once!"

"You are not Zeus," the jailor replied.

"I never said I was."

"Your friend, he was able to heal the cripple."

"God healed him. He spoke in the name of Jehovah, the only God."

"There are many gods."

"No, sir. There is one. Let me tell you about him. And let me tell you about his son, Jesus the Christ."

This jailor was a young Greek-speaking man, with a dark brown beard, and he leaned toward Barnabas. He seemed willing to listen and drew up a chair, allowing Barnabas to explain himself. Where had they come from? Why had Lycaonians ever thought they were gods?

In the meantime, they took Paul—the devil himself, who had healed a lame man in the name of his foreign god—to the outskirts of Lystra near the city dump.

Thinking of Jesus in his time of trial, Paul didn't resist, not even when one of them hurled a large stone at his head, knocking him to the ground. Another man kicked him in the back so hard that he could hear his spine crack, while further stones rained on his head, and Paul believed that what happened to Stephen on the outskirts of Jerusalem would happen to him. It was not a pretty death, and not what he expected from Lystra.

Yet Paul refused to resist. "In Jesus there is neither Greek nor Jew," he whispered.

But these were not Greeks, not exactly, and they were certainly not Jews.

They stepped on Paul and kicked him in the ribs, pummeled him with stones. And left him for dead. Paul's eyes rolled back in his head, leaving ghastly white globes without life in them. Blood poured from his left ear.

"He's dead," said one of his attackers.

In contrast, the jailor looking after Barnabas listened to him intently and then prayed with him. Soon the Holy Spirit overwhelmed his soul. Without a thought to the consequences of his action, he opened the door of the cell, saying, "Go with God!"

Barnabas walked unmolested into the alleyway, strolled into the marketplace, then out of the gates of the city. And nobody paid the least attention to him, although a young girl with an angelic face approached and touched his hand as soon as he stepped outside of the walls. He could see that she wanted him to follow her, and he understood that God had sent her as a messenger.

She led him to the dump where Paul lay dying.

Blood pooled around him, dampening the dirt. One ear was battered, torn. Barnabas bent to pray over his companion's limp body, asking God to accept his soul.

"This is thy humble servant," Barnabas said. "Take him, dearest Lord."

"Not yet," said Paul, in a gravelly voice. He opened one swollen eye.

"You are not dead!"

Now three or four young men approached, and Barnabas was afraid they would finish off Paul and stone him as well. But they lifted Paul gently, settling him on a litter, and carried him along a pebble-strewn path to a racing stream. They lowered him into the cool water, and one of them washed the blood from his head, using his hand to clear the skin. Paul wakened fully now, his eyes wide.

"God has spoken," Barnabas said.

The stream poured into a marshy area below, and they watched a dozen or so long-beaked white storks fishing for frogs, while buzzards circled above them on black wings.

Barnabas and the young men lifted Paul onto a mossy bank, where he lay with a tuft of grass beneath his head. One of the men tended to Paul's torn ear, bandaging it with muslin.

Later that day, a couple of women brought them food and drink.

Paul lost consciousness again, falling into an expressionless cold sleep. When after several hours he hadn't wakened, Barnabas began to fear for Paul's life. He put a palm to the apostle's mouth, which was slightly ajar, and could feel a faint breath: the only sign of life. Paul lay there like a barely smoldering fire, his flames liable to flicker and turn to blue ash at any moment. But before darkness fell, his eyes opened, and he managed a single word: *Jesus.*

Barnabas said to him, "Yes, Paul. Jesus. Jesus."

Chapter Ten

PAUL

I would not be beaten, cast aside, and left for dead by the evil Lycaonians without God's intervention. He had raised me up, allowed me to proceed. I confess, though, I'd been shaken. Was this God's way of refining my spirit, of tempering my steel? Did I need this abuse? Did I have to stare into eternity at such close range?

One night not long after the hideous events in Lystra, I found myself cursing heaven in my prayers. *Who do you think I am, God? What sort of maker would abuse his creation, allow one of his most faithful servants to suffer and nearly die?*

Those words had hardly escaped my lips when it occurred to me that Jesus himself had been more frightfully abused, beaten and scourged, nailed to a tree. His flesh had been shredded. He had bled to death. I, on the other hand, had merely been assaulted, left to die by myself beyond the city walls, abandoned. I suffered greatly but did so for his sake. And this helped me think about what had happened without rage and resentment.

It was easy to destroy a man. We are poor creatures, all of us, readily discouraged. We fall short of our divine nature, and miserably so.

Barnabas and I closed the circle of this journey by returning to Antioch, the city where our mission had begun a few months earlier. We had taken ourselves out, begun to test our message about the Kingdom of God. We met resistances, some of them coming from within, such as the difficulties between John Mark and myself. To a degree, I had to resist my own unwillingness to listen to God, to make myself vulnerable, and to fail. I would need to fail again, fail in huge ways, much as Jesus had failed, then found himself through failing.

I could hardly know what fruits might come of my travels with Barnabas, although I saw that we had spread seeds that might put out shoots after a period of dormancy. I would, I swore to myself, return to each of these places in the future. I was like a gardener coaxing delicate plants to life, these fresh gatherings of the Way. But for now, Antioch would absorb my attention.

The Way flourished here, as gentiles came to the gatherings in unforeseen numbers to share the sacred meal on the First Day, to read the scriptures, talk, pray, and sing. The excitement of this drew me forward, and I knew that Luke, Phoebe, and the others would be happy to hear stories about our travels, to tell me what had happened in Antioch in the months of our absence. They did, from the beginning, encourage my presence at their meals, inviting me to offer reflections, and I would attend as many as I could.

Hardly a few days passed without meeting Luke. He had made a little progress on his life of Jesus, and I read some passages. He had such an array of sources now and worked diligently to organize them. In the meantime, Phoebe gave me a lovely room overlooking the garden of her villa, a place where I could recuperate from my injuries in Lystra. My neck had been nearly broken, my head crushed, one ear damaged, and my back had twisted in ways that would cause trouble for years to come. In this refuge I could read quietly and write, pray, and meditate, or spend hours in conversation with Luke. Phoebe suggested I should meet with those who had recently joined us, helping them to understand the message of Jesus and how they might grow closer to the reality of God. It struck me that I could find the Christ in these conversations, as God happens when people of faith meet. "Where two or three are gathered, there you will find me," Jesus said—a saying that Luke would quote.

But impediments arose, threatening to overwhelm our circle. A small group led by a man named Jacob arrived from Jerusalem, sent to us by James. Like the brother of our Lord, these messengers failed to understand that Jesus was the Logos, present before and after time, and so present before his birth. They questioned the eternal and Godlike nature of his being and, in keeping with James, regarded Jesus as the mortal offspring of Joseph and Mary, a natural child of natural parents, one who gradually discovered the voice of God rising within his breast. By strict obedience to the Law of Moses, he became the Christ. James and those in his sway followed the Law to the letter precisely, as they imagined Jesus did. They insisted on circumcision for all God-fearing gentiles who wished to join the Way and enforced dietary laws, believing that Jews and Greeks could never sit happily together and share a meal. For them, the Jesus movement must be considered a reformed extension of Judaism, and all attempts to move into the Greek community troubled them.

Phoebe took me aside soon after their arrival. "This man, Jacob," she said, "brings a message from James. He and his friends Enoch and Nachum insist that all Greeks refrain from eating the sacred meal with us. But of course this threatens everything we've accomplished here."

She knew that the whole of our project, taking the Good News into the larger world beyond Palestine, would collapse if we could not admit honest Greeks to the Lord's Supper, as we had begun to call it. This meal, and the growing rituals associated with it, had become the mystical core of our gatherings, our symbolic community itself. We did as Jesus commanded, remembering him when we came together. As we knew, the Lord had held up the loaf in his hands, saying, "This is my body, given for you."

It was a complex metaphor, one that drew me toward it eagerly. The sacred circle would be broken if we could not admit into our circle Godfearers, gentiles, pagans, anyone who trusted God and hoped to participate in his coming kingdom. Yet we must take seriously this intervention from James. In the old days, I would have insisted we ignore Jacob and his friends, with their message of exclusion. Now I sensed we must tread carefully.

"Where does Peter stand?" I asked Phoebe.

"You might ask him," she said. "He is here."

I thought she must be joking. But Phoebe was not the sort of person to make such a joke. Indeed, the favorite disciple of Jesus sat on a cushion in her tablinum.

She led me into the light-filled room where Peter hunched beside a blue vase of terebinth sprigs with a book in his hands, quite absorbed in thought. I hadn't seen him in some time but recognized the wide flat nose, rutted as if a cart had trampled over it. His fleshy lips had a purple tint and the skin flaked badly. His ears seemed to have grown, having a vegetable look about them. His hair was silvery white, cut short across his forehead, almost like a cap. And he had put on weight.

"Peter!"

He stood abruptly now, a little sheepish. "Paul, our friend!"

We embraced, and I felt the honesty of his intentions. One could trust Peter.

"How long have you been in Antioch?"

"A few days. I'm staying with Apphia."

Apphia hosted the only gathering of the Way in Antioch to rival Phoebe's, and she remained less open to the Greeks than I would have preferred. It didn't surprise me that Peter had gravitated toward her.

"How is dear Apphia?" I said. "The same as ever?"

Peter heard my astringent note and drew back. "She is always Apphia, yes, opinionated to a fault. A little annoying at times. And yet she has brought any number of Godfearers into our circle in the past year."

"A change of heart?"

"She has never discouraged Godfearers, not in general." He looked toward Phoebe knowingly. "Of course they must bow to Jehovah and obey his laws."

I discovered that, on the previous evening, Peter had dined at the home of Lucius, a wealthy Greek merchant who traded in silks. The resources that men such as Lucius could bring to our movement didn't escape Peter, who paid close attention to our financial prospects, not only in Jerusalem but everywhere, even though the expansion of our circle to include pagans worried him. He must have known that, soon, he would lose the ability to retain close control over how the Way of Jesus broadened. The Christ principle, the divine spark itself, had set a grass fire that would rush through the world without restraint. I felt the joy of this in ways that Peter could not.

"I'm glad you sat down with Lucius and the others," I said. "I would suppose not all of the meat at their table was properly slaughtered, but what can one do? Antioch is not a Jewish center."

"It's best to avoid that subject," Peter said.

"The time draws near, and we can't avoid this conversation.

Jesus will return within weeks or months, and we must forge an understanding."

"There is truth in what you say."

I found him anxious to please, but awkwardly so, at times ingratiating. For all this, I much preferred him to James or even John or Andrew. That he liked to appease those around him opened the possibility of compromise. On the other hand, I worried I could not trust any arrangements we made. Peter might change his mind to accommodate the next person who spoke to him.

Phoebe invited a large group to a dinner at her house that evening, and I knew the conversation would prove uncomfortable for many. The guests included Peter as well as Jacob and his friends, who had apparently invited themselves. Everyone was seated on low cushions against the eastern wall of the triclinium, while half a dozen slaves moved from guest to guest with large goblets of wine that would surely loosen tongues.

Luke was eagerly talking to a young man called Silas, who had recently joined our ranks, while Barnabas lounged in one corner of the room by himself, fully rested after our exhausting travels. And even fatter than I remembered him. He was barefoot now, his black toes spreading wide, and he lifted a hand to acknowledge me—hardly a robust gesture of friendship, especially given our recent travels. Several leaders of the Way had come from villages on the outskirts of Antioch, and I recognized them and smiled in their direction. That nobody felt comfortable was obvious.

Peter greeted everyone warmly and claimed to have heard "great and marvelous things" about the work of the Holy Spirit in Antioch.

I could sense a level of anticipation in the room, as it meant a good deal to dine with a man who had been a close friend of our Lord. To be frank, I envied Peter his associations. That he had lived beside the Christ, had walked with him in Galilee and Judea for nearly three years, bestowed authority. On top of this, Peter was full of anecdotes, sayings, parables. He carried all of this well, without pomp or undue pretense. And his geniality of manner helped to ease tensions.

The trouble began when the food arrived: grilled lamb and vegetables, figs, loaves of warm bread, roasted pigeons. I noticed that one of the party, a young Godfearer whom I barely knew, took a cluster of grapes from a bowl on one side table and fed himself greedily, licking his fingers, passing a plate to another. I never imagined that the God-fearers among us—including Luke—would retreat to another room for their meal.

But Jacob stood, red-faced and breathless, eager to speak. "You will excuse me, please? We are mostly Jews here and cannot eat with those who are not part of Israel," he said, pushing the words out as if his teeth formed an invisible fence that must be overcome.

Peter dithered, looking at Barnabas—as if he might help.

"Jacob is right," Barnabas said, standing. "The scriptures don't allow for this. The Jew and the Greek must eat separately."

I restrained myself, though I recalled dozens of occasions where Barnabas and I had eaten with Greeks in recent months. Had he experienced a change of heart?

Jacob nodded, turning to the Greeks. "You must understand, none of us mean to cause offense. We do welcome you to our gather-ings, and we feel grateful for your support." He sniffed and looked around. "As you see, there is another room, adjacent. Phoebe will provide food for you there."

"I have no plan to send them away," Phoebe said. "We share the meal together in this gathering. It is our custom."

I loved her firm stance, the sense of authority and dignity. Phoebe never disappointed.

"I think it might be better, at least for now, if they ate separately," Peter said to her. "We will sort this out."

A small fellow, a Jew from Antioch, called out in a loud voice, "These matters do need clarification!"

"But perhaps not tonight," said Peter.

"Hypocrite!" I said.

My voice bounded off the walls, and eyes swung in my direction. I don't think anyone could imagine such an accusation hurled at the great disciple, but I had no ability to restrain myself.

"We belong to Jesus, all of us," I said. "We follow the Way. And everyone is included here."

"I'm sorry, but we can't remain in this room if the Greeks must dine here," said Jacob, and his friends nodded. "Jewish law is quite clear on this."

"Don't speak of Jewish law!"

"Think of Daniel, the prophet, who would not eat at the royal table."

"In Jesus there is neither Greek nor Jew," I said. "For Daniel, the problem had nothing to do with Greeks but with strange and unaccustomed food." My time with Gamaliel had not been wasted.

"But we all make distinctions," said Jacob.

I said again, "Neither Greek nor Jew."

Phoebe added dry twigs to the blaze. "Before long, Jacob," she said, "you will insist that Hylos and Glaucon should be circumcised." These men were prominent Greeks in Antioch and passionate advocates of the Way.

"Of course they must," said Jacob. "James would never admit them into the circle without this, as you know."

Glaucon smiled and said, "I shall not be mutilated."

I turned to Peter. "We have discussed this before, in Jerusalem. I thought we had an arrangement? Godfearers do not need circumcision to join the Way."

"This warrants further discussion."

"Discussion!"

Barnabas fell silent, perhaps ashamed. He and I had talked at length on our journey about circumcision, and we agreed that Greeks who became Godfearers and members of our circle did not need to submit to this ritual cutting. It would only discourage them, and Jesus had opened his door wide to the world.

Jacob said, "Do you understand that circumcision is a mark of God's own?"

I knew very well that every Jewish male underwent this ritual surgery on the eighth day of his life, a gesture of atonement in the shedding of blood. I often heard Gamaliel explain to a roomful of pupils that circumcision was God's gift to the men of Israel, a way of allowing us to perfect ourselves in the eyes of the Almighty. He said it was "Adam's curse that drew upon us the need for this intervention." Born of a woman, in shame, every young male was separated from his mother by what Gamaliel called "this ritual of amelioration, an act of self-perfection."

"Only God perfects us," I said, as if answering Gamaliel, who frequently rose in my mind as interlocutor. "We can't perfect ourselves."

Luke smiled at me, delighted by my rejoinders. And as he had not been "perfected" in this way, he doubtless appreciated my support.

"Did not Abraham perfect himself?" asked Jacob.

I understood that Abraham had circumcised himself in old age, in order to become part of Israel, a Jew at last. This "fruitful cut" was recommended by God in the context of telling Abraham that his seed would prove abundant. The male children of the patriarch would multiply, filling the earth with his progeny, but this could only occur after the ritual curbing of circumcision, an act of humility before God, a sacrifice of the flesh that signaled obedience to the divine will.

Yet I also understood that Jesus had changed everything by allowing his own flesh to be mortified. A "fruitful cut" indeed . . .

Not surprisingly, the Greeks in the room felt unwelcome, and they left Phoebe's house abruptly and without further word. It was sad, and I wondered if we would ever see a number of them again. It was a brief triumph for Jacob and his friends, but it caused disgruntlement and confusion among us, and I determined to reframe the relations of Judaism and the Way of Jesus. There was further work to be done here.

I bid Peter good night and went to my room without eating, determined to pray until dawn. I certainly had no appetite for sharing a meal with this group under these circumstances.

†

Luke said to me, "Before we go into the West together, you must travel to Jerusalem, sit with James and Peter, and come away with a clear sense of what is possible. We can't have these confusions." He insisted that we should settle this once and for all. Do Greeks actually require circumcision to join the Way? Can Jews eat with, consort with, and even marry gentiles and remain within the circle? Everything—the future of God's kingdom—would depend on the answer to these questions.

And so I went directly to Jerusalem, firm in the convictions that God had laid upon my heart. To set forth without the approval of the Pillars on these matters seemed foolish. And so, for much of an hour, I waited in the foyer of Peter's rooms above a noisy market in the Upper City. This had once been, for me, a familiar part of Jerusalem, though much had changed since my last visit, when I made a hasty exit, having been so unexpectedly saved by Aryeh. There had been skirmishes and a good deal of unrest in recent years, and now the presence of Roman legions on the streets had multiplied. I found the atmosphere oppressive, even though I remained a citizen of Rome and valued this status, which offered a form of protection.

Voices rose behind the braided curtain, and I could identify James by his pinched, nasal way of speaking. "We have only one Way, and it's a Jewish Way," he said. "My brother was a rabbi, a Jew who addressed the Jews."

Peter said, "We risk confining ourselves, limiting the possibilities."

Another voice, thin and ethereal, said, "I don't see why there is controversy. We must pray for the healing of division." I recognized this speaker as Andrew, who avoided conflict whenever he could. "And we must consider Rome. They will not rest easy. Look about you, friends."

I liked Andrew, whom I had met several times, but I found him self-serving. It surprised me that Jesus had chosen for his disciples such imperfect men, exasperating men. Today I saw that, in fact, Jesus wished to make a point, suggesting by his choices that nobody was perfect in this life, and that even the most flawed of his followers had the capacity for love. Like God, Jesus worked with the material at hand.

James almost shouted, "Rome will smother us if we lose our grip, if we don't stand together as the people of Israel. Remember Caligula!"

That summons to memory inflamed the Jews, who never for a moment forgot that the mad emperor had wished to place a statue of himself in the Temple, and had sent Petronius into Palestine with a plan to overwhelm Judea and establish complete Roman domination. Caligula would become their true god, not merely a son of Jehovah. Fortunately for the Jews, he was killed—assassinated by the Praetorian Guard—before this desecration could occur.

Peter worked to appease Paul, but James did not easily give way, reminding everyone that Jesus had been his brother. "Jesus hated Rome, and the emperor's vanity appalled him. 'When you see the abomination standing where it should never stand, in the Temple itself, let everyone know: All of Judea must flee to the mountains.' That's what my brother said. He loved the Temple. He was a Jew above Jews, with no need for gentiles."

At that point, unable to bear the drift of his argument, I stepped into the room without the benefit of invitation. It was surprisingly dark and stuffy in there, candlelit in the afternoon, with the curtains drawn. The walls glowed a sickly pallor, and there was something subversive in the atmosphere.

"Welcome, Paul," said Peter in a most unwelcoming voice. "We didn't expect you quite yet."

"I would refer you all to the prophet Isaiah," I said, avoiding the niceties. "God told the people of Israel not to exclude gentiles from their land. He said to make them joyful." I looked at each in turn. "'Joyful' is a strong word, but it's God's own word, not mine."

The truth of the scriptures sounded in the room, and it silenced them.

"Do sit with us," said Peter, after a few moments, gesturing to an empty cushion. "You raise an interesting point. That doesn't surprise me."

Andrew said, "You've lost most of your hair."

I smiled, unhappy with his observation, but I didn't remark on his gauntness or that look of a man pursued by wild animals. He already had one foot beyond this veil of tears.

"We should avoid discord," said James. "You and Barnabas did excellent work in Cyprus, this much I've been told. We've had reports from Paphos."

"So condescending," I said. "Do you actually hear yourself when you speak?"

James shook his head in a sad way, as if barely tolerating me. The toga that he wore had not been washed in several years, gritty with the dust of Jerusalem, and he obviously didn't eat much; his thin body had acquired a skeletal aura, his skull visible beneath the skin. He still spent much of every day in the Temple in prayer, where many regarded him as a kind of fixture, an eccentric who walked the streets at night in conversation with God. I felt more pity toward him now than anger. It was notable that Mary, his mother, had little to do with him, even though he apparently saw to her care.

"James meant no harm," Peter said. "There is no reason for a dispute."

"There is every reason. The Way can hardly prosper, even survive, if we simply become like the Pharisees, obsessed by every point of the Law, unwilling to let the Holy Spirit rise among us and lift us."

Peter sighed, perhaps feeling the force of my logic. "I don't see that we must choose between the Greeks and the Jews," he said. "God speaks to the nations in their own tongues. That should be a sign."

"If we exclude those who wish to join us because they are not circumcised," I said, "we must content ourselves with small numbers, a mere handful of advocates for the kingdom. But Jesus is the universal lord. He will not reject a man because he isn't circumcised or fails to adhere to the Law of Moses."

"My brother, you see, had a deep respect for—"

"Your brother! You had very little interest in your brother during his lifetime."

"Who says this?"

"Paul, please," said Peter. "This is pointless. To be personal at a time when—"

"Everything is personal. Jesus was personal."

"You must consider—"

"No! I've come a good distance to meet, to discuss these matters, and you know it's not safe for me in Jerusalem. We must have a clear understanding. Those we gather into the fold, if Greek, are not subject to Levitical regulation. It could not be more simple."

Peter sucked in a slow breath, rubbing his temples with his fingers. He didn't look well.

"I do need clarification," I said. "I'm sorry."

Peter replied, "If you don't mind, I would like to have a few words with James and Andrew. We have only the interest of the Way at heart." He looked nervously at the others, who showed no sign of agreement or disagreement.

"I, too, have in mind the interest of the Way," I said.

"I'm sure this is true. Could you possibly return at this time tomorrow?" I saw that sweat dripped from his forehead into his eyes, and that he winced. "We'll have thought carefully about all of this by then. I promise."

And so I left them to their deliberations. They knew what I thought. And I would not trouble myself if they decided against me. God stood beside me, so did I require anyone else?

I had found a room in a narrow alley near the Fish Gate in the house of Judah, an old and trusted acquaintance, and I returned there later in the evening. I noticed the jagged roofline of the Temple as I walked through the Upper City, looking about me in every direction, aware that if word of my presence reached the wrong ears, my life could be at risk. It was, of course, difficult to appraise the actual level of risk, but I assumed that any number of influential men in Jerusalem remembered me, and far from fondly.

It worried me greatly that the Way might soon diverge, and this would harm everyone who worshipped God in the spirit of his son. Sadness overwhelmed me, and I stopped by a wall to pray, letting my head sink against the rough stone. *Thy will be done*, I prayed, over and over as the sun dipped low in the western sky.

Shadows filled the streets with a kind of gold-tinged soot, and I drew a raspy breath, recalling my years in Jerusalem with mixed feelings. It was unlike any other city, with its mingling odors of incense and charcoal, camel dung and cat piss. The residual stench of blood from an infinite number of sacrificial offerings hovered in the air. Slowly I made my way along the worn cobbles, pausing to summon earlier days when I walked these passageways, my head filled with language from the Torah. I had always imagined myself writing commentaries one day, filling empty margins of sewn books with brilliant responses, which generations of scholars would encounter and contradict or, perhaps, confirm as erudite and wise.

In my tiny chamber, I sat at a small table before a pitcher of wine and some cold meat with sesame paste that had been left out for me. But it had been a long day, and I fell asleep in my chair, resting my head on the table.

I didn't waken until I heard the floorboards creak and, aware of the dangers, sat upright. A figure stood before me in the dusky light and I braced, thinking he would thrust a knife into my breast.

"Who are you?"

"Paul, do you still chatter about Plato and Antipater?"

Even in the dim light I recognized the bent nose, the familiar smell.

"How did you find me here, Aryeh?"

"Our friend Judah, of course." He paused. "He told me you had come back. As you see, I've grown fat."

We embraced, with his coarse beard pressing against my ear.

"I began to attend gatherings a few years ago," he said. "For me, Jesus has opened a way to God."

"Do you belong to the Temple Guard still?"

"That's for younger men."

"You're not so old."

"Nor you."

"I began life as an old man," I said. "You once said that. I won't forget your insult."

"You are hunched, bald, and bandy-legged," he said. "But otherwise appealing."

I had forgotten that he liked to make these humorous comments, and smiled at him. "You may insult me, dear friend," I said. "But my loyalty remains. And my affection."

We crouched together on feathery cushions after I lit an oil lamp, and I poured a cup of wine for each of us. He sipped, explaining to me that Gamaliel, before his recent death, had been a voice for reason in the movement, and that he often spoke of me.

"He is dead then? Gamaliel?"

"Only a month ago."

I had not heard this, and it shocked me to think of this man's passing. It had meant so much that Gamaliel had turned to Jesus, and that his great learning had become a part of our tradition. He apparently gave wonderful talks to the Jerusalem circle, bringing his knowledge of the Hebrew scriptures to bear on the story of Jesus. "Blessed is he who comes in the name of the Lord," Gamaliel would say, quoting the Psalms of David, which he called "a carpet unrolled for the feet of the coming Christ."

We talked about our teacher's alluring presence, and I recalled that Gamaliel, more than anyone, had shaped my thinking. His approach to argument—fierce, unafraid—became mine. He understood tradition as a living and ever-shifting body of thoughts and customs, an "accumulation of rhetorical moves," as he once suggested. God, he declared, speaks now, and to each of us. "The fire still burns," he said, whenever we spoke of the burning bush and Moses. "Get as close to the flame as you can manage. You won't fry!"

Perhaps I preferred the afterglow of an emotion to the burn itself, and considered this a fault of mine, not a virtue. I wanted to be somebody who would stand in the fire, in God's holy flame.

"God in me, God without, God everywhere," I said, repeating the words of Gamaliel.

Aryeh said, "Those words are . . . so beautiful."

"What is your life now?"

"I have a wife and two sons."

"I would like a son," I said. "Two sons, even better."

"You never took a wife?"

"There is no time for marriage." It seemed pointless to explain.

"You have a mission, a passion."

"God has chosen me. On my way to Damascus—"

"I heard this story. It circulates still, and I'm glad for you. The sky filled with angels?"

"A gleaming choir," I said. "And sounding brass. The ground shook, tilting in air. I was blinded by God."

"You haven't changed," he said.

We prayed together before he left, something I never thought would happen.

"God be with you," I said.

The next day, I woke with barely enough time to make my way back to Peter's house, and my stomach clenched as I pushed through the curtain into the room where, as before, I must face the Pillars.

Peter and Andrew would deliver the verdict, and I took this as a good sign.

"We have a clear vision," said Peter.

I raised my eyebrows.

"The Greek must become part of the Way," he said.

"I agree."

"We know you do. James disagrees, I must tell you. But we have overruled him. No Godfearer, no Greek must undergo circumcision to join the Way. That isn't necessary." He paused. "It would be a choice, of course. And one that we recommend."

"A sensible approach," I said, concealing my delight.

"As for diet, they must follow the Law."

"Which aspects of the Law?"

"We must keep this simple, otherwise there is no way to control whatever happens. If an animal has been sacrificed, or strangled, or has been mauled by another beast, its meat cannot be consumed. And the Greeks shall not drink blood. Blood is forbidden."

I could see where they were headed. Saving face would mean something to James. He would insist that they had agreed to a compromise. He must bring this news back to his constituents within the Way, who formed a tight influential circle within our movement in Jerusalem. This outcome could hardly please them, as it opened doors that could never be shut.

"We can eat at the same table, however," I said. It was a statement, not a question.

"Yes," Peter said, without elaborating. "And one further thing. Fornication is forbidden."

"And how do we define that?"

I had witnessed the whole range of fornication with my own eyes at the governor's palace in Cyprus, where mere copulation was the least of it, and was myself subject to urges that unsettled me, producing feverish dreams. I knew I must never relinquish control over my body to these animal spirits within me. Discipline was essential in this, as in all things.

"Do you wish to explain?" I asked.

Peter didn't answer. Instead, he broke off a piece of barley bread, giving it to me.

"There is a question of judgment in all things," said Andrew. "I would suggest that you pray deeply about these matters. God will show the way."

"I shall pray hard and long."

Peter smiled. "Very well, good."

He told me that I must try the honey that lay in a small clay pot on the table. "It comes from Ananiah, where we have a small gathering. I can't recommend it enough."

"Ah, yes. On the way to the Dead Sea."

I didn't mind the deflection. It was better to talk about honey than circumcision or dietary laws or, for that matter, the details of fornication. It had been a mistake to prod. Fornication must remain within the domains of individual judgment, as the word itself covered a range of behavior. Was a light kiss on the forehead enough to cross the line? Could one touch someone from the opposite sex on the bare wrist without hesitation?

I left them as soon as it felt it was polite to do so, and found myself almost rising to my toes, giddy with the success of this meeting and of the journey itself. I had settled these important questions, and to the benefit of the Way. A path forward opened broadly, with the sky's bright unending blue above the bluest heaven.

Chapter Eleven

LUKE

Paul arrived in Antioch in high spirits, buoyant but perhaps overwrought as well, his eyes blinking rapidly as he talked, his lips twitching. It had not been uncomplicated to secure an arrangement with the Pillars, though he had surprised himself by his achievement. The compromise with James, in particular, surprised him. It was perhaps true that James wanted Jerusalem to himself, and it probably made sense to let Paul loose among the Greeks.

According to Andrew, James thought that Paul would never succeed in the West. He was "too mad, unpredictable, and temperamental," James said. "His passion is dangerous."

He underestimated Paul.

Now the apostle planned to move into the Greek world without delay, believing the Holy Spirit would fill his sails. Jesus had appeared to him again as he traveled from Jerusalem, urging him to expand his ministry beyond Asia, to think about "Greece and beyond." To my amazement, Jesus also told him, "Luke will be your ideal companion."

It pleased me to have this affirmation.

Paul gathered the leaders of the Way in Antioch at Phoebe's house, and explained to them this compromise. It came as a relief, and they cheered his victory. Yet there was a triumphal note in Paul's explanation that didn't sit well with everyone, including a cousin of mine, who said, "What an impossible man!"

"We will travel well together," Paul said, once again, as we sat in Phoebe's garden.

"Where are we going exactly? It would be wise to plan."

He gripped my arm at the wrist, digging his yellow nails into my skin. "We'll tell out the greatness of the Lord and his love. God will suggest the right places for our work. Westward, though. I know he calls us westward."

That was an odd phrase but moving. *Tell out the greatness of the Lord and his love.* And the idea of going westward had its appeal as well.

How could one resist Paul's eloquence and passion, his childlike enthusiasm, even his mad energies? I decided to leave everything in Antioch behind, for now. I didn't care about money and was relatively free of worldly ties. I had no intention of marrying again, as one loss on that level was enough for a lifetime. No relatives apart from a number of cousins and one elderly aunt encumbered me. Nothing fixed me to Antioch except my villa on the southeastern edge of the city, with its view of Mount Silpius from the rooftop terrace, and I knew my cousins would happily occupy it in my absence.

"We should plan to travel for a period," Paul said. "I would like to cross the Taurus into the land of Japheth. Bithynia awaits! Have you been to Bithynia?"

I had not even been to Phrygia, which was closer. And yet I had longed to visit the territories stretching along the Black Sea. Macedonia and Anatolia rang in my head, these luminous and exotic names. News of their wonders had reached my ears, since Antioch was a crossroads, full of visiting merchants, soldiers, wandering teachers and mystics, many of them from Greece, which appealed to me as a destination. I had read the epics of Homer and seen plays by such masters as Aeschylus and Agathon and often thought wistfully about this legendary region beyond the setting sun, with so many islands in the sea.

Perhaps that day had arrived.

"Say something," Paul said, drawing close to my face.

"I'm thinking."

"Don't think. Come! The Kingdom of God is at hand!"

"I'm coming," I said.

Paul had already enlisted Silas, an Aramaic-speaking Jew from Judea, as another companion. This stocky young man, recently settled in Antioch, had limitless patience, as I had already seen. He listened keenly to Paul, and—though his Greek was never perfect—could warm to strangers, who found him appealing. I soon joked that Silas would "soften up" an audience before Paul took over. And this was especially true in synagogues, where his Judean origins counted for something. Like Paul, he was also a Roman citizen, and this played well on remote imperial roads, where one had occasionally to pass through military checkpoints.

Our plans fell into place over several weeks as we met at Phoebe's house for long and abundant dinners. We would stop in Tarsus, Paul said, before pushing into Bithynia by way of the southern Galatian towns of Lystra and Derbe. He was quite determined to meet the population in Lystra once again, even after they nearly stoned him to death, at first mistaking him for Hermes and (unbelievably) taking Barnabas for Zeus.

"We could bypass Lystra," I said.

"God has spoken to me," Paul said. "And it's better to face into the wind. There is a spiritual hunger in Lystra. It only requires appropriate feeding."

I could hear a hesitance in Paul's voice as he said that, and guessed that he covered over his terror. How could it be otherwise? They had nearly killed him. And yet this part of Galatia had become more amenable to our message in recent years, with a gathering that centered on Eunice, a confident woman of means who had opened the doors of her house to the Way.

One day in late spring we set forth, a band of three with a donkey, climbing along a gravel path beside a gorge. We followed in the wake of a camel train from Persia, although we made sure to keep our distance. Paul had brought a small tent, and we could shelter from stormy weather as needed in that waterproof hutch. My own bag contained a sheaf of papyrus as well as reed pens with a pumice to sharpen them. I kept a quantity of dry black ink made from gum and lampblack. I hoped to send letters home to Antioch and knew that Paul planned to correspond with gatherings in many distant parts, which had become a habit of his.

"We shall have dueling accounts," Paul said.

This journey through the Tarsus range could be dangerous, as highwaymen lay in wait for travelers, but Paul never cared about such things. "I believe Silas will keep them off," Paul said. "Tell him, Silas: You are quite vicious."

Silas embraced this description, keeping a sword in his belt to ward off potential attackers. I wondered if Paul had not, after being stoned in Lystra, wished for more protection. Perhaps Silas, without his knowing it, had been engaged to confront potential enemies or to protect Paul from their wrath. It is never good to make anyone feel like a fool, and those who mistook him for Hermes must still, even with the passage of time, harbor resentments.

We paused to look back on Antioch from the rust-brown crest of a hill several miles from the city, seeing a rainbow arc across the valley of the Orontes. Paul, as he would, took this for a sign.

"God will protect us," he said, lifting his arms to heaven.

I said, "You should feel relieved, Silas. It was your job earlier in the day."

We stopped in Tarsus for a few weeks, staying in Paul's family house, and met with many in his circle there, a gathering of thoughtful people dedicated to God's gradually realizing kingdom. It quite surprised me to see Paul in this context, in a place so familiar to him, and where the ghosts of his childhood scurried under the blue mosaic tiles in his old home. I noticed that even the slaves there seemed more like old friends and family members than servants.

"I could never live here again," Paul said. "It's oppressively comfortable. I look for, but never find, the child who lost himself in these rooms."

Setting off with fresh supplies, we trekked into the Galatian lowlands, arriving in Lystra late one evening. I noticed how anxious Paul seemed, looking around with a special alertness, ready for someone to recognize him. We made our way to Eunice, who seemed delighted to welcome us. In her spacious compound we slept on low beds in a wooden shed at the back of her garden, which teemed with cedars and aromatic bushes. Slaves brought us dinner on ceramic platters, which we ate outdoors beside a trellis covered with ferns and yellow roses. I watched Paul relax into the setting. He seemed happy that nobody had lurched at him or tried to drag him to the dump for stoning as before.

We took great pleasure in Eunice, a brisk, intelligent woman who led her gathering with a sense of joy. Her late husband had been a high-ranking provincial governor, and she had brought a considerable dowry to the marriage. It occurred to me that so many leading figures in the Way, without whom our movement could not survive, were women of means, often with political influence. They were, almost to a fault, benefactors who wished to use their fortunes to improve the lives of those who had not shared in their good luck.

With her coppery hair and somewhat wild-looking big eyes, Eunice held our attention. Her wry sidelong smile set her apart, as did her humor. She was adorned by layers of silver and brass necklaces and bracelets, so that when she moved she made jingling noises. Her dress billowed around her.

"She carries her own tent," Paul whispered.

"A tentmaker would notice."

On our second day in Lystra, Paul addressed the gathering at Eunice's request. It was the First Day, and she wished to show us the breadth and energy of her circle, which was composed mostly of former Godfearers, although she had attracted a number of outright pagans. Her sacred meal included readings, singing, and a variety of reflections. All listened keenly to Paul, asking questions late into the evening. The following day several of them came to the house and, to everyone's surprise, asked to be baptized by Paul, who agreed, leading them to a nearby stream—the same one, it so happened, where he had bathed his broken body on his last visit to Lystra.

A key member of the gathering was Timothy, Eunice's self-possessed son, now in his early twenties. He took to Paul at once and insisted that the apostle baptize him that morning, though he had been a participant in the Way for a few years by now. He was a quick, rangy fellow with tight red-and-gold curls. His blue eyes were the color of wild hyacinth, and he held one's gaze. He had a quick smile that engaged those around him.

"I caught a glimpse of you when you last came to Lystra," he said to Paul over dinner on our first night. "A remarkable entrance!"

"You didn't think I was Hermes?"

I had not known Paul to engage in this kind of banter.

Timothy grinned. "All of Lystra was agog," he said. "Zeus and Hermes had condescended to join us."

"Everyone still talks about that visit, but I never understood the fuss," said a woman who was sitting beside Eunice.

"Paul healed a man with a withered leg," Eunice explained. "He and his companion were taken for gods."

"It was only in the name of Jesus that I healed," Paul said. "I would never dare to heal in any name but his, with the power of God."

"A crippled man could walk again," said Timothy. "We haven't had so many miracles in Lystra, not since that day. If word gets out, there is no telling who will visit us."

I liked him already, the way he teased Paul while remaining affectionate. It was good to see a confident young man without fear of his elders, willing to frame opinions and yet open to correction, as I sensed he was. No doubt his assurance derived from the gift of his position in the world. He was a fellow with connections, with purchase on the world. A slave or poor man could never speak so freely. And having a strong mother like Eunice must have played a role in his formation as well.

That night, after dinner, Paul sat with Timothy in the garden on a bench under an umbrella pine, and I could see that he relished this contact with a younger man who obviously admired him. They shared a large jug of wine as twilight shifted into darkness and while household slaves circled the enclosure, lighting torches. From a distance I could feel the animation of their talk, whatever its subject, as Timothy employed an array of elaborate hand gestures, and Paul leaned in, nodding, his arms folded across his chest. This was, I thought, a fine tableau—almost like father and son.

Wrapped in a wool cloak, I crouched by myself in a corner, inhaling as a bed of white flowers tilted their lovely scent into the crisp night air, and soon dozed off. In the middle of the night I nearly fell off my seat and, clumsily, slipped back into the room in our shed to sleep on a pallet beside Paul and Silas. I closed my eyes and prayed: "God, thank you for these people, all of them, and this chance to serve you."

The next morning, over a dish of yogurt and dates, Paul announced that Timothy would join us on the journey to Bithynia. "He's got an uncle near Mysia," Paul explained. "A villa on the Sea of Marmara. He says we'd be very welcome there."

At first I didn't think we required a fourth companion, as it would make accommodations more complex. It had been difficult to fit the three of us into Paul's tent on the nights when it rained, and four would never work.

"We shall need another tent," I said.

Paul thought I was being foolish, and even Silas agreed. "You like it out under the stars," he said.

"Hailstorms are another beast."

"It makes good sense to have two couples," Paul insisted, "so we can split into pairs when we enter a city. It's a good strategy, and a further guard against thievery."

Silas liked Timothy, I could see, and this helped. He asked him about his family origins.

"My father was a Greek, from Corinth," Timothy said. "And I was never circumcised."

"That doesn't matter," Paul said. "We have a new dispensation."

"To me it does," said Timothy. "I want to belong, as a Jew."

Paul raised an eyebrow.

"I hear that you often visit the synagogues first," Timothy said. "You put yourself among Jews, who worship the true God. You know their language and customs. If they trust you, there is a start. They bring in Godfearers. The circle widens from this center. A good strategy."

"But circumcision is unnecessary," Paul said. "We have an arrangement with the Pillars in Jerusalem."

"But will Jews everywhere trust me if they suspect I'm not one of them?"

Paul shook his head sadly. He thought he had put the matter of circumcision to rest. But now it reappeared loudly, annoyingly.

"I must do what God is asking me to do," Timothy said. "I have prayed about this for many months. And I want to commit fully to the God of Israel. And to Jesus, who is the Christ."

"I do hear what you say," said Paul.

"That settles it," Timothy said. "But I would like your blessing and want you to perform the rite."

"It's not really my gift, you see—"

"I have a very sharp knife," Timothy said. "It isn't difficult, from what I gather."

When Timothy left the room, I tried to dissuade Paul. "You

might botch it. I have heard stories about how wrong this can go. A young man died in Antioch only last year, as you may know. He bled to death."

As a doctor, I had treated several Godfearers who came to me in anguish with their genitalia mutilated or inflamed, spewing green-and-white pus from the tip of the penis. I had to perform castration on one young fellow, removing the offending part altogether to save his life. Another poor man, in his mid-thirties, died in my care because he refused castration, and the agony of his passing did not bear description.

"I know the risks," Paul said, "and I will ask the Lord for guidance."

The Lord must have spoken quickly, because in Timothy's mother's house the next day, we stood in a circle, five of us, all men—including me, a Greek! Timothy entered the room and looked shyly at us before he lay on a divan, as instructed by Paul, who lifted the white linen tunic to expose his genitalia in a profuse nest of reddish pubic hair. Timothy turned his head to one side, and I could feel his fear.

I put a hand on his shoulder. "I'm a physician," I said. "You should feel safe with me here."

It was a lie, however reassuring. What would I do if the boy bled profusely, as some did? Briefly I thought about stopping the procedure altogether by saying: "This is madness! The Pillars have spoken! There is no need!" But the occasion had its own momentum, and I could not summon the will to intervene. It would probably have meant nothing, in any case.

Timothy's pale stomach shone, as smooth as his thighs, and his penis was slightly swollen with expectation.

Somewhat to my surprise, Paul knew exactly what to do. He put a cloth on the thighs, close to the groin, and removed the knife that Timothy had provided from its sheath, saying, *"Blessed art thou, Almighty One and King of Israel. Thou hast commanded us in this deed. Blessed art thou, O Lord."*

A burly textile merchant called Aaron, whom Timothy's mother knew, sat in the honorary chair of Elijah, named for the angel of the Covenant, saying, *"This is the Covenant of Abraham, our father."*

Without hesitation, Paul reached for the shaft of Timothy's penis with his left hand, in the action known as *milah*. With a single stroke of his right hand, he cut away the outer layer of the foreskin, which he had pulled tight. When Timothy shrieked, Silas gave him a piece of leather to bite on.

"God, help me!" Timothy said, craning his neck to see a gusher of blood. The wound seemed to gape and stream, and the white cloth turned crimson-dark and wet.

Paul, according to custom, bent forward and put the damaged penis in his mouth and sucked it clean. He kept it there, in his mouth, for a long time, allowing the flow of blood to subside. I winced to see the corners of his mouth drip with blood when, at last, he removed it from the site of the wound.

At once he wrapped a piece of linen around the disfiguration and told the young man to hold to it tightly. This would staunch further seepage.

"It's still bleeding," Timothy said.

"That's quite normal," Paul said.

But it was not normal. This could never again be normal, not in the age of the New Covenant. I could hardly believe that Paul succumbed to this request from Timothy, and that he had been willing to engage in a ritual that only a short while before he had roundly dismissed as inessential for admittance to the Way, even an impediment to our progress in the West. Any hope of gathering the Greeks into our fold would fail if we insisted on this sort of butchery as the price of entry.

Timothy rebounded quickly, however, much to my relief. And showed no signs of being damaged by the experience.

After a week of recovery for Timothy, we set off westward—Paul with a spring in his step, as he had escaped any real notice in Lystra apart from those in our circle, who had no wish to draw attention to the presence of a man who had been left for dead outside the city walls. I saw at once that Silas and Timothy matched well, being near opposites in disposition. And I considered myself a useful counterpoint to Paul, bringing forward a cool, commonsensical approach that balanced against his hot radical flame, which often torched the dry landscape around him.

The idea that we should take the Good News into Bithynia consumed Paul at this point, though he had little knowledge of what lay to the north—apart from being aware that natives of Thrace had migrated into that province centuries ago and, by reputation, harbored a willful streak of independence that posed a threat to Roman dominance in the region. These poor farmers and shepherds apparently spoke a strange local dialect, and their rural villages would be lonely and bereft of culture, full of superstition and prejudice. How they would react to Paul, or to any of us, was hard to predict, but I began to worry about our encounters. Anything might happen.

We continued northwest into the Galatian lowlands, pausing at Pisidia, which Paul had visited a few years earlier, and where he had struck up a friendship with a man called Adam, whose gathering of the Way had grown. We headed directly to Adam's house, where he and Paul greeted each other as long-lost brothers.

"It's the nature of my life, and not a good thing, that I make friends but must abandon them so quickly," Paul said. "Often I never see them again."

He and Adam walked into the lush countryside outside of the town, passing three days in each other's company, and Paul presided over a sacred meal there and offered eloquent reflections on our mission. It seemed that Adam, though a rabbi by training, knew a good deal about Greek ideas because he had lived and studied in Athens as a young man. I knew that Paul would have liked to remain with Adam for some days, as their conversation enlivened them both, but Timothy urged us on, and we departed one morning with fresh supplies, even an extra donkey. I rarely felt again such buoyancy in myself or in the others.

It was thrilling to cross the mountains that had risen for weeks in the middle distance, this jagged purple line that widened across the horizon. It had snowed at the higher elevations, and the air stung with a peculiar brightness. Sometimes a sharp wind blew up from below, and I was happy to have brought a heavy woolen cloak with a hood as well as leggings made from sheepskin. For his part, Paul seemed oblivious to the cold, or didn't mention his discomfort. Nor did he do more than put on an extra tunic and socks.

After long days of climbing, often along steep icy patches where the slippery path gave way on one side to precipitous drops and scree, we came down into a fragrant spring valley below the snow line, and I marked the wildflowers everywhere in profusion. Vast fields of them appeared in a variety of colors, like an audience with their eyes wide open. The earth itself softened, and we could hear a running stream, invisible but loud, with a cracking of stones. Then the sun hit us, its wide flat blade against our cheeks, and it felt almost too hot. It was as if we moved through several climates within hours.

We camped in the valley by a black lake with a fringe of white stones like chunks of ice. And that evening, as the donkeys lay down in the wet grass, their big ears tilting forward, we slept in the lee of a cave. At midnight or so, Paul suddenly rose, stepping over us into the dark, and I sensed his urgency, although this puzzled me. What was going on? It was a night of a big orange-tinted moon, and in the distance wolves raised their howls on a great leash of sound, perhaps racing through evergreen forests.

Or were these black spirits that were making such a racket?

Worried about Paul and his apparent agitation, I followed him from a distance and discovered him standing by the water's edge, in apparent conversation. Yet nobody stood near, even though he spoke in a heated way, gesturing. I could hardly intrude and waited by a clump of juniper, trying to listen.

After he settled, and a long silence followed, I called his name.

"What? You, Luke?"

"I couldn't sleep," I said, in the way of excuse-making.

"Ah, nor I. But I was summoned."

"By whom?"

"Gabriel."

"The angel?"

"He is active in these parts. And insists that we divert our mission," he said. "Avoid Bithynia! So he commanded, and without equivocation."

"But our plan—"

"It's easily aborted. We *shall* abort it, in fact. *Go to Troas*, Gabriel said. The gateway to Macedonia. The Greek world beckons, my dear friend. It's beginning to make sense, all of this. We wander in the dark, then it's light again." He drew close to me, his face bathed in moonglow. "God has spoken plainly," he said. "The angel urges us to go to Macedonia. They need us there. He had a man from Macedonia at his side. I am persuaded."

A man from Macedonia? What could this mean?

It probably didn't matter. I knew that Paul had convinced himself that we must follow this urgent plea from beyond, possibly from Gabriel himself. At breakfast the next morning, Paul explained our abrupt change of direction to Timothy and Silas, who both found it quite wonderful that God had sent a significant angel to speak with Paul. God obviously had our mission in mind and valued our work.

"What did Gabriel look like?" asked Silas.

"Dear Lord, such large green-blue eyes," said Paul. "And he swept into my presence on gold wings." He reached out his arms. "Such a wingspan!"

"Gold wings!"

Timothy said, "Gabriel appeared to the prophet Daniel, an interpreter of visions."

"A good memory," said Paul. "You have studied the scrolls."

Paul saw me gathering my wits.

"And what do you know of Gabriel, Luke?"

"When Mary was in her sixth month, Gabriel came to her. This was in Nazareth, in Galilee. He terrified her, with those green-blue eyes, those brilliant turquoise eyes. And the wings! He said, *Don't be afraid. God has shown you his grace. You will give birth to a son, whom you must call Jesus. He will rule over the people of David. He will be the son of the Almighty God. His kingdom will come and continue.*"

"This is good," said Paul. "You must write that down."

"How do you know all of this?" Silas asked.

"Andrew told me."

As a disciple of the Lord, Andrew spoke with authority, although not everyone trusted his stories because he had a gift for the fabulous, a love of the extraordinary, even the peculiar. I explained to Silas and Timothy that I had begun to gather material for an account of the life and teachings of Jesus, and had already collected a good deal of material, including the sayings and many fresh parables that had animated his teaching. I'd talked at length to several disciples about his activities in Galilee and Judea, and had isolated—at least in my head—the stories I would use. (I loved dearly a tale about a wayward son who returned to his father after a long and wasteful absence, and who was greeted affectionately, as if nothing was amiss: a sign that Jesus would not leave anyone behind, even those who rejected him in life. And there was a parallel anecdote about a lost sheep that I knew I must include.) One day in the future I would speak to Peter and James about their experiences with Jesus, although I was not sure how much fresh information they could provide. James, in my view, was probably unreliable and prone to turn the story in directions that supported his own ideas.

The life of Jesus meant so much to me, but it would take some effort to convince Paul that knowing the details of this life actually mattered.

"Jesus emptied himself of himself," said Paul, repeatedly. "He shows us the way to God. He died so that we might live. Do we need to know more? Are the details of his life relevant?"

"I want to know about his childhood," Silas put in. "I believe he worked with his father. Was he a stonemason or leatherworker?"

"Or a joiner?" Timothy said. "He would have framed houses. That is what I have imagined, though I know nothing. One hears rumors."

Paul squinted at me. "What interests me is the Holy Spirit and its activities, here and now, in the name of Jesus."

"Why Macedonia?" I asked, just to alter the course of this conversation, which had begun to trouble me.

"And why not?" replied Timothy. "I've always wondered about Athens."

"And what have you wondered?" Paul asked.

"I think of Plato, in the Academy. What a vision!"

"Socrates, the great teacher," I said.

Paul grew intense, as we had struck one of his favorite chords. "I've read Plato's work carefully, especially the *Dialogues*. I can't tell you how exciting it was to encounter such holiness of thought. He was the first follower of the Way."

I found this impossibly strange and pointed out that Plato had lived many centuries before Jesus. Where was the chronology here?

"Jesus was alive then, even before Plato. When I think about body and soul, and how they complement each other, this point was made by Jesus as well as Plato. Certainly Plato understood everything as a reflection of God on earth in his time. Jesus arrived in fulfillment of these ideas, the divine Logos, though in human form."

This was peculiar and adventurous thought, if incomplete. Paul was following a path that would in due course enable him to speak plainly to the Greeks, who knew nothing of Abraham and Isaac, Jacob, Joseph, Moses, or the Tree of Jesse. I often marveled at how the Greek and Hebrew worlds had evolved in such distinct ways, separated only by a short expanse of the earth's surface.

Silas said, "Jesus was a Jew."

"We're all Jews," said Paul.

"More or less," I responded, having neither been raised a Jew nor circumcised.

Timothy said, "I've cast my lot with Israel."

In his most diplomatic fashion Paul said, "God smiles on this affiliation, these affections, I'm quite sure. But he calls us into Greece now. The Way is wide, and it's opening on the western flank. One day the emperor himself will bow down, calling Jesus his Lord and the Christ."

This was speculation, and in the wrong company could lead to death, as it was broadly subversive, a challenge to the authorities. But it pleased me to sit among such friends, my companions on this journey, and to think about the conversation and debate that lay ahead of us. The idea that Gabriel would bring a man from Macedonia to stand by Paul's side continued to puzzle me, of course, especially as the man apparently said nothing. Yet I did my best to restrain my skepticism. With Paul, it never paid to question things too closely.

Chapter Twelve

PAUL

I t's the problem of visions: They glisten, splash their thunder with bolts of light, flash and fade. But is there any truth or reality in them? Why had Luke not seen the angel, the luminous Gabriel, nor the man from Macedonia? Certainly the angel spoke in a distinct voice, so loud I nearly covered my ears.

Luke feigned approval of the diversion from Bithynia to Macedonia. He did so, I think, for the sake of Timothy and Silas, knowing that young men adore visions. They dream dreams, and these dreams possess a near-corporal reality for them. And they live in the afterglow of these visions for months or years. I, on the other hand, was hardly a youth by any standard of measurement, and yet I had no doubt that God continued to seek me out, to send messengers, and to court my attention. I could have but didn't touch Gabriel's face, terrified that my hand would blaze, my fingers burn like twigs on fire.

Too often I felt like a leaf, my body fragile, scarcely a suitable container for the spirit that seethed in me. I was hungry for the real life beyond this fleshly existence, these pale rags hanging on a crate of bones.

I knew I must accept whatever awaited us in Macedonia, and without fear. God had willed me in this direction. And the Almighty provided a ship for us, a three-masted merchant vessel that carried us with our two donkeys to the port of Neapolis, where (after a night's layover on Samothrace) we landed late in the morning. The West had arrived!

An eerie, enchanting music played in my head as we disembarked. "What are you humming, that wonderful tune?" Timothy asked. "It's something I hear," I said.

My companions, however admirable, didn't quite hear or see what

I could hear and see. I seemed to live with one foot on this good earth, the other in that heavenly country beyond our ken, a place discovered more usually in inklings, moments of anticipation, omens, oddments of thought or feeling. And I had nothing like a deep confidence in these encounters or thorough understanding of their name or nature.

If anything, I felt like a beginner. A beginner in the spirit world.

+

Neapolis, this tiny fishing village in Macedonia, surprised me by its expansive and busy harbor, where we inquired after the where-abouts of a synagogue, assuming one could be found in this region. We were directed to an old man selling pieces of fine purple cloth from a stall by the docks.

He looked at me with keen attention.

"Jews?"

"We are Jews," I said.

"My employer is a Godfearer, Lydia. Go to her. She knows all the Jews in Philippi," he said. "Her business is flourishing."

"What is her trade?"

"Purple dye."

I knew this profession well, as my father had a friend who had been a purveyor of this rare and precious color, the hue of kings and emperors. It derived from a species of snail, which fishermen along the coast of Macedonia brought to her shop by the thousands in wooden barrels. As I would learn, Lydia and her workers extracted the dark violet dye from the mucus of a gland, an intricate process that involved piercing the shells with a needle. The mucus flowed with a milky shade, but when combined with vinegar and salt and left to dry in the sun, the purple tint emerged. And the effort paid off handsomely, as this dye sold widely through the empire, more expen-sive than gold or silver. Lydia's purple, many would say, had a peculiar radiance of its own, shading into deep violet-red at times.

The old man sent us to Philippi, several miles north of Neapolis. "You will like her hospitality," he said. "Your mission will interest her."

"Do you trust this man?" asked Silas, whose suspicions were

beginning to wear on me. Did he not trust the Holy Spirit to support our efforts?

"He is probably an angel," I said. "Angels are everywhere."

We set off with our donkeys toward Philippi, arriving in the city as the evening sun cast a hash of shadows on the streets. It was the dinner hour, and we could smell roasted meat coming from doorways. With surprising ease, we found rooms at a public inn near the marketplace, an expense we could hardly afford but our younger companions suggested it, as this sort of accommodation was a novelty. It was often better to accede in small matters, thus keeping our companionable spirit afloat. Travel was burdensome enough without having to contend with abrasive feelings.

Philippi impressed with its grand colonnade, its open sunny spaces, its abundant natural springs. I had rarely seen such a mix of vegetation, with flora fed from the water that rushed belowground, out of sight. My eye was drawn to Mount Pangaeus in the distance, with its skirt of yellow clouds and spiky peak.

"I like it here," Silas said.

This unleashed Timothy, who opened his drawer of knowledge. "The city was named by Philip of Macedon," he said, "the father of Alexander."

Silas never liked displays of information. "Why don't you become a guide?" he asked.

"Shut up," said Timothy.

I didn't like to see the boys squabble, not over petty things. Unity was all. But I held my tongue, and soon this ripple of tension passed. I worried, however, about the likelihood that we could maintain a sense of harmony for long, even though we had done quite well thus far. Pettiness is the plague of groups that travel as one, and discord always begins with small matters, minute cracks in the porcelain bowl that widen into fissures and weaken the larger structure. The object must crumble.

The next day was the Sabbath, and we heard that Lydia and her friends met at a nearby river, the Gangites. It was a well-known gathering, where Lydia led weekly prayers on a flowery bank. We followed the river north from the city and found a dozen women and two men in prayer beside the running stream, one of the women standing with her skirt raised to her knees in a bed of watercress. Without saying anything, we sat among ferns, cross-legged, lifting our palms to heaven.

A black buffalo hulked alone in the shallows, drinking, as Lydia's strong voice carried through the trees. Her spangled dress and copious purple head scarf set her apart.

"You are strangers," she said, coming toward us when she had finished her prayer, "but welcome. Are you Jews or Greeks?"

"I'm Paul of Tarsus, of the tribe of Benjamin, a Pharisee, trained at the school of Gamaliel in Jerusalem. My friends are Jews as well."

Luke didn't accept my sweeping inclusion. "I was a Godfearer, in Antioch. Almost a Jew, but a Greek."

"I'm from Judea," said Silas. "But I follow a special rabbi."

Only Timothy felt no need to explain that he had recently been circumcised and simply offered his name.

"Can you recite from the scroll?" she asked.

I launched into a long passage from Isaiah, by memory. And this opened her eyes: I was not an imposter. She smiled, and her circle drew around me eagerly when I had finished, whereupon I took this as my first opportunity in the West to speak of Jesus.

"We come with news from Jerusalem. My younger companion, Silas, has mentioned our teacher. Rabbi Jesus has arrived in this world, the Christ."

"He is the Christ?"

"A great teacher, with a new truth. And yes, the Christ himself. He is among us now."

"Here?"

"He is always present. Crucified under Pontius Pilate, he died in terrible pain. But he rose again after three days." I paused. "It was a glorious resurrection, and we shall rise in him, all of us, Jew and Greek."

This confused them, I could see. And Lydia gave their hesitation voice: "A man who is crucified can really be the Christ?"

"He is the Christ, here before and after."

This passed over their heads, drawing puzzled expressions, so I took another approach. I had only begun to learn what to say in these circumstances and what to hold back. The release of knowledge in the right order, in appropriate quantities, was key. And I must always find a language appropriate to the moment, one that took on the hues of the local surroundings and lodged where it must, in the listener's heart.

"Jesus received his powers from God, as do I, and you as we," I explained. "Each of you on this riverbank in Philippi is a child of God, empowered by him. Jesus opens the way to God, because that way involves suffering. We all suffer terribly, as part of what it means to live." I looked at each one slowly. "Haven't you all?"

"My husband died—a very young man at the time," Lydia told us. I could feel anguish in the expression of that sentence.

"I'm sorry for you, Lydia," I said. "But what the cross means, for me and for you, is that suffering leads to resurrection. It's not a hole. And the fact of resurrection changes everything."

I could feel the spirit talking, not me, Paul of Tarsus. I became his vessel, and he moved my tongue, figured my words. I was astonished by what I said, the cascade of metaphors, phrases, and images that tumbled from me, effortlessly. "Every suffering soul draws closer to God by praying in the name of Jesus, the beautiful one, who has shown us the face of God by his pain. His pain becomes our pain. His relief is our relief."

Timothy spoke after me, and he was eloquent, talking about the Kingdom of God and how we worked to bring it forward. I had made the right choice to bring him along. And I knew that his beauty enchanted the women, who gazed at him attentively as he talked, with the light of his hair like a halo in the morning sun. The spirit whirled around and through us, and that very day I baptized everyone in the river that flowed into Philippi. I poured the icy water over their heads, saying again and again in a strong voice: *In the Christ, there is neither male nor female, neither slave nor free man, neither Jew nor Greek.* I saw that the idea of "neither male nor female" delighted Lydia, who quite rightly regarded herself as representing a new spirit and time.

That night, at her invitation, we adjourned to her house. It doesn't suffice to call this a "house," as it was an array of buildings on the river, a dozen structures, which included offices, workshops, and storage areas. She invited us to occupy a cottage by the water, putting three slaves at our disposal, and told us over a dinner of many courses about her early days in business after the death of her husband. Through trial and error, she had perfected her process of extracting dye from mollusks, and this was her "very own secret." She had obviously prospered in this commercial venture.

It mattered, she said, that Philippi had a special status, and those who owned property or businesses here could work without taxation by Rome. The city had been rebuilt by Augustus, she explained, calling to mind the Battle of Philippi, where Mark Antony and Augustus (then Octavian) had defeated Brutus and Cassius, the slayers of Julius Caesar. "We have been designated as *ius italicum*," she said. "This imperial exemption has allowed me, as a woman, to create my wealth and live independently, without legal interference."

This was a city of many gods (including the Greek gods), emperors, and Egyptian deities such as Isis and Serapis, Lydia said. Innocent Silas found this shocking. "We are among pagans!" I smiled, telling him to think of this as an advantage. "The spirit is awake here, opening doors." Lydia agreed, saying that she would happily finance our work in Macedonia.

"God will reward you," I said. "There's no time to spend your fortune, not in the years that may never come. But a greater fortune awaits us all: the return of the Lord." I noted that few of us in that room would undergo death in the usual way. "Death itself will die," I said.

That evening we met Isola, a willowy, sad-mouthed girl with prophetic powers who was owned by Lydia's influential neighbor, Abas, who had a seat on the city council. Lydia said Isola had proven invaluable to Abas, as people would pay astonishing sums for the use of her gift of foretelling the future.

The girl lingered, standing beside us as we finished our meal, watching us eat. Perhaps fifteen years old, she had the miles-long stare of the mad, her eyes cindery, sunken below the skin, orbs that looked inward, not outward. Her skin had a mossy cast, while black hair tumbled in clumps to her waist. A sour smell pushed us away from her.

"It's quite uncanny, even unnatural, what she does," said Lydia.

At this, Isola stepped near to me, too close for ease. The odor of sweat in her filthy dress appalled me, and I disliked seeing her stained toenails and mud-splashed ankles. Her battered shins were indecently exposed. Silas sat beside me, and the girl's hand touched his cheek below the eye, drawing a line to his chin with her thumb, and he stared back at her in revulsion.

"You will die by the blade of a dull ax," Isola said to him. "Your skull will crack in the dust. The birds will devour your eyes and pick clean your bones."

This was definitely not the sort of thing one said to Silas, who rose, trembling. "Get away from me! Take her away!"

I grabbed her shoulders with both hands. "Look at me, Isola."

She stared up at me with mindless intensity, her lips apart. I flattened the palm of my right hand on her forehead, pressing into the bone of the skull.

"Kneel, Isola," I said.

She obeyed, still looking up at me.

"You will die by the blade of a dull ax," she said.

"Me as well, then?"

She nodded, and I realized she could see with unusual clarity into the future, and I did not doubt the truth of her observation. Nor did I care.

"You are possessed by demons," I said. "Do you wish to remain like this?"

She wept, shaking her head.

"In which case, Isola, repeat my words: *God, my Lord in heaven, take away these demons.*"

"God, my Lord in heaven, take away these demons."

"Let us repeat. *God, my Lord in heaven, take away these demons.*"

"God, my Lord in heaven, take away these demons."

"Do you believe in God's power to accomplish this?" There was no response. "Answer me, Isola. Your life depends on your response."

"I do, my lord."

"I am not your lord! Isola, there is one God." I paused. "Do you believe in God's power to heal you?"

"I believe in God's power," she said.

That was the phrase. Now she trembled with a violence that disturbed everyone in the room. Her mouth foamed, her arms flapped and beat the air like windmills. Her eyes popped wide, and she screamed with a vile scream, a single searing note. Falling with a slap to the floor, she writhed. And I crouched beside her, lifted my hands in the air, and called loudly to heaven, "Jesus, help your servant, Isola. Jesus, Jesus."

Timothy knelt beside me, lifting his arms, crying, "Jesus, Jesus."

A great storm passed through her body, after which I could see a light coming into her previously dead eyes.

I pointed to Luke. "This is my friend, Luke. Can you tell me how he will die?"

She drew herself up slowly, precariously, then stepped close to Luke, inspecting him. "I know nothing of this," she said. "I see nothing."

Silas said, "What about me?"

"I know nothing."

Lydia began to clap, and the rest of her associates clapped as well.

The next day, however, as Silas and I walked along the cobbled pavement into the market, four guards apprehended us.

"What's this about?"

"Our master, Abas, has charged you with unlawful sorcery."

"I'm no sorcerer!"

"We've done nothing!" Silas shouted.

But they paid no attention to our protests, and we were brought forcefully before Linus, the local magistrate in Philippi. Abas stood there, arms folded across his chest. Then he pointed to me.

"Are you Paul?"

"I am."

The magistrate looked bored, slumped in a chair behind a table in his gray toga. His beard was caught up in black snarls. He asked me if I practiced sorcery or dared to break laws established by Rome.

"I heal in the name of Jesus. I do nothing except by God's grace."

"And which god do we speak of?"

"Jehovah."

"You're a Jew?" Linus asked.

"A Jew and a Roman citizen." I paused. "I would, of course, never do anything against Roman laws. I respect the temporal authorities."

The word "temporal" gave him pause. "Why have you come to Philippi?"

"A very good question, sir," I said. "To proclaim the kingdom, God's unfolding kingdom. I speak in the name of Rabbi Jesus."

"So you're an agent of a foreign power, and a Jew."

"Not an earthly power, sir, a heavenly one. Rabbi Jesus was the embodiment of God."

"I have no idea what you're saying."

"Until the heart softens, knowledge fails. The truth cannot be observed from without."

This seemed only to inflame the magistrate.

"Honestly, Paul. Do you wish to go to jail? You and your friend?"

"You can't take away my freedom," I said.

This alarmed Silas, who began to protest that I hadn't fully understood the question. He explained that we had done nothing wrong, although this had no effect on the magistrate, whose guards seized us, tied our wrists behind our backs with hemp, and took us to a jail on the via Egnatia, several miles north of the city.

"I doubt there is much criminal activity in Philippi," I said to Silas. "This will provide amusement."

I had scarcely released the words when Roman guards dragged us into a rocky yard behind the jail. They stripped us both, then tied us to a post, whereupon they flogged us with braided whips, drawing fat welts on our shoulders and the backs of our legs.

Silas wailed inconsolably, and I wished I could help to ease his pain. But there was nothing for it.

The jailor, whose name I later learned was Matthius, brought us cups of water and bits of bread, with salted fish.

"You must eat," I said to Silas, who sobbed uncontrollably. Before this I had not quite realized the fragility of my young companion. His sobbing continued into dusk, and it didn't stop until darkness cloaked us.

I found the night air quite soothing in a strange way, as it had been miserably hot throughout the day, and the slight chill in the wind touched our wounds like a soft invisible hand and, to a small degree, lessened the pain. I asked Silas to pray with me. This was impossible for him, but at least he listened and, almost imperceptibly, moved his lips: *Dear God, Almighty father, help us in our distress. Help us, Jesus, aid us. Our defeat is your victory. Thy will be done, father.*

Matthius sat on a block of wood beside us, watching with interest. He had probably not seen many prisoners pray to God. The name of Jesus had certainly never been invoked in this setting. In fact, I suspected that few in Macedonia or Greece had yet heard the name of Jesus, my Lord, the Christ.

"What is your name, sir?" I asked.

He told me, and I thanked him for bringing us the water and food, which I was able to eat. Silas, beside me, slumped in his chains, unable to speak. He had resisted those who beat him, and this proved wrongheaded. Long ago I had learned to allow an assailant to complete his work, having become aware that anguish is pain intensified by the struggle to resist it.

"Do you want to hear about Rabbi Jesus, our wonderful Lord?"

He nodded vaguely, though I could detect no enthusiasm. In the boredom of his life, he could not refuse to hear news of any kind. I explained to him that we must all die soon, and yet there was one God in whom we could trust. When I told him about what happened to me on my way to Damascus, he seemed to awaken. I explained to him that Jesus was an aspect of God, and that he was alive, in spite of being crucified at Golgotha. I also told him that I had been commissioned by God himself to bring this news to the people of Macedonia.

"Do you wish to pray with me, Matthius?"

He didn't and made that clear. But he thanked me for what I told him, and said his wife might like to know about this. They had recently lost a child to fever, and she had not been well. "She weeps in her sleep and cries out," he said. "I'm unable to help her."

"What is her name?"

"Endora," he said.

I prayed loudly: "Dear God in heaven, Jesus, son of God, please comfort Endora in her distress. Please do this, Lord. In the name of Jesus."

Matthius explained that he would sit with us through the night, as it was his duty. His superiors had apparently been worried about our escaping. We must not escape, he said, or he would fall into jeopardy with the courts. This was, he said, "a dangerous time," and the Romans had become concerned with foreign visitors, especially those who might be subversives and wished to undermine imperial authority.

"We have no wish to do this," I said. "I'm a Roman citizen."

As night darkened the room, Matthius lit three torches on the wall. I don't know how much time passed, but I fell asleep late, possibly after midnight. I startled awake, however, sensing what felt like a minor tremor in the distance. At first, I thought it was something in my legs, not the earth itself, that moved, having experienced muscular tremors before. I noticed that poor Silas had his eyes open.

"How do you feel?" I asked.

He didn't reply.

"You should try to drink some of that water."

But the water, in a clay jug, slid off the little table beside us, spilling into the dirt. Then the walls themselves began to vibrate and crack, with stones collapsing upon stones. One roof beam cracked in the middle, and the plaster of lime fell from the ceiling. Matthius leaped to his feet.

"Oh God, liberate us!" I cried. "Tear down these walls!"

So the ground juddered, and the jail itself spun in a wild cyclone, with a high-pitched whine. More of the roof fell onto the floor, and beams split.

"Fall to your knees, Matthius! Ask God to help us!"

Matthius obeyed and dropped to the ground, his knees tucked into his stomach, his arms splayed in the dirt as stones dislodged from the walls, one of them striking Matthius in the leg, though he didn't move. Within moments, the whole roof now tumbled in upon itself.

"I'm free!" Silas said. "Free!"

His chains, like mine, had released.

The earthquake went on for a few minutes, then stopped, as dust hung in the air, and the room held its breath.

We lay still, none of us quite sure what to do next.

Feeling I must act, I bathed the wounds of Silas with cold water from a bucket, and he did the same for me. I was surprised to see that,

almost miraculously, his wounds healed. Mine, too, receded. We
stepped back into our clothing, which had been piled in one corner.

Now I bent beside Matthius, who wept inconsolably, putting a
hand on his shoulder.

"If you run away," he said, "they will abuse me. You don't know
what they are like. I have three living children."

"We aren't going anywhere," I said.

"Why are you so kind to me?"

"I love you, Matthius, as one of God's own children," I said. "Do
you wish to speak to Jesus?"

"Yes," he said.

We prayed, the three of us together, and I baptized Matthius
with the remaining water in the bucket.

"You're a new man," I said. "God is your shield now! Fear nothing."

Matthius accepted this, inviting us to his house, some minutes
from the jail, and we told Endora about Jesus, too. Her husband's
enthusiasm moved her, and when I asked if she wished to be baptized, she knelt and wept, and I poured water over her head. And
soon their slaves joined us, and everyone knelt with me and held
hands as I prayed.

Silas said, "Our Lord likes the unexpected."

It was touching to see him gathering the world into phrases he
could accept, attempting to make sense of unlikely circumstances.
But I feared for him. Reality never breaks in expected ways, and it
can't be described easily. The scaffolding of language often collapses
beneath us, leaving only the dust of experience.

We slept in Matthius's house that night, and at sunrise walked
into the town, going straight into the courts again, where Linus sat
alone at his desk. He looked up and was startled to see me. When
I told him what had happened, he stood in amazement and said, "I
must ask you to leave Philippi at once."

We returned to Lydia's house, where Luke and Timothy wrapped
us in their arms. They loved our stories, even though Silas still complained about the lashes. After a night of rejoicing, we left the next
morning. I promised Lydia that I would send regular dispatches from
my travels and would return when I could to assist and encourage her
gatherings.

Only a week later, on the way to Thessalonica, I paused for a day to write at length to Lydia and her companions, missing them sorely. "My dear friends, sisters and brothers in Jesus," I wrote. "Your many kindnesses will remain with me, and I know I speak for Timothy, Luke, and Silas as well as myself. You are the first fruits in this country. That is precious to me. I would ask you to remain as close to God as possible, speaking to him through his son, Jesus the Christ. All I ask of you is to practice what through God you have received as wisdom. Keep in mind only whatever seems true and worthy, just and pure. Stay close to what is attractive, beautiful, high-toned, and excellent. If you do these things, always in the name of Jesus the Christ, without losing sight of God, peace will flood your hearts, and you will stand in the river of love."

We traveled along the via Egnatia for some three days, stopping briefly in the cities of Amphipolis and Apollonia, arriving in Thessalonica at midday on the most brilliant of summer days. The city perched on a hill overlooking the indigo waters below, its houses white as dice tumbling downhill to the pebble-strewn beach. Mountains were heaped behind it, and we could see the white crown of Olympus in the distance.

The synagogue, our first destination, lay on the street called Patros, close to the harbor, in a tight enclosure with its shutters drawn, eager to remain unmolested by pagan curiosity. I found one of the elders rocking in prayer, draped in his shawl, and sat quietly beside him until he had finished. At the appropriate moment, I told him about our mission, identifying myself as a faithful Jew who brought word of a great new rabbi.

"Jason will help," the old man told me.

Indeed, Jason proved more than helpful, this strong young man with a business that included tanning and exporting hides. He welcomed us with enthusiasm, embracing me as if we were old friends when I told him about my family's commercial interest in tents, and how I had shipped hides from Jerusalem in my early days. He was an intelligent fellow and questioned me late into the night, having invited us to remain as long as we liked at his house. Within days, he accepted that the Way of Jesus made sense, and I baptized him, using water from a swift stream that flowed behind his house into the bay.

I soon realized we could establish an important outpost here, in Thessalonica, as the synagogue teemed with Godfearers, many of them well-trained in Greek philosophy as well as Jewish scriptures: a perfect combination. I began to see that the teachings of Jesus married well with those of Plato. And could actually picture God as the One described as a spirit anticipated by Plato in his *Phaedrus*.

We soon met Aristarchus, Jason's best friend, a gentle young soul with cobalt eyes and strong limbs who worked in the leather trade as well. He and I had long conversations after many First Day gatherings. He seemed to follow me wherever I went in Thessalonica, eager to hear my reflections. I liked him, with his soft but persistent manner, his innocent but intelligent questions. One day he asked me to baptize him, and I felt a surge of joy in bringing him more closely into our circle. Luke, too, admired him a great deal, and shared with him a collection of sayings by Jesus, which Aristarchus committed to memory. I often thought of him as almost the ideal new member of the Way, with his sincerity and depth of feeling. Soon I joined him and Jason at their workshop, which enabled me to draw on my skills. Charity was fine, I told my companions, but one must earn the respect of those in any community by working *with* them, side by side. Even if we had plenty of funds, this labor was necessary. It established ties, enlarging the web of community. The Way of Jesus would only prosper in this context.

Thessalonica enchanted us, with its open paved streets and a marble-tiled forum that had become the administrative center of the city. During the day it overflowed with carts and stalls, with commercial travelers from distant parts. Everything was bought and sold here, as in Tarsus or Antioch. There was a large stadium in the eastern quarter, with seating for some four hundred, and one could attend games there or, on occasion, see a play. We went to the synagogue on the Sabbath, and I would read to them from the scriptures at their request, but I took every opportunity to speak about Jesus. For the most part, they accepted my teaching, and we met with interested parties at Jason's house each week on the First Day, singing hymns and sharing the sacred meal.

My skills in tent-making proved useful again, as one of the men in Jason's gathering had a small factory where he produced tents and canopies. The speed of my work surprised them, and I found myself spending long hours at my table. Silas and Timothy joined me on occasion, when they weren't in the shop with Jason and Aristarchus, and we made a good team.

The Thessalonians folded us into the life of their city.

But, as one could have foreseen, a number of the Jews resented the successes of Jason's gathering, which grew week by week, and they hardened their hearts against the Christ and, as his representative, me. I tried to meet with them, and one of them (a man named Elon) acceded, and we had long and serious conversations. He, like the others, resisted all changes to what was considered the core of Jewish practice. I reminded him that Jesus was a Jew, and nothing he said or did obliterated that fact.

"Only God matters," Elon said.

"And how do you know anything about God?"

"We know him by his actions."

I pressed here. "What might those actions be?"

"The creation of the world!"

"Ah, yes. But that was not a single event in the past," I said. "Creation is an active and continuous process."

This puzzled, even annoyed him.

"The world dawns every day," I said, "and it's always new. The creation overwhelms us with its beauty, its changes. Such beautiful changes."

"You're talking nonsense," he said. "God gave us the Law."

"God is mysterious," I said. "We can't know much about him, not in this life. Even the Law remains a mystery. But he has chosen to reveal himself through Jesus, who is the point of intersection between the infinite God of this universe and mere human beings. We can only know of God what Jesus has shown us."

My arguments failed to impress him, that much I could see. And the next day, I heard from a friend at the shop that a number of Jews planned to apprehend us, charging us with treason and blasphemy. Blasphemy had no meaning here, not among the Romans, but the ears of the imperial authorities twitched when they heard any mention of treason, and they reached for their swords. Traitors to the empire would be dealt with harshly. I knew very well the potential outcome of this charge and rushed home to my friends, insisting they pack at once. Thessalonica could no longer be imagined as a haven, as we had hoped.

Why did God never let us rest?

We left the city even before Jason arrived home for the evening, when—so I heard a few weeks later—he encountered an irate group of Jews, who seized him instead of us, bringing him before a magistrate that evening.

I certainly did not wish, after our experience in Philippi, to subject Timothy and Silas, or Luke, to flogging and imprisonment.

But God drew us forward, opening a way in the thick underbrush of antipathy.

I hoped we would have less trouble with the noble Bereans.

Chapter Thirteen

LUKE

Although Timothy worshipped Paul, he was also wary of his mentor at times, as the apostle could be intrusive, paying too much attention to the boy's moods. He loved Timothy, of course; this affection shone in his face whenever the young man entered the room. In his presence, Paul grew alert, even giddy at times, laughing at the slightest remark, finding cleverness and spiritual depth in what struck me as mundane remarks. I knew enough not to say anything about this, as Paul would never understand. He would regard me as excessively critical. In fact, he often said that my "logical and interrogative" manner undermined him and the movement of his thought: "I leap over the stream. There is no need to wade through it."

He said I failed to appreciate Timothy, which was untrue.

Timothy was, now and then, something of a wit, and I admired that. But his thoughts about the Kingdom of God rarely surprised or interested anyone. At his best, he could parrot Paul's ideas with reasonable clarity, and this was enough to make him attractive as a speaker. He assumed even Paul's minor gestures, as when he would shake a finger at someone or fall into thoughtful silences in the middle of a sentence. He even began to stutter like Paul, which was odd. He had not stuttered when we first met him.

Silas felt pushed to one side, and he complained to me about his treatment, recalling that he had gone to jail with Paul in Philippi, had suffered a flogging with him. He had been a dedicated soldier in the Lord's army. But Paul largely ignored him. I suspect that he disliked the crudeness that at times made Silas an embarrassing companion. For instance, in many Roman-style houses the toilet occupied a corner in the kitchen, and Silas would not uncommonly choose to evacuate himself in front of company, even while a number of us assisted the slaves in the preparation of a meal. He pulled astonishing faces and grunted, and he had unimaginable odors that prompted me, a physician, to wonder about his health.

Timothy called him "Shitting Silas," much to the amusement of the slaves, but I refused to join this merry chorus, worried that Silas might, at any moment, abandon us. It upset me to think of the young fellow being ridiculed, and that Paul played into this derision by failing to acknowledge his dedication, his steadfast trust in God's love.

It also worried me that Timothy might one day object to Paul's fawning. Barnabas had hinted darkly to me that Paul, on their visit to Cyprus, had lavished unwanted attentions on John Mark. "He frightened the boy away," Barnabas had said. The same could happen here.

It might have been wiser for Paul to marry, thus weakening his need for contact of a kind that brought discomfort to others. It might also have dampened his occasional rages about fornication.

The Pillars discouraged fornication among all who followed the Way of Jesus, and we told those who wished to join our movement that they must refrain from sexual relations outside of the bounds prescribed by the rabbis and Jewish tradition. Mosaic Law had much to say about these matters. Not myself having been trained in Jewish legal traditions, I refrained from comment. The Jews had so many rules and prohibitions!

Paul himself never tired of explaining to me their intricate and eccentric laws, especially those governing sexual behavior, as formulated by centuries of Jewish sages. It was, he said, indecent under Mosaic Law for a man to have anal intercourse with another man, as this controverted the law against wasting one's seed. Masturbation was, likewise, a waste of this precious substance, since it clearly had nothing to do with procreation. Within marriage, according to Jewish tradition, any sexual act was permitted, but there had been commentators on the Torah who warned against "rooster-like activity" on the part of the male. The prohibition against Jews having sex with gentiles continued among Jews and, to a degree, had currency in Jerusalem among followers of the Way. But surely the New Covenant allowed for the marriage of Jew and gentile: This happened in any case, and it would have been self-destructive for the Way to ban the practice. Paul prayed for guidance on this subject, as he frequently advised young couples. (It surprised me how many came to him for counsel, given his celibate life.) He believed passionately that inter-marriage caused no offense to God. "Remember that in the Christ there is neither Jew nor Greek," he would say.

Yet he often taught it was "better to marry than to burn," which—as Timothy noted—was "not a great recommendation for marriage."

In Paul's way of thinking, it made no sense to marry, since the purpose of marriage was to fulfill a commandment from God: *Be fruitful, and multiply.* This multiplication had already been accomplished, in his view. He brought to mind what Gamaliel had taught the young men in his school about sexuality, making the traditional distinction between the *yetzer ha-tov* and the *yetzer hara*: the impulse to good versus the impulse to evil. But he always made a further point that these represented two sides of the same coin, and that one must have both sides for the coin to exist. "I don't believe we should think of good and bad in simplistic ways," Paul said. "Every bright flower has its roots in dark soil," he said, quoting Ion of Chios.

Paul could be wonderfully attuned to the man or woman who stood before him, asking questions, patiently seeking the truth. On the other hand, he occasionally showed very little sense of audience, and often mistook silence for assent. I don't, for instance, believe the Thessalonians had warmed to us, not to the extent that Paul imagined. I always felt their skepticism, and it worried me that Paul was blind to this.

His anger at our expulsion from that city didn't surprise me, but I tried to reassure him that Thessalonica was only a stopping point. We had planned to take the Good News into the wider western regions, well beyond the borders of Macedonia. And Athens remained a goal of sorts: Paul loved Plato and had studied the *Dialogues* as a very young man. His earliest tutor in Tarsus had been a scholar of Greek literature, and while in Jerusalem he had continued his studies in Attic philosophy. Gamaliel saw that Paul had a synthetic mind and knew this gift could prove useful one day. He never discouraged his pupil's love of Attic writing. The Greek thought world and the Hebrew thought world had been profoundly different, conceived and birthed in unique cultural circumstances. But the Way of Jesus, as

Paul argued, must draw together these separate strands. He noted that Homer and the Hebrew scriptures arose quite independently: "But there is one God who inspires the poets, Jew and Greek alike."

Since our arrival in Macedonia, Paul's talks and thinking had grown more passionate, speculative, and perhaps even wild. As he refined his ideas about the meaning of Jesus as the Christ, his language deepened in complexity. On one of our last evenings in Thessalonica, he addressed a gathering of perhaps two or three dozen followers in Jason's garden while peacocks with their shimmering blue necks and combs spread their fans among the lemon trees. He stood on a small flat stone with the setting sun at his back, wearing a colorful tunic, with Timothy and Silas on either side.

I watched in amazement as he leaped from metaphor to metaphor. This was not the kind of discourse I usually preferred, but it delighted me that evening. It was not how physicians were trained to think. We moved slowly and carefully, amassing evidence, making our deductions. But Paul didn't operate in this manner. His energies poured out freely, touched his listeners in unexpected ways, and the world around them blazed with new meaning.

And sometimes he angered those who heard him.

One young rabbi in Thessalonica had complained to me that Paul made things worse for everyone. "The Romans don't like us," he said, and by "us" he referred to the Jews. This expansive and ever-expanding empire could only sustain itself by the use of brutality, and he argued that one day soon the ax would fall, and Jewish heads would topple into the dirt. "I have no hopes for the survival of the Temple," he said, hinting that all of Jerusalem would burn one day, and perhaps soon.

The retreat from Thessalonica played in my head like a nettlesome dream. I recalled the night that Paul and I sat in the garden when Aristarchus rushed toward us. "They know what happened in Philippi," he said, "and they accuse you of treason. The penalty is death." He tried to control himself. "If you're here in an hour, they will seize you both, and we will never see you again."

"We must leave at once," I said.

Paul glared at me, and I knew he would try to remain in place.

To make my point again, I rose to my full height, towering above

Paul. "I will get my things, and leave. You may choose to stay if you like."

"But Timothy—"

"I will tell him you've gone," said Aristarchus.

"And where exactly will I have gone?"

"Berea," I said.

"I don't want to go to Berea," Paul said.

"Go wherever you will," said Aristarchus, "but stay out of Thessalonica. The Bereans will welcome you. I feel sure of this."

Paul was angry, though reality had begun to freshen his wits. "I shall go, but tell everyone my absence is temporary. When things settle . . ."

It was unfortunate that Timothy and Silas had traveled that week to Salumi, a nearby village, where a small gathering of the Way had established an outpost. We had no choice but to leave without them, asking Aristarchus to tell them we had gone to Berea. And to warn them to get away quickly.

We hurried off, as I insisted, taking only one of our two donkeys, and left by an unobtrusive road, heading southwest, passing through an array of villages, entering a broad plain where only sheep and goats grazed, with a few shepherds to look after them. We slept that night perhaps ten miles from Thessalonica in a tiny hut by a stream, where we filled our skins with fresh water after bathing in the morning.

Above us, hawks hung steady in a high wind, which augured a storm.

"Trouble ahead," said Paul, seeing the blood-bright clouds.

"Trouble behind as well."

It was miraculous that Paul had not died with Silas beside him in the Philippian jail. An earthquake shook the entire city and damaged the prison. The roof collapsed and the guard had been beside himself, sure that the Roman authorities would hold him responsible for whatever happened. He had been a simple man, without sides, and he took to Paul and, it seemed, Silas as well. He begged them not to flee, and Paul, as he would, assured him that he would speak to the magistrate before leaving Philippi. This jailor must not suffer on his account, Paul told him.

Paul told this story frequently, shifting details. In some versions they had been cast into a crowded jail, and he had preached the Good News to a substantial crowd, all of whom fell to their knees and wept, asking for the mercy of God. In another version, he and Silas had been alone with their jailor, whom Paul baptized with water from a jug. Paul had surely *not* been as badly beaten as he imagined, as I could tell from the wounds on his back. I applied my salve, and the cuts healed quickly. Silas had, for whatever reason, been more severely treated, and the inflamed skin of his back had taken two or three weeks to calm. His scars would, as I knew but didn't tell him, never dissolve.

I worried that his wounds could flare up repeatedly, as this could happen, especially among travelers who moved about the countryside as we did. We slept on hay quite often. Movement and good health lived in conflict, and we all suffered an array of skin inflammations, joint pains, muscle weaknesses, and agues. Rest became important, even critical, but difficult of access.

And Paul did not rest. Quite the opposite. He leaped from chair to chair, preferred standing to sitting, sleeping only a few hours, rising early to walk into the world on his own. He rushed to meetings, summoned the company of others, and took the lead in most conversations. He moved uphill and down with the same extraordinary speed, exhausting the rest of us, although Timothy proved a fair match for him.

"Timothy is my son," Paul said as we left for Berea without him.

"Well, he is not actually your son," I said.

"Parentage is not only physical," he said.

I would not have this. "Silas would feel slighted."

"Silas *is* slighted. We should never have brought him. He does nothing to advance the Kingdom of God."

"Not true!"

"Oh, please, dear Luke. You must not try to defend the boy."

"He suffered beside you in Philippi."

"I wiped the tears from his eyes."

"You are impossible."

He liked this description and smiled. Impossible Paul!

"Timothy will join us soon," Paul said, comforting himself.

"And Silas," I added.

We climbed a small hill before noon, with summer assuming its full-throated cry. Bees lumbered from flower to flower, giving the air a loud buzz, and gnats pulled their little nets around our heads. The sun tore a hole in the sky, heating the grass and the stones where we sat for a few moments to eat crusts of bread with the raisins, nuts, and figs that Paul had brought from Thessalonica: a gift from Aristarchus. We watered our donkey as well, letting him feed by rooting in the weeds.

"There is famine in Palestine, in Judea," Paul said, drawing this thought from nothing that had been part of our recent conversation. Had he heard fresh news of this problem, perhaps in a dream?

"It is sad," I said. I could not imagine why, out of nowhere, this problem in Judea began to interest Paul.

"It's tragic. We must help them."

"We're in Macedonia now. What can we do?"

"Those in our circle—our people—are starving, so we must find money to pay for their supplies. Jesus fed the poor. You have heard about feeding the multitude?"

"It happened soon after the death of the Baptizer."

I knew this story well and had been writing about it. It happened near Bethsaida. Jesus had been praying in silence, alone in the hills, as was his custom. When he came down, he met a throng of well-wishers who asked him to heal their sick, to make the blind see again, and to cast out demons. Andrew told him that the people lacked food, and that the nearest place to get supplies was miles away.

"What do we have?" Jesus asked.

"Only five loaves of bread and two fish."

Jesus looked at the crowd, which seemed to grow before his eyes. He directed Andrew and the other disciples to gather the crowd into groups of fifty.

"Feed them all," said Jesus.

Andrew shook his head. "We have only these few loaves and a little fish."

"It will satisfy."

So they walked among the people, and everyone had more than enough to eat.

"It was God's will in the world," said Paul, whose mind often landed on this tale. "God's wish to feed the people. It's the first and last miracle. And it's how we know what God wants for us. He supplies every need. This is love multiplied beyond counting."

Paul continued to dwell on the problem of the famine in Jerusalem, in Judea, and wondered how we could help.

In Berea, after a few days, we gathered in a synagogue with a handful of faithful Jews, who listened as Paul read from the scriptures. He focused on the passage where Moses proclaimed: *The Lord your God will raise up for you a prophet like me in your midst, from your own brethren.* "The prophet has already come," he said, "and he's with us now, although they killed him. He is not dead, I assure you. We have talked, face-to-face. Through him, God has spoken."

Aharon, the rabbi, sat upright when he heard this. He recognized a brother in Paul, a man suffused with God's energy and grace. Instead of hostility, we encountered openness of mind in Berea.

"You will become the seat of our Lord in Macedonia," said Paul to the rabbi. "The light of God will shine from this small hill."

Over the next week we sat with the leaders of his congregation and studied the scriptures with them, and everyone admired Paul's knowledge. He could refer easily to passages that most didn't know existed. His head teemed with verbatim quotations, in Hebrew as well as Greek. His reflections startled and informed at once.

One evening in the synagogue, as we sat in a circle, Timothy and Silas appeared at the edge of our group, as Paul had confidently predicted. He nodded toward them, offering the slightest of smiles as he kept talking. When he had finished, he introduced "our dear friends, angels of the Lord."

Over a late dinner in the garden of Aharon's house, where we stayed, Paul nearly shimmered with the joy of this reunion. He even put a hand on Silas's neck and kissed him on the forehead, provoking a surprised look from him. But Timothy brought unfortunate news. "Those fools in Thessalonica will arrive soon, and they will murder us. They have not been appeased."

"They know we're here?"

Timothy nodded, while Silas dipped his head. I could sense guilt there, its pervasive odor like damp in an old house.

Aharon said, "You must go at once. I will deal with them."

"Silas and I know these men," Timothy explained. "We can talk to them. Talk sense into them."

Paul liked Timothy's bravura. They wanted to murder Paul, as so many did, but this plot might distract them. He trusted that Timothy, who had no wish to die, knew what he was doing. "Go back to Thessalonica with them, if you think that will work," he said. "There is no end of need for the mercy of God. Explain to the Way there that Jesus needs their help. They must give you money for Jerusalem, a donation for our collection, a gift for the poor who are starving there. There is so much wealth in that city. As followers of Jesus, we must help each other." And Aharon agreed to go with them.

"This is a good plan," said Paul. "But first, I must baptize you in the name of the Christ. Do you want this?"

"I do."

Paul asked a slave to bring a cask of water, inviting Aharon to kneel in his own garden. "I baptize you, Aharon, another child of God," he said. "Remember that in Jesus there is neither male nor female, neither slave nor free man, neither Jew nor Greek."

A silence followed that was happily filled by a nightingale in a lemon tree behind the house. "This is the teaching of Jesus, and you need only remember and repeat it. Tell the world!"

"I will tell everyone," said Aharon.

"Praise to God," said Timothy, on his knees beside Aharon.

Silas joined them, as did Paul, who fell to his knees in concert with the others and raised his arms to heaven and began to sing. At last, I joined them, although they sang a song I didn't know.

It was memorable, the sight of this visionary company, everyone praising the Lord and singing, though I myself felt out of joint.

✝

The next day, I asked Paul why he would let Silas and Timothy return to Thessalonica, but he would not give me a satisfactory answer.

"God has a plan," he said. "Timothy will not only survive, he will prosper. This is the promise of heaven." He did not mention Silas.

The next day Paul and I left, with a guide supplied by Aharon.

He led us to a coastal village where, without difficulty, we joined a small ship traveling to Crete with a layover in Athens. "Athens is the center of the intelligent world," said Paul, in a buoyant mood. He shook the dust from his heels again and again, rarely looking back. But I was less easy about the people we abandoned to uncertain fates in our wake. The Roman authorities, now controlling Macedonia and much of the world we traveled, feared and despised what they considered treason. They could tolerate Jews as long as this restless fringe of fanatics kept to their own habits, lived within their communities, and didn't interfere with the life of the larger body politic. The Way of Jesus was another matter, less easy to understand and potentially a threat, as they proclaimed the kingship of their leader.

I had explained to wary Godfearers that the Way of Jesus wished only for *heavenly* kingship. We posed no threat to the local authorities and certainly the emperor should never worry about our movement. Disloyalty to the imperial powers never figured in our discussions; in fact, we often cited a famous line of our Lord: "Give to Caesar what belongs to Caesar."

Caesar could hardly disapprove of that sentiment!

But we occupied a highly wrought, aggressive, and intensely political world. The Pax Romana persisted, with the imperial "peace" guaranteed by the use of selective brutality. It would never be simple to follow the Way of Jesus without offending someone, and I worried about what might happen now. I lacked Paul's massive faith in the future, though I prayed to God to sustain me despite my disbelief, my cowardice and befuddlement.

The two-day journey by ship to Athens absorbed me. We often sailed close to the shoreline, smelling the sweet grasses, the unruly banks of thyme and purslane. Sheep bleated and dogs barked in invisible notches above the hills, and in the distance I got a good view of Mount Olympus as we passed the coast of Thessaly. Without much wind, we lay by for a whole afternoon outside the port of Athens, about half a day's journey from the city. The sea there was a green slick, with a few dead fish floating belly-up, pecked by gulls and other seabirds. The lungs of jellyfish lay open, festering.

"I don't know if this is a good sign or a bad sign," said Paul.

"Our lack of motion or the dead fish?"

"I hoped for better."

That evening, just before sunset, the winds picked up, the air turned cooler, and we sailed into the ancient port.

I knew a smattering of Greek history, and it was not difficult to imagine the Persian Wars, when Darius invaded Thrace and Macedonia, then tried to overwhelm Athens, without luck. The intellectual vigor characteristic of Athens was accompanied by military prowess, and they defeated the Persians roundly at the Battle of Marathon. A great age began, when playwrights and poets flourished. Soon Plato established the Academy, where he taught for many decades, wandering with the young amid the olive groves or sitting in the shade. These scholars devoted their lives to self-perfection, imagining a virtuous world—which of course meant trying to isolate the virtues deserving of replication.

"Jesus brought the ideals of Athens to Judaism," Paul said. "As a child, he would have encountered merchants from Greece, many of them on their way to the East."

Ideas from Persia or even the Kush may well have arrived by travelers heading from east to west, I suggested, and this excited Paul, who had met such men in Jerusalem as a young man as well as during his time with Musa in the desert.

After docking, we made our way toward the looming Acropolis, which rose above the plain, this dazzling white outcrop, which was composed of several structures that, according to Paul, "mirrored the perfection of the soul."

It was a sight we had longed to see, and it satisfied our longings.

The next day, we climbed to the Pantheon and the Erechtheion, where votaries of Athena gathered. "God has brought us here to reveal his entrance into the world, his interruption of history," Paul said, to nobody in particular. "The name of Jesus will one day live on every tongue in Athens." His plan was not merely to speak in the marketplace but to engage the wisest of Athenians. He said that philosophical thought itself emanated from this city, and so every remark had weight here. One could not proceed lightly with an argument but needed ballast, the weight of authority, and sound logic, all of this lifted by the Holy Spirit. I could see that being here had forced his concentration.

On the third day in Athens we visited the synagogue, a small limestone house at the end of a white-dust road in the Jewish quarter, although it took a while to summon any Jews, who were sparse on the ground. An elderly man led us to Enoch, a revered rabbi about whom Paul, as usual, seemed to have prior knowledge. In a low rumble, Enoch explained to us that pagans overwhelmed the city, as ever. "They imagine gods are everywhere, and yet they trust nobody. Zeus or Hera, Athena, Poseidon—one hears the names, but they carry no meaning. Philosophy reigns here, but this is not what Plato meant. They are Stoics and believe the world cannot be trusted."

"It cannot," said Paul.

The rabbi ignored him. "They spend much of their time reminding each other that time is short, that life is a flicker that fades in a moment."

"And this is true."

"But they see virtue as patience, forbearance, allowing the rational mind to adjust to circumstances."

Paul considered this proposition. "Life," he said, "is propositions about life."

Enoch leaned toward him, scratching his long, grizzled beard. I doubt he had encountered anyone quite like Paul thus far in his long life.

"There are unwholesome propositions," said Enoch. "But we, in our small circle, know the true God. We have the Law of Moses."

"No longer," said Paul.

This worried the rabbi, who asked Paul to elaborate. And Paul, as one might expect, told him that a New Covenant had replaced what God handed to Moses. "Not supplanted, not exactly," said Paul, "but Rabbi Jesus has become the new Moses."

Enoch was a simple man, with natural wisdom, as I could see. There was a sweetness about him that appealed to us both, and Paul did astonishing work now, convincing this rabbi that Jesus was the Christ whom everyone had long expected. It is never easy to change an old mind.

When the Sabbath arrived, Enoch invited Paul to read from the scrolls and talk about Jesus, which he did with renewed energy, as if discovering his ideas in the process. This was, I realized, the secret

of Paul, that he could wipe his mind clean of past expressions, beginning anew each time he spoke in public to discover his thoughts, to
frame them again. And so every time he stood before an audience of
any size he appeared to have only just found his footing in the expressions he put forward.

I watched closely as he tested his verbal skills in the marketplace
in Athens, where on any given day one could find wealthy young men
who flocked here from distant parts to talk about ideas, the purpose
of life, the nature of the gods, and the fate of this world. The names of
Crates, the great Theban, of Epicurus, and of Zeno, the philosopher
from Cyprus, circulated. Zeno had walked in the colonnade here,
teaching his disciples that virtue creates peace in the soul, and that to
live in accordance with nature was the most effective approach to life.
He had learned from his teacher Polemon, accepting the notion that
one could never know the purpose of the gods but had nevertheless to
protect oneself against their whims and depredations.

It excited Paul to move among these brisk thoughtful people, and
he engaged one after another, telling them about Jesus the Christ.
Their skepticism was boundless, however, and one of them mocked
Paul, repeating what he said in an irritating voice. But Paul waved a
hand to dismiss him: "The pigeon squawks! Away, bird!"

An uncomfortable space opened between how Paul viewed his
experiences with others and what I actually saw, and it worried me
that he could be less than candid with himself about what occurred,
even self-deceiving. But I had no inclination to make this point
because it would only enrage him, and I didn't imagine it would
change anything.

We spent many of our Athenian days in the public areas, though
it was hot and humid, unbearably so, with even the locusts gasping in
the fields of long grass at the edges of the city. We paused for a drink
by a well one afternoon, sitting in the shade of a broad plane tree.
Overwhelmed by the heat, Paul trembled as we drank from a cup that
a man passed to us. I thought he would swoon.

"Are you all right, Paul?"

"I wish Timothy could be here," he said, as if Timothy might protect him from the carping of these young philosophers and the heat
of the sun.

We stayed in a tiny house adjacent to the synagogue, once a stone barn, with a packed-dirt floor and no windows. Good Enoch had given us this place to sleep, however cramped and unappealing. It had a flat roof, which we climbed up to in the early evening to drink wine and look at the chalk-white glimmer of the Parthenon perched on its promontory like a prehistoric bird. The sea beyond, at sunset, upheld a thin yellow band of clouds, and the sun plunged into the horizon, turning the whole bay into a bath of blood-bright vermillion.

One morning three young men appeared at our house, a make-shift delegation, inviting Paul to the Areopagus, which the Romans called Mars Hill. It was a legendary outcrop where public trials occurred in ancient times, and where debates could be heard any day of the week. One could easily imagine Socrates in his toga here, the squat and craggy philosopher defending his unconventional approach to the instruction of Athenian youth. This moment of ancient history—it could not have lasted many years—continued to fascinate Paul, who often referred to Plato (a pupil of Socrates) as "the first follower of Jesus," much to the confusion of many in Athens.

On that blistering day Paul seized the occasion and rose among the scholars to submit to their questions, as did anyone visiting Athens who wished to walk in the footsteps of Plato. I counted at least thirty people in the crowd, few of them more than twenty years old. And one of them appeared quite belligerent, behaving as if Paul had offended the tradition of Attic reason by suggesting that a peasant from Galilee represented God on earth, and that he had been cruci-fied and lifted up to new life after three days.

"We can only tolerate what is absolute and true," the man called from the back of the circle.

"Come forward," said Paul. "What is your name?"

"Damian."

Damian stepped to the front of the crowd, and many snickered. Cleverness seethed in him; indeed, he seemed to fizz with excitement, savoring his role as interlocutor with Paul.

"I know something about Athens," said Paul. "I studied Plato as a young man, and I know about your Stoics. Everyone here talks about them. I'm aware of Metrodorus as well and have heard his criticism of the Stoics."

I worried that Paul had wandered onto unstable ground here. Was his knowledge of these thinkers ample enough to sustain a lengthy and very public argument? On the other hand, it rarely paid to underestimate Paul, who had surprising byways in his learning.

But Metrodorus!

"What is your religion?" asked a tall, thin young man with a black beard, who pushed to the front and stood beside Damian.

Paul said, "I know in Athens this is a serious question. Everyone in this city is concerned with the soul, and religion is the practice of soul wisdom."

I had never heard anything like this before, nor had they. *Soul wisdom!*

"As I moved among your many statues in Athens, each of them a place of veneration," Paul said, "I discovered an inscription that worried me: TO AN UNKNOWN GOD. You are intelligent, thoughtful, articulate men. So consider this proposition: An unknown God is no God whatever. Let's reason by analogy. The poems of an unknown poet are, quite simply, not read. They make no impression on the world, as the words fail to exist. *My* God, let me tell you, is the only true God, himself the creator of this universe. But he was far removed from us and scarcely knowable. In an act of compassion, he decided to make himself known to his creation. He erupted into our lives in the person of Jesus of Nazareth, who showed us what God is like, gave him a voice. Jesus became the human face of God."

I saw that Paul was alert today, radiant in his manner, comfortable in himself as he spoke, or God spoke through him, shaping the words that formed on his lips.

"God made this outcrop, and—see there—Mount Olympus." He gestured in that direction, and their eyes followed his finger. "The sea itself is his doing. The fish and fowl. You, me, all of us. We are creatures of his invention, sustained by his affection. And he dwells in every man and woman, in the rocks, wildflowers, within the far hills. When the wind surrounds with its invisible arms and seizes a forest, this is God rocking the world."

Paul insisted on this elaborate figuration in his speech. But it was sometimes, as here, overwrought, too pretty in its frivolities of association. Nonetheless, every eye fixed upon him. And nobody wished to interrupt the flow.

"He created you and me, and every nation, and he breathes life into everything around us. He orders and appoints the faithful seasons. He determines the boundaries of our habits, the width and breadth of our being. I don't believe he is far away, like Zeus and Hera, Aphrodite or Artemis, or Apollo. No! He's in my breast. He's in your breast, too. In him we live and move and prosper. Your own poet, the great Ion of Chios, once wrote: 'Bone of their bone, we grow from the gods. / Every finger and toe extends from them.' But there is only one God, the Almighty, the center of being."

"What does your God want from us?" asked Damian.

"You must change," said Paul. He touched his temples with both hands, then gestured as if lifting or releasing his skull to the sky. "Open your mind to the wider mind of God, and you will be healed, enlightened."

"What if we prefer being as we are?" one wry fellow asked.

"You are broken, as we all are broken," Paul answered. "Only God can heal us. You have transgressed—stepped over a line. We have all done things we should never have done. We resist doing the virtuous thing."

"We must be virtuous?"

There was some laughter in the crowd.

Paul raised a hand to silence them. "God asks for nothing but perfection. As Jesus was perfected by God in his death upon a cross in Jerusalem, you shall be perfected. This is wholeness and health. Jesus was crucified and buried. On the third day after this atrocity, God lifted him to new life. He is here."

One young man at the back spoke up: "So the dead come back to life? Is that what you're telling us, old man?"

"Stone him!" someone shouted.

But of course the Greeks had no taste for the Jewish practice of stoning dissenters, and this produced only laughter.

"We should go, Paul," I said, tugging his arm.

He looked at me as if wakened from a trance and followed me. I noticed that Damian and his friend, a woman introduced to us as Demaris, walked beside us, asking more questions.

"I want to hear more about your Galilean," said Demaris.

Paul had an eye for loveliness in young people, and he reached out to touch her arm.

"What a good thing," Paul said. "I will tell you everything."

That night, leaning with his back against a wall in Enoch's house with a large cup of wine in his hands, Paul talked about what had happened that day on Mars Hill. He understood that his afternoon in the sun had not changed anything. Not markedly. He had not been nearly as persuasive as he might have been, not as eloquent or rational as when the spirit filled him. This long-awaited moment in the Attic sun had passed without much effect.

"They were impervious to reason," Paul said, "which seems quite ironic, in the house of intellect."

He had clearly drunk too much, or spent too long in the sun that day, as his words slurred, even tumbled over each other. I told him not to fret about his performance, that he had planted seeds and these might take root in unexpected ways. One could never know what might follow from this or any work. I quoted the saying of our Lord about the Kingdom of God being like a mustard seed—a line that Paul often used.

"Don't humor me, Luke," he said.

Enoch didn't like to see Paul in this black mood and removed himself from our company.

"I will always tell you what I see," I said. "Depend on my frankness."

I wondered if I should end my association with Paul. Vanity had inflated him in Athens, and he had lost sight of our plan to alert everyone to God's plan for humanity. One could not, by syllogism or analogy, conjure the spirit or explain the message of Jesus. Paul's efforts on the Areopagus became a display of his powers of intellect, testing the force of his will. Once, I had heard him say that "in Jesus we lose ourselves, our will to shine over others." Where had this Paul gone?

Sometimes patience is called for, I reminded myself. And I loved Paul. I must allow for him to stumble, as I must stumble as well.

"We shall go to Corinth in the morning," Paul said.

This shift of plans came abruptly, and he rarely mentioned Athens in later years.

Chapter Fourteen

PAUL

We left Athens unhappily. It had not gone as well as I hoped, and I could see no point in remaining. The Athenians had only a limited understanding of the workings of the spirit, and their cynicism had overwhelmed their intelligence. Perhaps I would go back there one day, if the Almighty Lord pushed me in this direction, although I worried that the time drew short and that little would change in this city before the end of history. It occurred to me that Luke, however resilient, had no interest in rhetoric or inquiry. My sense of Athens as a place of high argument and philosophic inquisition failed to move him. He had not been schooled in Plato, in the Attic poets and playwrights, as I had. And he held a low opinion of the young men who gathered in the olive grove to walk where Plato had walked and taught. Wealth and position, he said, had blinded them to truth.

Now the prospect of Corinth—a gaudy jewel in the diadem of the Achaean world—brightened on the horizon. It was our next destination, and we moved forward without regret. I was learning this hard lesson, how to leave what must be left, how to accept failures, to adjust to them, and to face the days ahead unhampered, unbowed.

We stopped at Eleusis at my insistence, though Luke dismissed it as "a cesspool of superstition." I knew something of the parades that arrived twice yearly by torchlight, descending on Eleusis with hope as well as trepidation. And I admired the compulsion of these pilgrims to understand the mysteries of the site, whatever the cost. I thought of them as we walked along the Sacred Way, which led out of Athens to this holy place and its cypress grove.

Throughout the year, seekers engaged with the priests here, learning about resurrection, as taught through the tale of Demeter and Persephone. Musa had possessed a knowledge of these mysteries, and he didn't dismiss the truth of what lay behind this Greek story of death and rebirth, with its rites of initiation. "All truth comes to us obliquely," he told me, "through stories. A myth is a story that isn't just true; it's more than true. It marks a tear in the fabric of reality."

Musa insisted that resurrection must occur each day, if not several times each day. Once I asked him about death, and he said, "Life comes, at birth, as a glorious sunrise. I have no reason to expect anything less of death." He spoke often of Demeter, the goddess of nature, and her beautiful young daughter, Kore, with her curly auburn hair, who had been kidnapped by Hades, the master of the underworld. Demeter searched in vain for the missing girl, coming to rest in Eleusis, full of despair. In the guise of an old crone, she looked after the queen's son, dipping him in cool liquid fires that made him immortal. He became a splendid princeling, devoted to the cultivation of crops and the seasonal rounds of agriculture. But in sympathy the crops failed as Demeter's grief for her daughter increased year by agonizing year. Seeing this pain, the prince asked the gods to intervene, and Zeus obliged him, persuading Hades, the dark master, to allow Kore—now renamed Persephone—to return to the world of light, although she had been tricked into eating deadly pomegranate seeds, which meant she must spend half of each year in the land of the dead.

The story embodied a great mystery: the dying of the natural world in the autumn, its revival in springtime. Eleusis taught the truth of this mystery, and transmogrified all who understood its message and thereby lost their fear of death, becoming aware that death is simply part of life. But Jesus, as I knew, signaled the end of this cycle. He put death to death, by his own death and resurrection. Just thinking of this truth, its ferocity and wonder, I felt emboldened. I would bring Corinth to the foot of the cross. We would excite and transmogrify the Greeks, this wise and spirit-filled people, who would join us in our efforts to create the world again, once and for all.

I had planted seeds in Athens, that much I knew, and these seeds would drift toward Corinth, perhaps would populate the whole of Greece one day.

Several votaries stood outside the Hall of the Mysteries, a formidable temple erected to shelter those devoted to the spirit of this place. As many as three thousand worshippers came in the autumn and spring at appointed times to celebrate the story of Demeter and Persephone. Those who dared to brave the mysteries would be led by a priest into a dark cave, descending with him into the underworld, where they encountered in that twilight world the ghosts who lived there. The goal of this descent was to reemerge in daylight, coming back to life from a kind of death.

"It's not unlike baptism," Luke said, when I explained this.

"How strange to see a parallel there," I said.

He didn't mind when I mocked him. Indeed, I liked Luke because of his infinite capacity for humiliation. (And tried very hard not to take advantage of this.) That he would make occasional jokes at my expense didn't matter; my resilience overrode this. I indulged him, appreciating his loyalty and the fact that I could throw ideas against the wall of his mind, see them scatter and reassemble. At times he drew me toward the earth. His clarity had a calming effect, prompting me to think of those lines of Horace: "Reason and sense promote tranquility, / Not villas that look out upon the sea."

We sat in the pooling shade with a number of intelligent young men, and I found in them fertile ground for persuasion: Greek minds eager to understand the mysteries of life. They took a keen interest in our stories of Jesus, and one of them, seized by the spirit of God quite unexpectedly, asked me to baptize him in a nearby stream.

"He doesn't know what he's doing," Luke said to me.

"Let the spirit do its work. Don't interfere!"

To be frank, I wished for more like this young man, and for a violence of conversion, for masses awakening to the call of God through the voice of Jesus. It was not always necessary for a man or woman fully to comprehend what I said. Understanding might come slowly, in time—if time was allowed. To rest in God mattered more than anything else.

The journey from Eleusis to Corinth took us southwest along a coastline of sheer cliffs, where we stopped in tiny villages and sat with the Greek fishermen, who fed us sardines wrapped in fig leaves and steamed over hot coals. They had no interest in hearing about Jesus but politely listened to our stories. At Megara, with its beach like a half-moon of sand, I watched long-legged boys with spears who waded up to their thighs in green surf and stabbed the fish that swam close.

"Call me a fisher of men," I said.

"One of the best lines of our Lord," Luke said. "It will go into my story." As ever he gathered quotations for his life of Jesus and regularly sent versions of this book to Rome by messenger for safekeeping. Our travels were such that we could never depend upon arrival, but we could count on dear Patrobas, who had collected written material for the Way for some years, welcoming everything that Luke would send.

And yet I wondered if Luke's work would ever see daylight. His meticulous nature might impede his ability to finish a final version of this life of Jesus. (Already other accounts circulated in various drafts, and I had read two or three of them, frustrated by their apparent contradictions and lack of focus.) That Luke planned to write a narrative of our missionary journeys did worry me, as he saw everything strictly in his terms, believing in his own truth as the universal reality, always proceeding along the most logical lines. This was, perhaps, a consequence of his medical training.

On the other hand, I felt lucky to have Luke walk beside me.

⁓

We arrived in Corinth on a brilliant afternoon. It had none of the stuffy and self-congratulatory atmosphere of Athens, and I was relieved to enter this swarming and abundant city. From its ports at Cenchreae or Lechaeum sailors arrived in vessels from the world over, and the markets pulsed with a variety of hucksters who had things to sell: leather goods, silks, woolen blankets, baskets, jewelry, bronze and clay pots, glassware, paintings, silver platters, and exquisite pieces of marble sculpture. Everything opened to the eyes and ears: temples and monuments, bathhouses, public fountains, an amphitheater for games, and a capacious odeum for the recitation of poetry and song. Statues of one goddess or another rose in nooks and crannies, some gilded or cloaked in scarlet masks. There were porticoes and long colonnades on the main streets. The massive bronze figure of Helios, the sun god, took dominion over the principle gate to the city, with its big brass doors. Helios rode in a chariot with his son Phaëthon, and this seemed fitting, as the sun flooded Corinth, which had become a prized colony of Rome.

We stopped to gaze at the city from a nearby hill, with a view of the Gulf of Corinth and the surrounding mountains. A golden river slipped past Corinth, then emptied into the harbor below. It rippled by the Temple of Priapus, that rustic god of fertility, whose obscenely swollen member adorned statuary throughout the city. One could feel diverse erotic energies at work here.

The Temple of Aphrodite crowned the Acrocorinth, where alabaster columns suggested a purity it did not possess. The structure—really a sequence of buildings and open spaces between them—swarmed with more than a thousand whores, "priestesses" who offered their wares to sailors who made a point of stopping at this port. And this sordid aspect of Corinth reached back many centuries: Plato had referred to a whore when he used the phrase "a Corinthian girl." I mentioned this to Luke, who recalled a lurid Greek epigram of unknown origin: "The lively girls of Corinth never slack. / One finds them in the temple, on their back."

It surprised me that Luke, of all people, should allow such a fragment to stick in memory.

I had seen promiscuity and fornication before, often in grotesque incarnations, as in Cyprus at the governor's palace, where the most insolent acts took place in public view. But Corinth seethed on another level. Commerce ruled here, and the Corinthians brought carnality to a feverish level, as any physical desire could find fulfillment for a price. Anything or (nearly) anyone could be bought or sold in this city.

I knew something of their history. The original Corinthians had fled two centuries ago to the island of Delos, chased out by marauding armies. In recent times they had returned, eager to compete with Greeks from elsewhere, outwitting Syrians, Egyptians, and Jews from the farthest corners of the empire. The Jews had a pervasive presence here, and one or two of the prominent synagogues attracted Godfearers, ever the most receptive audience for our message.

As always, Luke and I sought out the Jews, and I did my best to capture their attention by proclaiming myself "a Pharisee of the tribe of Benjamin, trained under Gamaliel." It was my opening pitch in most synagogues, but here it drew only sighs of indifference. I did manage to read from the scrolls on the Sabbath, as they had few enough readers who could actually read aloud in Hebrew or Aramaic; but my reflections on Rabbi Jesus attracted neither rebuttal nor assent. One elder at the synagogue on Melus Street said, "I believe that many new voices have arisen, and your rabbi is one among them." He told me that Apollos, an Alexandrian Jew, had quite a following. And Apollos had apparently been baptized by John himself in the Jordan.

Luke said, "We should meet this Apollos."

I was skeptical: Our world teemed with wandering mystics and mountebanks, healers and tricksters. It seemed unlikely that Apollos would interest me, except in that he had won admirers throughout the eastern empire.

It wasn't a month before we met Prisca and Aquila. They had been among the Jews expelled from Rome by the emperor, who now and then took against those who refused to acknowledge his divinity. They worked in leather and made a handy living in the repair of tents and sails in the western district of Corinth, where craftsmen labored in small workshops, and attended a synagogue led by Crispus, a kind and receptive rabbi who would prove an advocate for our circle in Corinth. I quickly liked this young couple. Prisca was shockingly clever, with an ardent manner and blazing tongue. But I never was afraid of her. Aquila, her husband, was by contrast laconic, offering only a few words on any occasion. But I trusted him and understood that Prisca thrived in his presence. They were devoted to God and had come into contact with the Way in Rome.

I wasted no time in telling them about my encounter with the Christ on the Damascus Road, my subsequent years in the desert with Musa, and my travels among Jews and Godfearers throughout Asia, Macedonia, and Greece, where many of those I met had opened their hearts to the energies of the spirit, all in preparation for the establishment of the kingdom. I mentioned the gatherings, too.

"We've been to such gatherings in Rome," said Prisca.

She didn't say more, as if she didn't yet trust me.

Prisca was taller than Aquila by half a foot, lean and lithe. Luke said (to my annoyance) that she "looked like a young man." She certainly wore her hair shorter than women commonly did and carried herself in a confident way. Her eyes lit up when she talked. When she sang, she did so in a sonorous, lovely, low-pitched voice. She liked people, and her long fingers often reached out to those around her.

It surprised me, pleasantly, that when we held our first gathering at Corinth, Prisca spoke so eloquently about the Kingdom of God and "the New Covenant of the Christ." Her grasp of the Way impressed me, as did her reflections on the scriptures. I had not imagined I would meet such a follower of the Way in Greece, one with such knowledge and aplomb. Her father, she told me, had been a rabbi, and he had taught his beloved daughter to read the Torah in Hebrew. Most women never actually learned to read, and few gatherings of Jews admitted them to their inner circle. Her way of talking mirrored my own, and she often echoed my words as well, giving back what I said in clarified form, shaped in her own way. I loved her peculiar energies, the way she brought life into a room. I admired, even envied, Aquila for his connection to Prisca and his own wise silences.

Had I been younger, and Prisca not married, I might have wished for a closer friendship. That I could imagine myself married to her quite shocked me—I had never had such a thought before. It made no sense to me. But perhaps life makes less sense than I would have preferred, and I must accept this as one of its limitations.

To my dismay, I was unable to expel fantasies of sexual relations in Corinth, as hardly a day passed without a whore approaching me. Beautiful young men, too, winked at me, asking if I wished to walk away with them, for a price. I never knew what to say to these steadfast workers in the flesh, whom I did not disdain or rebuke. Had not Jesus been willing to talk with whores?

One night, as I walked alone in a public garden, a young woman, not unlike Prisca in outline, with long legs and arms, with a sloping neck and short hair, approached me, stepping from the shadows of an umbrella pine in the burning moonlight. Her eyes sank their hooks into my heart.

"You would like to spend a little time with me?" she asked.

Her voice was like a boy's, fluting and steely, as were her thin hips, her lanky form.

"I have very little money," I said.

"Whatever you have is fine," she said, drawing close to me, putting her arms around me.

Her honeyed breath lured me toward her, and I kissed her mouth, then touched her breasts with my tongue. The salty sweetness appealed to me, and I let myself kiss her belly as well. Her arms pulled me toward her with such force. And I lay with her that evening on the grass under a million stars, in a shower of comets, allowing her to press herself against me, letting the length of her inform me, becoming a part of me as I became a part of her. I touched her in ways I had only imagined in the years before this, savoring each moment as she pressed upon me, her body rising above me, enveloping my manhood as I held my hands against her tight buttocks and let myself go.

I walked home in the dawn light in a state of mingling excitement, confusion, and remorse.

I wept, then prayed desperately on my knees the next morning: *Lord, forgive me for what I have done. I have not listened to your voice. I have turned my back on you. I am sorry. And I will turn away from this. I promise now with every fiber of my being. I promise!*

Luke appeared behind me and stood with a hand on my shoulder.

"Is something wrong, Paul? You didn't come home last night, and I was afraid for you. I almost went out looking. The darkness is unsafe."

"I'm fine," I said.

"You look well enough," he said. "But I don't think you are fine. No."

"Do you believe—deeply in your heart—that God forgives us, again and again? No matter what we do?"

"Have you done something in need of forgiveness?"

I broke into tears and revealed everything to Luke. I could not hold back, not now, and not with him. That would have been pointless. In deep sympathy, he sat beside me on a divan, with an arm around me. "You have only been human," he said, "and God asks no more of us than our brokenness."

It was a kind thing for him to say in this circumstance, and useful as well. Suddenly I understood in a most visceral way the crooked timber from which God had fashioned us, and knew it was impossible to live in the purity to which I aspired. That had been a fantasy of mine.

"I'm broken," I said.

"You can't understand God's forgiveness if you can't forgive yourself. Have pity, my friend, on your own heart."

I never loved dear Luke more than on that quiet morning in Corinth. I felt truly human for perhaps the first time in my life, and utterly exposed as well, knowing at last that God had forgiven me, as he forgave everyone. As I forgave myself, and I did.

✢

I surprised Prisca and Aquila with my skills at tent-making and the repair and manufacture of sails, and they invited me to work every day beside them in the shop that they recently opened in Corinth. It felt good to plunge into this task again, reviving old skills. I was able, for instance, to procure hides from local temples, where sacrificial offerings meant an abundance of goatskin, which we dressed with alum—perfect for certain kinds of sails. The demand for our strong sails only increased when it became clear they could withstand heavy weather at sea, and soon we had to employ others in the task of production.

It delighted me to see Prisca and Aquila so happy with these results.

"We must put a fair portion of this money aside for the Jerusalem gathering," I said.

News of the drought in Palestine had been filtering in for months, with reports of a desperate famine, and I explained to my friends that we should follow the example of Jesus and give as much, even more, than we could afford. *Cast your bread upon the waters, and it will after many days return to you*, one read in Ecclesiastes. This rang in my heart as the height of ethical wisdom. God would only reward our loving with more love. There was a glorious circle of affection that we could describe.

It also mattered that we should not lose the confidence of the Pillars, who must regard us as supportive, not peripheral or oppositional. Though we differed on certain matters, we worked in our separate ways to make the world ready for the return of the Christ, helping to realize the Kingdom of God. "Many messengers," I would say, "but only one message."

I never planned to stay in Corinth for nearly two years and longed to return to Macedonia, sensing that the spirit breathed a deep life into the assembly at Philippi, Lydia's gathering, which could become a base for our movement in the West. Lydia had begun to gather money for the Jerusalem collection after I had written to her about this project, responding as I knew she would. I hoped to return to transport her gift, and those of others, to Judea myself. I would go with Luke and Timothy at my side, and perhaps Silas as well. It would be a kind of triumph for us, for our movement in the West.

But I worried about Timothy, whom I had sent back into Thessalonica. What had become of him? And what would I tell his mother if I never found him again?

The question of Timothy preoccupied me as I sat at my table in the shop, surrounded by sails and canvases. I suffered now, filled with a strange and horrible longing I could not quite assuage or understand.

Aquila said little, which was true to his nature, but Prisca told me countless good stories about the assembly in Rome, where the Way now prospered, and I prodded her for more details. What had Peter said to the circle when he passed through the capital? Did Andrew come as well? The Good News had begun to flood the synagogues at the heart of the empire, and the Way attracted a growing number of Godfearers in the emperor's court, even within his own family. All of this boded well for us.

Roman seamen came frequently to our shop with sails to repair, and they added to my fund of stories. As ever, I longed to go to Rome, to see for myself the Forum where Cicero had walked and talked. And the Circus Maximus, which owed its grandeur to Julius Caesar. This great city continued to grow as a destiny in my imagination, and I knew that God called me there. One day I would stand on the Palatine Hill and proclaim the glory of God and the healing energies of his son, Jesus of Nazareth. I would stand at the imperial center.

Prisca never tired of my questions about her city, and said, "Well, you must go there."

"One day," I said.

+

Luke and I moved among the synagogues on the Sabbath, expanding our contacts within the community of Corinthian Jews. And we held meetings each week on the First Day in Prisca and Aquila's house, which Luke and I shared with them, on Corvo Street. Our assembly multiplied week by week, spilling into their garden, where eventually we had as many as three dozen worshippers, mostly Greeks, who saw the love of God expressed in the face of Jesus and labored in the anticipation of his return. We shared the sacred meal, and I would talk afterward about whatever passages in the scriptures had caught my attention in recent days. Luke would sometimes read sayings of Jesus culled from one or another of his collections.

I would sit in the garden alone with Prisca at twilight, drinking wine, listening to the nightingales and owls, which lifted their songs over the constant thrumming of the cicadas. Thousands of fireflies flashed and failed in the dark, a mirror of my soul, which tingled as we leaned into each other.

How can I talk about this with moderation? I loved Prisca. And thought about her constantly.

"Your obsession with her is evident, and it's unhealthy," Luke said.

I didn't agree. One knows God through people and in people. I felt the love of God in Prisca, in the way her sympathies lit my day. I wanted simply to live in her company. I wanted to know her, more and more, finding out everything about her. The slightest detail from her past interested me, such as what she liked to eat as a child, what stories her father told her before sleeping, how she liked to play a flute in the family garden or walk alone by the river through the great city, dreaming of the vast imperial web of roads and remote outposts she would visit one day.

She knew the writings of Plato and Heracleitus quite well, and we talked at length about the meaning of Logos. "Everything passes, changes," said Heracleitus, "but the Logos remains, it's what we hold in common." Even before I could articulate the association, she compared the Logos to God and his manifestation in Jesus. It was, she said, "what Jesus had in common with God, the core element of his Christhood." At times Prisca went a little far, perhaps revealing too much, as when she said, "Aquila and I, let me say . . . we do enjoy our bodies. We live inside each other. But our souls are conjoined as well, and the spirit exceeds the boundaries of our flesh."

I didn't need to be told this, because I had a room adjacent to their bedroom and had been shaken by their cries in the night. I knew only too well the configurations of their physical love and could imagine their ecstasies. Love among the married was not a sin, of course, unless it was misused. Lust itself was human and necessary, as it drew a man and a woman together, a gift from God, a way of intersecting souls and creating the race. But hadn't the time for generation ended? Was it not the right moment to cast our thoughts beyond the mortal world?

I understood their dilemma, of course. I knew as well as they did that lust overwhelms us, as I myself had been overwhelmed.

I wanted to lie with Prisca, that was true. But I knew I must banish such thoughts, and I prayed fervently, asking God to spare me, to relieve me of the images and feelings that made me weak in her presence. I begged him to pluck me from these flames.

I began to worry about Timothy now. Had he been killed or imprisoned? There was nowhere to send a letter to him, though I tried to get information about his whereabouts as best I could.

"You're mad, Paul," Luke said, when I revealed my worries. "The young take care of themselves. Timothy and Silas are competent men." After a pause, he said, "Silas in particular."

This gave me no comfort. Having promised Timothy's mother that I would look after him, what had I done?

Luke heard rumors that a number of missionaries from Jerusalem had passed through Thessalonica and Galatia as well, and they had severely contradicted the message I had brought from the Pillars. It was even worse. They insisted that James had strongly condemned my teachings, calling me a false prophet, a derogator of the Law of Moses. He claimed that Jesus would not have found anything I said plausible. I was a manifestation of Ha-satan, the Adversary.

Me!

I took it upon myself to write sharp letters to the gatherings where these evil things might be believed. It was tedious, the way I must repeat myself. The mysteries must remain mysteries, as we possess only a partial view, and our vision is distorted; we look through a milky glass. It became clearer to me each day that God addressed the whole world in Jesus, not only the Jews, as James would have it. God was God, of course, and still Jehovah, in love with Israel, but Israel itself would expand to include the whole of the human race. No man or woman in the end would be lost.

I fear that some of my darker energies got into my reflections, and Prisca upbraided me after one of my weekly talks. "You often lose me, Paul. I can't follow your thinking," she said. "Is something wrong?"

I didn't really answer her, but I leaned close, eager to smell her breath.

Luke saw this and said, "You look at Prisca in ways that make me, and probably her, uneasy. You sigh plaintively in her company. Your longing is palpable, and Aquila has noticed this as well. He is restrained but not blind!"

Such nonsense, I told him. But I knew what I had done and felt guilty as charged. I slumped into a darkness of the soul, and no depth of prayer relieved me or could take me out of this hole. Perhaps James was right, I thought. I was a pawn of the Adversary, lost in the well of my own black soul. Night after night I lay awake, fearing that the dawn would never come. And then I was afraid it would come, and I would have to walk into the daylight exposed as a fool, adrift. The sun would kill me with its blaze, tear me apart. I prayed, as Jesus had prayed in his worst hour: *God, my God, why hast thou forsaken me?*

But then, in springtime, everything changed.

I was sitting by myself in the garden when, unannounced and unexpected, Timothy stepped into the sunlight. I had never seen anyone more radiant.

Had his hair turned gold?

I could barely stand. He approached with a sweet shy smile, and I opened my arms and held him without saying a word for such a long time. "My son, you're here, and safe," I said at last.

He brought news of Thessalonica, and the stories were worse than I had feared. The Way had slipped into strange ideas, narrowing their view of what Jesus had said and what his life and sacrifice had meant. Hearing this, I knew I must get back there as soon as possible. It seemed impossible, how we advanced a step or two, then slipped back. Whatever did God have in mind?

Over Timothy's shoulder I could see Silas, who had gained weight. His jowls hung loose, his feet splayed, and his toes looked black as dates. I knew I must send him away, although I hated to do this and didn't know how it might happen. I must pray for guidance, I told myself. God would explain everything and guide me. But he had a lot of explaining to do!

I didn't, in fact, know what trouble lay in store in Corinth itself.

The Jews in the city, unbeknownst to me, resented our accomplishments and regarded me as a threat. A few of them thought I exaggerated the accomplishments of Jesus and wondered if he was the actual Christ promised in the scriptures. "He is Lord and king," I said in a synagogue one day, though my words were met with hostility, with Abel Ben-Ezra, the most respected rabbi in Corinth, taking me aside.

"I know you mean well, and that God has touched your heart," he said. "But you should leave Corinth while it remains possible." He told me that a new proconsul was making his way from Rome, a man called Gallio, the brother of Seneca, the well-respected philosopher. "He may be hostile to the Way," he said, adding that he "wants to squash all potential forms of rebellion." Our popular gathering of the Way in Corinth was "not in any way good for the Jews," he added. "We live always on the fringe, as you know. We can't arouse their suspicions."

The day after this exchange with Ben-Ezra, which worried me badly, I came upon a crowd that had gathered to see the new leader's arrival. They stood four and five rows deep along the roadside cheering him as he passed. And I thought of Cicero and his return to Rome from exile in Thessalonica. After a dreadful separation from power, from his family and friends, his homecoming was delirious for him and his multitude of admirers. For miles and miles the masses—Roman workers and slaves, freemen, tradesmen—lined the roadside to catch a glimpse of the great orator, this representative of Reason and Good Sense, who would restore the republic to its democratic origins, bring calm again after years of autocratic misrule and brutality.

Gallio's presence delighted the Corinthians, who believed a new broom might sweep the stables clean. This was always the fantasy when new regimes came into power. But this proconsul's strong presence inspired my enemies, who appealed to him in person at the palace, calling me "a subversive, a traitor to Rome." They began to harass us at our gatherings, too: shouting from the back of the room, claiming that we taught a twisted version of Judaism, contravened the Law of Moses, made light of circumcision, allowed Jews and Greeks to fornicate, and served meat that had been sacrificed to idols. (They knew that I purchased sacrificial goats from temples for sails and tents and had somehow convinced themselves I would make a meal of these poor creatures before tanning their hides.)

One morning I was apprehended on my way to the workshop by a gang of young thugs, who bound my hands behind my back with a rough piece of rope. One of them boxed my ears, while another spat at me. They tossed me into the back of a cart and wheeled me to the basilica, where Gallio presided over a once-a-week Court of the People. I was brought before the bald, overly ripe Gallio, whose forehead bulged, inflated with thought and self-importance. His nose was large and soft, with flat nostrils. He sat on a throne of sorts between potted plants and two Roman guards in bronze helmets. A number of menacing lictors flanked these guards, ready to apprehend and flog those whom Gallio considered guilty of breaking the law.

I had heard terrible things about the Corinthian prisons and could not imagine myself in custody there. So fear squeezed me in its tight fist. I should have listened to Ben-Ezra and left while it was still possible.

"What is the charge against this man?" Gallio asked. He looked rather annoyed by this intrusion on his time, dipping his eyes to one side, as if mesmerized by a tiny green lizard on the floor.

Susthanes, a leading Jew in Corinth, said, "This man is a Jew, a Pharisee who studied in Jerusalem under a great scholar. But he teaches that the Mosaic Laws don't apply to him and his associates. He doesn't care if a Jew and a Greek dine together. He eats the flesh of unclean animals."

"Does any of this matter?"

"It does to us, sir. As you know, Roman law protects us. We have the right to conduct our lives in a manner that accords with Jewish traditions and practices."

"Oh, dear," he said. "Has this been written into law?"

"I know the emperor agrees."

"You and the emperor, I assume, are friends?" There was laughter in the hall, and even the lictors could not suppress their smiles.

"What I say is commonplace knowledge."

"Not to me! Are you saying I don't know what I'm doing?"

"I'm asking for justice."

"Ah, yes! Justice! Excellently put." He looked at me directly. "And who are you?"

"Paul of Tarsus, a Jew in good standing. I studied in Jerusalem under Gamaliel, as this fellow has said. But I mean no harm. I'm a Roman citizen, and I support Roman authority."

Gallio sighed, turning to Susthanes. "Has anyone been hurt?" Silence followed. "Has this man stolen anything, broken anything? Has he fomented violence? A riot, perhaps? We do not want riots in Corinth."

"He disregards Jewish law."

"You don't seem to realize that I have no power over such things. Jewish laws don't interest us. Do you not have priests, a tribal council of some kind?"

"Trouble will follow from his teachings."

"The trouble is with you, sir!"

Gallio caught my eye again. "Go back to where you came from, Paul of Tarsus. I don't want to hear about you again." Then he fell upon Susthanes. "You have wasted my time. We have important cases to deal with, not squabbling among Jews over laws that do not concern anyone beyond your circle." He stood now, furious. "Take him away from me! That one!"

He gestured to the lictors, who seized Susthanes.

From what I later discovered, they beat him badly. But I can't say that I didn't believe he deserved this treatment.

I returned home to inform Prisca and Aquila that we must leave, as soon as possible, and urged them to accompany us. Why not help to spread the Good News abroad? The leather shop would continue without us, as we had employed a dozen others and taught them well.

I expected resistance, but they agreed to go with us for a time, believing that the end drew near and that the Christ would return soon.

"Jesus will find us in motion on his behalf," said Aquila.

It was one of the finest things he ever said, I told Luke.

"And one of the only things," he said.

Silas, much to my relief, asked to remain in Corinth. He and Crispus had founded a gathering of their own at the western edge of the city, by the Windy Gate, on the steep hill near Lechaeum. In every respect, this solved a problem that had tormented me, and I gave him my blessing.

"God will stand behind you, Silas," I said.

Luke looked at me askance, but I ignored him.

The following day we secured passage on a merchant vessel bound for Syria with a plan to lay over at Ephesus for a time. From what I already knew of Ephesus, I could only believe that God wanted us there. It was the obvious next point on our journey home.

Chapter Fifteen

LUKE

Under duress, we set off for Antioch by way of Ephesus with Prisca and Aquila. And Timothy. Paul had managed to leave Silas behind. I thought about objecting to this, but in so many ways it helped to abandon Silas. Paul considered him a distraction, which inevitably turned him into one.

I had not expected this displacement. We had settled into a good life in Corinth, and I would have liked to remain longer in that grand if complicated city. My medical skills, and my salve, had found an audience there, and opportunities for telling people about the Good News mounted day by day. But a number of influential Jews had taken against us after we made inroads into their tight community, attracting many Godfearers away from Sabbath worship altogether.

One could, perhaps should, observe the Sabbath and, the next day, take part in one of our gatherings. That much we explained to everyone, although Paul seemed increasingly less interested in the Jewish community or its observances. Less frequently now did he open his remarks in a new synagogue by saying, "I am Paul of Tarsus, of the tribe of Benjamin, a Pharisee, trained under Gamaliel."

"Tarsus is enough," he said, when I asked about this.

The plan was to return to Antioch, laying over in Ephesus. The eventual trip to Jerusalem, with our famine relief in his possession, loomed heavily on Paul's mind. He had been restless for some time, coming to a boil inside, less communicative than usual, frantic, sleepless, eager for the return of our Lord. I could hear him weeping in the night, and this was new. What troubled him so?

"It's a matter of days before his coming in glory," he would say, month by month, though each time he said it his voice weakened.

I didn't say it again, but I knew that time meant nothing to God.

Ephesus had long been in my sights as an arresting city with a famous past, and I disembarked eagerly. Coming up from the busy harbor, we entered through the magnificent Gate of Augustus, making our way to the Jewish square in the eastern part of the city, where a large number of Godfearers could be found. Their hearty welcome buoyed us: Paul's reputation had, from what I could tell, preceded him; in any case, he had no need to explain his origins or mission.

We walked into the city with a rare feeling of anticipation, as each of us had heard much about its glories. And certainly the Temple of Artemis proved equal to its reputation, a wonder of invention. More than a hundred pillars rose to the sun, a grand and serial display of organized light. We noted the intricate mosaic floor in many colors and the airy hallways, and I spent much of one day studying the images in statuary on pedestals representing Artemis Ephesia, the object of worship here. She was the great and generous mother goddess, with multiple large breasts as symbols of nurture. Here they called her "Our Lady of Ephesus."

I should note that this Artemis bore no resemblance whatsoever to the popular goddess by the same name whom the Greeks adored: the sister of Apollo, the virgin huntress, with her narrow waist and tiny breasts. Artemis Ephesia was, perhaps, her mother, too: a goddess of fertility.

Her priests were eunuchs, castrated at birth, and so had nothing to fear from the sexual energies this goddess unleashed. In their yellow robes and glass beads, they presided over festivals that brought young men and women together under the temple roof to feed on the provender of animal attraction. Fertility was everything in these halls.

"It's such a waste," Paul said.

"Don't disparage this goddess," Prisca told him, "just because she is everything you are not."

"Darling!" said Aquila, who often tried to curb his wife's ungovernable tongue.

"Let her speak," said Paul. "I don't mind if she challenges me, as long as she smiles with her eyes."

"I hope I do more than challenge you," she said.

"You annoy me, too," said Paul.

I could not fathom their relationship. It was as if *he* were her husband. Or wished to be her husband. Certainly Crispus had made any number of droll comments on Paul's infatuation, and referred to Paul as "the holy virgin father." Needless to say, I didn't participate in such nonsense, knowing we must not make fun of each other, as this sort of palaver—though amusing in the moment—interfered with our mission.

Among the most eager of Godfearers in Ephesus was a quick-witted young man called Titus, a silversmith by trade who had recently come on business from Antioch and remained in this "city of silver," as he called it. He knew of Paul and introduced himself to us as "a friend in Jesus." Paul swept him into our fold, noting that Titus and Timothy had much in common.

"They could be brothers," Paul said.

Titus, too, had curly hair with a coppery tinge, although he lacked the feline graces of Timothy. Nor did he have the same sharply sculpted features.

Paul focused on these young men, eager for their attention, flattering them, inciting conversations that seemed much too personal. I wished for him to remain avuncular, a presiding figure in our movement, with no human appetites or flaws. Great generals—Alexander, Pompey the Great—never indulged in such behavior, remaining aloof. A campaign was demanding, and we had embarked on a great campaign in the name of the Christ.

One evening as we sat in the colonnade, near the agora, Paul and I saw the four others of our company drift by in pristine white tunics: Prisca and Aquila, Timothy and Titus. Paul sighed and bit his lip.

"Is anything wrong?" I asked.

"We have lost our youth."

"I never had mine."

"Neither youth nor age matters, not anymore," Paul insisted. "But I feel this longing at times. I want to go back to the beginning." He put out his hands. "Look at my skin, how it sags, like bark on a dead tree. I find it difficult to turn because my back is sore. I think my vision is far less sharp."

"Was it ever sharp?"

"Somewhat sharper, in any case."

I had no gift for theoretical exposition, nor did I understand the principles of rhetoric, but I could see that he countered his own arguments at every turn. If neither youth nor age mattered, why grumble about these losses? The contradictions held on a larger scale, too. He would tell a gathering of the Way to heed the laws of Rome, not to make waves but accept the imperial authorities. "Break no laws!" he warned them. And yet he wished to bring down walls and rumble foundations. The civil authorities annoyed him, and he dismissed them readily. His ideas were naturally disruptive. Jesus was King of Creation, he would tell us. "He overturned the tables in the Temple courtyard."

No Roman magistrate would find this kind of talk anything less than subversive, even treasonous. Paul created discontent wherever he went, as perhaps he must: The message of the Christ was disruptive, arguing for radical equality. Paul certainly refused to acknowledge that slaves had fewer rights than free Roman citizens like himself. His defense of the Christ often accompanied a denunciation of Mosaic Law: "It means nothing now. Jesus is the new Moses! We have a New Covenant with God!" Yet he remained a Pharisee, at least in name. "God's laws are eternal," he would argue, even as he dined with Greeks and pagans, women and slaves. I had frequently seen him eating meat of no specific origin, and I doubted the cooks who prepared it knew how any butcher had slaughtered it or where. Their servants would in any case have found the meat in the first place, and it might well have been sacrificed to some pagan deity.

Paul frustrated anyone who hoped for consistency.

"I follow the spirit, the Christ's voice breaking in my heart," he said when I tried to point out a contradiction in one of his letters.

"But consistency!" I said.

"The dead are consistent," he replied.

He expected me to notice if he framed a memorable comment or aside, and to write it down. Often I felt like Cicero's secretary, endlessly taking dictation, wearing out stylus after stylus. We required sheaves of papyri wherever we traveled, and these were expensive and easily fouled. And yet Paul didn't care about money, often dipping into the funds he hoped to bring to Jerusalem within a year or so.

Once I put forward an objection to what we spent on writing materials, and he seized the stylus from my fingers.

"Do you want to murder me?" I asked.

"I want you to take my dictation and to hold your tongue."

"Do your words mean so much to you?"

"My life is these words, written by a stylus dipped in blood."

How could anyone respond to that? What even did it mean? These tense moments between us were infrequent, or I could never have stayed by his side over many years. But it's worth recording that his imperfections troubled me, that he could act in irrational ways, and that I prayed for guidance.

It was during our months in Ephesus that word came from Rome that Prisca and Aquila could return. Political attitudes toward the Way had shifted as the number of Godfearers in positions of civil authority had swollen, and many of these men and women attended gatherings. Junia, a leader of the Way in Rome, had written to Prisca telling her to come, suggesting they could safely rejoin their beloved community in the capital. She nearly begged for their help, and they decided to go, with Paul's sad but genuine blessings.

"When the Lord gestures," he said to them, "you must respond."

We put them on a ship only a few days later and watched as they pulled away.

Paul wept openly that day, and even Timothy failed to comfort him.

"I'll never see them again," he said to me that night.

"Oh, you will. When you go to Rome."

"I had a dream, a very evil one. They will never make it to Rome."

I dismissed this roundly, though I could not avoid a rush of forboding. Paul could well be right.

✢

News came in bursts, often unpleasant ones, and we soon heard that a number of disputes had arisen over doctrine in several of our communities, including Corinth and Macedonia. This intelligence puzzled and upset Paul, and he decided to send Timothy to those places as our emissary, once again risking his friend's life. "You know the truth, Timothy," he said. "Go now, for me. Be my voice in Corinth and Macedonia. Then rejoin us in Antioch when it's possible. We'll work together in the same field soon."

Timothy looked unhappy, and I thought he might object.

"Don't resist me," Paul said to him. "We've done good work in these cities. It's important that we don't lose what ground we have gained."

Paul's ferocity and sincerity—lethal in combination—could overwhelm objections, and I never did see anyone who could stand up to him for long. Increasingly he believed that the Christ occupied his mind, and that he spoke with authority much as Jesus did. He acted boldly on every impulse, finding truth there, convinced of his rightness. This began to worry me, and I resisted his unrelenting presumption of authority. But he was a prophet, and one could not gainsay him. One had to accept that God had commissioned Paul for a purpose, and that the apostle could discern this purpose in his own soul, even when others doubted him at times.

We visited a few gatherings of the Way in and around Ephesus, and wherever we went Paul asked that money be put aside for the relief of famine in Jerusalem. The Collection, as he now called it, mattered to him greatly, and he sent a part of these donations by messenger back to Phoebe in Antioch. Paul would take this great gift to Peter and James when the amount was sufficiently impressive and, as he said, he would present the Collection himself, which would as he said "bind the two limbs of the Way, showing that we represented one body in the Christ."

Ephesus held my attention. The public agora there was livelier than the one in Corinth, much of it devoted to the trading of silver. One could also buy or sell slaves, jewelry, tents, leather sandals, wine, or wool. An adjacent small square was devoted to pottery and cookware, and I liked especially to walk among these items, though the merchants frowned upon men taking an interest in such things, as the preparation of meals was a female task. Near the Bath of Varius, crowds gathered to witness magicians and sorcerers, who came reciting their chants, casting out demons, healing the lame and sick. For a price, they would meet any challenge, and I marveled at their wizardry, as when the withered stump of an elderly man's hand unfolded like a flower in my presence, his fingers sprouting. How was this even possible? Was the Adversary at work here?

The abundance of sorcery in Ephesus interested Paul, who saw an opportunity.

"The spirit is surely at work in this city like no other place," he said. "Matters are ripe here. The kingdom begins in Ephesus!"

I admired his optimism: always the first response from Paul.

Within days, he found a leatherworking shop owned by an articulate Jew called Abel, spending a bit of time there each morning, once again repairing sails, always eager to earn his keep and contribute to the community. As with Corinth, Ephesus offered a safe, deep anchorage for vessels from the world over. Old sails required constant patching, and new sails must be made. So this enterprise prospered.

Soon Abel was swept into the Way and baptized by Paul, and this inspired other Jews to consider the teachings of Rabbi Jesus. As one might expect, of course, there was dissent as well, and Paul's manner of speaking, his love of this "strange rabbi from Galilee," upset many Jews. Undercurrents of gossip and dissent began to ripple in the community, and these would soon create mayhem. It seemed that Paul, though himself a Jew, ran afoul of Jews wherever he went.

On the Sabbath we frequently attended the congregation of the venerable Rabbi Sceva, who had been trained under Gamaliel's father in Jerusalem, long before Paul's time. His seven sons, none of them young, had acquired the skill of exorcism, and this had proved a profitable enterprise for the family and the synagogue, as demonic spirits proliferated in Ephesus, causing a variety of afflictions—from loose bowels, headaches, ague, back ailments, and lameness to madness itself.

I had useful skills in healing, yet I could hardly compete with those who exercised power over evil spirits. I was reminded that Pliny had denounced exorcism and magic as a form of vanity, one that "compounded madness with further madness," although I had seen with my own eyes the effectiveness of those who practiced the dark arts.

One day at the synagogue our worship was interrupted by a man with a mad daughter, whom he brought forward to the rabbi. Bound by ropes, she howled and raved about the devil, crying that she had copulated with him "a thousand times a thousand times." Her lan-

guage set my teeth on edge, and many in the congregation winced
and asked the man to take her away. She bit her father when he drew
near and refused to let anyone touch her. Her name, as we learned,
was Hoglah.

The rabbi called his eldest son forward, and he stood close to the
girl and bellowed, "Hoglah! Hoglah! I denounce the one who con-
sumes your mind! Out of you, devil, out!"

She grew still, then shuddered, foaming at the mouth, choking
and spitting. She fell to her knees, then struggled to her feet again.
Then in a raspy voice that seemed to belong to the demon inside her
she called out, "I know Paul, the apostle of Jesus, who stands among
you. But you, Paul! Who are you?"

That the demon who possessed Hoglah knew the name of Paul
created a shock of fear in the room. Rabbi Sceva and his sons were
alarmed that Paul, by his mere presence in the congregation, had dis-
rupted the exorcism of Hoglah, and (after they led the mad girl away)
they discouraged us from observing the Sabbath among them. From
that day forward we avoided this synagogue on the Sabbath, traveling
to other congregations, some of them on the far outskirts of Ephesus. And we continued to meet with gatherings of the Way, which
grew week by week as our stay lengthened, drawing Greeks and Jews
together. It astonished me how quickly these added numbers and
how faith in God, in the name of Jesus, blossomed.

Paul saw this, and it pleased him, but he itched to find a younger
and more philosophically minded audience for his ideas, as in Athens, where his failure still troubled him. These ambitions (which I
tried to discourage because they were the product of vanity) led him
to the Lyceum, a school in Ephesus, with its long peristyle forming a
sequence of white pillars under a portico, with gardens at either side.
There amid the anemones, asphodels, and poppies were small groups
of young men who walked and disputed with their teachers in a way
reminiscent of the Athenian school during the time of Plato.

The most popular and revered teacher in this city was Tyrannus,
whom the Ephesians called "our Socrates." He was a tall, dark-skinned
Stoic, trained under Attalus, the teacher of Seneca, and known for
his vast intellectual resources and droll charm. Tyrannus read literature in many languages and once had lectured to substantial crowds

in Rome. The child of a Spanish father and Greek mother, he had made a fortune by attracting wealthy pupils in search of philosophic understanding from distant parts of the empire.

Wearing a white toga and straw sandals, he surrounded himself with admiring young men who gleefully absorbed his witticisms, asked him polite questions, and listened to his digressions on ethics or metaphysics in the shade of a tree. Out of curiosity, I visited the Lyceum on a few occasions and found Tyrannus entertaining and, frankly, eloquent. He had read Plato carefully, and in many ways created his own versions of the famous dialogues with his students. And he entertained novel theories about the universe.

I listened with some astonishment as he suggested that the sun blazed at the center of our heavens, and that we occupied a large rock that moved around this fiery object. It was a strange notion, even preposterous, but attractive to the students, who sought unusual explanations for the obvious. Tyrannus explained: "Think of this Lyceum as an example. I am the sun, the light. All of you whirl about me. You reflect my ideas, and quote me nicely or—in some cases—to ill effect. It's a system, this arrangement of bodies; you glow reflectively in my glow. If I fade, you fade. It's the same with the universe, only less amusing."

One could not dislike this man, despite his self-absorption, and I urged Paul to attend his lectures. He did and came back with a definite view.

"It saddens me to see such intelligence go to waste," he said. "If only we had one or two like him in Ephesus as followers of Jesus, we might overwhelm the city. Tyrannus knows that the gods they worship represent nothing real. He has no faith in their power."

"Did you speak with him?"

"We had a good talk in the garden at the end of the day. I've never seen so many fireflies. Like ideas. They popped, sparkled, tantalized. But there was no heat from that light. It was not sustained and sustaining. Summer lightning?"

I was not sure if he referred to Tyrannus or the fireflies. "You told him about the Kingdom of God?"

"Yes. And he was not dismissive." Paul grew uncharacteristically silent.

After a while, I asked him if he would return to the Lyceum.

"Oh, it's more than that. Tyrannus teaches in the mornings, and he said I could have the afternoons in the Lyceum to myself. I have accepted this offer. It's an opportunity. Shall I wear a toga?"

I was startled.

"I think I shall," Paul said. "The news will spread to Athens, mark this!"

"You don't have any pupils."

"I haven't begun, have I?"

I should have known never to dismiss Paul's fantasies or discount his ambitions. Within weeks, he had one, then two, then a dozen pupils. Some of those who sat or walked through the cool hours of morning with Tyrannus returned after a meal at midday to sit or walk with Paul, who found his ideal spot under a leafy tamarind. I would stop to listen, and one conversation stays in my mind.

"Carpus, Carpus ... you are so terribly clever," Paul said to a brown-eyed boy of perhaps eighteen who sat before him on the grass with his legs crossed. Carpus was an Athenian youth, as I discovered, and the son of an aristocratic landowner. He had found the school at Athens wanting and came to Ephesus.

"I don't know how your idea of God differs from what Plato taught," the boy said.

Paul brightened. "Plato understood everything. He was a defender of the Logos, which is the center of being. This is God."

"Or gods?"

"Plato didn't have precise knowledge of the one true God. But if I've read the *Timaeus* properly—and I believe I have—he anticipated our awareness of God."

"He refers to a Craftsman."

"Who is God, of course! You can't imagine several Craftsmen, can you? The Hebrew scriptures say that, in the beginning, God created the heavens and the earth."

"So why did your God make the universe?"

"For the same reason that Plato's Craftsman went to work. To embody goodness."

"You keep referring to the Logos—"

"We have no choice but to find a word that stands in for the reality we intuit. Logos, God, the Craftsman. I often say: God is the center."

"You should be more specific."

"It's the problem of being human. We're frail, insubstantial. Our souls lodge in this flesh, but so briefly. Plato understood that. Jesus did, too."

"Why do you bother with Jesus?"

"Let's call our creator the Craftsman. I'm satisfied with that term. But where does he exist? If he made heaven and earth, heaven and earth came into being at a point in time. Jesus is often called the Logos, the Word who existed before time, and who will exist long after."

This caused a murmur of confusion, and I worried that Paul had lost his footing. The natural turn, I thought, was for him to refer to Jesus as the voice of God, his way of communicating with his own creation. But nothing along these lines emerged, not at this moment.

"Did Plato have an idea of time?" asked another boy.

"He understood eternity as a mode of existence unconditioned by time. In this luminous and mysterious reality, there is no before, no present, no afterward."

A couple of the young men scoffed.

Paul hardened himself, accepting nothing of their guff. "I do believe that Jesus, more than our Jewish sages, or even Plato, understood eternity and time in original ways," he said.

He pushed them closer by the day to his understanding of God, made them aware of the way Jesus had swept through the universe and mopped up time, liberating himself and, in the miracle of his resurrection, liberating us all. With an ease that surprised me, he brought these youths, who had little knowledge of Jewish teachings, into line with his own thought. Soon enough, he baptized Carpus, who would become a leading figure in the Way. And others followed.

We never intended to remain in Ephesus for such a long time, as I kept reminding Paul. But he didn't want to leave, because he had made such inroads among the younger generation here, and he believed we should stay until this phase of our work was done.

It was lucky for me that, since we had settled in for a considerable time, I acquired a number of patients in Ephesus, where I found that my knowledge of herbal medicines attracted a steady clientele. I began, once again, to manufacture salves for skin rashes and insect bites, preferring a mix of marigold and Hypericum, which I combined with olive oil and the crushed pods of tamarind, adding the dust of pigeon bones to draw these strands together. The salve proved effective, and I could hardly make it in sufficient quantities to meet the needs of the Ephesians.

The real surprise was the arrival in Ephesus of Apollos, the wandering teacher, whose fame preceded him. He had been baptized by John the Baptizer in the Jordan, and proclaimed himself a proponent of the Way, even though his understanding of Jesus lacked definition. He turned up at the Lyceum one afternoon, standing at least a full head above Paul, in ragged clothing and sandals. His nut-brown, lean body and long arms conveyed strength and endurance. He was a severe-looking fellow, with a circular scar on his left cheek and abundant gray hair and black eyes. I confess he frightened me a little: a wild creature come out of the desert to terrify us, a scorpion in the shape of a man.

Paul immediately rose to the occasion.

"For whom do you speak?" Paul asked him.

"God, the Almighty."

"Not his son?"

"I know the Way."

"The Way of Jesus?"

"The Nazarene? I believe he was a great rabbi."

It puzzled me that Apollos could have been dipped in the Jordan by John and yet have such little awareness of the Christ. Paul revered him, I could see, recognizing in Apollos a true messenger of God, although one who had been diverted. He saw his task as that of informing him about the meaning of Jesus, his suffering and his resurrection. Apollos had only the vaguest awareness of these truths and listened keenly. He was not, like Paul, a man of disputation, deep learning, or philosophical musing. He maintained a rocklike solidity, an impressive stillness, and gave away little of his feelings.

I could only admire Paul's way of working with Apollos, appealing to his mystical side, telling him about his own visit to the third heaven. He spoke of Musa and his time in the desert, and showed a knowledge of esoteric scriptures that startled me and appealed greatly to Apollos as a man who had spent decades by himself in the Arabian wilderness, in a profound well of prayer.

"I have heard of Musa," he said. And before a further day had passed, he said, "I will follow."

Paul wisely replied, "No, Apollos. You will lead."

They joined forces in Ephesus, drawing more and more God-fearers to our assemblies, often taking the platform together. The Jews, by and large, found these public conversations irresistible, and attendance at the synagogues began to falter. Not surprisingly, this agitated the rabbis, who worried that a marginalized group like the Jews could hardly afford to lose support from its own people. Paul and Apollos threatened them. The atmosphere of resentment, even hatred, began to resemble what we had encountered elsewhere, most recently in Corinth.

The depth of Jewish resistance became clear when I met Jonas, the eldest son of Rabbi Sceva, in the agora. He pushed me to one side behind a stall, gripping my throat.

"Listen carefully," he said. We want you and Paul, and this madman Apollos, to leave us in peace. Get out of Ephesus!"

"What do you mean?"

"Have I minced my words?"

I felt emboldened by the spirit and said, "When God wants this to happen, we shall go. But not before the appropriate day."

"Well, God is talking loudly, my friend. And I'm a friend, because I know that the silversmiths—the men who actually run this city—are *not* friends. And they're afraid they will have much less to do in the coming year if you persist. Who will ask for statues of Artemis now, or miniature replicas of the temple? Should they make statues of Jesus?"

He lifted a knee into my groin, and I dropped to the ground. What a friend this was!

"I won't kick you in the head, old man," he said. "But I do hope you value your life. It won't be worth much in a few weeks."

When I told Paul about this exchange, he said, "Pay no attention to Jonas, or Sceva. God protects us, as the Day of the Lord is coming."

✝

If anything, the opposition of the Jews spurred Paul on. The task before him opened with clarity, and he took it upon himself to counter the influence of the magicians and necromancers who moved among the Ephesians and twisted their souls. He organized a public burning of sorcery books one night in the amphitheater, drawing a crowd. This bonfire attracted both praise and scorn from onlookers.

"What is he doing?" a man asked me, his face licked by the light of the flames.

He worried that Paul's form of "magic" would simply replace another form, and that the cult of Artemis would fade.

"It's an act of purification," I explained.

Our bonfire also sent a brilliant signal throughout Ephesus that Paul the apostle was here, and that he brought a powerful spirit into the city.

The Festival of Artemis began a week later, at the peak of spring, when the plum trees blossomed in the grove outside the temple. Whole families descended, coming from the far ends of Greece and Macedonia. The streets of Ephesus overflowed with their chants, their music, with wanton dancing in the agora, in Curetes and Marble Streets. Young couples on the brink of marriage arrived by the hundreds, bidding for the grace of Artemis, which would assure them of an abundant family. The brothels boomed as well, as the spirit of Artemis inflamed men of every age.

For Paul, this was a ripe time for spreading the Good News, and yet opposition grew in proportion to our success, with discontent rising among silversmiths and other tradesmen, who worried about a potential decline in custom. It was difficult enough to survive without commercial headwinds from the Way.

One day, quite unexpectedly, Paul said, "I have prayed, and I think it's finished, my dear Luke."

"What is?"

"We should go to Antioch."

The retreat to Antioch at this moment confused me, and I realized I had less desire to go home than I expected. I had become quite used to living on the road with Paul. Yet he understood that the opposition to our presence in Ephesus had become an ungovernable force, and we must retreat. We had, in the past, waited too long.

Once again, in fact, we had not moved quickly enough. Jonah, the rabbi's son, and his friend Demetrius, who headed the guild of silversmiths, managed to convince a pliable Roman magistrate that Paul led a "subversive cult" and now "stirred unrest." They had Paul arrested at the Lyceum one afternoon, dragging him from his students, who protested in vain. They took Paul to a particularly filthy prison at the eastern gate of the city, where he would await a hearing before a Roman tribunal—always an uncertain proposition in Ephesus. The prison itself teemed with petty thieves and murderers, pickpockets from Thessaly, and the usual complement of madmen, who ate their own feces or drew faces with it on the walls of the cells. Of course Paul's familiarity with prison life was such that he didn't panic. He had, by his own estimate, been imprisoned at least fifteen times, and he used to say, "I don't know why, but I feel even closer to God in chains, among the least loved."

After a brief search, I found him. Among those unfortunates in his cell was Onesimus, a delicate young man with a red beard and flinty eyes. He was a slave who belonged to Philemon, a friend of ours from Corinth; apparently he had stolen money from his master and fled to Ephesus, where the authorities apprehended him for pickpocketing. Now Paul promised to write to Philemon, asking him to take back this wayward servant, and without punishment. Paul had brought the Good News to Onesimus, baptizing him with a cup of water. The young fellow responded by speaking in tongues, filling the cell with rapturous if incomprehensible chants, frightening the other prisoners but amusing Lucius, Paul's jailor, who was himself a Godfearer, someone we had met at gatherings.

Lucius told me I was welcome to visit at any time of day or night. "We have no restrictions," he said, "especially among those who are not criminals." I asked if I could bring food and wine, and he said, "As you like, sir. The slop in this prison would horrify a starving pig."

The prison smelled of dung and death, and the clay floor was rank with piss, pain, and terror. Fear hovered in the air like motes of dust in the lamplight. One morning I watched them execute a young man of perhaps sixteen in the yard behind the prison, binding him to a post with hemp, beheading him with a dull sword so that his throat bled but he did not die for a long time. Everyone in the prison could hear his agonized dying and fell silent in horror. Any of them could be next, as once you had been imprisoned the guards could seize and execute you with impunity by claiming you were "a threat to the peace."

Paul was, by his very nature, a threat to the peace, and I began to worry. Somehow I must secure his release. But how?

Every day I brought bread and cheese, even salted fish when I could. And Paul asked me to bring writing materials one afternoon, as the spirit had begun to move inside him. Indeed, a blizzard of letters followed, dictated as he paced the narrow room of his cell.

"I should never say this," he said, expanding on an earlier observation, "but I think more clearly in prison. I do! The closeness of the walls and the lack of mobility—all of this frees the mind."

He used his time in prison wisely, as he often did, and wrote passionately to the testy Galatians about their internal disputes; to Lydia and her friends in Philippi, discussing the Collection; to Crispus in Corinth about his continuing conflict with the Jews; and to Philemon as well, urging clemency for his runaway slave. He wrote affectionately to Timothy, although we did not know his whereabouts with precision. We sent letters to Prisca and Aquila, whom we assumed had made it to Rome by now, and to Phoebe in Antioch. I would dispatch these epistles with friends who traveled among the assemblies, several copies at once by different hands.

Rome in particular interested Paul, who heard many stories about our success in the capital, where the Way had flourished in the hands of Epaenetus, Mary, Andronicus, Junia, and Josephus, among others. (These were but names to me, without faces or voices to attach to them, although gossipy Prisca had brought them to life.)

This creative period in Paul's life pleased me. I worked, as ever, closely with him as his scribe, taking notes as rapidly as I could during the day and at night revising what he said, working by candlelight, sleeping little, suffering from boils and loose bowels. But I sensed the occasion, the fire of his imagination that burned in the dank of that prison cell in Ephesus. I had never before seen my friend in such a state of frenzied concentration—an oxymoron, but that is how it struck me.

Paul told me one day, abruptly, that he wished "once and for all to address the problem of the flesh." He called this "an intriguing side of our fallen nature," observing that "men who wished for dominance engaged with younger men, their pupils, at the time of Socrates." I think he could read the shock in my expression, and he teased me, asking if I had never wished to behave in such a way.

"I'm quite tame," I said.

"Don't mock me, Luke. You know what I mean."

I did, but frankness on this order did not suit me, and I had no wish to engage with him on this subject, as it could lead to unwanted distractions and misaligned thoughts and feelings. And, in truth, I felt few urges of the kind he described.

"Do you wish to lie with someone?" he asked me.

"I would never lie with anyone again."

"You must look into your heart."

"I have looked, and it's empty."

"That does you a disservice," he said. "Your heart is full. In any case, God forgives everything."

"I make it easy for him," I said.

Paul brushed this aside (I could see I disappointed him roundly) and began to dictate his beautifully wrought letter to the Romans, a task that absorbed him thoroughly, as he took this opportunity to reconsider many thoughts that had, over the years, vexed him. The question of fornication continued to bubble over in his soul. "God watched them—men and women alike, Jew and Greek—falling prey to dishonorable passions," he said. "These obsessions block the Holy Spirit. But there is hope in him, the Christ, who understands and forgives."

"This is good," I said. "You move to brighten their hearts. They will like it very much."

"It's no matter to me whether the Romans like or dislike what I say, whether they feel happy or sad," he told me, with excessive sternness. "I tell the truth, as God reveals it to me."

"You offer judgments," I said.

"I do not judge anyone!" He seized on this remark, and asked me to write this down: "'Dear men and women of Rome: When you judge another, you judge yourself. Only God can judge us. And he wishes to lead us to sound judgment and repentance. On the last day God's own judgments will be revealed. Until then, we must not condemn anyone.' Is that good, Luke?"

"It's very good."

Indeed, I knew I could work with this, as it chimed nicely with one of the sayings of Jesus, and I teased out from Paul some of its implications. He had, since the trouble in Antioch some years earlier, thought deeply about the nature of the Law, its implications for the Greeks who came to God through Jesus. He now recited a flurry of quotations from the scriptures, combining them into a hymn of his own, finding a fresh tempo:

> Not one is righteous, no, not one!
> No one seeks God.
> All turn aside from him, do wrong, do no good thing.
> Their throats are graves!
> Their tongues deceive!
> The venom of the asp lies under their lips.
> The way of peace eludes them.

"This is all so good," I said. "One hears the voice of David in your phrases. But what about God's role here, and the path that Jesus opens?"

Paul twisted in thought. I had never seen him so convulsed, so eager to forge a view, to separate the strands of argument and lay his meaning bare. When he burst out with language, I could hardly write down everything he uttered, though he would mercifully pause and say, "You've got that, I hope?"

I got fragments, which I would rework in the evening, making them whole. My methods had evolved over the years, and I had some confidence in my ability to complete Paul's thoughts, to emend and revise them. I knew what he intended, or believed I did. God was, I think, working in me, moving my hand.

He nearly bit the air as he spoke now. "The righteousness of God has been made evident apart from the Law, although the prophets and the Law reveal it: We who emulate the faithfulness of Jesus are, like him, made whole. Everyone has sinned and falls short of God's glory. We are splintered but made whole by God's grace, the gift of his son."

I liked this, however rough and scattered, and knew I could improve upon it. The trick was to anticipate the direction of his thought, to complete in reality what he had begun in hope.

Over several days, Paul churned through ideas about redemption, the meaning of the fall of man, the grace of God at work in the world, even the meaning of the Christ's death and resurrection. "All thinking in the Way is resurrection thinking," he told me. "We die to ourselves. Lose our little selves. We take on the larger mind of the Christ, hiding in him as he lodges in us."

"Remember that we must live in this world," I said, "at least for now."

He raked his beard with scrawny fingers. "Write this: 'Do not be conformed to this world. Resist it. Find the will of God, and be transformed in the flesh. Find whatever is good, acceptable, and perfect.'"

"Perfection? Can we ask them for this?"

"God works for the benefit of those who love him, who are called according to his purpose."

I reminded him that Prisca had wondered about the relation of body and soul.

"There is no soul apart from the body," he said. "And no body that does not flourish in the soul. So I will appeal to them all, by God's will and mercy, to put forward their bodies as a living sacrifice, holy and acceptable to God. The Christ showed us with his body how to perfect himself before heaven."

"This is going to be difficult in practice," I said.

"Tell them that God asks only what is possible, in the measure of their faith. No more, no less. Tell them to give everything they have. But not more."

Not more than everything! I would need to consider that again. Would anyone understand? Or find it possible?

Paul defended his role as apostle to the Greeks, saying that he had a plan. He would go first to Jerusalem, would meet with the Pillars, and then make the journey to Rome. A clear path opened in his head, a trajectory, with Spain as a distant goal, a step beyond Rome to what he called "the farthest edge of the world as we know it."

I reminded Paul that some would find his assertions troubling and provocative.

In response to this, he added a warning to the Roman circle: "Take note of those who create dissent and trouble, opposing the good things you have been taught. Avoid these people. For they do not serve the Lord our Christ as they attempt to satisfy their own appetites; they flatter and deceive. I would have you wise to what is good and guileless to what is evil."

After several further weeks of reading over what we had done, I realized that we had assembled the core of the Good News in a succinct and suggestive manner. With a feeling of triumph, I dispatched this letter to Phoebe, who would soon be making her way to Rome. (I gave another copy to Quintus, a commercial traveler we had met in Corinth, who had business in Rome as well. This letter was so good, and so useful, it must find its destination.)

The Roman letter marked the end of our time in Ephesus, which concluded in a flourish of sparks. A number of our friends in the Way had been seized, and they would be taken into the amphitheater for an interrogation led by Demetrius, the intemperate silversmith, who had convinced so many of his fellow tradesmen that the Way posed a threat to their livelihood. The Jews in this city had seized on and multiplied the resentments against us, hoping to drive us away.

Lucius, Paul's jailor, told us about the forces marshalling against us, and he took it upon himself to liberate Paul, saying: "I believe they will come for you and kill you. So take note. The door will be left open briefly tonight, when I step outside after dark. You will know what to do."

Paul kissed Lucius on the forehead and thanked him.

That night, after the others had fallen asleep and when Lucius stepped outside into the yard, Paul gently pushed at the door, and it swung free.

Outside, Lucius said, "You must leave Ephesus in the morning. It's not safe here, I assure you."

"Will you be in trouble for my sake?"

"It doesn't matter," Lucius said. "We have enough prisoners here."

Paul came to my room that evening, and at first I thought it must be a ghost.

"We must go to the amphitheater in the morning," said Paul. "I can't abandon them."

"But you can't help them. They will murder you."

"I've been murdered before. Yet here I am. Do you recognize me, Luke?"

I could only smile. But I would not, under any circumstances, allow him to go to the amphitheater.

"You're telling me what to do?"

I said, "I've devoted myself to you. I think you know this. And there is work to be done elsewhere. Antioch calls us. And we have the Collection."

Paul sighed. And I knew that, for once, he would listen.

Chapter Sixteen

⁜

LUKE

On the night of our arrival in Antioch, we were shown such a quantity of gold—Phoebe laid it out on a table in her house, the glittering coins—that I wondered how we might safely transport this bounty to the Pillars. It would be dangerous to send it ahead with messengers, and of course Paul relished the idea of putting the Collection on a similar table in Peter's house himself, with James standing to one side and wringing his hands.

"We carry this ourselves," said Paul.

Timothy had recently joined us again, so we had three men to transport the Collection. The famine had, sadly and cruelly, continued in Jerusalem without respite, and grain was beyond the reach of the poorest in our circle. We heard rumors of children and the elderly dying for lack of nourishment. The rest could manage, but uncomfortably. This gift had become more than symbolic. It would save many of them from starvation.

We set off quickly, as Paul saw no reason to wait, sailing for Troas in the hot, unblinking sun. Paul looked triumphant as he stood on the foredeck and gripped the rails, his face turned upward. He was the earth itself, hard-packed, with cracks in his face like a baked mudflat. He had aged, his sparse beard going white. Hair had mostly disappeared from his head, with a slight fringe at the back and sides, a few isolated strands on top. His eyebrows bushed, unruly and white as well. But the quick eyes always caught you, alive with movement. As ever, he leaned close to talk, too close, whispering or shouting, depending on his mood.

We rounded a spar with purple cliffs and entered the calm harbor, where the water was so clear one could see schools of orange fish that burst into light and faded into shadow. Troas had once been famous for a school established by Aristotle, and we still thought of it in these terms, although the philosophical rumblings had long disappeared. There we called at once on Judah, a prosperous fishmonger who owned several vessels and was a member of our circle, and he invited us to stay with him for as long as we found it useful.

We shared our sacred meal in his good company on the second story of his narrow house overlooking the harbor and held a gathering with a dozen or so members of the Way, who were drawn from local Jews and Greeks. Paul led the meeting and, afterward, preached for three full hours. I hadn't seen him so enthused in a while, with language pouring from him. The room seemed to relish the stories about what had happened to us in Galatia, Corinth, and Ephesus, and Paul drew everyone forward in their seats with excitement, and some of them would call out in affirmation to whatever he said. This was the purest kind of performance, theatrical in manner, with Paul taking on voices like a man possessed.

But the evening took a dark turn when, toward the end of Paul's reflections, the son of our host, a boy of eleven, fell backward through the open window and landed on the path below. His name was Eutychus, a skinny talkative boy who looked younger than his age, with wide brown eyes and curly auburn hair. Paul had been charmed by him and spent more time than usual in his company, telling him stories about our adventures.

"The boy is a wonder," Paul had said, "with pressing questions. All good questions."

We ran outside and watched in horror as Judah cradled the boy in his arms, kneeling in the dirt with him, weeping. Blood bathed the boy's face, pouring from a wound just above the brow. The eyes rolled back in his head, the whites marbled with red. The mother wept as well, standing at the side, held aloft by two friends.

"He is gone," Judah said, and several women trilled their tongues in grief.

I never saw Paul so focused or determined to summon the spirits. He knelt beside the boy and held a hand out over him, and he prayed passionately, "Dear Jesus, Jesus, Jesus! Hear me, son of God, Jesus, our Christ. Heal this child. Heal! Almighty father, waken the boy from this slumber. In the name of your beloved son."

After only a moment, as if thinking it over, Eutychus opened his eyes, wiped a swash of blood from his brow with one hand, looked dismissively at the vermillion smear on his small palm, and smiled, saying, "I'm fine, Mother. Why are you crying? Why is everyone afraid?"

Judah knelt before Paul, still in tears. I thought he would kiss Paul's feet.

"Stand, Judah. I did nothing," Paul told him. "God will, if he chooses, answer prayers offered in his son's name. With him, anything is possible. I have seen this. The spirit rises when we bow before the throne of the Almighty with the name of Jesus on our lips."

Paul knew how to handle these situations, and he had God's ear, that much I knew.

I myself thought that Eutychus had tumbled to his death. It was a high window, and the fall was precipitous, the ground unforgiving. But once they cleaned the blood from his face with a wet cloth, he seemed even better than before, even quite happy, moving easily among the gathering. He chattered and basked in their love, now amplified by his revival.

Paul never appeared livelier, or more spirit-filled.

Taking Timothy aside after the meeting, Paul said to him, "Walk with me in the morning, if you will. To Assos. I need to stretch."

Paul asked me to accompany them, too, but it was a steep climb over a stony pass in the hot sun with near-vertical patches. I preferred to go by ship, and I didn't actually mind a few days away from Paul. I had been deeply in his company for some time and looked forward to a break from that torrent.

Paul was glad, in any case, to walk with Timothy, who was eager for his mentor's company. I watched them shrink into the distance, the slight young man with curly hair and Paul, hunched and brown and bald, always with a stick in hand since he could lose his balance unexpectedly. (It was for this reason I tried to discourage his walk to Assos, but he ignored my plea for caution.)

A number of friends joined us there, including Aristarchus, that quiet but lovely young man from Thessalonica, who had worked with Jason in the leather trade. That he had come such a distance to find us moved me. I had forgotten how much I liked him.

Paul and Timothy joined us three days later in Assos, where we all boarded a large sailing vessel that took us to Miletus, stopping along the way at the port of Mytilene on the southeastern edge of Lesbos, the home of Sappho, the lyric poet who wrote so heartbreakingly about love. We also stopped briefly at Chios, the birthplace of Homer and Ion. I knew this pause in our journey would excite the apostle, who appeared to hold in memory all of Ion's ten thousand lines.

"There is poetry in the air," said Paul.

I stood beside him on a shingle of bone-white pebbles that scrambled after the tide with a rhythmical sucking sound, and there he recited Ion in a voice that carried over the knock of waves against the rocks:

> And the long white cloud continues,
> This dear world wherein we dwell:
> Part heaven and part hell.
> So the gods allow us to be fed
> With fruit of words, these openings to worlds
> Beyond our present: fragrant portals
> Where we enter, linger, breathe, begin
> these orisons, with tongues of many angels.

Nobody in my experience could recite poems with such feeling, the words and phrases ravishing the air. Paul had no ear for music as such, which had surprised me. He simply could not sing, however much he tried, often to the amusement or despair of friends at gatherings. Instead, language was his instrument, and he played it well, summoning the music of ideas.

"God spoke to me last night," Paul said that morning. "He has asked me to prepare myself for the conclusion of this mission. My work is done. I've given what I have, though—I confess—I long to go to Rome, even to Spain."

We would donate our Collection—an impressive sum—to the Way in Jerusalem, and it would surely help them through a dark time of famine and self-doubt. Perhaps the diverging roads of the Way would merge again, if luck held. But I wondered if our gift would really provoke a change of heart. Gifts can also stir resentments, as nobody actually likes to stand at the receiving end of charity. Gratitude is a difficult emotion to master. Perhaps I should have kept my worries to myself, but I asked Paul directly if James and Peter would appreciate our work on their behalf.

"You ask me things I can't answer," he said. "It is annoying when you do this."

I did my best to let arrows like this skim off my breastplate. I had a good deal of natural armor and could withstand occasional attacks by the apostle. But I prayed that God would fortify and protect me from these unnecessary jibes. I never quite knew what provoked them. It was better to put my head down and proceed, as a vision of loveliness opened before us.

At Rhodes, perhaps the most beautiful of the islands on this coast, our ship stopped for two days to unload a quantity of grain in heavy sacks and to collect crates of amphorae filled with wine and oil. From the deck we could see the ruins of the Colossus, a bronze statue of unimaginable proportions. It had once stood aloft in the brilliant sky, improbably balanced, before an earthquake toppled it. One could not hold even the thumb of this figure in one's arms, it was so mammoth. Now untold quantities of bronze lay at the harbor's entrance, glistening at dawn, a ruined Leviathan asleep in these green waters, never to waken.

"Why does this make me so sad?" Paul asked, gazing over the rail of our ship at the ruins.

Was this yet another omen, a sign of his demise?

Timothy would have none of Paul's dark mood. "The pagan world must fall, must fail. It has already failed! This statue—I see it as a kind of false triumph. I hope the sea carries it away."

Paul smiled at his protégé. "You say wise things, my dear friend."

Timothy often said foolish things, in fact, but I had no wish to correct him. The young speak confidently in ways that must embarrass anyone over a certain age. I know that I, as a young man, believed quite firmly that I had a complete knowledge of medical science. That "complete" knowledge dwindled year by year as I came to know how little I knew or could possibly know. I grew increasingly wary of predictions. As Herophilus, the legendary anatomist who taught in Alexandria, once said, "Don't predict. Observe and be still."

When I mentioned this to Paul, he said, "You're a fount of irrelevant quotations, dear Luke. Herophilus! Another of your medical mountebanks."

I forgave Paul for this and other rebukes, knowing he couldn't help himself. As we set sail for Palestine, I saw he was fearful, unhappy, and overwrought, as if he understood that nothing could go as we hoped, not in Jerusalem, where so many in the Way had no understanding of Paul's vision. His words would feel oddly discordant to them, and—with so many angry Jews on full alert—he must have understood that he faced the challenge of his life. From what we had heard, James lay in wait for us, eager to make light of our gift.

We changed for another vessel in Patara, on the southern coast of Lycia; its hold was filled with a large quantity of timber, and it listed ominously to port. Which meant the captain kept urging us to stand at the starboard rails: never a welcoming command. We hugged the shoreline closely on our journey to Caesarea, stopping for a full week at Tyre, a major port in Phoenicia. With so much timber in store, the ship required twenty men to unload it, and this cargo was immediately replaced by copper and iron, as well as hides.

A true son of his father, Paul always showed interest in commercial dealings, and he spoke at length with the Greek captain about his experience with hides in Jerusalem some decades ago. "They paid too much for these hides, I suspect," Paul said.

Alerted to our arrival, a number of followers met us in Tyre. It astonished me how word traveled in our circle, leaping from harbor to harbor. Paul knew many of them, as a few had once lived in Jerusalem but fallen out with James, who continued to expand his influence. To this gathering, after the sacred meal, Paul spoke freely. I saw that, to them, he was the true apostle of the Christ, although one of their number claimed that, in a dream, he had been warned by an angel that Paul should not proceed to Jerusalem. "It's unsafe for Paul," the angel had said.

Paul took no notice of this. "There are too many angels," he said. "And each of them has an opinion."

We set off again, sailing past Cyprus, which prompted Paul to recall his months there with Barnabas and John Mark, whom he referred to as "that plump little toad." I noticed that Paul, for the most part, looked away from the island, as if shielding his eyes from a version of himself that provoked discomfort. I never understood what had gone amiss on that journey, though scandalous rumors spread among Paul's enemies.

From the deck I watched in awe as the limestone Promontory of Zeus swelled before us.

"Mount Carmel," Paul said. "It's where Elijah confronted the priests of Baal. A brave moment for him."

"What's that again?" My weak knowledge of history was on display now.

"Gamaliel always spoke of this incident with a kind of special energy. The Canaanites would make unholy sacrifices there. I'll never set foot on that hill, believe me. It's full of evil spirits."

I believed him. Not being a Jew, I relied on Paul's knowledge of such things, and he liked to play the wise rabbi with me. Timothy, of course, could never get enough of this, and I listened as he questioned Paul about the Canaanites. Who were they? What did they want? Where had they gone? So many questions . . .

"Alexander sat beside Aristotle," I said to Paul one day, with Timothy listening.

"What does that mean?"

"I'm thinking of you and Timothy."

Paul raised one eyebrow. "I believe you've just been compared to Alexander the Great, my boy," he said. "Perhaps you will conquer Palestine one day."

+

The arrival in Jerusalem, where political tensions had reached a threatening level, frightened me, and confrontations in the streets between Jews and Roman soldiers had risen to a level of violence unknown in recent decades. I revealed my misgivings to Paul, and this was always risky.

"How can they harm us, with God as our protector?" he asked me as we drew near Ptolemais, one of the ports along this coastline. In a moment of peculiar self-revelation, he added, "I'm more spirit than flesh these days."

"It's one of the benefits of aging," I said.

We disembarked with our treasure and were joined by another band of followers led by Philip. They came with camels and donkeys, who swelled this caravan taking our gift to the Way. A sense of something awesome, without precedent, filled me; almost no one in our company spoke, as if aware of our moment in history. We moved in grandeur, with respect for the deed before us, which could unite everyone in the love of the Christ.

Apparently Philip had known Paul in Jerusalem many years ago, and he admired a holy man named Agabus, who occupied a lonely shepherd's hut above the city, where he lived on honey and locusts. He came to meet us as we drew close, summoned by Philip, and said to Paul directly, "Do not proceed to Jerusalem. They want to kill you there."

"You had better listen," said Philip.

This was his second warning, and I suggested he take it seriously. He could return to Antioch, and a few of us—less conspicuously—could drop off the Collection and retreat as well. The less splash we made, perhaps, the better.

Paul shrugged. "I trust in God. And go where I go. If I should die in Jerusalem, I die for the one I serve."

I bit my tongue, as it was not my place to argue with Paul about his destiny or vision. Yet a gloom settled over me as we set off for Jerusalem the next day, with Paul intensely conscious of the fact that this could well be the final leg of his meandering journey through life. At least he didn't climb up on a donkey as the walled city loomed, this mirage that grew into reality before us, with its amber walls and the Temple gradually asserting itself, that sacred center of the world, rebuilt after the Babylonian captivity by Ezra and Nehemiah. We stopped for a meal by the roadside and listened to Paul, who had such a memory for the details of history that everyone marveled. He recalled that Herod had added the impressive Second Wall between the Jaffa Gate and the Temple Mount.

"I don't know Jerusalem well," I said.

Paul looked at me sternly. "Pay attention, Luke. This will be important for your writing."

Art is an act of attention, and I was writing down everything at night, making notes while the rest of our company slept. My story of the adventures of Paul would attract readers. How could it not? Someone had to remember everything that had happened, what we did, what Paul had said and accomplished. In his letters, he refused for the most part to talk about himself, addressing problems at hand in Galatia, Thrace, Thessalonica, Philippi, Derbe, Cyprus, Corinth, Antioch, and Ephesus. Everywhere unique conflicts and tensions arose, and Paul did his best to advise them, offering the fruits of his prayers.

As it was, no fanfare greeted us as we entered Jerusalem, no buzzing cloud of witnesses, clanging cymbals or drums. No feathery palms spread before our path. No wreaths of laurel.

Paul was anonymous, for a time. And it was good that we attracted no attention since the gold in our possession made us a clear target for thieves.

"Mnason the Cypriot is expecting us," Paul said.

Surely enough Mnason, a wealthy dealer in olive oil, welcomed us to his large house only half a mile from the Temple. The Jews disliked him, this man with no roots in their tradition; he had been, as Paul explained, "a disciple from the beginning, only briefly a Godfearer." I believe that Peter had often engaged him, seeking financial advice if not gifts for the Way.

"Their incompetence annoys me," Mnason said. "James would have everyone a pauper, and Peter can't manage his own finances."

I worried that Mnason had no sympathy for those affected by the famine, but I didn't mention this, as Paul caught my eye with a look that, of course, I understood. It was as if he could read my mind and objected to my remarks even before I made them.

Mnason said we could stay with him as long as we liked, though Paul had very little sense of how long we might remain. Would we simply return to Antioch after giving the Collection to Peter and James, accepting their thanks and bowing in retreat? That would have pleased me, as I could then reclaim my family home, perhaps resume my medical practice. We had done the work we set out to do, and the Kingdom of God would unfold in its proper time. One could not hurry the Christ. God's plan for his creation remained his own, and we could not expect to understand everything now.

"We're going to Rome, in due course," said Paul, vaguely to Mnason but also to me.

Always Rome. And I knew that I, too, would be drawn to the center of the empire with him. My dream of settling in Antioch for good was, alas, short-lived.

✦

Paul could hardly wait to bring the Collection to Peter and sent a message announcing our arrival. Peter replied warmly, saying we should go to the house of James the following day. The brother of Jesus lived at the edge of the Upper City, in a villa with a surprisingly large interior garden.

"A gift from an admirer," Paul whispered.

The next day we arrived, several of us, with the box. Anxiety pulsed in the villa, where any number of unknown faces appeared: The Way in Jerusalem had acquired its own complexion, and we had lost touch with them. Everyone looked out of sorts, unhappy to see us. Even when we presented them with our gift, they barely acknowledged us. James, in particular, reacted with only a quick, nervous glance at one of his associates, who remained impassive.

Peter tried his best now to make us comfortable. "I can hardly thank you enough, all of you. Especially you, dear Paul. We will put this gift into service. The poor among us will benefit. Nobody will starve, even if there's another dry season."

Sitting in a wicker chair, arms folded across his chest, James sighed. He had grown very old and strange-looking, with dark hollows in his cheeks. John the Baptizer could not have appeared more haggard, wizened, or otherworldly. He mumbled to himself continuously, as if in dispute with some invisible spirit. His eyes twitched, these tiny red orbs with black circles beneath them.

"You look tired," Paul said to James. "Do you live on locusts?"

"I eat no meat," said James. "But locusts are fine."

"So you pluck the wings of these poor insects, and eat them

greedily," Paul said. "Is that right? Should we not consider locust as a form of *meat*?"

James's mouth puckered slightly, as if a lemon had been pushed into it, and the skin of his brow tightened. Did Paul really wish to cause offense at the moment we should have been reconciled, at last, with the Jerusalem contingent? Peter looked glumly at me when I caught his eye.

"I don't know where you hear such things," said James.

"One hears things, especially about you. Of course I dismiss most of what I hear. Gossip is tedious."

Somehow I didn't expect Paul to taunt the brother of Jesus.

Peter made an effort to shift the conversation onto happier ground. "Tell us where you have been, Paul and Luke. And Timothy. We hear rumors, but we can't keep track of your travels in the West."

"The West," said Paul, "is larger than you know." He launched into an account of our travels, observing that many Godfearers and Greeks had come into our circle, and that the Kingdom of God drew ever closer. "We have seen our numbers grow, our gatherings spilling over. The seeds we planted have taken root, often in stony soil. The little green shoots push through the dirt. There are flowers, here and there, and there is fruit!"

He went a little overboard—Peter and James might have preferred a modest answer—but Paul could not restrain himself.

James looked quietly angry as Paul continued in a manner that most would consider boastful.

"They say you teach the Jews who live among Greeks to ignore the teachings of Moses altogether," James said. "The Law of Moses is irrelevant, that is apparently what you say to them. They find our traditions ludicrous, or irrelevant. Even the Jews refuse to circumcise their sons. They eat meat that is improperly slaughtered. Do they eat pigs now? Do they fornicate as well?"

Paul said, "We had an agreement, I believe, some years ago. Am I mistaken? I have only done as we agreed. Jews are Jews, and they should follow the Law to whatever degree accords with their hearts."

I was quite relieved that he didn't bring up what he had written to the Romans, where he said without equivocation: "No, my friends, no! A man is a Jew inwardly and not by circumcision. I call this circumcision of the heart, by the spirit, not in accord with any written code. We do not obey the letter of the law but understand its spirit. A man who has been transformed by the spirit seeks praise only from God, not from others."

James had something in mind now, and said, "We have four men among us who are newly admitted to our circle. They are Jews. Show them that you are a Jew, a Pharisee, of the tribe of Benjamin. You observe the Law yourself, as I understand. So take them into the Temple for the ritual purification. Pay for the shaving of their heads. And shave your own head, Paul!"

Paul was so bald it would take the most superfluous effort to shave his head, and I could see this vaguely amused him.

"I shall do as you suggest," he said.

"Do you love my brother, Paul?"

It was another odd remark by James. Did Paul love Jesus? Here was the man, after all, who wrote to the Roman assembly: "For I am convinced beyond doubt that neither death nor life, nor angels, nor rulers, nor present things, nor things to come, nor powers, nor height, nor depth, nor anything else in this whole of creation, will be able to separate us from the love of God in Christ Jesus, our Lord."

And yet James would not let it go. "You do love my brother?"

Paul said, "As much as you, shall we say?"

That seemed to end it.

The next day we met at the steps of the Temple with the four young men who had been raised as Jews but vowed to serve only Jesus, our Christ. The Temple Guards watched us nervously, while Jews crowded the courtyard in more than the usual numbers, hovering in conversation on the steps. Many still recalled Paul as a fellow worshipper, though it had been a long time since he had been among them in this way. Paul certainly understood the rituals of the Temple and what was required. Now he stood with the four men and said, "I will take you in. They will shave our heads, as you know. Remember that we do this as Jews who understand that Jesus is the Christ, that we give ourselves to his mind, God's mind in ours. Enlightenment is at hand. The night is gone, far gone. The day arrives."

I don't think they quite understood this overcharged declaration, nor did I. Not exactly. Paul doubtless had an impulse to define this moment for the young men in ways separate from what the ritual portended. He searched to find a language adequate to the experience at hand, but he had not found it, at least not this time.

Having never been a Jew, I stayed well beyond the boundaries. In truth, I didn't understand their passion for dividing lines and directives. Paul had told me about the priests, the children of Aaron, who guarded the Holy of Holies with a jealousy beyond comprehension to a Greek. One entered this area at risk of death. A gentile could not go anywhere near the inner courts, and I could see the guards with their swords ready to slay any intruder. An aura of menace hung over the place, and it failed to inspire the love of God in me.

As we all knew, the high priest of the Temple had recently been murdered by a zealot from the Galilean hills, who had been immediately stoned to death by Temple Guards. The potential for disruption terrified the civil authorities, too, and Roman soldiers gathered at the entrance to the Temple, keeping watch. The imperial army was omnipresent in Jerusalem, in encampments outside the city walls, prowling the streets, guarding the entrance to the Temple. They feared, with justification, that the beginnings of a large revolt could erupt anywhere, anytime, and one could not predict how this destructiveness would end.

The world did seem near its end.

Leaving me to wait by myself in a shady spot, Paul took the young men into the Temple. They emerged a few hours later, their heads shaven. They all looked quite happy, chattering among themselves. Paul walked in the center of their little circle, and I could see that he was full of stories.

Suddenly a large, gruff man began to shout at Paul from nearby, shaking a fist. I could not easily comprehend the accusation he made, though I heard the name of Trophimus. Paul had recently been seen in the company of Trophimus, a well-known Ephesian, who had been visiting Jerusalem on business. We all knew Trophimus well. He was a friend. And Paul and I had certainly walked in the street with him the day before, even stepping briefly into the courtyard of the Temple while Paul explained certain things before we passed on.

"He took a Greek into the Temple, into the sacred place!" the man cried, as the mob intensified in number and heat. Others shouted accusations of blasphemy.

Paul refused to answer them, even to acknowledge their shouts.

"He is innocent!" I said as loudly as I could.

One of them hit me in the jaw, and I fell to the ground, losing consciousness briefly. Paul rushed toward me, wanting to help, but they held him back. Where had they all come from? As they would, the well-trained Roman guards knew exactly what they must do in these circumstances. A riot must not happen. They had been instructed to isolate and calm an uprising before it actually started, and they were told to arrest the culprit at once and disperse the mob by any means necessary.

They quickly identified Paul as the instigator.

"He's not the one!" I said as clearly as I could. I would do anything to protect Paul, but someone kicked me in the head as I tried to sit, knocking me to the paving stones, and the last thing I saw was the apostle, my dear friend, being led away in chains.

꙰

Chapter Seventeen

PAUL

I had never seen the Roman presence in Jerusalem in such profusion, with legionaries on every street as Passover approached. They watched keenly, even warily, while visitors spilled through the eleven gates of the city. Guards on horseback stood in the dark shadow of the Temple Mount, swords drawn for use if needed. I saw a man arrested for shouting at a huckster in the marketplace, another seized for staring at a soldier. Violence had erupted near the Zion Gate the week before, with the death of a Roman policeman, the first in a few years. This act only intensified the imperial glare.

The whole of Judea, and Palestine more broadly, had been tense for years, as Jews clashed with the occupying forces, who misunderstood and probably hated our people, our culture, our God. Outlaws and rebel groups roamed the countryside, with occasional skirmishes, some of them deadly. For the most part, the disturbances had been isolated in Galilee and the northern provinces, with their long Maccabean history of rebellion, but now Jerusalem had become a flash point and flames could easily engulf the holy city.

These walls would not stand for long, that much I foresaw. And thought of the words of Jeremiah, the prophet: *O Jerusalem, wash your heart from wickedness, that you may be saved. How long shall your vain thoughts lodge within you?*

In the past weeks, a fiery Jew from Alexandria, one Ezekiel, had entered the city under cover. This zealot had been massing rebels in the distant hills for months, and he wished to incite further trouble in Judea, calling himself "the new Maccabeus," reminding those who gathered around him that Judas Maccabeus had overthrown the Seleucid occupation many centuries ago with far fewer men. "It's not the size of the rebel forces," Maccabeus famously said, "it's the size of their fury." He and his men shattered the pagan statuary that Antiochus Epiphanes had put in the Temple, restoring Jewish worship, making the Holy of Holies a sacred place once again. The name of Maccabeus rang of resistance, with the aura of victory.

Despite my misgivings about the directions the Jews had undertaken in recent decades, and how they had turned their backs on the Christ, I understood the wish to rid our ancient and sacred land of invaders—there had been so many over the centuries, and we as a people recalled with sorrow the long exile in Babylon. (My father never ceased to remind me of Babylonian atrocities, as if they had happened a week, and not centuries, before.) But the Roman Empire had overwhelmed us thoroughly and definitively, and it made little sense to fight against them, especially now, with the Kingdom of God at hand.

The Christ would conquer every army with the purest love.

Dear Luke often called me an "apostle of love," and I would not contradict him on this. I tried to follow the Lord's directive: *Love God and love your neighbor as yourself.* There was no higher commandment.

Jesus would heal all divisions between God and man, as he had done in my own life.

I was a young boy, visiting the Holy Land with my father, when I had first seen Herod's restoration of the Temple. I recall standing below it, peering up at the gold-clad façade, this accumulation of glory. "It is brighter than the sun," my father had said. He told me that one day I would sit among the elders and would see for myself the high priest as he stood before the Holy of Holies, his robe glinting with emerald, onyx, beryl, jasper, and sapphire, his miter of linen tied by a blue ribbon, his golden crown in which the four letters symbolizing the name of God had been lovingly engraved. My father never tired of ceremonial details, and he had fixed them permanently in my head.

Temple life had meant so much to me, and I had, in my years under Gamaliel, often gone to pray there, mounting the fourteen steps, lifted on a chorus of the Levite choir, whose lovely music was, my father reflected with uncharacteristic grace, "so beautiful and yet a pale reflection of the choir that sings to God."

I missed being near the Temple, with the sheen of its walls, the glow of its limestone ashlars at sunset, the mix of gold and bronze that answered the sunrise back with as good as it gave. I missed the slightly sweet smell of burnt offerings, and the noise of pigeon wings and mewling goats in the courtyard, where sacrificial animals were sold. I had returned several times to this sacred place in the past few days, as if drawn to the source, its axial power, and the hush that lay behind the colorful veil enclosing the Holy of Holies.

One morning I took Trophimus into the Court of the Gentiles. He was a friend from Ephesus, a Greek convert to the Way who often stopped by our leather shop to tell stories and listen. A cheery silver-smith, he was not much younger than myself but could boast a stout belly and loose jowls, which he considered a mark of his prosperity. Blood-red ears and a purple nose distinguished his face.

"Such a colorful fellow," said Timothy, who could never restrain himself.

Trophimus had come to Jerusalem on business, his first visit to the city where our Lord had been crucified. He heard from an acquaintance in the Way that I was here. Word traveled in our circle quickly, more so now than ever.

"Show me the Temple," he said, as we walked in the city, arm in arm.

I knew exactly how far to take him into the Temple grounds, being well aware that the established barrier—so clearly marked—must never be crossed by gentiles under any circumstances. I had once, as a young man, witnessed a visitor from Thrace, a Greek merchant, step blithely beyond the boundaries, ignoring threats blazing out in Hebrew, Latin, and Greek: "No gentiles beyond this point!" The poor fellow lasted perhaps ten minutes before Temple Guards swooped. They led him outside the city walls that same morning and stoned him to death without needing to inform the civilian authorities.

The Romans allowed for these "religious executions," as they called them, shrugging their shoulders at our "brutal cultic habits." A Jewish matter, in their minds, was beyond their jurisdiction, some-thing they preferred not to consider, dismissing Jewish rules and practices as a kind of fanaticism beneath contempt. Toleration had been the official policy of Rome for decades, and one that had benefited everyone. But now a terrible war loomed, as anyone could sense, though I hoped our Lord would return before it began.

War solves nothing. It never does. As Jesus well understood. And it would be unbearable to see this shining Temple destroyed yet again, as it certainly would be.

I told Trophimus about Solomon's Temple, the magnificent predecessor to this one, and how it had been destroyed by the Babylonians. I explained that we had rebuilt it slowly over centuries. "Herod took all the credit for this," I said, "but it was a project much larger than him." That day Trophimus left the Temple grounds without incident.

The inundation of visitors to Jerusalem at this time of year added to political anxieties that shifted in the air and upset the Roman authorities, who knew how little it took for a riot to become a revolutionary surge beyond their control. Those in our circle found this disturbing, as we felt more vulnerable than even the Jews, having so many enemies.

Josephus lived here, one of the Antioch Jews who had despised and condemned every Jew who dared to call Jesus the Christ (he particularly disliked Phoebe, in part because of her wealth and influence). He and his many allies claimed that our movement had insolently rejected the Law of Moses, the heritage of Israel itself. "They eat meat that has been sacrificed to idols, they dine with gentiles, they refuse circumcision," he complained. "The Temple means nothing to them!" Did we fornicate with pigs as well?

A rumor circulated that I, an apostle of the Lord, had burned a scroll in plain view of one congregation of Jews "somewhere in Asia." Such nonsense. But rumors can be difficult to contain, especially when they are florid and play to the excitability of gullible listeners. It never worked simply to say: I did not do that, I burned nothing!

As Timothy exclaimed when I told him this, "You have become, Paul, a rumor in your own time."

The sad thing is that Josephus in his fury reminded me of myself at twenty, a hater of those who followed the Way, eager to wipe out this persistent sect that threatened and made a mockery of everything I prized.

I heard that Josephus and his followers regarded me as the Adversary. He said he would do his best to see that I stood accused of the foulest crimes, including blasphemy. My skull would be crushed by Jewish stones. "We shall erase the name of Paul!" he proclaimed.

I didn't care a whit about the name of Paul—I was nobody, nothing. I had erased myself in the name of the Christ. Josephus either didn't understand this or had not listened closely to my words.

A pack of Jews led by Josephus now took me by surprise as I stood in the heat of the sun in the Courtyard of Gentiles with the four young Jews who had shaved their heads and gone with me into the Temple for purification. Perhaps foolishly, I had come here to satisfy James, to prove my continuing devotion to God and Temple worship. But I never expected this treachery!

The attack began with a round of jibes and hisses, followed quickly by sputtering threats. "That's him!" someone cried. A crowd seethed around me, and a young man spat in my face.

At first I didn't take this seriously, and wondered who these people were and what I had done to elicit their wrath. Surely they mistook me for another. It could not be a crime to bring four pious young Jews into the Temple for purification. Had I not shaved my own head in obeisance to Almighty God and his descendants through Abraham and David?

The heavy Corinthian bronze doors of the nearest gate drew shut from within, a sign that the priests wished not only to protect their sacred area but also to hear nothing and to know nothing about what transpired in the outside world. Ignorance was their self-protective gesture in every awkward circumstance.

Then Josephus himself stood before me, pointing.

"He's the one, Paul!"

Was it pure hatred, that sharpness in his eyes, which narrowed like points of fire?

Two burly men seized me by the elbows, claiming that I had taken "an Ephesian, a filthy Greek" beyond the boundaries.

"This is a lie," I said.

But it seemed impossible to defend myself or reassure them that I had no intention of defiling this Temple. Was I not a Pharisee? Did they imagine I didn't understand the rules?

Escape routes caught my eye: a slight opening in the crowd. I had disappeared into the general surge and bustle many times, as one leaf in a forest becomes invisible. Yet I could not escape the invisible noose my accusers tightened around my neck that day. Temple Guards appeared in numbers, accompanied by Roman military policemen, who must have been summoned from the Antonia Fortress.

I looked up at the Temple, thinking of our Lord in the days before his crucifixion. He had said, "Destroy this Temple and I shall rebuild it, and it will take only three days." I had often dwelled on that uncanny remark. Perhaps Jesus referred to the temple of his body, which they would soon destroy, tearing him limb from limb over the course of Passover. He would be beaten and scourged, then crucified. But in three days he would rise to new life, his temple rebuilt, transmogrified.

His body was broken for us so that we might have new life. I had uttered this phrase many times at the sacred meal, in far-flung parts of the empire. They might break my body, too. But I had been changed forever on the Damascus Road, and would rise instantly to life in him, my Lord. A strange calm settled over me as I thought about the brief time ahead of me on this earth, knowing I could not be harmed. What could they do to me, with God as my shield? I turned my eyes to heaven in thanks, and saw a brilliant circle of light above my head. An angel? I heard its wings bell-beat the air. Then a voice spoke: "Paul, my son! Say only what is true, and I will protect you. Have no fear." The phrase "no fear" echoed and dwindled as the crowd fell silent.

Had they heard this voice as well?

I knelt on the paving stones, bowing my head. "Thy will be done," I said, praying as our Lord had prayed in the garden before his arrest.

"This is Ezekiel!" a boy shouted.

I lifted my head, looked into his emerald eyes and saw his coppery hair: He didn't seem more than thirteen. Was this Simon, my old dear friend? Had he come back to accuse me falsely of being a dangerous zealot?

I saw Luke now, and tried to rush toward him, but several of the mob restrained me, pulled me backward. Guards fastened my wrists with leather straps and lifted me to my feet. One of them pulled a chain around my neck, cutting the skin, and I bled. Unable to speak, dizzy, I tried to look at my accusers as the crowd lunged toward me, ripping my tunic, pulling my ears. I thought I might suffer dismemberment at their hands when a young man with appalling hatred in his eyes kicked one of my shins, drawing more blood.

I prayed to myself: *Jesus, how you suffered! I know how you suffered!*

The thorns dug into his scalp that day, the ignominious crown that mocked his pretense to kingship. My pain did not compare to his, but I felt strangely closer to him, to his experience on the hard but holy day of his torture. He had walked through the streets only a short distance from this spot, a rough-hewn heavy cross on his shoulders. He had stumbled and fallen, whereupon a benign passerby had assisted him, taking that instrument of death upon himself. If only I could have been there, able to help him. I would surely have carried that cross to the four corners of the earth.

I must have passed out, as I wakened within the Antonia Fortress, where Jesus had spent his last night before the crucifixion. I lay on the dirt in a filthy room where they interrogated prisoners, often torturing them, extracting false confessions before scourging and beheading them. Their shit, blood, and piss darkened the dirt, and the room swam in this stench of terror, an invisible steam of misery that lifted to the ceiling. There was no air in the cell, which had a single narrow window with an iron grate. A torch blazed in one corner, casting a pallor over the walls. And yet I felt safer here than on the streets, where I would never have survived. The thirst of a mob for vengeance cannot be contained.

One pathetic creature lay in a heap on the floor beside me, a tangle of limbs, and I thought he must already be dead. A broken thighbone pushed through a festering open wound, and I could see into his chest, where a knife had tunneled through the skin between cracked ribs. He was no more than sixteen or seventeen. His features had been severely distorted, his nose flattened, his auburn hair a sopping mat of blood. The eyes fell back in his head, and his tongue lolled to one side through a grate of shattered teeth.

He coughed now, surprising me.

"Can I help?"

"I'm thirsty," he said.

"Give the boy water!" I called to the guard, who sat by a wall.

He laughed, asking if I were a nurse.

The cruelty of this present world crushed me. The human misery before me was sin, error, transgression—a sign of our separateness from God. The fall of man was the fall into creation, but we would be lifted out of creation into new life at last. I recalled the words of Jesus as framed in one of the books of sayings that Luke had found in Ephesus: *My dear people, we are already the children of God. Only what lies in the future has not yet been revealed. All we know is that, on the proper day, we shall be like God.*

Poor Luke struggled to understand this concept, which I did my best to elaborate, and I prayed for him. As a physician, he trained his eyes on the things of this world, and he could be confoundedly literal. "Look elsewhere!" I would say, puzzling him. "Lift your eyes!"

I raised a palm in the direction of the young man, who in revealing his thirst had inadvertently echoed the words of Jesus from the cross. "Heal this prisoner, Lord," I said loudly. "Make him whole, in the name of Jesus!"

The boy's eyes focused. He smiled faintly, sitting up by himself, breathing deeply, revived before my eyes. His bloody wounds, the broken skin and bones as well, miraculously healed, as if weeks became moments. He opened a broad smile of relief.

Our befuddled guard, in astonishment and fear, brought him a cup of water and put some bread on a plate in the dirt beside him, and we watched him drink and eat.

"You are not an ordinary prisoner," the guard said to me.

"You're quite wrong, sir," I said. "I'm ordinary."

But I seized on this opening, asking to see Lysias, his superior.

Claudius Lysias was a Greek officer of some fame who had risen through his diplomatic skills to this key outpost of empire. In the past weeks he had commanded his soldiers to search throughout Judea for Ezekiel, the zealot from Alexandria, raiding houses in Bethany, Hebron, and Ziph. The results had been unhappy for everyone. One pious community of scholars in En-Gedi had been routed thoroughly, with several arrests and one beheading, though not the head of Ezekiel. The radical Egyptian would be caught soon, I guessed, and given a peremptory trial, then crucified, much like the ruffians who hung on either side of Jesus that day at Golgotha.

The guard led me to the commander's office at the end of a reeking dim corridor, saying, "Speak for yourself. He will listen."

I could feel God's hand at work that day.

It surprised me that command headquarters in the Antonia was such a stifling and narrow room, with a single desk in one corner and only a tiny window for light and ventilation. A slave took dictation from Lysias, writing on a wax tablet.

I stood before him, waiting.

Lysias paused, staring at me. "And who are you?"

I liked the look of this fellow: a tall man of perhaps thirty-five, with straight black hair, black eyes. His long nose arched at the bridge. His firm voice suggested experience and calm in the face of difficulties. One would like such an officer in charge in dangerous times, and I understood at once why the imperial army had chosen him for this job.

"You're staring at me," he said. "Speak! Who are you?"

"I'm Paul, an apostle of the Lord."

This provoked a slight smile, and even his slave grinned.

"So how may I assist you, Paul the apostle?"

"Why have you arrested me? I've done nothing, have offended neither civil nor religious laws. I'm not a zealot, certainly not Ezekiel the Egyptian. This is a mistake!"

He put down his papers and looked at me with cool interest. "You speak Greek without an accent."

"It's my native tongue. I had a wonderful tutor in Tarsus. Together we read Plato and the poets, the best of the Attic playwrights." I nearly quoted Ion of Chios but thought better of such a display of learning. Restraint is the beginning of wisdom, and it never paid off to intimidate—or try to intimidate—men like Lysias.

My response puzzled him, and he took a while to absorb it.

"You're not a Judean?"

"I came here as a young man from Tarsus to study with Gamaliel. His school was legendary. But I'm a visitor now, an apostle of Jesus."

"Who?"

"Jesus of Nazareth, who spoke for God, and who lives now, though he was crucified."

This produced another smile, a wider one, and I think he saw me as yet another religious madman. Palestine teemed with them. But he was curious as well, and asked me to tell him more. Who was this Jesus, and what was our connection?

I explained that my life had never been the same after a blazing experience "of light, of God's glory on the Damascus Road."

"The Damascus Road?"

"God spoke to me there," I said, "through Jesus the Christ."

"I see," he said, but he did not hide his confusion. It was there in his eyes. "There are so many sects. I don't understand the Jews. We give them so much freedom, you see . . ."

I was about to tell him about my Roman citizenship—always the right card to play in these circumstances—when we heard shouts beyond the walls of the fortress. A band of Jews had gathered outside, demanding that the Romans release me into their hands. An underling came into the room to explain all of this to Lysias, who listened with impatience. This was not how he had planned to spend the afternoon.

"Your people seem eager to see you," he said, with a wry smile. "You're apparently quite a figure. I seem to have missed out on your fame."

"They want to stone me," I said. "But let me talk to them."

"You're quite sure?"

I nodded, and he gestured to a guard to untie my wrists.

I stepped through the main doorway, in the shadow of the fortress, where perhaps twenty or thirty Jews had gathered and continued to shout, while Lysias stood behind me and watched with interest. The spectacle, I think, surprised him.

I lifted my hands to silence them, and to my astonishment, it worked. "Please, friends," I said. "You're mistaken. I'm a Jew, a Hebrew of Hebrews, a Pharisee, born of the tribe of Benjamin. I came to this city as a young man from Cilicia. My father was a tentmaker."

"You're lying!" one of them shouted.

I didn't answer him but continued: "I studied at the school of Gamaliel. I was, briefly, in the Temple Guard, a friend of Aryeh."

I should never have used my friend's name, as it might put him in jeopardy, and I regretted this false step at once. But there was a sigh of recognition, and I had their full attention. "I prayed every day in the Temple for many years," I told them. "And persecuted those who followed the Way. I hated their fraudulent Christ, the Nazarene."

I could have walked away then, without harm. In fact, one of them cried, "We've got the wrong man! Let him go!"

I said, "Please, hear my story to the end. I helped to stone Stephen, their first martyr. You remember him? I crushed his skull with my own hands! Then I was sent by the high priest to Damascus on a mission. I wanted only to kill those who caused us difficulties, who showed no respect for our tradition or the Law of Moses. We had enough to worry about, being Jews, without this. But a light in the sky overwhelmed and blinded me. A thousand times brighter than the sun it was! I fell to the ground, which shook around me, tilted in air. The Christ himself appeared, speaking in a clear voice beside me: *I am Jesus. I have come to make you one of my own.* And so I have labored these decades only for him. He will make us whole. Each of us, Jew and Greek, will be made whole in his name. The Kingdom of God opens before us, even within us." A few moments later, sensing a further opening, I said, "Each of you must find your own Damascus Road."

It was not my best speech, but I told them the truth. It remains hard to say what you mean in ways adequate to the experience before you. Words strain at the boundaries of thought and feeling, and mostly they fail us. Every word is an elegy to what lies behind it, the silence of its true meaning.

I would have liked each of these angry and puzzled men to bow before our Lord, to understand what powers lay within them, what immense possibilities might be uncovered, possessed or repossessed, in the name of the Christ.

"The end of this wretched life will arrive soon," I said, "perhaps within days."

I expected, awaited eagerly the coming apocalypse. I could sense its approach like a great storm that travels over the desert, gathering speed. Only a few nights before I had dreamed of pigs being born with the claws of a falcon and babies erupting from the womb with cloven hooves. Pigeons exploded in the sky, fell to earth like fireballs, setting fields of corn alight. I saw the massive walls of Jerusalem crumbling, a scrim of limestone dust where they had proudly stood. I saw pillars of fire where Herod's Temple once rose in glory.

Was this just a nightmare? Or did the return of Jesus loom? It could not be far away, though it was impossible to imagine the texture and quality of his return, his posture, the nature of his presence. All I knew was that he would not come as so many Jews imagined the Christ would come, on a white horse in the manner of Alexander, with a sword raised high. He was not another Judas Maccabeus.

"Kill him!" one of them yelled. "This is Satan!"

"Stone him!" another shrieked.

They threw handfuls of dirt at me, and at Lysias as well, who stood openmouthed beside me. Did they not realize he was the commander of the Roman army in Judea and beyond? Had the fabled insurrection of the Jews finally begun, and all because of my visit to Jerusalem?

"Take him back to the barracks!" Lysias told the guards. "I've had enough of this man."

It upset him that I was not acquiescent, not eager to save myself and, in doing so, to help him calm and disperse the crowd. I could have walked away, disappeared into the Jewish world, never to be seen again. I was clearly not Ezekiel, the dangerous zealot he sought. As a Pharisee and former student in the school of Gamaliel, an ally of the Temple Guard, this Jewish flock would simply have welcomed me into their fold. Or ignored me.

But this would not happen now, when hatred and fear hovered in the air like unhappy ravenous birds that settled and dug their claws in the dirt and fed at random.

The guards were supposed to return me to the barracks, as commanded, but they pushed me into a hot dusty yard, where they stripped me, strapped me to the pillar for scourging. Some underling had obviously decided to take matters into his own hands. But this could not have been what Lysias expected!

I hung there for what seemed like days, though it was hours, the sun licking and reddening my bare skin, raising welts on my neck and back. Mangy dogs prowled in a circle around me, baring their teeth, slavering. Did they throw human meat to these dogs? Did these starving animals finish off their victims, picking the bones clean?

A hard-looking lictor with iron forearms and blank, unfeeling eyes came toward me with his whip, the straps glinting with jags of metal and sheep bones at irregular points along strands of varied lengths. His whip would rip me to shreds. I had watched this torture unfold at first hand in prisons in Asia and Macedonia. The skin of the victim would break and tear, the sheep bones biting into layers of flesh, with the underlying skeletal tissue exposed so that it quivered and bled. Few survived a genuine scourging. I would never, at my age, outlast this tormentor.

"Dear Lord, I am coming home," I cried softly. "Gather me into your arms, Lord. I give myself to you."

"You will die here," said the guard, suddenly eager to open my neck, my back, my legs, and my arms.

"This is unlawful," I said, taking a long breath before I spoke so that the words came out with the force of will and clarity. "You may not scourge a Roman citizen. Ask Lysias, and he will explain. This is the law. I've not been tried, and I've never been condemned. This will cause you a great deal of trouble, sir. Do you want to risk everything? Is your life worth so little?"

My objections took him by surprise, and he fell back. He spoke to a comrade, and they discussed the circumstances of my scourging as I sweltered and scorched. My armpits ached, and I felt so dizzy it seemed impossible I could stay here longer, not in a living state. The earth itself spun around the post.

I begged for water, just before passing out.

And I woke to see Lysias before me. One did not dare to claim Roman citizenship without cause. Instant death would follow a false claim of this kind. My head would topple into the dust at my feet.

"You're a citizen of Rome? Is that true? Can you hear me, Paul?"

"I am."

Without guile, he said, "I purchased my freedom at great cost."

I seized on this opening: "I, sir, was born into this state."

He knew I had no reason to pretend to this status, as I spoke with confidence in his own language.

"I believe you're telling the truth," he said. "You're a learned and cultivated man. I don't know how or why you put yourself in such a position."

He told the guards to untie my wrists.

"I must speak to the Sanhedrin," Lysias said. "I know Daan, the high priest. Stay here while I consult. I will do my best for you."

"I will stay," I said, somewhat ruefully.

They put me into a cell with several other prisoners, with food and water. I waited for two days for further word, using the time for prayer. This was more like a place of temporary confinement than a proper cell, not like the horror of most prison enclosures, where light and nourishment became far and fanciful dreams, and where prisoners often preferred death over imprisonment, taking their lives at the first opportunity. The other three prisoners in this cell listened to me closely, and—here the Lord worked on my behalf, as my energies had slipped—I gathered them into the Way within hours. They were petty criminals for the most part, thieves and vagabonds without much knowledge of their heritage, although I have almost never met a man or woman who did not long for God, did not understand what it means to be taken into his arms.

I realized that Luke and the others would be frantic for knowledge of my whereabouts, and I tried to get word to them, but no guard would carry a message. One of them insolently slapped my face when I asked for this favor, and slapped me again when I said, "I forgive you, sir."

Late in the afternoon of the next day, I had an unexpected guest. I had fallen into a granite sleep on my pallet and didn't recognize my visitor, waking slowly to his presence.

"Paul," he said, touching my shoulder, "are you awake?"

"I know you," I said, "but memory fails me."

"I'm Joshua, your nephew," he said.

Esther was dead, but this was surely her son. I didn't doubt this as I searched his face, even touched it with trembling fingers.

"I'm well connected at the Temple," he said.

It moved me to see a member of my family, to encounter this physical connection to my deepest past. I could see my father in his visage, even in his slight stoop, with the head craning forward. The dimple in my father's chin had returned here, a dark purple indentation carried from generation to generation. He had my own massive ears, my bald head, although he must have been twenty years younger than me. Already his beard had begun to gray.

He sat on the floor beside me, crossing his legs, and there was an intimacy between us that could only have been familial. The force of this connection surprised me.

"Tell me what is happening, Joshua. Should I speak to the Sanhedrin myself?"

"At least forty men lie in wait for you at the Temple. I don't think you would survive the meeting." He paused. "There is anger, and confusion as well. I know they despise you."

"And why is this?"

"You have turned many away from the Law, from our traditions. That's what they say." He looked down at his unblemished hands, the hands of a man who had obviously never worked with them. "My knowledge of your past lacks detail, but I've heard terrible things about you, Uncle. I can't trust what I hear, of course. I weigh what they say carefully."

"You're a good man, and must listen, dear Joshua."

I told him my story with love, and with unusual specificity, going back to Damascus and my time in the desert with Musa. We talked as the room darkened, and I marveled at the focus of his attention. What I had to say appeared to move him.

"I want to know this man, Jesus the Christ," he said.

"Let me baptize you," I said. "It's our way of bringing you to our side, into the Way of Jesus. It's a symbol of rebirth. Like him, the Christ, you rise into fresh life." I looked hard at him. "Do you want this?"

He nodded, a lovely moment of acceptance.

There was a clay vessel of water on a table beside my pallet, and I asked my nephew to kneel. "Joshua, blood of my blood," I said, dribbling water on his head from a cup, "I baptize you in the name of Jesus. In him there is neither male nor female, neither slave nor free man, neither Jew nor Greek."

How startling: my own nephew, one of our circle. I sorely wished I had known his mother better. But we had remained distant, as if afraid to get too close. This may have had something to do with our shared loss, the loss of our mother. Or my father's reticence and hardness. I would never understand the unspoken divide between us.

I had barely finished baptizing my nephew when Lysias stepped into the room, with a torchbearer beside him.

"Trouble?" I asked.

"You are my trouble." He explained that a squadron of soldiers would escort me to Caesarea, where I would stand before the Roman procurator, Felix. He had written to him to explain my situation, outlining the accusations against me.

"I follow Roman law to the letter," Lysias added.

He was a decent fellow, and I could not fault him.

"God will bless you," I said.

He ignored this. "It's important that you leave at once. We don't want to attract attention, which is why you must travel by night. An escort is ready."

So I took leave of Joshua, saying that, God willing, I would meet him again, perhaps in paradise. I gave him the names of several members of the Way in Jerusalem, and told him to explain to them what had happened to me, and that everyone should pray for my welfare but understand that God directed my footsteps and that I rested happily in him. I urged him to contact Luke as soon as possible, as he would be desperate for news.

Of course Luke would follow me to Caesarea. I didn't doubt the faithfulness of my friend.

I blessed Joshua now, drawing an invisible cross with my thumb on his forehead. "With this sign, I deliver you into the hands of Almighty God, who will protect you as he protects his own." That was the first time I had ever used this gesture, and it felt right. God had moved my hands for me.

Outside the fortress, in a wide courtyard previously unknown to me, I was surprised by the contingent of cavalry with spears, and a squad of infantrymen, perhaps two dozen of them. I could hardly believe that Lysias had taken such trouble over me.

"Felix will receive you," said Lysias. "Or one of his magistrates. I wash my hands of you."

And so we left Jerusalem, descending into the night along a dirt road through a pine forest that drops onto the Plain of Sharon. We traveled some forty miles, passing through a part of country known for brigands, which is why I needed such an impressive escort. Near dawn, we came to the edge of the plain, where the threats of robbery and murder apparently dwindled. At this point, outside of Antipatras, the horsemen turned, heading back to Jerusalem. From this point, after camping by the roadside in a clearing, I marched slowly with soldiers toward Caesarea, arriving at the coast in the early morning.

As we stood above the curving sweep of the bay and the harbor, which spread its sheet of gold before us to the water's far horizon, we saw that a large number of ships lay at anchor, and I wondered what on earth God had in store for me.

Whatever happened, it would astonish me. God knew how to do that.

Chapter Eighteen

LUKE

Was this Paul or perhaps his ghost, this rumpled and hairless man who stood in my doorway in the shadows? When he said he was Joshua, Paul's nephew, I understood.

"Paul has spoken of you," I said.

In the decades I had spent in Paul's company, he had mentioned that he had a sister and nephew. He had no other family and, I think, required nothing but the branching family of the Christ to surround and comfort him.

"He's in considerable danger," said Joshua.

He explained what happened, and I had guessed as much. Having the details provided some relief. So I made haste to Caesarea, traveling with a caravan of strangers who, for a few coins, protected me from the brigands who lay in wait for innocents on this road, one of the most dangerous in Palestine.

They left me alone above the city, and I continued by myself, descending along a rocky path to the harbor, which was in itself a monument to human invention. Not even the Colossus of Rhodes at full height could dwarf this spectacle. It had been elaborately conceived by Herod, who adored all physical extensions of his own ingenuity and grandeur, and it rivaled the Temple as a marvel, having taken more than a decade to construct. Monumental limestone blocks had been dropped into the sea, forming a breakwater that held back the surge of storms and roiling surf, giving merchant and military ships a quiet place to anchor in any season.

Herod had seized and reshaped what had previously been a nondescript village, laying streets in a pattern modeled on Alexandria. An elaborate complex of mercantile and residential structures rose in sandstone bricks, with running water, sewers, a vast amphitheater, even a hippodrome for chariot and horse races. Overlooking the city was a temple dedicated to Augustus, where one found statues of the emperor and Roma, a version of Hera, the so-called Queen of Heaven.

I had been in this port city several times, but it always stirred something in me, the idea that the mind can rebuild itself in such configurations, with a vain belief that places like this city can last, that glory inheres in the physical residue of human invention. This quest for immortality could only fail. Rubble to rubble, I whispered to myself, turning my eyes to heaven, where my true glory lay. Paul quite often referred to the treasures that awaited us, and they were not physical, not part of this poor ephemeral and fantastic world.

I puzzled over the delight that Romans took in gods and goddesses, their pantheon stolen from the Greeks but somehow impoverished in translation. All gestures of veneration missed the point that God is everywhere and requires no images. Idols were, at best, superfluous, and none of these could match what his reality, the Almighty Presence, means to those who live in the spirit.

The peace of God was sustaining, and yet the situation of Paul worried me hugely. Joshua said he had upset the Sanhedrin, who wished to have him murdered. They didn't actually want to put him on trial or listen to any arguments he might put forward. Reason and sense meant nothing to Daan or the Temple priesthood. Only revenge mattered. Getting back at the man who had opened the minds of so many in the West, turning them against Judaism as they defined it, this religion of observance and obedience to the Law.

Lysias had sent Paul to testify before Antonius Felix, a brutal man by reputation. A former slave himself, he had been freed by his owner, then married well—not once but three times. And at least two of his wives had royal blood in their veins, including Drusilla, the current spouse, the daughter of Agrippa II and a granddaughter of Herod the Great. Each of these wives had increased Felix's wealth and position in society, and he compounded this bounty by revealing a talent for bribery and graft.

Pallas, his brother, had been the slave of the emperor Claudius and then his courtier. In the latter role, he managed to assemble a fortune, acquiring contracts to import precious metals from Asia,

Egypt, and beyond. He persuaded Claudius to elevate Felix to the office of quaestor in Rome, where he had already proven himself as clever enough to impress his superiors, making them all very rich. Now Pallas was dead, the victim of court intrigues, but Felix—ever the survivor, a man who had begun life as a slave—served as the procurator of Judea.

It didn't take long to discover Paul's whereabouts, which was in Herod's praetorium, a stockade behind the palace where prisoners waited for a few weeks or months for a hearing. I found him by himself in a pleasant-enough room, with a curious guard who sat at the end of the hallway. This prattling young man told me I could come and go as I pleased. "We lack for decent company here," he said. "Just don't play any tricks."

Did I have any tricks?

When I saw Paul, in what struck me as a shrunken state in an unlit corner of the room that had become his cell, I nearly wept. What had become of him in such a short while?

"Dear Luke," he said, upon seeing me, "you didn't have to worry. I do believe I'm alive! Look at me." He wiggled his fingers impishly to show the life in them. "And you? You are alive, too?"

I had feared I would never see him again, having shared the presentiment with many others that he would die in Jerusalem. He had, after decades as an apostle, acquired too many enemies. And our procession into the holy city possessed, for him, a quality of doom that surprised and unnerved me. I'd never seen him so resigned and yet determined to finish his work.

I would not leave his side again. We had come far together, and I must honor this effort and not allow anything to come between us again.

Within days, a prosecuting party arrived from Jerusalem, eager to pursue the case of this man whom they considered the worst sort of traitor. Daan came, accompanied by Temple underlings and Tertullus, his lawyer, who evidently wished to destroy the Jesus circle as much as Paul, in his youth, had yearned to do the same. They scheduled a hearing with surprising speed and—at the appointed hour—I followed Paul into a palace chamber where the procurator sat on a gilded chair, with lictors at his side and a retinue of armed guards.

(He had been attacked only a month before in the marketplace by Jewish assassins and would take no risks.) Felix had the threatening look of an annoyed bull, with wide expanding nostrils and furious eyes like small holes drilled in his fat cheeks. He breathed coarsely through his mouth, eating tiny white cakes and Egyptian figs from a silver tray that a slave kept passing in front of him.

"Speak," he said, addressing the lawyer as he chewed. "I have only ten minutes for this nonsense."

Tertullus, a young prosecutor with a silky black beard and too many rings on his fingers, lifted his chest and coughed to clear his throat before speaking. He said at once that Paul was "a dangerous man." His voice grew forceful. "He's of course a well-known agitator throughout the empire. You know as well as anyone, Your Excellency, that we face the most uncertain of times. Unrest will be found in pockets everywhere around us."

"Stay on the topic," Felix said.

"I apologize," Tertullus said. "I will come straight to the point."

"Please do."

I realized that someone had prepared Tertullus well, as he now talked fluently about the difficulties in Antioch that had arisen in years past, noting Paul's unorthodox position on circumcision and dining with Greeks. He argued that Paul had "stirred the pot" among Jews in Asia and Macedonia, in Cyprus and Greece. The man was an agitator, imprisoned again and again, beaten by his own people, run out of town, scourged, even stoned. And, most alarmingly, "he dared to incite violence in Jerusalem during the days of Passover." He completed his speech by contending that Paul had brought a gentile across the boundary within the Temple grounds, inviting this "Greek stranger from abroad" into a place where only a Jew could stand, thus provoking a riot. "It took the wisdom of Lysias to contain what might have been a full-blown rebellion," said Tertullus in a grand finale.

One slave in the back of the room, unbidden, began to clap—the only one who did so. I suppose he had never heard such a good speech before.

Paul showed no interest in this oration. He listened half-heartedly to Tertullus, distracted, his arms folded across his chest. He ignored the glare of Daan from the other side of the room, where the high priest's subordinates huddled on a bench beside him, whispering throughout their lawyer's presentation.

Felix turned to Paul. "And what do you have to say? These accusations, they worry me."

Paul stood, but he looked away from Felix. The silence around him deepened as he failed to say anything.

"Well, Paul?" asked Felix, after a while. "Will you defend yourself?"

"I have not much to add," said Paul, in a pinched voice that surprised me. "I do only what my Lord, the great rabbi, Jesus of Nazareth, commands. I try to love others and to engender love. I renounce violence. I accept Roman law in every particular and refuse to join any resistance."

With this, he sat down.

Felix laughed heartily, for reasons not quite apparent. "And where is Lysias?" he asked, directing his question to Tertullus. "Without him, I can make no sense of this case." He suddenly rose, refusing even to wait for an answer, and left us there, wondering what had happened. We saw only the back of him as he swept from the room in his colorful robes. I suspected that Tertullus and Daan were annoyed, but they had no recourse. Felix had failed to deliver a judgment.

The guards took Paul back to the praetorium, and I followed. Of course we had no idea what might happen next, whether they would simply let us go or abandon us to Paul's accusers, who would surely kill us both before we even got back to Jerusalem.

Within a day, we were summoned again to the palace to face Drusilla, the procurator's wife, herself a Jew. She had asked to interview this man who claimed to be the apostle of Rabbi Jesus, having heard tales of this inspiring teacher, a man threatened by the Jews, though he had been a Pharisee himself, a student of Gamaliel.

Our guard in the praetorium had been full of stories about the procurator, and he informed us with relish that Drusilla, despite her young age—she was nineteen—had been married before. Felix stole her from her husband, a prince. He made a habit of stealing wives, especially if they had royal connections and abundant dowries. Like most prison guards, this one had little to occupy his mind, so rumors appealed to him, and he told us far more than we cared to know about

Drusilla and her personal adventures. He grew quite animated as he explained that after the death of her father, Agrippa I, the king's enemies had broken into his palace and stolen a number of prized alabaster statues of his beautiful daughter, then taken them into a brothel in Caesarea and abused them in a most obscene fashion: an act of revenge on her father that our guard described as "unspeakable, indecent." Like most hypocrites of his kind, only sexual indiscretions offended him.

Paul listened to this story with increasing discomfort. Royalty and their insipid, wasteful lives held no interest for him.

So he was led again to the palace to stand before Drusilla, who sat beside her husband, as if eager for the revels to begin. A number of courtiers sprawled on silk pillows on the floor beside her. The familiar white cakes appeared, with the figs, and Felix gobbled them as before.

"Tell us your story, Paul the apostle," Drusilla said.

"I know *your* story," said Paul.

Did he really say this to the granddaughter of Herod the Great?

"I believe everyone knows everything about me," she said.

Felix laughed, touching her arm with approval.

"You're a Jew," said Paul, "and immorality is not something we brag about before the world. The commandments prohibit fornication."

"Fucking?" she said.

They all smiled.

Paul said, "Your Excellency, we are only human. All of us! Imperfection is, well, our nature. But we must not take pride in our failures."

The story of John the Baptizer, who stood defiantly before Herod Antipas and Salome, came to mind. Paul had, like John, condemned their immorality without equivocation.

For John, it did not go well. Would Drusilla ask for this apostle's head on a plate as well?

Paul didn't hesitate: "Let me tell you about the restoration that awaits you and me, each of us here today." He swept a finger in a semi-circle, pausing on each figure before him on the raised dais. "Jesus is the Christ, and he arrived in this world for a purpose, having been sent by the Almighty. God had previously been obscure to us, an unseen force, inscrutable and terrifying. But now we see God himself in the face of Jesus."

I was relieved to see him speaking well again, inhabiting his voice. He continued speaking to Felix and Drusilla about righteousness and temperance, warning them about the judgment surely to come, when the Kingdom of God would arrive in its full glory.

"We shall not have to wait for long," he said.

Felix stood abruptly. "Take him away," he said to the guards. "He's a madman. I have heard enough!"

We left the audience chamber with Drusilla still sitting in her chair. I suspect that she found Paul's message both arresting and threatening. Paul had both intrigued and moved her.

It so happened that Felix, without evidence, believed that Paul was a man of considerable wealth and invited him back to the palace a few weeks later, saying that he had spoken well and that, for the right price, could go free. "There are boats every week for Tarsus," he said. "I shall make sure you get a safe passage. You can forget about those Jews from the Temple. Their accusations don't interest me. It's nonsense."

Paul explained that neither he nor I had access to money in the amount that Felix would think sufficient. He had given away everything he owned.

"Any sum will do," Felix said.

"Gold is only a color," Paul said. "It's a bright one, and some are drawn to it."

The procurator could make no sense of what Paul said, nor could I. But he did understand that he would not be getting a bribe from us.

"Take them away!" he said, waving a hand.

✢

For two years Paul was imprisoned in Caesarea, but it proved an oddly productive time, when he began to revisit his earlier thinking. The Lord had not returned as predicted, not in a sudden burst of glory to redeem history and proclaim the arrival of his kingdom. Paul must, it seemed, recalculate everything as he continued his correspondence with gatherings near and far, with individual leaders in the Way. So much was at stake, and there were few enough thinkers of Paul's quality, with his ferocity of intellect.

I slept in a tent in the garden of a family whom I met at one of several gatherings in Caesarea. And each day I walked to Paul's cell, where I took dictation and, as he complained, occasionally nodded off while he dictated letters, which the gatherings everywhere copied and read aloud at their meetings. Paul heard back from them as well, taking in their concerns, their failures, their triumphs. Many of them misunderstood what he said, and he would have to elaborate on what he had written and, now and then, make corrections. He often shifted in mid-sentence, telling me to cross out what he had just said. "Try it this way," he would say.

Once I noted that many of the gatherings seemed discouraged, even saddened, by the slow arrival of God's kingdom.

"There is joy and grief," he said, "but they exist in balance, each drawing on the other for energies."

"Is this true of good and evil?"

"Evil is separation from the good, and repair means union, or reunion."

I had, at times, to content myself with his Delphic propositions.

A period of great productivity followed, and over the course of twenty months he wrote as many letters as he ever had, or more. As usual, his learning amazed me. He could summon a quotation from the Greek scriptures without hesitation, verbatim. But often enough as he dictated his letters I could not tell if he quoted something or invented it. He wrote to assemblies in Asia, in Macedonia, in Cyprus. He replied again and again to Antioch, Thessalonica, Philippi, Corinth, Iconium, Ephesus, and Galatia. Often he reconsidered his previous formulations, trying again. "Everything is revision," he said. "Life is an act of revision, continual revision in the interest of greater understanding. It is the Way of Jesus. We remake ourselves daily and find fresh versions of ourselves."

My head spun as I attempted to catch and clarify his phrases, his accumulating sentences. I tried to write everything down, but his words too often had a riddling quality. And after our most recent visit to Jerusalem, his antipathy to the Jews worried me. So many Jews supported him strongly, and they remained the backbone of the Way in most of our gatherings. I pointed this out one morning, and he thought for longer than usual before responding.

"The Jews quite naturally dislike the idea of a crucified Messiah," he said. "They cannot accept it, it's their stumbling block. But to me, to you, to those whom we cherish in our circle, Jesus emptied himself of everything, taking on the power of God, the wisdom of God. This was the paradise he promised to the poor man who hung by his side. *Today you will dwell, with me, in the paradise of the kingdom.* What beauty one hears in that!" I listened carefully. "Please, my friend, write everything down!"

Paul spoke frequently about love in its different forms, often referring back to Plato. "Without love, we are nothing, we have nothing. Prophetic powers are useless without love. We can address the mysteries, even absorb them, but without love, everything is nonsense. Only God is love, and when we inhabit God, we find each other. In each other, we discover God. And, in everything we do, we proceed without fear."

He knew, of course, that his life lay in danger in Caesarea, that death itself loomed. "For me to live is Jesus. For me, dying is gain. While alive, I labor fruitfully, as I must. I'm caught between two worlds: light and darkness, life and death. But all I wish for, even desire, is removal into the hands of God, lifted by the Christ. To remain in the flesh may be necessary for the moment. We shall, my friends, rise together on the last day."

I wrote the last lines of this fine letter, which he sent to Philippi, with such gladness: "Rejoice in the Lord always. I say it again, rejoice! The Lord is at hand. Let nothing worry you. Make all your requests known to God, and he will listen, grateful for your supplications. He will listen and bring you a peace beyond the possibilities of human comprehension. Rejoice!"

These letters flowed, and I copied them out several times and sent them by a variety of couriers. By day I came and went, bringing food and wine. Often we shared in the sacred meal with others in the prison, singing and praying. And yet the conflict between the

Jews and their occupiers only deepened in Palestine, as rebel bands previously hidden in the highlands of Galilee fanned out through the countryside, and small but violent groups, such as the sicarii (Judas, the betrayer of Jesus, counted himself among them), made a specialty of assassination. Any number of Roman officers and representatives died from their infamous knife wounds. There had been several attempts on the life of Felix, and even Drusilla had barely escaped an attempt to poison her. She lay ill for six months in a state of near stupefaction, but recovered. According to Paul's talkative prison guard, Felix entertained himself during her convalescence with an Egyptian catamite—a tidbit of gossip that enraged and disturbed Paul.

Felix had thousands of troops at his disposal, and toward the end of our second year in Caesarea, in the midst of an uprising that threatened to undermine Roman authority in Judea and beyond, he razed whole villages. "All they understand is terror," he said. "Kill them!"

But violence begets further violence, and rioting in Jerusalem followed. This led to a crushing response by Lysias and, finally, the end of Felix. The emperor, now Nero, acted swiftly to change provincial viceroys when things began to go badly, as had previous emperors. And so Drusilla and her unpleasant husband prudently withdrew to a villa by the sea, southwest of Rome, in the shadow of Vesuvius. They were, I think, lucky to survive at all.

✝

Porcius Festus replaced Felix as procurator. He was a man of substance, with a noble lineage, unlike Felix, the former slave. He swept into Caesarea with imperial grandeur, surrounded by horse guards and courtiers, a clip-clop train of self-affirmation, a show of eminence and authority. With a brilliance that surprised even his supporters, he managed to suppress the rebellion, increasing the number of foot soldiers quite dramatically and executing in a ghastly fashion any rebel unfortunate enough to get caught. Spectacular violence was, as ever, a useful tool for controlling a population.

Several of these rebels had just been strung from a gate at one entrance to Caesarea, each disemboweled with their entrails hanging out and swarmed by flies. Their cries of agony lofted over the rooftops as I made my way to visit Paul one morning, and the voices sickened me. When I told Paul about this barbarity, he said, "There's no hope except in Jesus."

Despite his savagery, Festus generally found a receptive audience in Caesarea, encouraging theatrical displays and civic games, determined to turn this city into a little Rome, a marvel of sophistication in what he probably considered this barbarous outpost of empire. The amphitheater throbbed with entertainments, including plays—rather primitive ones, as I discovered after a visit one afternoon. The actors wore crudely painted masks, and mimes played beside them, clarifying whatever was said with vigorous (and often rude) gestures.

When I complained about the lack of value in this dramatic work, Paul smiled weakly. "This isn't the Athens of Pericles."

My impulse to visit the amphitheater baffled him altogether, but I had grown a little bored in Caesarea.

"Our time grows short," Paul said.

And he did not have to say more.

The Temple priests had never lost interest in Paul, and a further contingent arrived in due course from Jerusalem, again led by Tertullus, and they requested an audience with Festus. Paul's case must be reopened, they told him. He led a dangerous sect, one that threatened Jewish ways. Unrest was sure to follow, and this could not be good for Rome. (The implication, of course, was that it could not be good for Festus either.)

Festus refused to take their bait and showed no interest in hearing this case, saying Paul could rot in prison, and this would rid them of the problem.

A convergence of events changed his mind, however. It happened that King Agrippa II was coming to town with Berenice, his sister. He was apparently curious about this preacher whose following in the Greek world evidently terrified the Sanhedrin. He told Festus that he would personally hear the man's case, as it would entertain his sister, who had studied the scriptures and showed a fondness for religious disputation. Word of her intelligence and composure had, in fact, reached our ears before this.

"She has an interest in this Nazarene sorcerer, whom I believe this Paul once knew," Agrippa said. "They've got some sort of cult about him. Let us meet him and hear his arguments."

The news of a royal audience didn't frighten Paul; he had stood before Gallio in Corinth and before Felix only two years earlier. Agrippa and Berenice would not faze him. I, on the other hand, followed him into the chamber with the weakest of knees. No good would come of this, I felt quite certain.

What a scene greeted us! A retinue of military guards, trumpeters, and drummers preceded the king, who emerged in purple robes, with lots of jewelry in evidence. Berenice had green and blue feathers in profusion. Festus wore a flowing scarlet cloak.

Paul was chained at the wrist to a court guard, who stood beside him as he approached the dais.

Tertullus approached at the same time, bowing as he walked to indicate abject subservience to the royalty before him. He spoke first, as expected. With force, he condemned Paul once again as a radical Jew who led a dangerous rebel sect. "They pose a threat to us all, Jews and gentiles alike." He then drifted off into lofty generalities about society and the need to obey laws and respect traditions.

Agrippa fingered his beard, listening to the lawyer, who had grown mature since I last saw him, fuller in his face, with a tinge of grayness in his beard. The king gave nothing away with his impassive expression, making occasional grunts beyond interpretation. It struck me that the advocate for the Temple position had surely not managed to put forward a clear case against my friend, not one that would interest this judge. Abstract statements meant little in these circumstances. Only stories have the power to change hearts.

Berenice listened closely and whispered in her brother's ear, while Festus looked on with mild curiosity. He could see that Paul's case offered decent entertainment for his royal guests, and that was probably all he wanted from this hearing. The idea of justice surely meant nothing to him whatsoever.

"You shall speak for yourself, Paul," Agrippa said. "They say you talk rather well. I'm eager to hear your answer to these charges, which strike me as quite serious. No regard for the law? A rebel who wishes to overthrow imperial authority? Is that so?"

Paul lifted his chin, with its dimple looking cavernous and purple, saying, "I'm honored to have a chance to bear witness to my Lord, Jesus the Christ." He began with an account of his own lineage, setting the argument in his usual frame, then admitted to stoning the "great servant of God, Stephen," gesturing as he told about crushing the poor man's skull with a heavy stone. I could see the eyes of Berenice widen as he told about the poor man's "crown splintering, with a pool of blood and bone and flesh."

He soon recounted the story of the Damascus Road with a flourish that I had not heard in many years: "The skies opened, and there were trumpets—loud glorious trumpets."

"No drums?" asked Festus with a wry smile, and the king laughed. It was proving a good day for them, a jolly diversion.

Paul continued without pause, mounting phrase upon phrase as only he could do. "Angels—a thousand angels, with such gold wings that the sky changed color. The sun appeared to explode, and I went blind. I fell to the ground, which pulsed now, throbbing and tilting. I could feel the Adversary on one side and the Lord Jesus on the other. 'Come toward me, Paul!' cried the Lord. So I crawled toward him, and he held my head in his beneficent lap. I wept."

A new version! At first, I wished my friend had preferred a simpler version of the story, but he knew his audience, and Berenice rose from her chair, unable even to sit. She actually clapped and smiled.

Paul stopped talking out of respect, but she called, "Please, sir, do continue. This is splendid. Go on!"

The spirit of God possessed him now, and he shook, his lips quivering, his eyes seeming to fork lightning. Did I hear thunder overhead? Paul spoke suddenly in tongues, or so I thought. In the intensity of the moment, I lost track of everything, nearly swooning. I felt the hot presence of the Lord surging through the air, an invisible power. Apart from Paul's voice, only a quivering silence filled the room.

"What does God want of us?" asked Berenice, when Paul had finished.

Paul told her that Jesus opened a way to God, that we saw the Almighty in the face of our Christ. He said that death meant nothing. Jesus had conquered death. "We must hide ourselves in him forever," he said. "We must lose our petty names, these passing shadows to which the soul briefly clings. We live eternally in him, here and always."

I saw, and everyone saw, that Paul had moved Berenice, as her cheeks shone, and she wiped her eyes. Her brother also looked quite astonished and put a hand on his sister's shoulder.

Tertullus broke in: "You must let us have him! We'll take him to Jerusalem, and the Sanhedrin will hear him out. This is a Jewish matter, a Temple case!"

Paul silenced him by speaking over him, quoting the scriptures at length, saying that the prophets had long ago predicted the arrival of God's son. *And the Lord Almighty God shall raise up among you a prophet,* he intoned, from Deuteronomy, and he compared Jesus to Moses, who had met God on Mount Sinai. He recalled an eloquent passage from Isaiah, then a sequence from Daniel. And he concluded with a line from David's hymn: *Therefore my heart is glad, and my whole being rejoices, and this flesh dwells secure in the knowledge that God will not abandon us to the darkest place.*

The king was moved now, his features mobile, expressive. I could not tell his state of mind, but it was obvious that something had occurred inside him. "Paul, this is well spoken," he said. "But you have maddened yourself with so much learning. I confess, I'm almost persuaded by your arguments. This teacher, your Rabbi Jesus, he sounds like a man of wisdom."

Paul struggled to draw the right words into the open. "I only wish every knee would bow before my Lord," he said. "The Kingdom of God will arrive any day. It has already dawned in my heart, as in the heart of my friend here, dear Luke."

I wished that he had left me out of this, as I certainly had no wish to speak in court.

Tertullus repeated his request: "Let us have him, please. I ask in the name of Daan, our high priest. The Temple demands this."

The king nodded. "This is obviously a case for Temple elders," he said. "I do see that."

At this, Paul turned his palms up before the court, saying in a loud voice, "I am a citizen of Rome, Your Excellency. *Caesarem appello!*"

He appealed his case to Caesar!

Every Roman citizen of good standing and, more usually, in possession of wealth or influence, had this right of appeal. He or she could demand a hearing in the imperial courts, in Rome. But this was a bold and unexpected move, and Paul's utterance hushed the chamber. Agrippa turned to speak in the ear of Festus, who leaned toward him to hear. An exchange took place that I couldn't follow.

"You appeal to Caesar?" asked Festus. "Fine, then. That's where you shall go!"

Agrippa nodded with approval. They would send Paul to Rome under guard, by ship. He would have a hearing in the imperial city. Berenice nodded eagerly. This made sense to her, I could see.

When Tertullus objected, Festus told him to be quiet. "I don't want to see you again," he said. "Tell the high priest I have no other option."

With the roll of drums and the blaring of trumpets, the royal party, followed by Festus, left the chamber.

Chapter Nineteen

✕✕✕

PAUL

My voluble prison guard suggested they might just have let me go free, as the Temple Jews had no case against me. The imperial courts were not religious courts, and Berenice had said as much to Festus, urging my release.

"You should never have asked for a hearing," my jailor told me.

"How can you possibly know this?"

"The court has a thousand little ears," he said.

He annoyed me, and I tried to avoid conversations with him, without much luck. For his part, Luke agreed that I should never have appealed to Caesar, saying I should have held my tongue.

Me?

Was I not an apostle of the Lord, appointed by Jesus himself on the Damascus Road to proclaim his truth to the world? In accepting this call to prophecy, I had given up any right to my own volition, even to my body. I belonged to God now and had eternal life in him. The right to appeal to Caesar mattered, perhaps because it would lift the Way into a kind of prominence. I longed to put the case for Jesus as the Christ before Nero. This could become a final victory before the end of history, an appropriate one.

Much as I loved Luke, and I did, I saw that he often failed to understand the obvious: that God lives in us, and we live in him. And I must do as he commands. But the dear fellow never would abandon me, and this loyalty counted. As did his willingness to act as my scribe; that was a gift, for a man of his stature, and also an act of humility, a sign of his wish to serve God in whatever capacity seemed appropriate. He often said that my letters were a gift from the Almighty Lord, and that the Holy Spirit governed my tongue.

I could believe this, as I had no sense of my own voice when I wrote to the assemblies. I was simply a vessel, conducting God's word. I had no choice, no way to stop this language, which often felt oddly alien to me, as if I discovered exactly what my readers discovered. God's voice welled in me, broke into being. It was exhilarating but terrifying as well.

Our young friend Aristarchus appeared in Caesarea, having heard the news of our departure. His persistence surprised me, and I loved him for it. He wished to accompany us to Rome, he said, where he hoped to assist the gatherings, which had recently made such headway among the gentiles there. I knew that the future of our mission required men like him, so I agreed happily to this.

Rome would become the center of God's kingdom, not Jerusalem. Jerusalem was lost.

It was obvious that the war between the Jews and the Romans would intensify, leading to chaos and, in the end, a woeful scattering of the tribes. The sacking of Solomon's Temple by the Babylonians would find itself reenacted, a repetition that could not be stopped. Herod's Temple would become a heap of holy rubble, a smoldering expanse. Exile and sorrow lay ahead, a consequence of Israel's rejection of Jesus, their Christ. Of course the Kingdom of God could well arrive even before this crash, before the complete ruin of Israel. Perhaps the Lord did not wish to see his Temple crumble but to oversee its transformation?

It was pointless to try to predict the sacred plan, as God would reveal everything in his own time. I kept reminding myself to pray as the Lord had prayed, saying, *Thy will be done.*

I stood with Luke and Aristarchus on the dock, eager to board our ship for Rome, as a dry wind crackled the pines. Julius, a young centurion, had been appointed to escort us, and I liked him from the outset. Nonetheless it astonished me, and Luke as well, that a man of such rank in the imperial army had been assigned to this task. Did Festus wish to send a message to Nero? How was it even possible that my case had aroused such interest? Surely this was God's invisible hand at work, I told myself.

"Winter is almost upon us," Aristarchus said. "It is late in the year for a voyage."

Our accomplice and friend rarely spoke, but when he did it was often in empty statements, as I realized now. I loved him but knew I must accept that the obvious appealed to him.

It was, of course, clear to everyone that we had left this journey late in the calendar year.

Listening to Aristarchus, I badly missed Timothy, his wit and goodwill. I wondered if he had made it back to Galatia, as he had planned. I'd sent a letter to him in care of his mother, but no reply had come. Now Aristarchus proved a poor substitute, this sweet but inarticulate young man.

But I must put Timothy out of mind. I must think of Rome.

Winter journeys by sea rarely end well, that much I knew, and the prospect before us left me feeling uneasy, even a little frightened: a rare feeling, in fact. I could usually dispense with doubts, allowing myself to rest in God, and to trust that he had something in mind for me. Luke had, perhaps wisely, asked to delay our passage until spring, but Julius explained that we had no choice in the matter. Festus ordered us to go, being somehow afraid that our mere presence in the city represented a threat.

Julius reassured us, saying we were not alone in setting out at this time. A dozen or so ships lay at anchor in Caesarea, most of them laden with amphorae of wine and olive oil, bags of figs and dates and nuts, woolen goods, marble, silver, and iron ore. This would be the last shipment of the year for most, and I did recall hearing of even later sailings. Roman navies, indeed, depended on the wisdom of Fortuna, the goddess of luck.

Yet the season was out of sorts.

Not even Caesarea's legendary breakwater could hold back the surge of the sea, which foamed in pilings around the docks and bristled in the rocks. The air smelled of salt and rotting fish, with a sharpness that worried me as I watched other prisoners boarding. Twenty or more of them marched aboard in close formation under heavy guard. The crew stood to one side, warily. Everyone looked to Julius as an authority—our fine imperial escort, with his straight black hair and eyes like ebony. And a centurion no less! Perhaps all was well if a centurion was about to board this ship.

Luke didn't like what he saw of the other prisoners. "Murderers, thieves," he said.

I had spent months, even years, among men like this in a variety of prisons, and I found this characterization painful. Many had looked at me askance, assuming that this vicious criminal named Paul deserved whatever he got. I always pitied a prisoner, whatever the case against him. He was so alone, even in the midst of a crowded cell.

"All prisoners are God's own," I said to Luke.

Julius smiled warmly at this, beginning our unspoken collusion.

I had noticed from the outset that our guardian and escort treated us as equals. He accepted without question that Luke and Aristarchus would accompany me to Rome, and refused to let anyone tie or chain me, saying I could come and go as I pleased, as long as I boarded the ship when asked to do so.

"An ill wind blows," said Luke, raising a wet finger in the air.

"What do you think, Aristarchus?" I asked.

He drew a long breath, puzzling his brow. "I have no opinion, as I know nothing of the sea," he said. "The waters seem happy enough."

"I assure you," I said, "they are without feeling."

In general, Aristarchus impressed me with his devout habits and sincerity. He prayed fervently each morning and night, and sang loudly in our meetings. As I explained to Luke, God needed every hand in these fervid and unpredictable final days. We could tolerate his empty comments, which were probably a result of fear, not genuine stupidity. I said that he might, in due course, surprise us all.

Later than expected, with several unexplained delays, we boarded and set sail, heading toward Sidon. It proved a tranquil enough passage, surprising the pilot and captain with a brisk tail wind that seemed to lift and push at the same time. Even Luke relaxed, standing at the bow rail, his chin forward. At one point, he lifted his arms.

"You're a gull in the wind," I said.

"I so dislike metaphors."

"But you're a writer, Luke. Metaphor is your trade."

He shook his head, knowing he would avoid metaphor as often as he could. It was, he suggested, "a natural inconvenience, at times useful, often a terrible excess."

"Not so terrible," I said.

My dear Luke wrote well, I must say, with a grace of precision, often improving upon my dictation. His Greek recalled for me the style of Herodotus, that historian who had mastered (or created) a stylish form of Ionic Greek. He wrote with such fluency and poise, and his life of our Lord—should he actually complete it—would surely attract a following. I saw a luminous scroll opening in one vivid dream, and I knew it was Luke's.

When I mentioned this, he said, "Paul, you are seeing things."

"It's what I do," I answered.

We sailed happily for two days, putting in at Sidon, a familiar port, where Julius agreed I could wander ashore without a guard. We had a lively circle of the Way there, led by Seth, a feisty, clever rabbi who had studied under Gamaliel in my time. Our visit coincided with the First Day, so we shared the sacred meal with these good people. As ever, they invited me to read from the scroll and speak. It was largely a Jewish group, and I marked this, saying that God would save the whole of Israel in due course.

"Not all of them," shouted Seth.

"All of them," I repeated. "Do you think God will let anyone go? He has fashioned us, flesh and bone, for his pleasure, to expend his love. Love binds us, and Jesus perfected his faith in the love of God. Never doubt this, my friends."

In the prison in Caesarea, I had realized in a swoop of understanding that God would never let us go, not a single one. We do not let a child go, however wayward that child. We are all of us the prodigal children of our Creator. He will not prefer this one over that one. In the fullness of days, each soul unites with the whole, finding a center in God. I knew this perfectly now, as if for the first time, and understood why our Lord had not taken me away in Jerusalem.

I had further work to do.

But Seth scoffed at me, continuing to object, saying that Adam had ruined everything. We had been cast out, landing somewhere east of Eden, aliens under heaven. Humanity was flawed, stained by our forefather's seminal act of disobedience.

I refused to let him have the final say in this because he was wrong. "In Adam we die, each of us," I explained. "But in the Christ we blossom into new life." I recalled what I had written to the Roman circle. "How shall we compare the gift of God in Jesus to the sin of one man, Adam?" I asked those who gathered in Sidon the same question. "Death reigned for a while, yes, because of one man, Adam, who represents our sinful aspect. We step over the line repeatedly, according to our nature. But consider the abundant provisions of God, who in his son models forgiveness and makes us whole!"

I wished I could stay longer with my brothers and sisters in Sidon, as their responses to what I said encouraged me, and even Seth appeared to relent, but I had promised to return to the ship. And Rome called.

✝

Sailing close to the wind, we headed northwest, with the shoreline in view, its brown undulating hills and evergreen forests, the sheer sides of cliffs, the inlets of white, rocky shingle. Sheep and goats dotted the hillsides, and I saw the lonely stone huts of shepherds and wondered about these isolated lives. The margins between land and sea always provoked deep thoughts in me, calling me to the boundaries of flesh and spirit.

In years past, I had taken comfort in the company of shepherds, and slightly envied their still and present lives, their absorption into a landscape, with its familiar contours and profound silences, how they adjusted to the passing seasons, the alternating rhythms of day and night. I wondered if, in the next world, I would meet these shepherds again. Would I even know them when we met? Would I know my friends, my family? Or did we become pure spirit in the end, removed from our petty past lives?

I put these questions to Aristarchus, who stood beside me on the deck, and he answered after a pause. "I share these questions. My life is all questions, but this is what God has allowed us—questions, not answers." Then he added: "But such wonderful questions!"

I kissed him on the forehead, delighted by this response. I had, perhaps, tried too hard to supply answers, when questions sufficed. The simplicity of dear Aristarchus moved me now. And I realized how much I could learn from his straightforward approach to complicated matters.

The winds picked up, gusting and baffling our pilot, who tacked to port and starboard with unusual skill as we came off the coast of Cyprus toward Lycia, beating past Pamphylia into the harbor at Myra one afternoon as the sky streaked with black-and-vermillion clouds and a dull thunder rattled over the city. This port was well placed for grain ships from Alexandria, and the docks spilled over with sailors who spoke with strangled Egyptian accents.

Julius explained that we would continue to Rome on a larger vessel, an Alexandrian ship bound for Italy, its hold packed with massive sacks of grain from the latest harvest. Since the time of the Republic, Roman politicians had ensured that grain was available in the capital, even free for the neediest, as hungry citizens were dangerous citizens. Expediency fueled their compassion. Now the captain told me that Nero, who required the love of his people (not just their obedience), had allotted six or seven bushels a month to each family in Rome: a generous allotment that bought their support if not their love. In response, wily and avaricious Alexandrian merchants had built their fleets, creating wide floating cargo transports that had little maneuverability in heavy seas but had proven reliable enough.

I had seen these vessels before, but only in the distance; the size of them up close startled me. Their cargo as well as their ballast and double planking for stability weighed them down, and they rode the waves like giant turtles. They carried a substantial crew and assorted passengers, and often shifted prisoners from one dismal location to another for a small sum, which the Romans happily paid. We had more than two hundred and fifty men on board this particular vessel, seventy of them—like me—in custody. The rest were divided between Roman troops and the Egyptian crew. Our pilot, I was told, was "almost a Phoenician," meaning that his navigational skills could be trusted, though I had heard this before and doubted its truth.

This information inspired Luke, who offered us a quietly learned dissertation on Phoenician history and their legendary seamanship and journeying to the farthest rims of the earth, recalling that "they gave to the world the gift of alphabetic writing."

It was indeed a gift, and one that Luke, in particular, delighted in. The patience he had shown in Caesarea, writing and rewriting my letters to the Way, amazed me in retrospect. I could not easily have taken another man's words and put them down as faithfully, not without altering something at every turn. I tended to revise my own thoughts even before I had them, aware that God himself guided this impulse toward perfection.

"She is remarkable," said young Aristarchus, surveying our ship from dockside. He asked about its exact measurements and capabilities, and one of the crew supplied the details. "A sturdy vessel," he said.

It was so. The prow rose to a mythic bird's head and beak, and the stern swept its tail broadly. It boasted one tall cedar mast with a smaller one up front, some yards from the bow. A pilot's cabin squatted on the aft deck, with a desk inside where he could consult charts or escape from a stiff icy wind to collect his thoughts. They told us to sleep below, in rows like sacks of grain, but we would resist this confinement, asking to sleep up top if possible, as surely the hold would reek of fear, rat droppings and human excrement, ancient layers of piss and sweat, and the usual creeping sea damp that infested all vessels belowdecks where there was inevitably seepage between the strakes.

Julius, bless him, understood our wishes. "I don't think anyone will protest," he said, "and if they do, refer them to me. In fact, I'll speak with the captain right away." He would sleep in one of the cabins reserved for officers, in an actual bunk with blankets.

As dark fell on our first night out, I slumped against a starboard-side bulwark in a rough wool shroud, with Luke and Aristarchus beside me. We had some bread and cheese, and a handful of figs and nuts—almost a feast, although I worried that the quantity of food would dwindle before we set foot ashore again. Aristarchus lay back, humming, with his face to the heavens, lost in his own music. I felt an unexpected surge of affection for him and was glad, after all, that he had joined us.

The sea swelled as we set off, with a peppery mist in the air, not quite rain but its harbinger. We mounted each wave to its peak and slid down the other side—an undulating sweep that sickened my companions. (Aristarchus heaved over the rail and felt better afterward. Or, at least, he bravely chose to say that he felt "much improved.") The water hissed and curled around the hull.

As I knew from past journeys by sea, the cloudy sky posed a

dilemma for the pilot. Without a clear view of the pole star, finding our way to Sicily could not be easy. Sailors, for the most part, relied on point-to-point navigation, keeping as near as possible to the shore, moving from landmark to landmark. But this was not always possible, especially with these deep-hulled ships, which sailed close to any coast at their peril.

I made a point to befriend Dymas, the pilot, a furrow-browed and laconic Alexandrian who inspired confidence by his manner. He eyed me with respect, in part—or so I imagined—because a centurion had been assigned as my personal guard. He had not seen that before. Prisoners on these ships were generally treated as livestock, though with less care for their comfort and safety.

"You must be important, sir," Dymas said.

"An illusion."

"Either an assassin or a politician," he said.

"Or both."

I could have been specific about the actual charges against me but didn't actually wish to sink in his estimate. Temple violations would not impress him. And my elevated status as a prisoner of some consequence might prove useful in circumstances I could not yet envision. As ever, I simply liked being close to the pilot because the craft of navigation interested me.

Early the next morning we drew into Cnidus, a harbor village on the long, rocky spike of a peninsula that pushed out between Rhodes and Kos. We planned to lay over there, counting on a westerly breeze, but it proved impossible to anchor, with an easterly blow fouling our approach. The harbor glimmered in the distance, tantalizing and yet beyond our reach. I recalled stopping there many years ago and walking into their temple, which was dedicated to Aphrodite, and then strolling beyond the village boundaries to a sloping necropolis, where tombs called out to our vulnerability.

I advised our pilot to seek the leeward side of Crete, and he agreed. It was the best we could manage, under the circumstances, as we plunged into cold rain that stung like nettles. The sea frothed, white-capped, chaotic. Driftwood passed beside us, scattering its white bones on the water, and I took this as an omen, knowing the tides and winds worked against us and would push us off course. The captain stood alone on the foredeck, pensive. He spread his legs to brace himself, holding to the rail. The fraught look on his face struck me, and I knew he feared the worst. In winter, most prudential seamen refused to venture abroad, heeding the so-called mare clausum—an unwritten code that forbade travel by sea during the worst season.

We rounded the escarpment of Cape Salmone under a black sky, then made for the coast, keeping land in view as we hauled against a driving northeasterly. Somehow, for two days, we managed to lay near Fair Havens, a relatively quiet bay, with the sun occasionally beaming through a part in the cloudscape. I suggested to the captain and Dymas that we should consider spending the winter here. The wind would only grow stronger, less predictable by the day, and it blew the wrong way. At our current pace, we would never make Sicily before the depth of winter overwhelmed us, and the consequences could be dire.

The captain listened to me politely but said that Fair Havens would never suit us, as it had few resources, such as food or shelter. It was, he maintained without sufficient evidence, "the equivalent of a mirage." He suggested we continue in the direction of Phenice, "a better harbor, with an abundant village. Perhaps a couple of days' journey," the captain said, "if the weather cooperates."

The pilot glanced at me, and I understood what his look meant. The captain had no deep knowledge of these parts, or he was counting on optimism to lift us over the worst.

"A typhoon is coming," I said.

"Is this man a prophet?" the captain asked, winking at Julius.

Julius rejected the notion of wintering in Fair Havens. "Phenice, I think, might be preferable," he said. "It's a question of supplies. We have a lot of men aboard."

The captain agreed, and so we headed into the first flush of a storm. Within the hour, black waves splashed over the gunwales and sopped the deck, which rolled fiercely, while the sails cracked and sputtered. The crew scattered in various directions, doing their best to follow the captain's helter-skelter commands, which alarmed me. I wished I could help, but there was nothing for it. I would have to watch this catastrophe unfold without the authority or even the knowledge to be useful.

I huddled with the pilot, who insisted I should advise him. The captain was too frightened or befuddled to object, so I pressed beside Dymas with the charts—an old Phoenician map, which was spread out before me as we skidded along the island's southern coast, sailing as close to the wind as we could get, though we drifted erratically and gained almost no purchase on our course.

At last a steady blow came behind us, and we moved forward, rounding what I assumed was Cape Matala, whereupon the sky emptied itself. Gushers of wind blew us off course, and our pilot had little control of our direction. We had only a brief respite one afternoon, sailing in the shelter of Clauda, a tiny treeless island that looked woefully alone. In that pause, the captain insisted that his men bail the longboat, which had been following in tow. He had mere survival on his mind now, and we took the usual precaution of frapping, which meant pulling cables around the ship and using a windlass to tighten them. This made good sense, as I could easily imagine our ship bursting apart in hurricane winds without this wrapping. I suggested that we strike sail, too, since we had no hope of keeping our course, but the pilot knew our captain would never assent.

The prisoners and soldiers belowdecks were ordered to bring up the grain sacks and toss them overboard, a sign of our mounting desperation. I saw amphorae filled with wine rolling overboard, sucked into foamy whirlpools. Crates followed, so heavy it took a dozen men to upend one of them into the deep. Any number of grain sacks followed, our most precious cargo.

The clamor of the wind subsided for a few hours, and hope briefly caught fire when the sun blinked between clouds, scalloping the sea with sharp blades of light.

"We'll be fine," the captain said, more to himself than to anyone beside him. It occurred to me that human beings cannot for long abide the thought of their own demise. They cast doubts overboard, making false assumptions.

Soon the rain picked up, as I knew it must, driving hard from the east, pricking our faces with a fine, cold, horizontal drizzle. Before long, the storm had caught its breath and blew up, snapping the sails. I imagined us being blown off course into the invisible sandbanks off Tripoli, the well-known graveyard of countless ships over many centuries. We would be driven onto what Ion once called "the hard black rocks of dreams, whereupon we die."

Then the worst began as zigzag lightning struck the mast with a bold crack that startled us all. It toppled to the deck, striking a young sailor and killing him at once. Even with our aft paddles deep in the water, we had little purchase, the wind spinning us in circles until we suffered a complete loss of control. We drifted toward the nearby shore, where I could hear the loud seethe and pluck of the surf as it smashed upon what I guessed was a line of hidden rocks.

Our doom lay there. I knew that perfectly well, as a vision of our fate had flashed before me. I knelt on the deck and lifted my arms to heaven. "Thy will be done!" I prayed loudly.

Following orders, the crew heaved our four anchors overboard: a final effort to stay ourselves. But they attached to nothing, the depth of the seas being unknown; on the other hand, our landward skid was slow, as the winds had no consistent direction. The rigging whined a miserable song that returned again and again to its sad single theme: our demise.

Then we suddenly caught, hovering above what must have been a sandbar, one or two of the anchors holding. I doubted we could stop our fatal drift for long, but optimism rose, and I saw a couple of the sailors cheering.

"We can wait this out," the captain said to Julius.

His inexperience poked like bone through skin. But I said nothing. Reality would assert itself, and soon.

Waiting doesn't begin to describe the days that followed, empty days without sun, moon, or stars. Time could not find itself and stood to one side, breathless. The dull glow of daylight hung for several hours before, once again, the dark enveloped us, with a stillness that belied our peril.

"Where are we?" the captain asked the pilot.

It is never a good thing to hear a captain say this.

"West of Crete somewhere," Dymas said, catching my eye.

Truth could be found in that statement, but it hardly meant anything. We had no idea where in the world we lay. Or if we had somehow sailed beyond this world altogether.

Hunger and fatigue became brothers, each pricking and agitating the other. We passed around lumps of unleavened dough, raisins, and small quantities of salted fish heads. These dwindled within five or six days, producing violent tempers. The prisoners erupted one night in shouts and fistfights, and irritable guards wasted no time in killing the ringleaders. I watched the blood-soaked bodies tumbled overboard, counting eight splashes.

Hope frayed, and one dark morning a member of the crew leaped into the sea and disappeared quickly: a suicide, the first of several.

I moved among the men belowdecks, praying with them, offering hope and the Christ's faith in God, with Luke and Aristarchus beside me. One dying prisoner looked at me in terror. "Was Jesus God?" he asked. I gripped his hand tightly. "He humbled himself before God, before his father, taking on human flesh," I said, "these tatters, our bodies. He emptied himself for us. His life was perfect, as our lives are imperfect. You will die, my friend, but only to live forever in the warm and blessed arms of the Almighty. Trust him."

"I trust him!" he cried.

At this, I dribbled water from a cup onto his forehead, baptizing him. And soon others asked for this as well.

The agony of these days proved, for me and others, a useful time of prayer and reflection. In times of crisis, spiritual progress becomes possible. I had so often in my life found myself advanced by suffering, brought closer to the breath of God. Any semblance of pain recalled the blessed pain of the cross.

Luke and Aristarchus followed my example, and so we moved together among the men, day after day, hearing their confessions, their hopes, their fears, giving comfort, offering baptism. It was often enough to listen, to hold someone's hand in the simple ministry of presence.

I knew I would not die in these waters, as God wished for me to stand before Nero himself, to proclaim the greater glory of Jesus. One night in half sleep I dreamed of Odysseus with Ithaca in mind and dear Penelope waiting on her island and fending off suitors. Odysseus had plied these same waters, long ago. He trusted in the journey home, as I did. But my home was heaven.

One day I woke to screaming. It seemed as if a madman were tearing out his hair: The storm had found its voice again. It shrieked now like a mad, unruly child. The waters turned from gray to black, roiling, and the ship rocked from aft to stern, even spun in a circle. The anchor lines snapped, and I knew we had broken free and would splinter on the rocks. I could actually see and hear this splintering before it happened.

A dozen crew tried to haul in the longboat, and I called out, "Stay with us! It's safer!"

A soldier used his sword to cut the line to the longboat, and several of us watched the sea, and the gray swirling fog, absorb it.

One poor man wept on the deck, bending to his knees, curling into himself, shaking, then becoming still. I don't know if he died or fell into a stupor.

We all stood on the deck, a crowd of horror.

Within the hour, we heard the lashing of waves on nearby shoals, the boom and tingle of the surf. An island swung into view, ringed by a stony black outcrop. Beaching the ship would not be easy, though we had no other course but to make for the narrow inlet. I watched with admiration as the pilot managed, without sails, to steer us using only the rudder paddles toward the most plausible landing.

"Ready!" he cried.

We heaved onto a cluster of granite blades with a crunch and hung motionless for a moment, as if caught in the beak of some prehistoric bird. The ship groaned and suddenly split in two on the rocks, with the stern lifting its shadow above the prow as the deck splintered underfoot. I rushed to the bulwark, clinging to a stray line, looking for Luke, who lay on the deck nearby calling for me, desperate. I saw Aristarchus jump overboard.

His leap shocked me. I knew he could swim, but that act of heaving himself over the rails defied everything I knew about him. Was it complete terror, a loss of control, or an act of unexpected self-confidence? Had he caught some glimmer of eternity? Or imagined he could best survive by himself? Had God perhaps called him to jump? Anything was possible.

Then I saw many of those who could swim leap into the icy waters behind him, though a number of soldiers attempted to slay their prisoners before they could escape, as was customary. Guards often killed those in their custody in these circumstances rather than see them escape, but Julius—that dear man—cried out, "No murder! All who can swim, let them leap. Others, find a piece of the ship. Any fragment will do. Hang on for life!"

The world blew apart now, furiously. And I found myself in a plume of salty foam, with a stout length of the mast in my hands and Luke beside me.

I called for Aristarchus, but he didn't answer.

We moved with the current, slipping sideways toward shore. A slantwise rain drilled the surface of the sea with a din like a thousand hammerheads on iron. I was cold but numb, and did my best to see that Luke didn't drown, drawing him toward me, holding on to him as well as the mast. He looked half dead, his face blue, with seawater spewing from his mouth.

I thought of Jonah, and how the whale had vomited him at the Lord's command.

And so God commanded the sea to heave us in a violent belch that left us on the shore, with loose strands of golden wrack around our arms and legs, and brown seaweed mixed with the sandy remains of cuttlefish and crab. Half a dozen drowned men bobbed in the surf or washed onto the beach, while survivors—four or five foam-white men—lay beside us. One of them smiled weirdly at me, and I nodded to him. The brotherhood of the living.

Not being dead today counted for something.

We lay there for a time, trying to gather ourselves, even to speak. I knew that God had something in mind for me in Rome, and therefore I would not die on this island.

But where was Aristarchus?

On wobbly knees I walked up and down the beach, hoping to see our good companion, our friend in Jesus for whom my fondness had recently grown. I had not quite realized how much I loved this young man, and I prayed for his safety, lifting my palms to heaven.

Luke raised his head with difficulty when I returned, his slick beard streaming water. "Aristarchus?"

"I fear the worst," I said.

Luke frowned, but I knew that anything but the truth would only further upset my friend, who faced reality with a brave but tender heart. He too admired and loved Aristarchus and would miss him.

He might be drowned, but he might have been swept to another part of the island. In these fierce, unpredictable currents one could hardly hope to control one's drift.

Men from a local village rushed to the water's edge, eager to assist us, this pathetic straggle of exhausted, starving, wet, nearly frozen men heaved onto their coast. They explained that we had landed on an island that was part of the Maltese archipelago, and promised food and shelter. One of our men begged them to light a fire, saying we required warmth more than food or shelter. And I agreed, setting off by myself to gather twigs from a nearby brush for tinder.

As I bent to pick up a stick, it suddenly rippled into life, taking the form of a viper: the most poisonous of snakes. According to Maltese legend, anyone attacked by a viper was a murderer, and the villagers shouted and shrank back, watching me struggle with the snake.

"Satan, let go of me!" I called.

The viper died and dropped from my hand, falling into the sand, and I kicked it to one side.

This provoked an outcry of wonder from the Maltese, and one of them shouted, "This is a god, not a man! He has come to visit us from the bottom of the sea!"

Shades of Lystra, and my strange adventures there with Barnabas, rose before me.

I objected, saying I was not a god, but had no luck in dissuading them. They required a god, it seemed, and I was too exhausted to evade my apotheosis. They lifted me on broad shoulders and carried me into the village, no more than a scattering of huts, taking me to the thatched mud house of their mayor, Zacharias, whose father lay ill on a low bed of straw. The elderly fellow, gaunt and pale, had not left his pallet in four months. I held his loose-skinned, skeletal hand, telling him about Jesus and what he meant to me, to everyone who called on his help in times of sadness, terror, or affliction. "The Christ loves us in our sorrows," I said.

I was not sure the old man could hear me, but he offered a toothless smile, dribbling onto his chin.

Zacharias asked me to help him, saying, "You're a god. Do what is necessary."

"I can only pray for his recovery in the name of Jesus."

"So do this, my friend!"

I put a hand on the wasted fellow's burning forehead, asking God to heal him, in the name of Jesus.

"Do you trust in God?" I asked the invalid.

He nodded vaguely.

"Heal!" I called. "In the name of the Christ!"

Within moments this ghost of a man threw off his coverlet, swung his stick legs to one side of the pallet, then—reaching for his son's hand—jerked himself to a standing position. He took a step forward, gingerly at first, and began to glide, as if walking on water.

The gasps in the room thickened, lifting to a roar.

"He is truly divine, this man from the sea," Zacharias said.

I protested, but nobody heard me.

For the next four months we lived among these people, Luke and I in a stone barn with a roof of tightly bound shoots. Being a god in their eyes had its benefits. And yet I did my best to teach them about my Lord the Christ, and I brought many of them into our circle, praying with them, baptizing at least twenty villagers. Julius grew closer to us than I would have guessed, and (after many hours of vigorous conversation and prayer) I baptized him as well.

The saddest thing, however, was the loss of Aristarchus. Luke would stand on a promontory with a view of the sea, searching the horizon, hoping for our friend to reappear, but Aristarchus never came. I prayed for his soul, continuing to hold out hope to Luke, saying that perhaps he had landed far away and found a hospitable village. It was always possible, given the swift and unpredictable currents. But he could just as easily have drowned, and probably did.

To our relief, wintering in Malta proved acceptable, even palatable, with decent company and log fires. We drank our share of wine from local vineyards, which had been stored in wooden barrels, and ate well: Fish and fowl could be found in abundance. We had fresh eggs and small green apples. There were seeds, olives, almonds, and sycamore figs. One elderly woman brought us loaves of coarse-grain bread that had been baked over hot stones.

Our new friends even secured a quantity of papyrus for writing.

I was tempted to ask Julius if we might not remain among them forever. I was an old man and could easily have spent the rest of my days on this dun-colored hump of rock in the bluest sea. The Maltese would have welcomed me. I could imagine a gathering here of those who lived in the Christ. It would not be a bad way to end my days if, indeed, the final hour of history failed to come before I died.

Spring arrived, as it did in these parts, with a flourish. Flowers broke into life: the snowy apple, the pink cherry, with blooms like snow on black branches. I watched an almond tree burst into a cloud of bees. There were carob, prickly pear, and lemon trees in profusion. I lay by a stream one afternoon on a bank of green-gray moss, which felt warm to my hands.

Could paradise itself have outmatched this fragment of Malta?

There is nothing quite like the sun in spring, when it wakens to its powers, with pillars of gold that drop through the bluest skies, with the surface of the sea like brass. I lay on the shingle on the sunniest days, counting myself part and parcel with the breathing gills of seaweed and the bleached driftwood: all flesh and bone, with everything belonging to the Almighty. I wanted nothing but God now, to be home with him.

But Julius would not disobey orders, and I would never let him disappoint himself.

And so in late spring we set off for the mainland, where we boarded another merchant ship—a small one from Alexandria—and sailed for Sicily.

Rome lay before us, that much I knew. And I would set foot there before I died.

God had spoken.

Chapter Twenty

We can't leave without Aristarchus," I said.
Uttering this, I knew perfectly well that Aristarchus would not join us, now or ever. He had not been seen since he leapt into the sea.

Enveloped in mist and sleet. Sucked into a swirl.

The horror of that shipwreck often returned, waking me in the night, shuddering through me when, for a few moments, my thoughts drifted toward it. We had splattered on the rocks with a loud crack, spun, and broken apart. Only the intervention of God Almighty saved Paul and me, as we clung to a piece of the mast that, quite miraculously, had passed in front of us.

God's big hand fathered us ashore.

We washed up, choking and cold, whereupon a number of kind villagers stumbled toward us, curious about what the stormy seas had disgorged. They showed us sympathy, offering food and shelter and a dry place to sleep. And they treated Paul especially well because of a peculiar incident involving a snake. It was so odd. Paul had simply shaken a dead snake from a stick. No more than that. But word spread among the Maltese that a god was among them. Hail, mighty Paul, son of Neptune! He had stunned the serpent with a glare!

Apparently this type of snake had peculiar meaning among them, and Paul had fit himself into their larger narrative. He had expressed divinity.

Why he refused to deny his status as a god puzzled me. He could have scoffed at those who elevated him, made everything plain with a simple statement to the contrary. But this glorified status served us well on the island where we spent the whole of winter in their safe-keeping. Divinity had its perquisites, which included regular supplies of fish and meat, loaves of good local bread, lemons, tart green apples, beans, and a variety of root vegetables. Amphorae of wine turned up once a week: a ruby-tinted, granular wine that we loved.

"Soon they will sacrifice sheep and goats in your name," I told Paul one evening after a basket of bream appeared at our door.

"I will eat whatever they bring," Paul said.

He could feign a cheery mood, but I sensed a shift in my friend, a diminishment of spirits, amplified by fresh infirmities. The shipwreck had weakened and darkened him in unexpected ways.

"What does God have in mind for me?" he asked.

We could hardly deny that the Kingdom of God had not arrived, not as Paul had once conceived it. "It's foolish to imagine anything in detail," he said. "Whatever you think will happen is what never happens. One might use this as a ploy: imagine the worst thing you can imagine, but only to forestall it."

I saw he did not engage the Maltese with quite the passion one might have expected from him. His energies had fallen away quite sharply, and he became an old man overnight. The gray of his beard bristled white, as did the hairs that poked from his ears and nostrils. His once rather taut, nut-brown skin now draped over his skeleton, a loose pallium of flesh. His stoop increased, so that he looked at the ground as he ambled forward, measuring each step. His vision grew worse and worse.

This was hardly the fiery, fiendishly bold apostle I knew from years gone by, the man who took on the armor of the Christ, braving everything for heaven's sake.

I tried my best to understand him, asking if he felt well. He stared at me without seeming to recognize my question.

"The sky is blue above Malta," he said. "The heavens unfold."

"I know you would prefer to spend your last days here, in a chair by the garden wall, with the voice of the sea in the background," I told him. "You can do this if you like."

"Really?"

"God will understand. It may well be the right thing."

By his pensive glare I knew I had uncovered a truth. He preferred to remain here and never to move again. Yet this could not possibly be an appropriate fate for the apostle, a man who had taken the message of Jesus to the wider world, among Jews and gentiles, among pagans. His words like spores had passed in the winds of empire, taking root in unlikely places, becoming whole forests of faith. (After so many years, I had learned the gift of metaphor from him, and felt more comfortable now with the device.)

"Rome is so far away, so far," he said.

I remained gentle with him, preferring to draw him back to our mission but aware that he must follow his nose on this matter.

"Perhaps I should stay," he said. "You go, Luke."

"The Roman circle, they remain our friends," I said. "Think how delighted they would be to see you in person. I'm sure that Prisca will be waiting. Your letters have meant a good deal to everyone in the capital. I'm sure of this."

"Peter went to Rome," he said.

The comment seemed dislocated in time, irrelevant. Peter was not, in his mind, a reliable ally or someone he should emulate. The disciple of Jesus had done nothing to protect Paul during our visit to Jerusalem, when we had delivered our gift, a generous sum by any reckoning. Perhaps worse, Peter had never acknowledged the weight or wonder of Paul's teachings. He felt uncomfortable among Greeks, even those who sought to emulate the Christ, "opening their minds to the larger mind of God," as Paul put it.

The Maltese villagers who had rescued us and allowed us to become their friends sat with us in the evenings by the dying embers of a log fire, listening to us recall our adventures and trials over many decades. Now we had Julius with us, though not Aristarchus, whose loss clouded our time on the island.

Since leaving Caesarea, we had delighted in the company of Julius, who in due course joined the Way, praying with us, seeking baptism. He would have allowed Paul to remain on the island of our shipwreck, but Paul—after long thought—decided to join us on our voyage to Rome. The chance to see Prisca again perhaps drew him forward, I could not say.

In truth, I felt much relieved by his decision. Rome without Paul was, for me, no destination I could imagine. I would instead simply return to Antioch by myself, bidding Julius farewell in the Italian port. Summer was, indeed, a good time for sailing, and I would have no trouble finding transport. I would miss Paul sorely, though, and perhaps might have remained with him to the end on the island.

In these months we had come to adore Julius, and Paul picked his memory for stories of his childhood, his youth in Rome. He grew up in a fine villa near the Palatine Hill, which Paul recalled was where Cicero had lived. His father moved in legal circles, and his family were aristocrats ("of a lesser variety," Julius would demur). He had been apprenticed to an influential lawyer, living in the man's home on the Aventine for three years. As was customary, Julius sat with the distinguished advocate as he consulted with clients, learning by listening or pursuing minor tasks. He accompanied his master to the Forum three times a week, acting as his scribe at one point. He was expected to wed the eldest daughter in the family, who was, as Julius remarked, "seven years my senior, with rust-colored teeth and stooped shoulders." Her breath smelled of "long-abandoned eggs." This marriage of convenience held no appeal for a handsome young man, however ambitious, and Julius rejected the opportunity to don the toga virilis of a gentleman and professional, preferring a military life.

With his aristocratic connections and legal training, he rose quickly in the ranks of an expanding imperial army. One day, as Paul boasted on his behalf, Julius might become a general, although our centurion liked the idea of politics as well. He would make a wise provincial governor, I suggested, addressing him as Pompey the Great.

Julius batted away this compliment. "Pompey's end was ignominious," he said, and recalled his assassination in Egypt.

"I meant the early Pompey," I said. "The consul, part of the Triumvirate."

"I'm no Pompey," Julius said. "Early or middle, even late."

I watched Paul carefully now, as he seemed both eager and reluctant to leave our new island home. One night I saw him sitting on the grass, under starry skies, where he studied a small creature, perhaps a small hyena or rat, as it nudged its way into a tuft of moonlight. I drew close to him. "You don't have to come," I said.

"I do, in fact. You were perfectly right."

"You've given everything. There is no need."

"No," he said. "I seem to be alive. As long as I breathe, I must continue to speak for the Christ." After a pause, he said, "I have heard a voice, and it calls me to Rome."

"To Rome, then," I said.

⸭

When the fair winds began to blow from the south, we boarded a merchant ship, another Egyptian vessel, though it bore no resemblance to our lumbering, ill-fated grain ship. I admired this vessel, with its prow distinguished by the figures of Castor and Pollux, the twin servants of velocity. As before, Paul ingratiated himself with the pilot, showing off his navigational skills. He kept a close watch by night, sighting the pole star and making the appropriate calculations. He might well have been a sailor in another life, although his bad luck with sea journeys suggested otherwise.

"You have studied the heavens," the pilot said to him.

"I've been there," Paul said.

The pilot grinned, but this was not a joke. Paul's infrequent but memorable vaultings into the upper heavens remained a key part of his sense of himself as an apostle of the Lord, a man changed forever on the Damascus Road. He already knew what it meant to rejoin the Almighty in the third heaven, to stand before the Ancient of Days, and I envied this.

My own spiritual longings had less clarity and occasion. I would make my way to God in my own time, I knew that with certainty. But I would never leap in the same fashion as Paul. That heavenly country, where the saints gathered in concert, illumined from within by God, would remain a fond wish, achievable in the course of time but still distant, an imagined destiny. For now, I must fare forward, mile by mile.

Favorable winds abaft the stern created a steady blow that drove us into the Sicilian port of Syracuse within days. We made our first landfall in Ortygia, where more than a dozen other ships anchored offshore in calm, clear water. I loved it there, with quivering schools of gold-and-silver fish below us. Houses tumbled down the hillside, their red-tiled roofs gleaming, while the Temple of Apollo loomed above the harbor, a grand example of human invention. It took away one's breath, with columns that formed a colonnade beneath its portico. One or two men in white togas strolled and talked, and their tiny shapes reminded us how tall the temple must be.

Julius said, "Think how they carried those columns uphill, and managed to erect them as well."

Like me, his mind often turned to practical details, while Paul, as ever, remained in the heavens. Ancient temples had simply fallen to the earth from the ether or sprung, like mushrooms, from the dirt. In our travels, I never saw him pause to admire the Roman facility for the construction of aqueducts or bridges, or their ingenious use of reservoirs and cisterns. The miracle of Roman roads never failed to impress me. But I was a different sort of person, one who longed to see the architectural wonders of Rome.

Julius had tantalized me with his memories of this great city, talking at length about the genius that lay behind the construction of the Pantheon, even though Paul disliked hearing about it. "God will find a better use for this building one day," he said.

Increasingly, he spoke of "one day," which was surely not "tomorrow." The Kingdom of God unfolded at the Lord's own leisurely pace, and we could hardly hurry the Almighty, who probably found our impatience both tedious and insulting. Why could we not simply trust him?

I could hardly help but notice that Paul's message carried less urgency than earlier, though it had become more interesting and complex, as least in my view. He told Julius that "God arrives in us each day," and the Kingdom of God was "always and now, alive and everywhere."

Mere equivocation? Perhaps. Or an adjustment to realities.

Julius took some convincing on this point, but in this he hardly differed from me, another of those who tend to count, weigh, and measure the things of this world. We see shapes and sizes, pinch points and parallels. We admire calendars and rules, their discreteness and specificity. Paul resisted all calculations along these lines, gesturing to the sea. "Listen to the surf, its rote insistence. How many times does it lunge to the shoreline and retreat. Is God counting the waves?"

He compared time and eternity to rivers and the sea. "We flow into God," he said, "trickling through the landscape, smoothing the pebbles, sloshing our banks, spilling over in seasons of flood. In dry times, we disappear underground, with hardly a trace of us."

I tired of these similitudes but had grown used to them, had even begun to adopt them. One accommodates to the modes of discourse that surround one, as close friends and companions in due course adopt a common tongue. I think I pushed Paul a little further in the direction of simplicity, plainspokenness, and concision as a consequence of his being my friend. But he could relapse, growing long-winded, even vaporous, though I liked to believe that my company made this kind of talk less likely.

We disembarked in the Ortygia harbor, with Paul eager to seek out a synagogue at the western edge of the city where a legendary rabbi named Yohanan had led a vigorous congregation for several decades. Paul remained alert to significant teachers throughout the empire, and he noted that Yohanan had written scriptural commentaries that had circulated in Jerusalem. He and Paul had exchanged letters at one point, although when I pressed him, Paul was reticent. I think he imagined that most people agreed with him and tended to discard opposition or counterarguments as mere annoyances. I wondered about Yohanan, who was reputedly a defiant and self-involved fellow.

Paul had lost a good deal of his argumentative vigor and had withdrawn while in Malta in ways that surprised me. I had never quite seen this version of the apostle, the old man with his white scruff of a beard who sat for hours in spring sunlight with his face lifted to the sun, occasionally smiling, even laughing to himself. He often spoke softly under his breath, as if conversing with spirits. Where was the ferocity, the torch, that passion that had made him the great apostle? But any flame dies, and it was possible that Paul's visionary fire had been extinguished and only embers remained.

All of us become cinders in the end. Some die on their feet, as my father had. I had seen the old fellow sleepwalking in Antioch and scarcely able to recall his own name. I addressed him respectfully to the end, as duty required, but he barely acknowledged me. A slight nod, perhaps, was all I could expect. In conversation, I had to supply memory, asking if he recalled this time or that. An occasional spark might glimmer, briefly even reignite. But never for long. Silence had become his preferred tongue.

In the end, as in the beginning, there is only silence.

Now Paul asked to visit Yohanan.

Julius said, "We depart in three days for Rome. So keep track." He himself was treating the apostle like an elderly man.

I looked at Paul, who glanced at the pavement. What was on his mind? Did he realize that Rome might well pose the greatest challenge to us yet, an opportunity to consolidate so much of what we had labored to achieve but with pitfalls one could hardly begin to calculate? Julius had seemed uneasy about the prospects for the Way in Rome, although he would never elaborate.

We found the synagogue in a winding alleyway behind the amphitheater. Sitting on a low stool, Yohanan looked up without seeing us. As he would, Paul got his attention, saying, "I am Paul, an apostle of Jesus the Christ. We knew each other in the past and have exchanged letters."

Yohanan stared at us. He was, like Paul, without hair except for a slight beard that had turned to frost. He had red hands like pincers, squat legs, and a large belly.

"We have come from Jerusalem," said Paul, trying to engage his attention. "We were shipwrecked throughout the winter on an island near Malta. We're going to Rome now."

Yohanan listened to this summary without apparent interest as Paul kept adding details.

"Tomorrow is the Sabbath," Yohanan said, when Paul had finished.

"I have lost track of the days."

"You will come?"

Paul nodded. "I'm a Pharisee," he said, "a student of Gamaliel."

"Like me." Yohanan smiled now, for the first time.

"I remember you," said Paul. "We sat in the same room. So many years ago."

"Did we know each other?"

"We exchanged a few words."

After a long pause, Yohanan said, "I remember your letter. You asked for my assistance in Sicily. But the Christ has not come."

"He is here."

Yohanan stood, alert. "He is not, sir. God is God, and he has sent no one to speak in his name with authority."

"Let me explain," said Paul. I could see the kindling flare in his mind.

Yohanan listened with his arms folded across his chest as Paul launched into the story of what happened to him on the Damascus Road, an abbreviated version, less dramatic than usual, although I could appreciate one or two flourishes. "A choir of beautiful young angels with golden wings sang above me," he said. This choir had unexpectedly become young and beautiful, with golden wings. Not bad, I thought. Even plausible.

Yohanan said, "The Law is the Law. I don't care about one Christ or another. They come through my doors at regular intervals. Each of them wags God's tongue, or claims he does."

"You must hear me, my friend. I do not speak lightly. I admire what you have written in the past. But Jesus is God's voice in our time, and beyond time. He was here before Adam and Abraham. And he will return soon, and remain forever."

"What about the Law?"

"He *is* the Law."

Yohanan told us that he had tired of false prophets.

"I'm simply an advocate for Jesus," Paul said, "the anointed one who shows us the way."

The lack of force or freshness in this comment worried me. Yet Paul had many devices, and knelt before the rabbi now, a peculiar gesture of obeisance. It was as if by giving in, he knew he could soften the heart of Yohanan. Julius and I exchanged skeptical glances.

Yohanan said, after a long pause, "I will pray about this, Paul. Come tomorrow."

"You should expect me," Paul said.

"I shall come, too," I said.

So we appeared on the Sabbath as promised.

"This is Paul, a Pharisee," Yohanan said to the two dozen men who crowded the room. He turned to Paul: "Will you read from the scroll?"

This was, as before, the opening Paul sought. He glanced only

briefly at the scroll. Seeing a passage from the Torah that was familiar, he chanted the holy scriptures with his eyes closed, his palms
lifted to heaven. This gesture of mastery caught their attention, as
Paul didn't simply recite from memory. He embodied the words, the
voice of God sounding in his mouth, echoing in his bones. Nobody
could doubt this gift of prophecy.

It was a fine day for Paul. He trembled as he retold the story of
Abraham and Isaac, always a favorite. Everyone gasped when, after
he finished the recitation, he launched into his own interpretation,
telling them that Jesus was Abraham's son, and that God had sacrificed his own beloved for everyone in the room. "Jesus allowed his
father in heaven to break his body. He bled because we bleed. He
showed us his trust in God by accepting his own demise, by shedding
his rags of flesh, taking on the light itself. After three days he rose,
as prophesied, assuming a glorified body. God lifted him into heaven
again after forty days. He now sits with the Almighty, and we shall sit
beside him. His throne is our throne. You are the Christ." He pointed
to each man in the room. "You! And you! Rise into the kingdom!"

I could see transformations happening as old men wept and the
younger ones jumped to their feet and lifted their hands in the air and
called out to God. One fellow, no more than twenty, fell to the floor,
speaking in tongues. An elderly man pounded his cane on the wall
hard, as if trying to knock God loose from the plaster.

Paul waited for them to settle, for a wave of silence, then told
them how he had tried to murder those who proclaimed Jesus as Lord.
He had "dropped the final stone on Stephen, crushed his skull. And
the blood pooled around, soaking into the dirt." He retold the story
of the Damascus Road. I had heard this tale a thousand times. But
this time, radiant and unexpected details, fresh and full of nuance,
emerged.

"I felt my guts spill into the earth," Paul said. "I was turned out
of this flesh, my soul a burning light. And the fire in me had nothing
of me about it, it was God's holy fire. I sizzled in that conflagration,
consumed as within a bonfire that takes everything away, lifts ashes
into heaven. Nothing was left of me. Gone, the young man driven by
his own pride. Gone, the foolish and overlearned youth. Gone, the
lustful and wrathful young man. I became light forever, lost in him.

I hid in his mind, the Christ mind. God consumed me whole, swallowed me in his flare. I had been lost. Now I was found."

Not a single man in that room refused baptism after that flight of language, not even Yohanan.

Julius said to me when we returned to the ship, "We have seen God blaze before our eyes."

"And we have seen his apostle," I said.

※

I almost didn't dare approach Paul as we boarded the ship, heading to Rome. He seemed to burn inwardly, and would have ignored my inquiries, or rejected any comments I offered with a blank stare.

"I shall die soon," he said, stepping beside me on the deck as the ship passed Rhegium, then beat into the harbor at Puteoli, from which Rome lay only a day's journey by cart. I knelt to pray, thanking God for a safe passage. And Paul knelt beside me, lifting a prayer as well.

We moved, again, in unison. For a time.

"This is a holy place," Paul said, as we disembarked, noting that Virgil was buried nearby, in Cumae, an antique city where the Greeks first made landfall in Italy. At Avernus, a crater lake near Cumae, Aeneas made his fateful descent into the underworld to meet his father.

Paul surprised me and Julius by reciting a passage from the great Roman poet, and with strong feeling. I had never heard him recite in Latin before, but he seemed possessed by this text.

"Virgil was an alien, a pagan," I said.

Paul shook his head. "No! The voice of God has always spoken through the mouths of poets as well as prophets. Virgil knew Jesus in advance of his coming into the world." He recited from one of the *Eclogues*, where the poet proclaims the birth of a male child who would find divinity within himself, holding sway over the cosmos. "Did you imagine the truth that Jesus proclaimed was not present before him?"

I knew nothing of Virgil or his work, but I accepted this, and Julius seemed quite knowledgeable about this particular poem. He nodded eagerly, quoting verbatim. "The cattle will never fear the young lions," he said, alluding to a line of verse that, as Paul observed, suggested that the calf and the young lion would rise together, led into glory by a small child.

That day we traveled to Avernus, a beguiling and violet-tinted lake, a near-perfect circle that quivered in the air, as if suspended. I watched as Paul hovered near what he perceived was the entrance to the underworld itself. It was twilight, and soon Paul's body dissolved in the dark. Then I felt a shudder of cold, and darkness overwhelmed me. It was the blackest night I had ever experienced, and I went looking for Paul, calling his name. But he was not there.

Julius said, "We may never see him again. And this should not surprise you."

We spent the next day together at our camp, waiting for Paul to return. It was the Sabbath.

Had Paul been swept into the underworld?

I woke on the First Day to find Paul standing over me.

Or was this Paul? I could hardly recognize him.

"Where have you been?"

"It has been a long journey," he said.

"I worried about you."

"There's no need to fear," he said.

Julius kissed him. "I know where you went."

Paul shook his head, offering a sly smile.

We must sometimes go places where no friend may accompany us. And we cannot speak of these journeys. That much I could understand.

But from this day forward, Paul was not the same man.

+

Julius conferred with a friend in the imperial courts, who explained that Paul's chances of a hearing in Rome were slight. Festus had been quite wrong to send him to the capital. It was, he was told, "absurd and irresponsible." The apostle's bold appeal to the emperor had no legal status, as no civil charge had been brought against him. Roman authorities would consider his conflict with the priests of the Temple in Jerusalem a ridiculous and petty quarrel within a remote and insular group. Such matters must be settled by Jewish elders within the Temple and, in Nero's time, nobody cared about such things.

Paul listened without understanding. "So am I still under arrest?"

"In theory," Julius replied. "Yet probably not."

Paul hated this ambiguity, but he had no choice. He was, in reality, a free man. Julius told him, indeed, to consider himself liberated. He could pursue the Way of Jesus in Rome as he saw fit. His life was, again, his own.

Paul moved into a house near the river with Junia and Josephus, two of our most faithful servants in Rome. They were friends of Stachys, whom Paul had known for decades, and he understood what Paul required: a quiet room with a small garden, if possible. A place to sleep, read, pray, write, and reflect. But great sadness overwhelmed him when he heard from Junia that Prisca and Aquila had not survived their journey several years earlier. Their ship had gone down off the coast of Sicily.

Paul wept so profusely it terrified me. This was not something I had seen before.

There was no room with Junia and Josephus for me, so I lived separately, some miles away, with Atilius, a new friend in the Way who had room in his house. Quickly I realized how much I liked having a distance between us, after so many years. It had never been easy to have Paul beside me, day and night, ever watchful, critical, argumentative. He was inspiring, of course, but I began to covet my solitude. I could come to Junia's house every day, or nearly every day, without feeling oppressed. And yet I could get away, as needed.

I confess to feeling a certain lightness in my step now.

Junia herself was a flamelike creature, and the success of the Way in Rome reflected her energies. She moved among the many houses where gatherings occurred. In each cluster a leader emerged, and all relied on Paul's teachings. Parts of his letters had been copied many times and distributed. Indeed, Junia led any assembly by saying from memory the words of Paul, which echoed those of our Lord on the night before his death in Jerusalem, "This is my body, broken for you. And this is my blood, shed for you."

I loved Junia, a gentile from Alsium, just north of Ostia on the western coast. She had hosted Peter a few years ago, bringing him to a dozen gatherings, and the mere presence of the first disciple of our Lord had inspired the Way throughout the capital. The Kingdom of God seemed closer than ever, as Paul said to Seth and his gathering in Sidon in one of his last letters, which I rewrote for him:

> My dearest ones in Sidon, I greet you, and only wish I could visit you again on that shore, with its view of the mountains. Luke and I, as you may not know, made it—after many trials—safely to Rome, where the Way has progressed as none of us could have imagined. God is alive here, and we shelter in his son, who lives in you, in me, in all of us.
>
> Lately I have gone into the depths, scouring the underworld. I hovered, as did our Lord, in a black Sabbath where I knew neither life nor death. My whole life—more than sixty years!—wavered in dim light. I could hardly see it: my father's workplace, his taciturn smile, his disbelief that I had gone (in his view) so far astray, having worked to become a scholar of Torah, having stood among the Temple Guard for a brief while, but with such hatred in my soul. As you know, everything changed with my journey to Damascus, when the glories of the heavens opened before me and Jesus himself appeared as I lay on the ground, tilting in space. I kissed his feet. I touched him, as his disciple Thomas had touched him after the resurrection.
>
> He told me to proclaim the coming Kingdom of God, anointing me as his apostle of love.
>
> I hovered by the lake of Avernus between the darkness and the dark. Was it years and not a day? Time failed me. Hanging in the balance was not less than everything, as I could hear a distant crackle, the thunder of the Lord's return. Was that what I heard? I woke to find myself standing on the lake, and walked to shore over the fiery dawn waters, with my friends still asleep. They slept at my feet, these dear friends in the Christ. And my love for them was great, as is my love for you.
>
> I have made this journey many times in my life, from the day of death to the day of resurrection. All our thinking must be resurrection thinking. We die to live.

As we know, in Jesus there is neither life nor death. There is only light, love, and the security of knowing our place in God's hands. We rest in him, now as before, then and always. We enter his flames of complete affection.

I feel this fire now. As I have said, imitate the faith of Jesus. In life as in death, he showed us the way to God.

That passage I copied several times for friends, and it would make its way through the Roman gatherings and far beyond.

I came to Paul every day, taking his dictation, offering such help as I could. He wrote letters to distant communities, revising them more obsessively than in earlier years, releasing them only after he had found exactly the right words.

"Will you ever write this long-awaited life of our Lord?" he asked one day. "It has taken a long time. I've seen only fragments."

"Writing takes a long time," I said.

My "long-awaited" life of Jesus had acquired something of a reputation, even though few had seen anything of it. A number of times I read from it at gatherings, at Paul's insistence, but these weak performances—I was never a good speaker—drove me back to the desk to rework my narrative. A life is not simply a chronicle of facts, which are in themselves without life. It's an assembly shaped by the imagination, a work of passion and discretion. One picks and chooses among countless examples. One suppresses. One highlights. One has to imagine the truth with fearlessness as well as humility.

Already numerous accounts of the Christ's life—his birth in Judea, his years in Galilee among the poor, his teaching, and, most crucially, the final drama of Jerusalem—passed from hand to hand, with collections of "sayings" in wide circulation, many of them bogus, and with variant quotations. Consistency would count in the years ahead, especially if the Kingdom of God were not realized at the pace we expected when our mission began.

I searched for those who had been a witness to the Christ, as their testimonies were invaluable. Once, for instance, I met an elderly woman in Rome, a Jew, who told me that her mother had been present in the Temple when a young couple from Nazareth arrived with a child. And there had been much talk of this infant's mysterious origins. Was this couple even married? She told me that an elderly man in the Temple named Simeon had been present that day, a legendary figure who came every day to pray for nearly eighty years. He had no wife or offspring of his own. It was known that Simeon had healing powers, and he was sought out by women with afflicted children, whom he often healed in the name of the Almighty God. As he had financial resources, he supported the families of those who could not manage their lives because of the needs of these children.

The Holy Spirit lived in him, and he was radiant with a love that everyone could feel. When Mary and Joseph brought their child to the Temple for consecration on the eighth day, he took the infant into his fragile arms and wept. He chanted: *Great Lord, sovereign one, king of creation: now I may go in peace. My eyes have seen the glory of your child, whom the world will soon observe. He will be a light for the gentiles and the glory of Israel. Make way for the Lord.*

He died within a day's journey of that experience, bathed in the glow of God's own child.

There was another Temple devotee, the elderly Anna, a prophetess, who knelt and wept before the infant and proclaimed him the son of God, as light streaked from her grizzled hair. Her eyes flashed, and Mary understood that her child would grow and prosper. "He will surprise everyone," she said to Joseph, who said, "I don't think any mother or father wishes to be surprised."

When I mentioned this to Paul, he said, "I would hesitate to put that into your narrative. Irony will never work here, not in this context. It's too much for the story to bear."

I pondered this, as I pondered so many things Paul said.

We spent hours talking about my life of Jesus, and what it should include or exclude. Paul insisted that the only thing of interest was his death on the cross, followed by his resurrection in glory. "Everything else is gossip," he said. "Do we really know much about the childhood of Jesus? What matters is the moment when he found, in himself, the eternal Christ."

I had in mind the beginning of my life of Jesus. Everyone likes a story of origins, where a tale begins. And rumors about the birth of this child in extraordinary circumstances interested me and others as well. So many in our movement wanted to know about his earliest days, which must have been wondrous. God entering human flesh! Why did we only hear about him at the age of thirty?

I heard any number of stories associated with the birth of Jesus, and these rarely conformed to a single idea. When I told Paul my intentions, he said I would have to choose how to approach the contradictions, how to unfold my tale in the plainest and most efficient and moving terms. He dismissed the idea, put forward by Thomas, the disciple, that Jesus had been whisked away to Egypt by his parents, a fugitive from Herod. The absurdity of this was self-evident, Paul said. "Why would he have gone to Egypt? Why would Herod in fact have wished him dead?"

Paul urged me to focus on the character of Jesus, and his perfection of life during his last years. He was, as Andrew had told me, devoted to the least among us, those who lived on the edges, and I knew I must dwell on this. He also said that Jesus would amplify his sermons with anecdotes, as with the story of a kindly Samaritan (an unpopular tribe if any existed) who went out of his way to help a traveler. "Remember that the Lord is our shepherd," said Andrew, "and Jesus often adopted stories and images from the countryside." It also struck me, from what I had gathered over the decades, that Jesus lived and worked among many women, and that these women meant as much to him as any of the men in his company, including the Twelve. They supported his ministry, not unlike the women who had stood behind Paul, such as Phoebe and Lydia, Prisca, Junia, and so many others.

I would present the life of Jesus in my own way, in the time I had left, gathering the disparate strands, creating a text that would truly represent our Lord, the Christ of heaven, and his teachings. As rumors about him surfaced, I felt an urgency, realizing I must get this narrative in place, correcting false information, shaping the story so that readers could appreciate the unique quality of this life. Jesus had modeled how to live, and how to experience suffering with grace and hope. He had treated women and slaves, the poor and desperately ill with respect. He had absorbed the scriptures, the Law itself, and reimagined a covenant between God and his creation. Jesus was, in sum, the Christ. The Almighty had taken flesh in his body, found the contours of human speech in his voice. And through his anguish, his death by execution, and his transformation, he had shown us a way into life that outlasts the ruins of time.

For nearly two years I moved with Paul around Rome, where we found a hunger for his teaching. His letters had been seeds scattered in the wind, and they had rooted here, blossomed and borne fruit. My friend the apostle had spent a life in the slow acquisition of spiritual knowledge, in prayerful conversation with God, and he still had much to say.

Now the great fire threatened to incinerate Paul's lifelong mission. The Way of Jesus had been singled out, demonized by Nero, and nearly eradicated in Rome. And it happened swiftly. I had been able to make my way with difficulty across the burning city to Paul's house, which had nearly been razed by the time I arrived. The only human beings alive in this fire were two small boys, the sons of Junia and Josephus, who had looked on me with terror. A blast of fire, and a spray of sparks, had pushed me to the ground. Coughing, I struggled to my feet in this hot cloud, calling to the boys, who had fled into a smoky passageway beside their burning house. The wood-framed villa was swept in flames, trembling, and ready to collapse.

"Boys!" I called.

I did my best to remain standing, my head spinning as I pushed along the alleyway. I could not let them rush into a blazing city, a world of indifference where they would never find help or comfort again. It was horrifying to think of them as slaves, as servants of some oppressive master. They might well live at the edge of the capital for a few years, skeletons of light, moving in the shadows. I had seen the lost children of Rome, with their faces blackened and wandering by themselves. I had seen small bodies floating in the Tiber or washed onto the shoreline, piled like rags in mounds, or burning on pyres. The remains of dogs and children lay everywhere, their white bones and sad fragments.

From dust we came, and to dust we return, we read in the scriptures.

And Paul had amplified this teaching when writing to Corinth, saying that "because death came through a man's deed, so the resurrection of the dead must also come through a man's deed. In Adam all men and women die. In the Christ, everyone lives again."

I plunged into the thick smoke wall, trying to find a footing, even to breathe. Fire poured around me, a stinging swirl of ash and sparks, as I called for the boys. But they had disappeared and doubtless had perished in the fires. How I escaped incineration only God knew or could understand: He had a plan for me, I realized. It was the only reason I had been spared thus far.

Somehow I made it back through the fiery streets to the house of my young friend, Atilius, this kind soul, and spent a night in recovery. He brought me fruit in the morning and sat beside me. But toward evening, against his wishes, I set off in search of Paul. The news that Nero had stuffed our friends into the skins of beasts and set wild dogs upon them had terrified me, and I already knew they had burned some of our people alive in the Circus, creating human torches. There seemed no end to this horror.

Determined to find Paul, I made my way to the Circus garden, once a holy place of prayer, where so often he and I had paused to reflect, to meditate, to beseech God, asking for strength and composure. This enclosure was the property of Agrippina, the mother of the emperor, and once her refuge. As I entered the gate, the brilliance of the night startled me. A blaze of torches lined both sides of the gravel path where I walked, in a baffled and frenzied crowd, pulling a shawl around my head, hiding my face.

I must not be recognized. That much I knew in my gut.

It nonetheless took a while to accept that the torches that appeared to shriek were human beings who had been fastened to posts, covered with tar and straw, set alight.

I had never been witness to such agony.

One man's blackened face dissolved before me, his hair aflame, his teeth like needles of light. The cheekbones flared. He reached for me in vain.

Another torch was a woman, and I vaguely recognized her. I paused, and she reached toward me as well, her hand shriveling in fire. It was Junia, her startled eyes drilling through the flames. I walked on, fearing she would recognize me. Embarrassed that I could do nothing for her.

Junia!

And there, not far along the row, blazed Josephus. His voice called out, begged for mercy. Did he, like the Christ, ask God why he had forsaken him? There was such anguish, disbelief, and fury in his voice. Even disappointment.

What could I do?

I followed along the serial display of horror and recognized others. Albanus, Caelia, Crispus, Florianus, Livia, and Marcus. I knew them all, at least by sight. Only weeks ago I had sat with them and prayed and sang.

At the end of the gravel pathway I saw, or believed I saw, Paul. Slowly I approached, trying not to catch his gaze. That would have been too awful to bear. I would cast myself down and die.

But it wasn't Paul.

I didn't know who this poor wretch might be, but he was certainly not alive and was not the apostle. His hands drooped at his sides like black flags of misery. They had ceased to quiver.

A hand suddenly grasped my elbow, and I thought I was finished. I would soon join those who had died in the service of the Lord of creation. They had me now.

But the figure said, "Be calm, Luke. Stay with me. Just walk on." It was Julius! "I know where they've taken him," he said. "Let's go. We might save him yet."

He hurried me to the Forum Boarium, near the Tiber, where we mounted horses that Julius had commandeered and rode through the night, under the archway of the Porta Trigemina into the dawning light along the via Ostiensis, a thoroughfare that led ultimately to the coast, although many large villas could be found along the way, some of them connected with the imperial household.

Our friend Lucina lived there in a light-filled villa. I had been with her only recently, and my heart lifted at the thought of her reassuring presence. She had been a source of funds to the Way, generous beyond measure, our companion in the Christ. As we rode into the pink sky of early morning, the wind cooling our cheeks, I convinced myself that she had rescued Paul and that we would meet again in her garden. Soon my friend and I would settle in a house she owned along the coast, and we would write at the same table with the surf rippling beyond our window.

"God bless you, dear Luke," Paul would say.

I could hear the sweet susurrus of her voice, a way of talking that soothed and satisfied.

The early-morning ball of sun cast a scarlet light along the eastern ridge of hills, where a patchwork of hayfields and vineyards unfolded. I could smell the odors of cooking and saw smoke rise from a stone house by the roadside. As we rounded one corner, I saw a group of perhaps a dozen men in the road ahead. They were Roman soldiers, with a few horses tethered to nearby trees. I saw Julius wave to them as comrades.

They acknowledged him as we drew close.

He dismounted and spoke to one of them.

I remained on my horse, allowing my scarf to disguise my features. Nobody would recognize me, I had to suppose. But it was best to leave nothing to chance.

When I saw a stump at the roadside, only slowly did I realize that it was a chopping block, a place of beheading.

We had stumbled upon an execution, not a mile before arriving at Lucina's villa.

"My dear friend," a voice called with a familiar flourish, unmistakable. "How I love you, and what we have accomplished! Rejoice! Always rejoice!"

I knew at once this was Paul's voice, and that he had never said such a thing to me before.

Quickly I dismounted, tying my horse to a tree. I made my way toward Julius and his fellow soldiers. Nobody looked in my direction, and Julius himself ignored me: not a good sign. Was he afraid? When at last he caught my eye, he nodded toward the roadside.

Paul's head had been separated from his body, and it lay in the ditch. His eyes were open, as if startled, his mouth wide. I could not restrain myself and rushed to his side, taking off my shawl and tunic, wrapping his head in the soft cloth. His blood soaked through the fabric immediately, and my hands turned crimson and sticky. I began to shake all over.

It might well have been dangerous for me, as nobody could doubt my allegiance to Paul. But Julius protected me, ushering the others away. He could use his authority in the right circumstances, and nobody would disobey a centurion.

"You will carry on, for me, for the sake of Jesus! For your own sake, Luke," a voice called.

"Paul!"

"I hear you," he said. "We are always together."

And those were the last of his words, the last I would hear in this present life. His voice faded from the air, and as the sun rose and the daylight found its footing, I was left with nothing but the empty bright space of everyday life.

"He will like it here," said Julius, a while later.

It was an odd remark, I thought, as we stood together in Lucina's garden. She had agreed to Paul's burial beside a tall stone pine, near an ancient cistern. Above us, an arc of doves rose and whirled in a great ring.

Lucina read from one of Paul's letters, where he said to the gathering at Corinth that "the splendor of heavenly bodies is of one kind and that of earthly bodies another. Just as the sun has its own splendor, the moon another, and the stars another. And so, with the resurrection of the dead, we should understand a final truth: The body that is sown is perishable; the body that is raised is reaped by the creator and will live forever." I made the sign of the cross as Paul had taught me and watched the birds wheel into the sun and disappear, and I understood at once that all would be well, as we—Paul, everyone who followed in the Way of Jesus, including myself—had already risen in the Christ. The waters of baptism had been a sign of our survival, our everlasting life together in the divine presence, and we would never be separate again.

My father was a Baptist minister, and he would often read the letters of Paul aloud at the breakfast table to the family. Later, I studied Paul's letters closely in college and graduate school, and I became intrigued by his unique voice, which is challenging, even unnerving, but memorable.

Like others, I often found his patriarchal tone off-putting and bristled at his views on homosexuality and the role of women in the church. But in recent years, when I came to read the best modern scholarship on Paul, I realized that only seven of the thirteen Pauline letters in the New Testament are widely accepted as being written by Paul: Romans, 1 and 2 Corinthians, Colossians, Philippians, 1 Thessalonians, and Philemon. The rest stand on shakier ground and were probably written much later and by those who considered themselves part of the "school of Paul."

The authentic letters offer a singular portrait of Paul, one different from that put forward in the later ones, which often work overtime to undo what the apostle had done. The real Paul believed in radical equality between men and women, between slaves and free men, between Greeks and Jews. He celebrated women—Phoebe, Lydia, Prisca, and others—as leaders in the Jesus movement, people in every way his equal. He comes across in these epistles as a visionary, a proselyte of extraordinary power and zeal, and a gifted writer himself, a thinker whose influence on Western thought is second only to that of Plato.

I determined to write this book when, some years ago, I was rereading the *Dialogues* of Plato and, to my amazement, kept stumbling upon phrases and ideas that Paul adopted as his own. That made sense to me because Paul was a Jew born in the Greek world of Tarsus, and he was surely as familiar with Plato and Greek philosophy as he was with the Hebrew scriptures. This Attic-influenced Paul brings a fresh sense of the man, his origins and development, and helps to explain his drive to Athens, where he lectured eagerly on the sacred ground where Plato had established his Academy in a grove of olive trees.

In this novel, I hoped to imagine what it was like for Paul and his fellow missionary, Luke, to live and move around the Roman world in the early to middle years of the first century. What did it look and smell like? What were its tastes and sounds? How did people talk? What were the religious currents that shaped their thinking?

Luke wrote both the Gospel of Luke and the Acts of the Apostles, and so it made sense to use him as a co-narrator in this novel, a contrapuntal voice that reflects a contrasting temperament. In fact, the writer of these texts may or may not have been the same man who traveled with Paul, but that is a traditional assumption that seems at least possible and worked for me as a novelist.

The Damascus Road is a vision of what might have happened, an attempt to take in the world of early Christianity. And it conforms largely to the sequence of events as narrated by Luke in the Acts of the Apostles, a chronology augmented by the letters of Paul, which represent the earliest Christian writings. My sources, apart from the New Testament writings, were varied, and it's almost impossible to give credit to every book or article I read in the course of the five or six years during which I researched and wrote this novel.

For a start, I could hardly have written the book without reading closely *The First Urban Christians: The Social World of the Apostle Paul* (1983) by Wayne A. Meeks, where the essential atmosphere of early Christian life is evoked with granularity. In addition to this, I owe a great deal to a range of modern scholars, from E. P. Sanders to John Dominic Crossan, Elisabeth Schüssler Fiorenza, and Douglas Campbell (who kindly shared with me one of his unpublished books on Paul). I drew on my friend A. N. Wilson's *Paul: The Mind of the Apostle* (1997), and benefited from serious conversations with him over the years about Paul and the meaning of Jesus. I found Karen Armstrong's *St. Paul: The Apostle We Love to Hate* (2015) useful as well. The scholarship of Amy-Jill Levine was crucial to my understanding of the women in Paul's life. And this is only to name a handful of the writers whose books and articles I have lived in over the decades as I studied this infinitely complex figure, the man who more than anyone is responsible for inventing Christianity as we know it.

During the writing of this book I also benefited from conversations with Shalom Goldman, a good friend and scholar of Jewish studies. He read early drafts of this novel and offered many helpful suggestions.

Again, the main source for this novel is the letters of Paul and Acts, which I read in various translations, often returning to the original Greek, working with *The New Greek-English Interlinear New Testament*, edited by J. D. Douglas (Tyndale House, 1990 edition). To me, it was worth rephrasing the language of the Bible as it has been passed on to us through the fourth-century Latin Vulgate to the King James and later translations. I often put into modern English key terms, such as *ekklesia*, which is usually translated as "church." It really means "gathering," so I avoid the more familiar term, as it mistakenly gives the impression that some form of institutional Christianity existed at the time of Paul. There was no "church" then, just a loose aggregate of followers with an unstable theology. There was no Christian priesthood, as such, and certainly women were the equal of men in the clerical role. I move away from loaded terms like "salvation," preferring "enlightenment" as a translation of *soteria*. I usually call Satan the Adversary, which seems like the best translation. On and on, in little and large ways, I rephrase terms that are so familiar their meaning is often lost. My intention is to give them a freshness, even a strangeness, that makes their interest and oddness visible again. Finally, I make sure to call Jesus "the Christ," as Christ is the translation of the Greek word for Messiah. And I rarely use the word "Christian," as it had no currency at the time of Paul.

I do, here and there, quote the familiar King James translation of the Hebrew Bible, especially when the phrasing is either too beautiful to dismiss or useful in the context. It's especially the Greek New Testament that I prefer to convey in my own versions.

In the course of my research, I did a good deal of traveling and have seen firsthand most of the places I write about. I also turned now and then for inspiration to some favorite travel books, such as H. V. Morton's marvelous *In the Steps of St. Paul*. I ransacked for images and ideas a range of relevant earlier books, such as Richard Chandler's *Travels in Asia Minor* (1775), T. R. Glover's *The World of the New Testament* (1933), and James Smith's incisive *The Voyage and Shipwreck of St. Paul* (1866).

This is, needless to say, a novel and not a work of scholarship per se. I wanted to imagine as fully as possible the world of Paul and Luke, seeing the men and women of the earliest Jesus movement with the usual failings, worries, and ambitions. I left out a lot of things, as one must: Paul (with or without Luke) zigzagged through imperial Rome freely, with abandon, and I skipped over parts of his life and conflated certain crises, as there was a certain repetitive quality to his adventures. Overall, I adhere to the agreed-upon facts of his life and travels, and my vision of Paul is an attempt to dream the particulars of this world in ways that could well be true.

ALSO BY

JAY PARINI

EMPIRE OF SELF
A Life of Gore Vidal

The life of Gore Vidal teemed with notable incidents, famous people, and lasting achievements that call for careful evocation and examination. Jay Parini crafts Vidal's life into an accessible, entertaining story that puts the experience of one of the great American figures of the postwar era into context, introduces the author and his works to a generation who may not know him, and looks behind the scenes at the man and his work in ways never possible before his death. Provided with unique access to Vidal's life and his papers, Parini excavates many buried skeletons yet never loses sight of his deep respect for Vidal and his astounding gifts. This is the biography Gore Vidal—novelist, essayist, dramatist, screenwriter, historian, wit, provocateur, and pioneer of gay rights—has long needed.

Biography

THE LAST STATION
A Novel of Tolstoy's Final Year

As Leo Tolstoy's life draws to a tumultuous close, his tempestuous wife and most cunning disciple are locked in a whirlwind battle for the great man's soul. Torn between his professed doctrine of poverty and chastity and the reality of his enormous wealth and thirteen children, Tolstoy dramatically flees his home, only to fall ill at a tiny nearby rail station. The famous (and famously troubled) writer believes he is dying alone, unaware that over a hundred newspapermen camp outside awaiting hourly reports on his condition. In *The Last Station*, Jay Parini moves deftly between a colorful cast of characters to create a stunning portrait of one of the world's most treasured authors.

Fiction

THE PASSAGES OF H.M.
A Novel of Herman Melville

With a masterly touch that made *The Last Station* so powerful, Jay Parini penetrates the mind and soul of another literary titan. Through the eyes of his long-suffering wife, Lizzie, we are introduced to an aging, angry, and drunken Herman Melville. He is decades past his flourishing career as a writer of bestselling tales of seagoing adventures. His epic but ungainly *Moby-Dick* was meant to make him immortal, but critics scoffed and readers fled. He spends his days trudging the docks of New York as a customs inspector and contemplating his malign literary fate. But within him is stirring, perhaps, one great work yet. In a narrative that shifts seamlessly between Lizzie's personal account and evocative snapshots of Melville's crowded life, Parini manages to humanize a giant of letters while illuminating the source of his matchless creativity.

Fiction

PROMISED LAND
Thirteen Books That Changed America

In this lively exploration of America's intellectual heritage, acclaimed poet, novelist, and critic Jay Parini celebrates the life and times of thirteen books that helped shape the American psyche. Moving nimbly between the great watersheds in American letters—including *Walden*, *Huckleberry Finn*, *The Souls of Black Folk*, and *On the Road*—Parini demonstrates how these books entered American life and altered how we think and act in the world. An immensely readable and vibrant work of cultural history, *Promised Land* is sure to appeal to all book lovers and students of the American character alike.

History/Literature

ANCHOR BOOKS
Available wherever books are sold.
www.anchorbooks.com